W9-CLJ-367

CHARLES DICKENS

HIS GRANDSON AND HIS STRANGE COMPANION.

CHARLES DICKENS

THE OLD CURIOSITY SHOP

VOLUME I

WITH ILLUSTRATIONS BY

C. GREEN

WALTER J. BLACK, INC.

NEW YORK

PRINTED IN THE UNITED STATES OF AMERICA

CONTENTS

ILLUSTRATIONS

THE OLD CURIOSITY SHOP

THE OLD CURIOSITY SHOP

CHAPTER I

ALTHOUGH I am an old man, night is generally my time for walking. In the summer I often leave home early in the morning, and roam about the fields and lanes all day, or even escape for days or weeks together; but, saving in the country, I seldom go out until after dark, though, Heaven be thanked, I love its light and feel the cheerfulness it sheds upon the earth, as much as any creature living.

I have fallen insensibly into this habit, both because it favours my infirmity, and because it affords me greater opportunity of speculating on the characters and occupations of those who fill the streets. The glare and hurry of broad noon are not adapted to idle pursuits like mine; a glimpse of passing faces caught by the light of a street-lamp, or a shop-window, is often better for my purpose than their full revelation in the daylight; and, if I must add the truth, night is kinder in this respect than day, which too often destroys an air-built castle at the moment of its completion without the least ceremony or remorse.

That constant pacing to and fro, that never-ending restlessness, that incessant tread of feet wearing the rough stones smooth and glossy—is it not a wonder how the dwellers in narrow ways can bear to hear it? Think of a sick man, in such a place as Saint Martin's Court, listening to the footsteps, and in the midst of pain and weariness, obliged, despite himself (as though it were a task he must perform) to detect the child's step from the man's, the slipshod beggar from the booted exquisite, the lounging from the busy, the dull heel of the sauntering outcast from the quick tread of an expectant pleasure-seeker—think of the hum and noise being always present to his senses, and of the stream of life that will not stop, pouring on, on, on, through all his restless dreams, as if he were condemned to lie, dead but conscious, in a noisy churchyard, and had no hope of rest for centuries to come!

Then, the crowds for ever passing and repassing on the bridges (on those which are free of toll at least), where many stop on fine evenings looking listlessly down upon the water, with some vague idea that by-and-by it runs between green banks which grow wider and wider until at last it joins the broad vast sea—where some halt to rest from heavy loads, and think, as they look over the parapet, that to smoke and lounge away one's life, and lie sleeping in the sun upon a hot tarpaulin, in a dull, slow, sluggish barge, must be happiness unalloyed—and where some, and a very different class, pause with heavier loads than they, remembering to have heard or read in some old time that drowning was not a hard death, but of all means of suicide the easiest and best.

Covent Garden Market at sunrise too, in the spring or summer, when the fragrance of sweet flowers is in the air, overpowering even the unwholesome streams of last night's debauchery, and driving the dusky thrush, whose cage has hung outside a garret window all night long, half mad with joy! Poor bird! the only neighbouring thing at all akin to the other little captives, some of whom, shrinking from the hot hands of drunken purchasers, lie drooping on the path already, while others, soddened by close contact, await the time when they shall be watered and freshened up to please more sober company, and make old clerks who pass them on their road to business, wonder what has filled their breasts with visions of the country.

But my present purpose is not to expatiate upon my walks. The story I am about to relate, arose out of one of these rambles; and thus I have been led to speak of them by way of preface.

One night, I had roamed into the City, and was walking slowly on in my usual way, musing upon a great many things, when I was arrested by an inquiry, the purport of which did not reach me, but which seemed to be addressed to myself, and was preferred in a soft sweet voice that struck me very pleasantly. I turned hastily round, and found at my elbow a pretty little girl, who begged to be directed to a certain street at a considerable distance, and indeed in quite another quarter of the town.

'It is a very long way from here,' said I, 'my child.'

'I know that, sir,' she replied timidly. 'I am afraid it is a very long way; for I came from there, to-night.'

'Alone?' said I, in some surprise.

'Oh yes, I don't mind that, but I am a little frightened now, for I have lost my road.'

'And what made you ask it of me? Suppose I should tell you wrong.'

'I am sure you will not do that,' said the little creature, 'you are such a very old gentleman, and walk so slow yourself.'

I cannot describe how much I was impressed by this

appeal, and the energy with which it was made, which brought a tear into the child's clear eye, and made her slight figure tremble as she looked up into my face.

'Come,' said I, 'I 'll take you there.'

She put her hand in mine, as confidingly as if she had known me from her cradle, and we trudged away together: the little creature accommodating her pace to mine, and rather seeming to lead and take care of me than I to be protecting her. I observed that every now and then she stole a curious look at my face as if to make quite sure that I was not deceiving her, and that these glances (very sharp and keen they were too) seemed to increase her confidence at every repetition.

For my part, my curiosity and interest were, at least, equal to the child's; for child she certainly was, although I thought it probable from what I could make out that her very small and delicate frame imparted a peculiar youthfulness to her appearance. Though more scantily attired than she might have been, she was dressed with perfect neatness, and betrayed no marks of poverty or neglect.

'Who has sent you so far by yourself?' said I.

'Somebody who is very kind to me, sir.'

'And what have you been doing?'

'That, I must not tell,' said the child.

There was something in the manner of this reply which caused me to look at the little creature with an involuntary expression of surprise; for I wondered what kind of errand it might be, that occasioned her to be prepared for questioning. Her quick eye seemed to read my thoughts. As it met mine, she added that there was no harm in what she had been doing, but it was a great secret—a secret which she did not even know, herself.

This was said with no appearance of cunning or

deceit, but with an unsuspicious frankness that bore the impress of truth. She walked on, as before: growing more familiar with me as we proceeded, and talking cheerfully by the way, but she said no more about her home, beyond remarking that we were going quite a new road and asking if it were a short one.

While we were thus engaged, I revolved in my mind a hundred explanations of the riddle, and rejected them every one. I really felt ashamed to take advantage of the ingenuousness or grateful feeling of the child, for the purpose of gratifying my curiosity. I love these little people; and it is not a slight thing when they, who are so fresh from God, love us. As I had felt pleased, at first, by her confidence, I determined to deserve it, and to do credit to the nature which had prompted her to repose it in me.

There was no reason, however, why I should refrain from seeing the person who had inconsiderately sent her to so great a distance by night and alone; and, as it was not improbable that if she found herself near home she might take farewell of me and deprive me of the opportunity, I avoided the most frequented ways and took the most intricate. Thus it was not until we arrived in the street itself that she knew where we were. Clapping her hands with pleasure, and running on before me for a short distance, my little acquaintance stopped at a door, and remaining on the step till I came up, knocked at it when I joined her.

A part of this door was of glass, unprotected by any shutter; which I did not observe, at first, for all was very dark and silent within, and I was anxious (as indeed the child was also) for an answer to her summons. When she had knocked twice or thrice, there was a noise as if some person were moving inside, and at length a faint light appeared through the glass which, as it approached very slowly—the bearer having to make his way through a great many scattered articles—enabled me to see, both what kind of person it was who advanced, and what kind of place it was through which he came.

He was a little old man with long grey hair, whose face and figure, as he held the light above his head and looked before him as he approached, I could plainly see. Though much altered by age, I fancied I could recognise in his spare and slender form something of that delicate mould which I had noticed in the child. Their bright blue eyes were certainly alike, but his face was so deeply furrowed, and so very full of care, that here all resemblance ceased.

The place through which he made his way at leisure, was one of those receptacles for old and curious things which seem to crouch in odd corners of this town, and to hide their musty treasures from the public eye in jealousy and distrust. There were suits of mail standing like ghosts in armour, here and there; fantastic carvings brought from monkish cloisters; rusty weapons of various kinds; distorted figures in china, and wood, and iron, and ivory; tapestry, and strange furniture that might have been designed in dreams. The haggard aspect of the little old man was wonderfully suited to the place; he might have groped among old churches, and tombs, and deserted houses, and gathered all the spoils with his own hands. There was nothing in the whole collection but was in keeping with himself; nothing that looked older or more worn than he.

As he turned the key in the lock, he surveyed me with some astonishment, which was not diminished when he looked from me to my companion. The door being opened, the child addressed him as her grandfather, and told him the little story of our companionship.

'Why bless thee, child,' said the old man patting her on the head, 'how couldst thou miss thy way? What if I had lost thee, Nell?'

'I would have found my way back to *you,* grandfather,' said the child boldly: 'never fear.'

The old man kissed her; then turned to me and begged me to walk in. I did so. The door was closed and locked. Preceding me with the light, he led me through the place I had already seen from without, into a small sitting-room behind, in which was another door opening into a kind of closet, where I saw a little bed that a fairy might have slept in: it looked so very small and was so prettily arranged. The child took a candle and tripped into this little room, leaving the old man and me together.

'You must be tired, sir,' said he as he placed a chair near the fire, 'how can I thank you?'

'By taking more care of your grandchild another time, my good friend,' I replied.

'More care!' said the old man in a shrill voice, 'more care of Nelly! why who ever loved a child as I love Nell?'

He said this with such evident surprise, that I was perplexed what answer to make; the more so, because coupled with something feeble and wandering in his manner, there were, in his face, marks of deep and anxious thought which convinced me that he could not be, as I had been at first inclined to suppose, in a state of dotage or imbecility.

'I don't think you consider—' I began.

'I don't consider!' cried the old man interrupting me, 'I don't consider her! ah how little you know of the truth! Little Nelly, little Nelly!'

It would be impossible for any man—I care not what his form of speech might be—to express more affection than the dealer in curiosities did, in these four words. I waited for him to speak again, but he rested his chin upon his hand, and shaking his head twice or thrice, fixed his eyes upon the fire.

While we were sitting thus, in silence, the door of the closet opened, and the child returned: her light brown hair hanging loose about her neck, and her face flushed with the haste she had made to rejoin us. She busied herself, immediately, in preparing supper. While she was thus engaged I remarked that the old man took an opportunity of observing me more closely than he had done yet. I was surprised to see, that, all this time, everything was done by the child, and that there appeared to be no other persons but ourselves in the house. I took advantage of a moment when she was absent to venture a hint on this point, to which the old man replied that there were few grown persons as trustworthy or as careful as she.

'It always grieves me,' I observed, roused by what I took to be his selfishness: 'it always grieves me to contemplate the initiation of children into the ways of life, when they are scarcely more than infants. It checks their confidence and simplicity—two of the best qualities that Heaven gives them—and demands that they share our sorrows before they are capable of entering into our enjoyments.'

'It will never check hers,' said the old man looking steadily at me, 'the springs are too deep. Besides, the children of the poor know but few pleasures. Even the cheap delights of childhood must be bought and paid for.'

'But—forgive me for saying this—you are surely not so very poor—' said I.

'She is not my child, sir,' returned the old man. 'Her mother was, and she was poor. I save nothing—not a penny—though I live as you see, but'—he laid his hand upon my arm, and leant forward to whisper—'she shall be rich one of these days, and a fine lady. Don't you think ill of me, because I use her help. She gives it cheerfully as you see, and it would break her heart if she knew that I suffered anybody else to do for me what her little hands could undertake. I don't consider!' he cried with sudden querulousness, 'why, God knows that this one child is the thought and object of my life, and yet he never prospers me—no, never!'

At this juncture, the subject of our conversation again returned, and the old man motioning to me to approach the table, broke off, and said no more.

We had scarcely begun our repast when there was a knock at the door by which I had entered; and Nell: bursting into a hearty laugh, which I was rejoiced to hear, for it was childlike and full of hilarity: said it was no doubt dear old Kit come back at last.

'Foolish Nell!' said the old man fondling with her hair. 'She always laughs at poor Kit.'

The child laughed again more heartily than before, and I could not help smiling from pure sympathy. The little old man took up a candle and went to open the door. When he came back, Kit was at his heels.

Kit was a shock-headed shambling awkward lad with an uncommonly wide mouth, very red cheeks, a turned-up nose, and certainly the most comical expression of face I ever saw. He stopped short at the door on seeing a stranger, twirled in his hand a perfectly round old hat without any vestige of a brim, and, resting himself now on one leg, and now on the other, and changing them constantly, stood in the doorway, looking into the parlour with the most extraordinary leer I ever beheld. I entertained a grateful feeling towards the boy from that minute, for I felt that he was the comedy of the child's life.

'A long way, wasn't it, Kit?' said the little old man.

'Why then, it was a goodish stretch, Master,' returned Kit.

'Did you find the house easily?'

'Why then, not over and above easy, master,' said Kit.

'Of course you have come back hungry?'

'Why then, I do consider myself rather so, master,' was the answer.

The lad had a remarkable manner of standing sideways as he spoke, and thrusting his head forward over his shoulder, as if he could not get at his voice without that accompanying action. I think he would have amused one anywhere, but the child's exquisite enjoyment of his oddity, and the relief it was to find that there was something she associated with merriment in a place that appeared so unsuited to her, were quite irresistible. It was a great point too, that Kit himself was flattered by the sensation he created, and after several efforts to preserve his gravity, burst into a loud roar, and so stood with his mouth wide open and his eyes nearly shut, laughing violently.

The old man had again relapsed into his former abstraction and took no notice of what passed; but I remarked that when her laugh was over, the child's bright eyes were dimmed with tears, called forth by the fulness of heart with which she welcomed her uncouth favourite after the little anxiety of the night. As for Kit himself (whose laugh had been all the time one of that sort which very little would change into a cry) he carried a large slice of bread and meat, and a mug of beer, into a corner, and applied himself to disposing of them with great voracity.

'Ah!' said the old man turning to me with a sigh as if I had spoken to him but that moment, 'you don't know what you say, when you tell me that I don't consider her.'

'You must not attach too great weight to a remark founded on first appearances, my friend,' said I.

'No,' returned the old man thoughtfully, 'no. Come hither, Nell.'

The little girl hastened from her seat, and put her arm about his neck.

'Do I love thee, Nell?' said he. 'Say; do I love thee, Nell, or no?'

The child only answered by her caresses, and laid her head upon his breast.

'Why dost thou sob?' said the grandfather pressing her closer to him and glancing towards me. 'Is it because thou know'st I love thee, and dost not like that I should seem to doubt it by my question? Well, well—then let us say I love thee dearly.'

'Indeed, indeed you do,' replied the child with great earnestness, 'Kit knows you do.'

Kit, who in despatching his bread and meat had been swallowing two-thirds of his knife at every mouthful with the coolness of a juggler, stopped short in his operations on being thus appealed to, and bawled 'Nobody isn't such a fool as to say he doesn't,' after which he incapacitated himself for further conversation by taking a most prodigious sandwich at one bite.

'She is poor now,' said the old man patting the child's cheek, 'but, I say again, the time is coming when she shall be rich. It has been a long time coming, but it must come at last; a very long time, but it surely must come. It has come to other men who do nothing but waste and riot. When *will* it come to me?'

'I am very happy as I am, grandfather,' said the child.

'Tush, tush!' returned the old man, 'thou dost not know—how shouldst thou?' Then he muttered again between his teeth, 'The time must come, I am very sure it must. It will be all the better for coming late'; and then he sighed and fell into his former musing state, and still holding the child between his knees appeared to be insensible to everything around him. By this time it wanted but a few minutes of midnight, and I rose to go: which recalled him to himself.

'One moment, sir,' he said. 'Now, Kit—near midnight, boy, and you still here! Get home, get home, and be true to your time in the morning, for there 's work to do. Good-night! There, bid him good-night, Nell, and let him be gone!'

'Good-night, Kit,' said the child, her eyes lighting up with merriment and kindness.

'Good-night, Miss Nell,' returned the boy.

'And thank this gentleman,' interposed the old man, 'but for whose care I might have lost my little girl to-night.'

'No, no, master,' said Kit, 'that won't do, that won't.'

'What do you mean?' cried the old man.

'*I* 'd have found her, master,' said Kit, 'I 'd have found her. I 'd bet that I 'd find her if she was above ground. I would, as quick as anybody, master! Ha, ha, ha!'

Once more opening his mouth and shutting his eyes, and laughing like a stentor, Kit gradually backed to the door, and roared himself out.

Free of the room, the boy was not slow in taking his departure; when he had gone, and the child was occupied in clearing the table, the old man said—

'I haven't seemed to thank you, sir, enough for what

you have done to-night, but I do thank you, humbly and heartily; and so does she; and her thanks are better worth than mine. I should be sorry that you went away and thought I was unmindful of your goodness, or careless of her—I am not indeed.'

I was sure of that, I said, from what I had seen. 'But,' I added, 'may I ask you a question?'

'Ay, sir,' replied the old man, 'what it is?'

'This delicate child,' said I, 'with so much beauty and intelligence—has she nobody to care for her but you? Has she no other companion or adviser?'

'No,' he returned looking anxiously in my face, 'no, and she wants no other.'

'But are you not fearful,' said I, 'that you may misunderstand a charge so tender? I am sure you mean well, but are you quite certain that you know how to execute such a trust as this? I am an old man like you, and I am actuated by an old man's concern in all that is young and promising. Do you not think that what I have seen of you and this little creature to-night, must have an interest not wholly free from pain?'

'Sir,' rejoined the old man after a moment's silence, 'I have no right to feel hurt at what you say. It is true that in many respects I am the child, and she the grown person—that you have seen already. But waking or sleeping, by night or day, in sickness or health, she is the one object of my care; and if you knew of how much care, you would look on me with different eyes, you would indeed. Ah! it 's a weary life for an old man—a weary, weary, life—but there is a great end to gain, and that I keep before me.'

Seeing that he was in a state of excitement and impatience, I turned to put on an outer coat which I had thrown off, on entering the room: purposing to say no more. I was surprised to see the child standing patiently by, with a cloak upon her arm, and in her hand a hat and stick.

'Those are not mine, my dear,' said I.

'No,' returned the child quietly, 'they are grandfather's.'

'But he is not going out to-night.'

'Oh yes he is,' said the child, with a smile.

'And what becomes of you, my pretty one?'

'Me! I stay here of course. I always do.'

I looked in astonishment towards the old man; but he was, or feigned to be, busied in the arrangement of his dress. From him, I looked back to the slight gentle figure of the child. Alone! In that gloomy place all the long dreary night! She evinced no consciousness of my surprise, but cheerfully helped the old man with his cloak, and, when he was ready, took a candle to light us out. Finding that we did not follow as she expected, she looked back with a smile and waited for us. The old man showed by his face that he plainly understood the cause of my hesitation, but he merely signed to me with an inclination of the head to pass out of the room before him, and remained silent. I had no resource but to comply.

When we reached the door, the child setting down the candle, turned to say good-night and raised her face to kiss me. Then, she ran to the old man, who folded her in his arms and bade God bless her.

'Sleep soundly, Nell,' he said in a low voice, 'and angels guard thy bed! Do not forget thy prayers, my sweet.'

'No indeed,' answered the child fervently, 'they make me feel so happy!'

'That 's well; I know they do; they should,' said the old man. 'Bless thee a hundred times! Early in the morning, I shall be home.'

'You 'll not ring twice,' returned the child. 'The bell wakes me, even in the middle of a dream.'

With this, they separated. The child opened the door (now guarded by a shutter which I had heard the boy put up before he left the house) and with another farewell, whose clear and tender note I have recalled a thousand times, held it until we had passed out. The old man paused a moment while it was gently closed and fastened on the inside, and, satisfied that this was done, walked on at a slow pace. At the street-corner he stopped. Regarding me with a troubled countenance, he said that our ways were widely different, and that he must take his leave. I would have spoken, but summing up more alacrity than might have been expected in one of his appearance, he hurried away. I could see, that, twice or thrice, he looked back as if to ascertain if I were still watching him, or perhaps to assure himself that I was not following, at a distance. The obscurity of the night favoured his disappearance, and his figure was soon beyond my sight.

I remained standing on the spot where he had left me, unwilling to depart, and yet unknowing why I should loiter there. I looked wistfully into the street we had lately quitted, and, after a time, directed my steps that way. I passed and repassed the house, and stopped and listened at the door; all was dark, and silent as the grave.

Yet I lingered about, and could not tear myself away: thinking of all possible harm that might happen to the child—of fires, and robberies, and even murder—and feeling as if some evil must ensue if I turned my back upon the place. The closing of a door or window in the street, brought me before the curiosity-dealer's once more. I crossed the road, and looked up at the house, to assure myself that the noise had not come from there. No, it was black, cold, and lifeless as before.

There were few passengers astir; the street was sad and dismal, and pretty well my own. A few stragglers from the theatres hurried by, and, now and then, I turned aside to avoid some noisy drunkard as he reeled homewards; but these interruptions were not frequent and soon ceased. The clocks struck one. Still I paced up and down, promising myself that every time should be the last, and breaking faith with myself on some new plea, as often as I did so.

The more I thought of what the old man had said, and of his looks and bearing, the less I could account for what I had seen and heard. I had a strong misgiving that his nightly absence was for no good purpose. I had only come to know the fact through the innocence of the child; and though the old man was by at the time and saw my undisguised surprise, he had preserved a strange mystery on the subject and offered no word of explanation. These reflections naturally recalled again, more strongly than before, his haggard face, his wandering manner, his restless anxious looks. His affection for the child might not be inconsistent with villainy of the worst kind; even that very affection was, in itself, an extraordinary contradiction, or how could he leave her thus? Disposed as I was to think badly of him, I never doubted that his love for her was real. I could not admit the thought, remembering what had passed between us, and the tone of voice in which he had called her by her name.

'Stay here of course,' the child had said in answer to my question, 'I always do!' What could take him from home by night, and every night? I called up all the strange tales I had ever heard, of dark and secret deeds committed in great towns and escaping detection for a long series of years. Wild as many of these stories were, I could not find one adapted to this mystery, which only became the more impenetrable, in proportion as I sought to solve it.

Occupied with such thoughts as these, and a crowd of others all tending to the same point, I continued to pace the street for two long hours; at length, the rain began to descend heavily; and then, overpowered by fatigue though no less interested than I had been at first, I engaged the nearest coach and so got home. A cheerful fire was blazing on the hearth, the lamp burnt brightly, my clock received me with its old familiar welcome; everything was quiet, warm, and cheering, and in happy contrast to the gloom and darkness I had quitted.

I sat down in my easy-chair, and falling back upon its ample cushions, pictured to myself the child in her bed: alone, unwatched, uncared for, (save by angels,) yet sleeping peacefully. So very young, so spiritual, so slight and fairy-like a creature passing the long dull nights in such an uncongenial place! I could not dismiss it from my thoughts.

We are so much in the habit of allowing impressions to be made upon us by external objects, which should be produced by reflection alone, but which, without such visible aids, often escape us, that I am not sure I should have been so thoroughly possessed by this one subject, but for the heaps of fantastic things I had seen huddled together in the curiosity-dealer's warehouse. These, crowding on my mind, in connection with the child, and gathering round her, as it were, brought her condition palpably before me. I had her image, without any effort of imagination, surrounded and beset by everything that was foreign to its nature, and farthest removed from the sympathies of her sex and age. If these helps to my fancy had all been wanting, and I had been forced to imagine her in a common chamber, with nothing unusual or uncouth in its appearance, it is very probable that I should have been less impressed with her strange and solitary state. As it was, she seemed to exist in a kind of allegory; and, having these shapes about her, claimed my interest so strongly, that (as I have already remarked), I could not dismiss her from my recollection, do what I would.

'It would be a curious speculation,' said I, after some restless turns across and across the room, 'to imagine her in her future life, holding her solitary way among a crowd of wild grotesque companions; the only pure, fresh, youthful object in the throng. It would be curious to find—'

I checked myself here, for the theme was carrying me along with it at a great pace, and I already saw before me a region on which I was little disposed to enter. I agreed with myself that this was idle musing, and resolved to go to bed, and court forgetfulness.

But, all that night, waking or in my sleep, the same thoughts recurred, and the same images retained possession of my brain. I had, ever before me, the old dark murky rooms—the gaunt suits of mail with their ghostly silent air—the faces all awry, grinning from wood and stone—the dust, and rust, and worm that lives in wood—and alone in the midst of all this lumber and decay and ugly age, the beautiful child in her gentle slumber, smiling through her light and sunny dreams.

CHAPTER II

After combating, for nearly a week, the feeling which impelled me to revisit the place I had quitted under the circumstances already detailed, I yielded to it at length; and determining that this time I would present myself by the light of day, bent my steps thither early in the afternoon.

I walked past the house, and took several turns in the street, with that kind of hesitation which is natural to a man who is conscious that the visit he is about to pay is unexpected, and may not be very acceptable. However, as the door of the shop was shut, and it did not appear likely that I should be recognised by those within, if I continued merely to pass up and down before it, I soon conquered this irresolution, and found myself in the curiosity-dealer's warehouse.

The old man and another person were together in the back part, and there seemed to have been high words between them, for their voices which were raised to a very loud pitch suddenly stopped on my entering, and the old man advancing hastily towards me, said in a tremulous tone that he was very glad I had come.

'You interrupted us at a critical moment,' he said, pointing to the man whom I had found in company with him; 'this fellow will murder me one of these days. He would have done so, long ago, if he had dared.'

'Bah! You would swear away my life if you could,' returned the other, after bestowing a stare and a frown on me; 'we all know that!'

'I almost think I could,' cried the old man, turning feebly upon him. 'If oaths, or prayers, or words, could rid me of you, they should. I would be quit of you, and would be relieved if you were dead.'

'I know it,' returned the other. 'I said so, didn't I? But neither oaths, nor prayers, nor words, *will* kill me, and therefore I live, and mean to live.'

'And his mother died!' cried the old man, passionately clasping his hands and looking upward; 'and this is Heaven's justice!'

The other stood lounging with his foot upon a chair, and regarded him with a contemptuous sneer. He was a young man of one-and-twenty or thereabouts; well made, and certainly handsome, though the expression of his face was far from prepossessing, having in common with his manner and even his dress, a dissipated, insolent air which repelled one.

'Justice or no justice,' said the young fellow, 'here I am and here I shall stop till such time as I think fit to go, unless you send for assistance to put me out—which you won't do, I know. I tell you again that I want to see my sister.'

'*Your* sister!' said the old man bitterly.

'Ah! You can't change the relationship,' returned the other. 'If you could, you'd have done it long ago. I want to see my sister, that you keep cooped up here, poisoning her mind with your sly secrets and pretending an affection for her that you may work her to death, and add a few scraped shillings every week to the money you can hardly count. I want to see her; and I will.'

'Here's a moralist to talk of poisoned minds! Here's a generous spirit to scorn scraped-up shillings!' cried the old man, turning from him to me. 'A profligate, sir, who has forfeited every claim not only upon those who have the misfortune to be of his blood, but upon society which knows nothing of him but his misdeeds. A liar too,' he added, in a lower voice as he drew closer to me, 'who knows how dear she is to me, and seeks to wound me even there, because there is a stranger by.'

'Strangers are nothing to me, grandfather,' said the young fellow catching at the word, 'nor I to them, I hope. The best they can do, is to keep an eye to their business and leave me to mine. There 's a friend of mine waiting outside, and as it seems that I may have to wait some time, I 'll call him in, with your leave.'

Saying this, he stepped to the door, and looking down the street beckoned several times to some unseen person, who, to judge from the air of impatience with which these signals were accompanied, required a great quantity of persuasion to induce him to advance. At length there sauntered up, on the opposite side of the way—with a bad pretence of passing by accident—a figure conspicuous for its dirty smartness, which after a great many frowns and jerks of the head, in resistance of the invitation, ultimately crossed the road and was brought into the shop.

'There. It 's Dick Swiveller,' said the young fellow, pushing him in. 'Sit down, Swiveller.'

'But is the old min agreeable?' said Mr. Swiveller in an undertone.

'Sit down,' repeated his companion.

Mr. Swiveller complied, and looking about him with a propitiatory smile, observed that last week was a fine week for the ducks, and this week was a fine week for the dust; he also observed that whilst standing by the post at the street-corner, he had observed a pig with a straw in his mouth issuing out of the tobacco-shop, from which appearance he argued that another fine week for the ducks was approaching, and that rain would certainly ensue. He furthermore took occasion to apologise for any negligence

Swiveller, after favouring us with several melodious assurances that his heart was in the highlands, and that he wanted but his Arab steed as a preliminary to the achievement of great feats of valour and loyalty, removed his eyes from the ceiling and subsided into prose again.

'Fred,' said Mr. Swiveller stopping short as if the idea had suddenly occurred to him, and speaking in the same audible whisper as before, '*is* the old min friendly?'

'What does it matter?' returned his friend peevishly.

'No, but *is* he?' said Dick.

'Yes, of course. What do I care whether he is or not?'

Emboldened as it seemed by this reply to enter into a more general conversation, Mr. Swiveller plainly laid himself out to captivate our attention.

He began by remarking that soda-water, though a good thing in the abstract, was apt to lie cold upon the stomach unless qualified with ginger, or a small infusion of brandy, which latter article he held to be preferable in all cases, saving for the one consideration of expense. Nobody venturing to dispute these positions, he proceeded to observe that the human hair was a great retainer of tobacco-smoke, and that the young gentlemen of Westminster and Eton, after eating vast quantities of apples to conceal any scent of cigars from their anxious friends, were usually detected in consequence of their heads possessing this remarkable property; whence he concluded that if the Royal Society would turn their attention to the circumstance, and endeavour to find in the resources of science a means of preventing such untoward revelations, they might indeed be looked upon as benefactors to mankind. These opinions being equally incontrovertible with those he had already pronounced.

he went on to inform us that Jamaica rum, though unquestionably an agreeable spirit of great richness and flavour, had the drawback of remaining constantly present to the taste next day; and nobody being venturous enough to argue this point either, he increased in confidence and became yet more companionable and communicative.

'It 's a devil of a thing, gentlemen,' said Mr. Swiveller, 'when relations fall out and disagree. If the wing of friendship should never moult a feather, the wing of relationship should never be clipped, but be always expanded and serene. Why should a grandson and grandfather peg away at each other with mutual wiolence when all might be bliss and concord? Why not jine hands and forget it?'

'Hold your tongue,' said his friend.

'Sir,' replied Mr. Swiveller, 'don't you interrupt the chair. Gentlemen, how does the case stand, upon the present occasion? Here 's a jolly old grandfather—I say it with the utmost respect—and here is a wild young grandson. The jolly old grandfather says to the wild young grandson, "I have brought you up and educated you, Fred; I have put you in the way of getting on in life; you have bolted a little out of the course, as young fellows often do; and you shall never have another chance, nor the ghost of half a one." The wild young grandson makes answer to this and says, "You 're as rich as rich can be; you have been at no uncommon expense on my account, you 're saving up piles of money for my little sister that lives with you in a secret, stealthy, hugger-muggering kind of way and with no manner of enjoyment—why can't you stand a trifle for your grown-up relation?" The jolly old grandfather unto this, retorts, not only that he declines to fork out with that cheerful readiness which is always so agreeable and pleasant in a gentleman of his time of life, but that he will blow up, and call names, and make reflections whenever they meet. Then the plain question is, an't it a pity that this state of things should continue, and how much better would it be for the old gentleman to hand over a reasonable amount of tin, and make it all right and comfortable?"

Having delivered this oration with a great many waves and flourishes of the hand, Mr. Swiveller abruptly thrust the head of his cane into his mouth as if to prevent himself from impairing the effect of his speech by adding one other word.

'Why do you hunt and persecute me, God help me?' said the old man turning to his grandson. 'Why do you bring your profligate companions here? How often am I to tell you that my life is one of care and self-denial, and that I am poor?'

'How often am I to tell you,' returned the other, looking coldly at him, 'that I know better?'

'You have chosen your own path,' said the old man. 'Follow it. Leave Nell and I to toil and work.'

'Nell will be a woman soon,' returned the other, 'and bred in your faith, she 'll forget her brother unless he shows himself sometimes.'

'Take care,' said the old man with sparkling eyes, 'that she does not forget you when you would have her memory keenest. Take care that the day don't come when you walk barefoot in the streets, and she rides by in a gay carriage of her own.'

'You mean when she has your money?' retorted the other. 'How like a poor man he talks!'

'And yet,' said the old man dropping his voice and speaking like one who thinks aloud, 'how poor we are, and what a life it is! The cause is a young child's, guiltless of all harm or wrong, but nothing goes well with it! Hope and patience, hope and patience!'

These words were uttered in too low a tone to reach the ears of the young men. Mr. Swiveller appeared to think that they implied some mental struggle consequent upon the powerful effect of his address, for he poked his friend with his cane and whispered his conviction that he had administered 'a clincher,' and that he expected a commission on the profits. Discovering his mistake after a while, he appeared to grow rather sleepy and discontented, and had more than once suggested the propriety of an immediate departure, when the door opened, and the child herself appeared.

CHAPTER III

The child was closely followed by an elderly man of remarkably hard features and forbidding aspect, and so low in stature as to be quite a dwarf, though his head and face were large enough for the body of a giant. His black eyes were restless, sly, and cunning; his mouth and chin, bristly with the stubble of a coarse hard beard; and his complexion was one of that kind which never looks clean or wholesome. But what added most to the grotesque expression of his face, was a ghastly smile, which, appearing to be the mere result of habit and to have no connection with any mirthful or complacent feeling, constantly revealed the few discoloured fangs that were yet scattered in his mouth, and gave him the aspect of a panting dog. His dress consisted of a large high-crowned hat, a worn dark suit, a pair of capacious shoes, and a dirty white neckerchief sufficiently limp and crumpled to disclose the greater portion of his wiry throat. Such hair as he had, was of a grizzled black, cut short and straight upon his temples, and hanging in a frowsy fringe about his ears. His hands, which were of a rough coarse grain, were very dirty; his finger-nails were crooked, long, and yellow.

There was ample time to note these particulars, for besides that they were sufficiently obvious without very close observation, some moments elapsed before any one broke silence. The child advanced timidly towards her brother and put her hand in his; the dwarf (if we may call him so) glanced keenly at all present, and the curiosity-dealer, who plainly had not expected his uncouth visitor, seemed disconcerted and embarrassed.

'Ah!' said the dwarf, who with his hand stretched out above his eyes had been surveying the young man attentively, 'that should be your grandson, neighbour!'

'Say rather that he should not be,' replied the old man. 'But he is.'

'And that?' said the dwarf, pointing to Dick Swiveller.

'Some friend of his, as welcome here as he,' said the old man.

'And that?' inquired the dwarf wheeling round and pointing straight at me.

'A gentleman who was so good as to bring Nell home the other night when she lost her way, coming from your house.'

The little man turned to the child as if to chide her or express his wonder, but as she was talking to the young man, held his peace, and bent his head to listen.

'Well, Nelly,' said the young fellow aloud. 'Do they teach you to hate me, eh?'

'No, no. For shame. Oh, no!' cried the child.

'To love me, perhaps?' pursued her brother with a sneer.

'To do neither,' she returned. 'They never speak to me about you. Indeed they never do.'

'I dare be bound for that,' he said, darting a bitter look at the grandfather. 'I dare be bound for that, Nell. Oh! I believe you there!'

'But I love you dearly, Fred,' said the child.

'No doubt!'

'I do indeed, and always will,' the child repeated with great emotion, 'but oh! if you would leave off vexing him and making him unhappy, then I could love you more.'

'I see!' said the young man, as he stooped carelessly over the child, and having kissed her, pushed her from him: 'There—get you away now you have said your lesson. You needn't whimper. We part good friends enough, if that 's the matter.'

He remained silent, following her with his eyes, until she had gained her little room and closed the door; and then turning to the dwarf, said abruptly—

'Hark 'ee, Mr.——'

'Meaning me?' returned the dwarf. 'Quilp is my name. You might remember. It 's not a long one —Daniel Quilp.'

'Hark 'ee, Mr. Quilp, then,' pursued the other. 'You have some influence with my grandfather there.'

'Some,' said Mr. Quilp emphatically.

'And are in a few of his mysteries and secrets.'

'A few,' replied Quilp, with equal dryness.

'Then let me tell him once for all, through you, that I will come into and go out of this place as often as I like, so long as he keeps Nell here; and that if he wants to be quit of me, he must first be quit of her. What have I done to be made a bugbear of, and to be shunned and dreaded as if I brought the plague? He 'll tell you that I have no natural affection; and that I care no more for Nell, for her own sake, than I do for him. Let him say so. I care for the whim, then, of coming to and fro, and reminding her of my existence. I *will* see her when I please. That 's my point. I came here to-day to maintain it, and I 'll come here again fifty times with the same object and always with the same success. I said I would stop till I had gained it. I have done so, and now my visit 's ended. Come, Dick.'

'Stop!' cried Mr. Swiveller, as his companion turned towards the door. 'Sir!'

'Sir, I am your humble servant,' said Mr. Quilp, to whom the monosyllable was addressed.

'Before I leave the gay and festive scene, and halls of dazzling light, sir,' said Mr. Swiveller, 'I will, with your permission, attempt a slight remark. I came here, sir, this day, under the impression that the old min was friendly.'

'Proceed, sir,' said Daniel Quilp; for the orator had made a sudden stop.

'Inspired by this idea and the sentiments it awakened, sir, and feeling as a mutual friend that badgering, baiting, and bullying, was not the sort of thing calculated to expand the souls and promote the social harmony of the contending parties, I took upon myself to suggest a course which is *the* course to be adopted on the present occasion. Will you allow me to whisper half a syllable, sir?'

Without waiting for the permission he sought, Mr. Swiveller stepped up to the dwarf, and leaning on his shoulder and stooping down to get at his ear, said in a voice which was perfectly audible to all present—

'The watch-word to the old min is—fork.'

'Is what?' demanded Quilp.

'Is fork, sir, fork,' replied Mr. Swiveller slapping his pocket. 'You are awake, sir?'

The dwarf nodded. Mr. Swiveller drew back and nodded likewise, then drew a little further back and nodded again, and so on. By these means he in time reached the door, where he gave a great cough to attract the dwarf's attention and gain an opportunity of expressing in dumb show, the closest confidence and most inviolable secrecy. Having performed the serious pantomime that was necessary for the due conveyance of these ideas, he cast himself upon his friend's track, and vanished.

'Humph!' said the dwarf with a sour look and a shrug of his shoulders, 'so much for dear relations. Thank God I acknowledge none! Nor need you either,' he added, turning to the old man, 'if you were not as weak as a reed, and nearly as senseless.'

'What would you have me do?' he retorted in a kind of helpless desperation. 'It is easy to talk and sneer. What would you have me do?'

'What would *I* do if I was in your case?' said the dwarf.

'Something violent, no doubt.'

'You 're right there,' returned the little man, highly gratified by the compliment, for such he evidently considered it; and grinning like a devil as he rubbed his dirty hands together. 'Ask Mrs. Quilp, pretty Mrs. Quilp, obedient, timid, loving Mrs. Quilp. But that reminds me—I have left her all alone, and she will be anxious and know not a moment's peace till I return. I know she 's always in that condition when I 'm away, though she doesn't dare to say so, unless I lead her on and tell her she may speak freely, and I won't be angry with her. Oh! well-trained Mrs. Quilp!'

The creature appeared quite horrible, with his monstrous head and little body, as he rubbed his hands slowly round, and round, and round again—with something fantastic even in his manner of performing this slight action—and, dropping his shaggy brows and cocking his chin in the air, glanced upward with a stealthy look of exultation that an imp might have copied and appropriated to himself.

'Here,' he said, putting his hand into his breast and sidling up to the old man as he spoke; 'I brought it myself for fear of accidents, as, being in gold, it was something large and heavy for Nell to carry in her bag. She need be accustomed to such loads betimes though, neighbour, for she will carry weight when you are dead.'

'Heaven send she may? I hope so,' said the old man with something like a groan.

'Hope so!' echoed the dwarf, approaching close to his ear; 'neighbour, I would I knew in what good investment all these supplies are sunk. But you are a deep man, and keep your secret close.'

'My secret!' said the other with a haggard look. 'Yes, you 're right—I—I—keep it close—very close.'

He said no more, but, taking the money, turned away with a slow uncertain step, and pressed his hand upon his head like a weary and dejected man. The dwarf watched him sharply, while he passed into the little sitting-room and locked it in an iron safe above the chimney-piece; and after musing for a short space, prepared to take his leave, observing that unless he made good haste, Mrs. Quilp would certainly be in fits on his return.

'And so, neighbour,' he added, 'I 'll turn my face homewards, leaving my love for Nelly and hoping she may never losc her way again, though her doing so, *has* procured me an honour I didn't expcct.'

With that he bowed and leered at me, and with a keen glance around which seemed to comprehend every object within his range of vision, however small or trivial, went his way.

I had several times essayed to go myself, but the old man had always opposed it and entreated me to remain. As he renewed his entreaties on our being left alone, and adverted with many thanks to the former occasion of our being together, I willingly yielded to his persuasions, and sat down, pretending to examine some curious miniatures and a few old medals which he placed before me. It needed no great pressing to induce me to stay, for if my curiosity had been excited on the occasion of my first visit, it certainly was not diminished now.

Nell joined us before long, and bringing some needlework to the table, sat by the old man's side. It was pleasant to observe the fresh flowers in the room, the pet bird with a green bough shading his little cage, the breath of freshness and youth which seemed to rustle through the old dull house and hover round the child. It was curious, but not so pleasant, to turn from the beauty and grace of the girl, to see the stooping figure, care-worn face, and jaded aspect of the old man. As he grew weaker and more feeble, what would become of this lonely little creature; poor protector as he was, say that he died—what would her fate be, then?

The old man almost answered my thoughts, as he laid his hand on hers, and spoke aloud.

'I 'll be of better cheer, Nell,' he said; 'there must be good fortune in store for thee—I do not ask it for myself, but thee. Such miseries must fall on thy innocent head without it, that I cannot but believe but that, being tempted, it will come at last!'

She looked cheerfully into his face, but made no answer.

'When I think,' said he, 'of the many years—many in thy short life—that thou hast lived alone with me; of thy monotonous existence, knowing no companions of thy own age nor any childish pleasures; of the solitude in which thou hast grown to be what thou art, and in which thou hast lived apart from nearly all thy kind but one old man; I sometimes fear I have dealt hardly by thee, Nell.'

'Grandfather!' cried the child in unfeigned surprise.

'Not in intention; no, no,' said he. 'I have ever looked forward to the time that should enable thee to mix amongst the gayest and prettiest, and take thy station with the best. But I still look forward, Nell, I still look forward. And if I should be forced to leave thee, meanwhile, how have I fitted thee for struggles with the world? The poor bird yonder, is as well qualified to encounter it, and be turned adrift upon its mercies—Hark! I hear Kit outside. Go to him, Nell, go to him.'

She rose, and hurrying away, stopped, returned back, and put her arms about the old man's neck, then left him and hurried away again—but faster this time, to hide her falling tears.

'A word in your ear, sir,' said the old man in a hurried whisper. 'I have been rendered uneasy by what you said the other night, and can only plead that I have done all for the best; that it is too late to retract, if I could (though I cannot); and that I hope to triumph yet. All is for her sake. I have borne great poverty myself, and would spare her the sufferings that poverty carries with it. I would spare her the miseries that brought her mother, my own dear child, to an early grave. I would leave her—not with resources which could be easily spent or squandered away, but with what would place her beyond the reach of want for ever. You mark me, sir? She shall have no pittance, but a fortune—Hush! I can say no more than that, now or at any other time, and she is here again!'

The eagerness with which all this was poured into my ear, the trembling of the hand with which he clasped my arm, the strained and starting eyes he fixed upon me, the wild vehemence and agitation of his manner, filled me with amazement. All that I had heard and seen, and a great part of what he had said himself, led me to suppose that he was a wealthy man. I could form no comprehension of his character, unless he were one of those miserable wretches who, having made gain the sole end and object of their lives, and having succeeded in amassing great riches, are constantly tortured by the dread of poverty, and beset by fears of loss and ruin. Many things he had said, which I had been at a loss to understand, were quite reconcileable with the idea thus presented to me, and at length I concluded that beyond all doubt he was one of this unhappy race.

The opinion was not the result of hasty consideration, for which indeed there was no opportunity at that time, as the child came back directly, and soon occupied herself in preparations for giving Kit a writing lesson, of which it seemed he had a couple every week, and one regularly on that evening, to the great mirth and enjoyment both of himself and his instructress. To relate how it was a long time before his modesty could be so far prevailed upon as to admit of his sitting down in the parlour, in the presence of an unknown gentleman—how, when he did sit down, he tucked up his sleeves and squared his elbows and put his face close to the copy-book and squinted horribly at the lines—how, from the very first moment of having the pen in his hand, he began to wallow in blots, and to daub himself with ink up to the very roots of his hair—how, if he did by accident form a letter properly, he immediately smeared it out again with his arm in his preparations to make another—how, at every fresh mistake, there was a fresh burst of merriment from the child and a louder and not less hearty laugh from poor Kit himself—and how there was all the way through, notwithstanding, a gentle wish on her part to teach, and an anxious desire on his to learn—to relate all these particulars would no doubt occupy more space and time than they deserve. It will be sufficient to say that the lesson was given; that evening passed and night came on; that the old man again grew restless and impatient; that he quitted the house secretly at the same hour as before; and that the child was once more left alone within its gloomy walls.

And now, that I have carried this history so far in my own character and introduced these personages to the reader, I shall for the convenience of the narrative detach myself from its further course, and leave those who have prominent and necessary parts in it to speak and act for themselves.

CHAPTER IV

Mr. and Mrs. Quilp resided on Tower Hill; and in her bower on Tower Hill Mrs. Quilp was left to pine the absence of her lord, when he quitted her on the business which he has been already seen to transact.

Mr. Quilp could scarcely be said to be of any particular trade or calling, though his pursuits were diversified and his occupations numerous. He collected the rents of whole colonies of filthy streets and alleys by the water-side, advanced money to the seamen and petty officers of merchant vessels, had a share in the ventures of divers mates of East Indiamen, smoked his smuggled cigars under the very nose of the Custom House, and made appointments on 'Change with men in glazed hats and round jackets pretty well every day. On the Surrey side of the river was a small rat-infested dreary yard called 'Quilp's Wharf,' in which were a little wooden counting-house burrowing all awry in the dust as if it had fallen from the clouds and ploughed into the ground; a few fragments of rusty anchors; several large iron rings; some piles of rotten wood; and two or three heaps of old sheet copper, crumpled, cracked, and battered. On Quilp's Wharf, Daniel Quilp was a ship-breaker, yet to judge from these appearances he must either have been a ship-breaker on a very small scale, or have broken his ships up very small indeed. Neither did the place present any extraordinary aspect of life or activity, as its only human occupant was an amphibious boy in a canvas suit, whose sole change of occupation was from sitting on the head of a pile and throwing stones into the mud when the tide was out, to standing with his hands in his pockets gazing listlessly on the motion and on the bustle of the river at high-water.

The dwarf's lodging on Tower Hill comprised, besides the needful accommodation for himself and Mrs. Quilp, a small sleeping-closet for that lady's mother, who resided with the couple and waged perpetual war with Daniel; of whom, notwithstanding, she stood in no slight dread. Indeed, the ugly creature contrived by some means or other—whether by his ugliness or his ferocity or his natural cunning is no great matter—to impress with a wholesome fear of his anger, most of those with whom he was brought into daily contact and communication. Over nobody had he such complete ascendancy as Mrs. Quilp herself—a pretty little, mild-spoken, blue-eyed woman, who having allied herself in wedlock to the dwarf in one of those strange infatuations of which examples are by no means scarce, performed a sound practical penance for her folly, every day of her life.

It has been said that Mrs. Quilp was pining in her bower. In her bower she was, but not alone, for besides the old lady her mother of whom mention has recently been made, there were present some half-dozen ladies of the neighbourhood who had happened by a strange accident (and also by a little understanding among themselves) to drop in one after another, just about tea-time. This being a season favourable to conversation, and the room being a cool, shady, lazy kind of place, with some plants at the open window shutting out the dust, and interposing pleasantly enough between the tea-table within and the old Tower without, it is no wonder that the ladies felt an inclination to talk and linger, especially when there are taken into account the additional inducements of fresh butter, new bread, shrimps, and water-cresses.

Now, the ladies being together under these circumstances, it was extremely natural that the discourse should turn upon the propensity of mankind to tyrannise over the weaker sex, and the duty that devolved upon the weaker sex to resist that tyranny and assert their rights and dignity. It was natural for four reasons: firstly, because Mrs. Quilp being a young woman and notoriously under the dominion of her husband ought to be excited to rebel; secondly, because Mrs. Quilp's parent was known to be laudably shrewish in her disposition and inclined to resist male authority; thirdly, because each visitor wished to show for herself how superior she was in this respect to the generality of her sex; and fourthly, because the company being accustomed to scandalise each other in pairs, were deprived of their usual subject of conversation now that they were all assembled in close friendship, and had consequently no better employment than to attack the common enemy.

Moved by these considerations, a stout lady opened the proceedings by inquiring, with an air of great concern and sympathy, how Mr. Quilp was; whereunto Mr. Quilp's wife's mother replied sharply, 'Oh! he was well enough—nothing much was ever the matter with him—and ill weeds were sure to thrive.' All the ladies then sighed in concert, shook their heads gravely, and looked at Mrs Quilp as at a martyr.

'Ah!' sighed the spokeswoman, 'I wish you 'd give her a little of your advice, Mrs. Jiniwin'—Mrs. Quilp had been a Miss Jiniwin it should be observed—'nobody knows better than you, ma'am, what us women owe to ourselves.'

'Owe indeed, ma'am!' replied Mrs. Jiniwin. 'When my poor husband, her dear father, was alive, if he had ever ventur'd a cross word to *me,* I 'd have—' The good old lady did not finish the sentence, but she twisted off the head of a shrimp with a vindictiveness which seemed to imply that the action was in some degree a substitute for words. In this light it was clearly understood by the other party, who immediately replied with great approbation, 'You quite enter into my feelings, ma'am, and it 's jist what I 'd do myself.'

'But you have no call to do it,' said Mrs. Jiniwin. 'Luckily for you, you have no more occasion to do it than I had.'

'No woman need have, if she was true to herself,' rejoined the stout lady.

'Do you hear that, Betsy?' said Mrs. Jiniwin, in a warning voice. 'How often have I said the very same words to you, and almost gone down on my knees, when I spoke 'em?'

Poor Mrs. Quilp, who had looked in a state of helplessness from one face of condolence to another, coloured, smiled, and shook her head doubtfully. This was the signal for a general clamour, which beginning in a low murmur gradually swelled into a great noise in which everybody spoke at once, and all said that she being a young woman had no right to set up her opinions against the experiences of those who knew so much better; that it was very wrong of her not to take the advice of people who had nothing at heart but her good; that it was next door to being downright ungrateful to conduct herself in that manner; that if she had no respect for herself she ought to have some for other women, all of whom she compromised by her meekness; and that if she had no respect for other women, the time would come when other women would have no respect for her; and she would be very sorry for that, they could tell her. Having dealt out these admonitions, the ladies fell to a more powerful assault than they had yet made upon the mixed tea, new bread, fresh butter, shrimps, and water-cresses, and said that their vexation was so great to see her going on like that, that they could hardly bring themselves to eat a single morsel.

'It 's all very fine to talk,' said Mrs. Quilp with much simplicity, 'but I know that if I was to die to-morrow, Quilp could marry anybody he pleased—now that he could, I know!'

There was quite a scream of indignation at this idea. Marry whom he pleased! They would like to see him dare to think of marrying any of them; they would like to see the faintest approach to such a thing. One lady (a widow) was quite certain she should stab him if he hinted at it.

'Very well,' said Mrs. Quilp, nodding her head, 'as I said just now, it 's very easy to talk, but I say again that I know—that I 'm sure—Quilp has such a way with him when he likes, that the best-looking woman here couldn't refuse him if I was dead, and she was free, and he chose to make love to her. Come!'

Everybody bridled up at this remark, as much as to say 'I know you mean me. Let him try—that 's all.' And yet for some hidden reason they were all angry with the widow, and each lady whispered in her neighbour's ear that it was very plain the said widow thought herself the person referred to, and what a puss she was!

'Mother knows,' said Mrs. Quilp, 'that what I say is quite correct, for she often said so before we were married. Didn't you say so, mother?'

This inquiry involved the respected lady in rather a delicate position, for she certainly had been an active party in making her daughter Mrs. Quilp, and, besides, it was not supporting the family credit to encourage the idea that she had married a man whom nobody else would have. On the other hand, to exaggerate the captivating qualities of her son-in-law would be to weaken the cause of revolt, in which all her energies were deeply engaged. Beset by these opposing considerations, Mrs. Jiniwin admitted the powers of insinuation, but denied the right to govern, and with a timely compliment to the stout lady brought back the discussion to the point from which it had strayed.

'Oh! It 's a sensible and proper thing indeed, what Mrs. George has said!' exclaimed the old lady.

'If women are only true to themselves!—But Betsy isn't, and more 's the shame and pity.'

'Before I 'd let a man order me about as Quilp orders her,' said Mrs. George; 'before I 'd consent to stand in awe of a man as she does of him, I 'd—I 'd kill myself, and write a letter first to say he did it!'

This remark being loudly commended and approved of, another lady (from the Minories) put in her word—

'Mr. Quilp may be a very nice man,' said this lady, 'and I suppose there 's no doubt he is, because Mrs. Quilp says he is, and Mrs. Jiniwin says he is, and they ought to know, or nobody does. But still he is not quite a—what one calls a handsome man, nor quite a young man neither, which might be a little excuse for him if anything could be; whereas his wife is young, and is good-looking, and is a woman—which is the great thing after all.'

This last clause being delivered with extraordinary pathos, elicited a corresponding murmur from the hearers, stimulated by which the lady went on to remark that if such a husband was cross and unreasonable with such a wife, then—

'If he is!' interposed the mother, putting down her tea-cup and brushing the crumbs out of her lap, preparatory to making a solemn declaration. 'If he is! He is the greatest tyrant that ever lived, she daren't call her soul her own, he makes her tremble with a word and even with a look, he frightens her to death, and she hasn't the spirit to give him a word back, no, not a single word.'

Notwithstanding that the fact had been notorious beforehand to all the tea-drinkers, and had been discussed and expatiated on at every tea-drinking in the neighbourhood for the last twelve months, this official communication was no sooner made than they all began to talk at once and to vie with each other in vehemence and volubility. Mrs. George remarked that people would talk, that people had often said this to her before, that Mrs. Simmons then and there present had told her so twenty times, that she had always said, 'No, Henrietta Simmons, unless I see it with my own eyes and hear it with my own ears, I never will believe it.' Mrs. Simmons corroborated this testimony and added strong evidence of her own. The lady from the Minories recounted a successful course of treatment under which she had placed her own husband, who from manifesting one month after marriage unequivocal symptoms of the tiger, had by this means become subdued into a perfect lamb. Another lady recounted her own personal struggle and final triumph, in the course whereof she had found it necessary to call in her mother and two aunts, and to weep incessantly night and day for six weeks. A third, who in the general confusion could secure no other listener, fastened herself upon a young woman still unmarried who happened to be amongst them, and conjured her as she valued her own peace of mind and happiness to profit by this solemn occasion, to take example from the weakness of Mrs. Quilp, and from that time forth to direct her whole thoughts to taming and subduing the rebellious spirit of man. The noise was at its height, and half the company had elevated their voices into a perfect shriek in order to drown the voices of the other half, when Mrs. Jiniwin was seen to change colour and shake her fore-finger stealthily, as if exhorting them to silence. Then, and not until then, Daniel Quilp himself, the cause and occasion of all this clamour, was observed to be in the room, looking on and listening with profound attention.

'Go on, ladies, go on,' said Daniel. 'Mrs. Quilp,

pray ask the ladies to stop to supper, and have a couple of lobsters and something light and palatable.'

'I—I didn't ask them to tea, Quilp,' stammered his wife. 'It 's quite an accident.'

'So much the better, Mrs. Quilp; these accidental parties are always the pleasantest,' said the dwarf, rubbing his hands so hard that he seemed to be engaged in manufacturing, of the dirt with which they were encrusted, little charges for popguns. 'What? Not going, ladies? You are not going, surely?'

His fair enemies tossed their heads slightly as they sought their respective bonnets and shawls, but left all verbal contention to Mrs. Jiniwin, who finding herself in the position of champion, made a faint struggle to sustain the character.

'And why *not* stop to supper, Quilp,' said the old lady, 'if my daughter had a mind?'

'To be sure,' rejoined Daniel. 'Why not?'

'There 's nothing dishonest or wrong in a supper, I hope?' said Mrs. Jiniwin.

'Surely not,' returned the dwarf. 'Why should there be? Nor anything unwholesome either, unless there 's lobster-salad or prawns, which I 'm told are not good for digestion.'

'And you wouldn't like *your* wife to be attacked with that, or anything else that would make her uneasy, would you?' said Mrs. Jiniwin.

'Not for a score of worlds,' replied the dwarf with a grin. 'Not even to have a score of mothers-in-law at the same time—and what a blessing that would be!'

'My daughter 's your wife, Mr. Quilp, certainly,' said the old lady with a giggle, meant for satirical and to imply that he needed to be reminded of the fact: 'your wedded wife.'

'So she is, certainly. So she is,' observed the dwarf.

'And she has a right to do as she likes, I hope, Quilp,' said the old lady trembling, partly with anger and partly with a secret fear of her impish son-in-law.

'Hope she has!' he replied. 'Oh! Don't you know she has? Don't you know she has, Mrs. Jiniwin?'

'I know she ought to have, Quilp, and would have, if she was of my way of thinking.'

'Why an't you of your mother's way of thinking, my dear?' said the dwarf, turning round and addressing his wife, 'why don't you always imitate your mother, my dear? She 's the ornament of her sex—your father said so every day of his life, I am sure he did.'

'Her father was a blessed creetur, Quilp, and worth twenty thousand of some people,' said Mrs. Jiniwin; 'twenty hundred million thousand.'

'I should like to have known him,' remarked the dwarf. 'I dare say he was a blessed creature then; but I 'm sure he is now. It was a happy release. I believe he had suffered a long time?'

The old lady gave a gasp, but nothing came of it; Quilp resumed, with the same malice in his eye and the same sarcastic politeness on his tongue.

'You look ill, Mrs. Jiniwin; I know you have been exciting yourself too much—talking perhaps, for it is your weakness. Go to bed. Do go to bed.'

'I shall go when I please, Quilp, and not before.'

'But please to go now. Do please to go now,' said the dwarf.

The old woman looked angrily at him, but retreated as he advanced, and falling back before him suffered him to shut the door upon her and bolt her out among the guests, who were by this time crowding downstairs. Being left alone with his wife, who sat trembling in a corner with her eyes fixed upon the ground, the little man planted himself before her, at some distance, and folding his arms looked steadily at her for a long time without speaking.

'Oh you nice creature!' were the words with which he broke silence; smacking his lips as if this were no figure of speech, and she were actually a sweetmeat. 'Oh you precious darling! oh you delicious charmer!'

Mrs. Quilp sobbed; and knowing the nature of her pleasant lord, appeared quite as much alarmed by these compliments, as she would have been by the most extreme demonstrations of violence.

'She 's such,' said the dwarf, with a ghastly grin,—'such a jewel, such a diamond, such a pearl, such a ruby, such a golden casket set with gems of all sorts! She 's such a treasure! I 'm so fond of her!'

The poor little woman shivered from head to foot; and raising her eyes to his face with an imploring look, suffered them to droop again, and sobbed once more.

'The best of her is,' said the dwarf, advancing with a sort of skip, which, what with the crookedness of his legs, the ugliness of his face, and the mockery of his manner, was perfectly goblin-like;—'the best of her is that she 's so meek, and she 's so mild, and she never has a will of her own, and she has such an insinuating mother!'

Uttering these latter words with a gloating maliciousness, within a hundred degrees of which no one but himself could possibly approach, Mr. Quilp planted his two hands on his knees, and straddling his legs out very wide apart, stooped slowly down, and down, and down, until, by screwing his head very much on one side, he came between his wife's eyes and the floor.

'Mrs. Quilp!'

'Yes, Quilp.'

'Am I nice to look at? Should I be the handsomest creature in the world if I had but whiskers? Am I quite a lady's man as it is?—am I, Mrs. Quilp?'

Mrs. Quilp dutifully replied, 'Yes, Quilp'; and fascinated by his gaze, remained looking timidly at him, while he treated her with a succession of such horrible grimaces, as none but himself and nightmares had the power of assuming. During the whole of this performance, which was somewhat of the longest, he preserved a dead silence, except when, by an unexpected skip or leap, he made his wife start backward with an irrepressible shriek. Then he chuckled.

'Mrs. Quilp,' he said at last.

'Yes, Quilp,' she meekly replied.

Instead of pursuing the theme he had in his mind, Quilp rose, folded his arms again, and looked at her more sternly than before, while she averted her eyes and kept them on the ground.

'Mrs. Quilp.'

'Yes, Quilp.'

'If ever you listen to these beldames again, I 'll bite you.'

With this laconic threat, which he accompanied with a snarl that gave him the appearance of being particularly in earnest, Mr. Quilp bade her clear the tea-board away, and bring the rum. The spirit being set before him in a huge case-bottle, which had originally come out of some ship's locker, he ordered cold water and the box of cigars; and these being supplied, he settled himself in an arm-chair with his large head and face squeezed up against the back, and his little legs planted on the table.

'Now, Mrs. Quilp,' he said; 'I feel in a smoking humour, and shall probably blaze away all night. But sit where you are, if you please, in case I want you.'

His wife returned no other reply than the customary 'Yes, Quilp,' and the small lord of the creation took his first cigar and mixed his first glass of grog. The sun went down and the stars peeped out, the Tower turned from its own proper colours to grey and from grey to black, the room became perfectly dark and the end of the cigar a deep fiery red, but still Mr. Quilp went on smoking and drinking in the same position, and staring listlessly out of the window with the doglike smile always on his face, save when Mrs. Quilp made some involuntary movement of restlessness or fatigue; and then it expanded into a grin of delight.

CHAPTER V

WHETHER Mr. Quilp took any sleep by snatches of a few winks at a time, or whether he sat with his eyes wide open all night long, certain it is that he kept his cigar alight, and kindled every fresh one from the ashes of that which was nearly consumed, without requiring the assistance of a candle. Nor did the striking of the clocks, hour after hour, appear to inspire him with any sense of drowsiness or any natural desire to go to rest; but rather to increase his wakefulness, which he showed, at every such indication of the progress of the night, by a suppressed cackling in his throat, and a motion of his shoulders, like one who laughs heartily, but at the same time slily and by stealth.

At length the day broke, and poor Mrs. Quilp,

shivering with the cold of early morning and harassed by fatigue and want of sleep, was discovered sitting patiently on her chair, raising her eyes at intervals in mute appeal to the compassion and clemency of her lord, and gently reminding him by an occasional cough that she was still unpardoned and that her penance had been of long duration. But her dwarfish spouse still smoked his cigar and drank his rum without heeding her; and it was not until the sun had some time risen, and the activity and noise of city day were rife in the street, that he deigned to recognise her presence by any word or sign. He might not have done so even then, but for certain impatient tappings at the door which seemed to denote that some pretty hard knuckles were actively engaged upon the other side.

'Why dear me!' he said looking round with a malicious grin, 'it 's day! open the door, sweet Mrs. Quilp!'

His obedient wife withdrew the bolt, and her lady mother entered.

Now, Mrs. Jiniwin bounced into the room with great impetuosity; for, supposing her son-in-law to be still abed, she had come to relieve her feelings by pronouncing a strong opinion upon his general conduct and character. Seeing that he was up and dressed, and that the room appeared to have been occupied ever since she quitted it on the previous evening, she stopped short, in some embarrassment.

Nothing escaped the hawk's eye of the ugly little man, who, perfectly understanding what passed in the old lady's mind, turned uglier still in the fulness of his satisfaction, and bade her good morning, with a leer of triumph.

'Why, Betsy,' said the old woman, 'you haven't been a—you don't mean to say you 've been a—'

'Sitting up all night?' said Quilp, supplying the conclusion of the sentence. 'Yes she has!'

'All night!' cried Mrs. Jiniwin.

'Ay, all night. Is the dear old lady deaf?' said Quilp, with a smile of which a frown was part. 'Who says man and wife are bad company? Ha ha! The time has flown.'

'You 're a brute!' exclaimed Mrs. Jiniwin.

'Come, come,' said Quilp, wilfully misunderstanding her, of course, 'you musn't call her names. She 's married now, you know. And though she *did* beguile the time and keep me from my bed, you must not be so tenderly careful of me as to be out of humour with her. Bless you for a dear old lady. Here 's your health!'

'I am *much* obliged to you,' returned the old woman, testifying by a certain restlessness in her hands a vehement desire to shake her matronly fist at her son-in-law. 'Oh! I 'm very much obliged to you!'

'Grateful soul!' cried the dwarf. 'Mrs. Quilp.'

'Yes, Quilp,' said the timid sufferer.

'Help your mother to get breakfast, Mrs. Quilp. I am going to the wharf this morning—the earlier, the better, so be quick.'

Mrs. Jiniwin made a faint demonstration of rebellion by sitting down in a chair near the door and folding her arms as if in a resolute determination to do nothing. But a few whispered words from her daughter, and a kind inquiry from her son-in-law whether she felt faint, with a hint that there was abundance of cold water in the next apartment, routed these symptoms effectually, and she applied herself to the prescribed preparations with sullen diligence.

While they were in progress, Mr. Quilp withdrew to the adjoining room, and, turning back his coat collar, proceeded to smear his countenance with a damp towel of very unwholesome appearance, which made his complexion rather more cloudy than it had been before. But, while he was thus engaged, his caution and inquisitiveness did not forsake him. With a face as sharp and cunning as ever, he often stopped, even in this short process, and stood listening for any conversation in the next room, of which he might be the theme.

'Ah!' he said after a short effort of attention, 'it was not the towel over my ears, I thought it wasn't. I 'm a little hunchy villain and a monster, am I, Mrs. Jiniwin? Oh!'

The pleasure of this discovery called up the old doglike smile in full force. When he had quite done with it, he shook himself in a very doglike manner, and rejoined the ladies.

Mr. Quilp now walked up to the front of a looking-glass, and was standing there, putting on his neckerchief, when Mrs. Jiniwin, happening to be behind him, could not resist the inclination she felt to shake her fist at her tyrant son-in-law. It was the gesture of an instant, but as she did so and accompanied the action with a menacing look, she met his eye in the glass, catching her in the very act. The same glance at the mirror conveyed to her the reflection of a horribly grotesque and distorted face with the tongue lolling out: and the next instant the dwarf, turning about, with a perfectly bland and placid look, inquired in a tone of great affection:

'How are you now, my dear old darling?'

Slight and ridiculous as the incident was, it made him appear such a little fiend, and withal such a keen and knowing one, that the old woman felt too much afraid of him to utter a single word, and suffered herself to be led with extraordinary politeness to the breakfast-table. Here, he by no means diminisned the impression he had just produced, for he ate hard eggs, shell and all, devoured gigantic prawns with the heads and tails on, chewed tobacco and water-cresses at the same time and with extraordinary greediness, drank boiling tea without winking, bit his fork and spoon till they bent again, and in short performed so many horrifying and uncommon acts that the women were nearly frightened out of their wits and began to doubt if he were really a human creature. At last, having gone through these proceedings and many others which were equally a part of his system, Mr. Quilp left them, reduced to a very obedient and humbled state, and betook himself to the river-side, where he took boat for the wharf on which he had bestowed his name.

It was flood-tide when Daniel Quilp sat himself down in the wherry to cross to the opposite shore. A fleet of barges were coming lazily on, some sideways, some head first, some stern first; all in a wrong-headed, dogged, obstinate way, bumping up against the larger craft, running under the bows of steam-boats, getting into every kind of nook and corner where they had no business, and being crunched on all sides like so many walnut-shells; while each, with its pair of long sweeps struggling and splashing in the water, looked like some lumbering fish in pain. In some of the vessels at anchor all hands were busily engaged in coiling ropes, spreading out sails to dry, taking in or discharging their cargoes; in others, no life was visible but two or three tarry boys, and perhaps a barking dog running to and fro upon the deck or scrambling up to look over the side and bark the louder for the view. Coming slowly on through the forests of masts, was a great steam-ship, beating the water in short impatient strokes with her heavy paddles, as though she wanted room to breathe, and advancing in her huge bulk like a sea monster among the minnows of the Thames. On either hand, were long black tiers of colliers; between them, vessels slowly working out of harbour with sails glistening in the sun, and creaking noise on board, re-echoed from a hundred quarters. The water and all upon it was in active motion, dancing and buoyant and bubbling up; while the old grey Tower and piles of building on the shore, with many a church-spire shooting up between, looked coldly on, and seemed to disdain their chafing neighbour.

Daniel Quilp, who was not much affected by a bright morning save in so far as it spared him the trouble of carrying an umbrella, caused himself to be put ashore hard by the wharf, and proceeded thither, through a narrow lane which, partaking of the amphibious character of its frequenters, had as much water as mud in its composition, and a very liberal supply of both. Arrived at his destination, the first object that presented itself to his view was a pair of very imperfectly shod feet elevated in the air with the souls upwards, which remarkable appearance was referable to the boy, who being of an eccentric spirit and having a natural taste for tumbling was now standing on his head and contemplating the aspect of the river under these uncommon circumstances. He was speedily brought on his heels by the sound of his master's voice, and as soon as his head was in its right position, Mr. Quilp, to speak expressively in the absence of a better verb, 'punched it' for him.

'Come, you let me alone,' said the boy, parrying Quilp's hand with both his elbows alternately. 'You 'll get something you won't like if you don't, and so I tell you.'

'You dog,' snarled Quilp, 'I 'll beat you with an iron rod, I 'll scratch you with a rusty nail, I 'll pinch your eyes, if you talk to me. I will!'

With these threats he clenched his hand again, and dexterously diving in between the elbows and catching the boy's head as it dodged from side to side, gave it three or four good hard knocks. Having now carried his point and insisted on it, he left off.

'You won't do it again,' said the boy, nodding his head and drawing back, with the elbows ready in case of the worst; 'now!'

'Stand still, you dog,' said Quilp. 'I won't do it again, because I 've done it as often as I want. Here. Take the key.'

'Why don't you hit one of your size?' said the boy approaching very slowly.

'Where is there one of my size, you dog?' returned Quilp. 'Take the key, or I 'll brain you with it.' Indeed he gave him a smart tap with the handle as he spoke. 'Now, open the counting-house.'

The boy sulkily complied, muttering at first, but desisting when he looked round and saw that Quilp was following him with a steady look. And here it may be remarked, that between this boy and the dwarf there existed a strange kind of mutual liking. How born or bred, or how nourished upon blows and threats on one side, and retorts and defiances on the other, is not to the purpose. Quilp would certainly suffer nobody to contradict him but the boy, and the boy would assuredly not have submitted to be so knocked about by anybody but Quilp, when he had the power to run away at any time he chose.

'Now,' said Quilp, passing into the wooden counting-house, 'you mind the wharf. Stand upon your head again, and I 'll cut one of your feet off.'

The boy made no answer, but directly Quilp had shut himself in, stood on his head before the door, then walked on his hands to the back and stood on his head there, and then to the opposite side and repeated the performance. There were, indeed, four sides to the counting-house, but he avoided that one where the window was, deeming it probable that Quilp would be looking out of it. This was prudent, for in point of fact the dwarf knowing his disposition, was lying in wait at a little distance from the sash armed with a large piece of wood, which, being rough and jagged and studded in many parts with broken nails, might possibly have hurt him.

It was a dirty little box, this counting-house, with nothing in it but an old rickety desk and two stools, a hat-peg, an ancient almanack, an inkstand with no ink and the stump of one pen, and an eight-day clock which hadn't gone for eighteen years at least, and of which the minute hand had been twisted off for a tooth-pick. Daniel Quilp pulled his hat over his brows, climbed on to the desk (which had a flat top), and stretching his short length upon it went to sleep with the ease of an old practitioner; intending, no doubt, to compensate himself for the deprivation of last night's rest, by a long and sound nap.

Sound it might have been, but long it was not, for he had not been asleep a quarter of an hour when the boy opened the door and thrust in his head, which was like a bundle of badly-picked oakum. Quilp was a light sleeper and started up directly.

'Here 's somebody for you,' said the boy.

'Who?'

'I don't know.'

'Ask!' said Quilp, seizing the trifle of wood before mentioned and throwing it at him with such dexterity that it was well the boy disappeared before it reached the spot on which he had stood. 'Ask, you dog.'

Not caring to venture within range of such missiles again, the boy discreetly sent, in his stead, the first cause of the interruption, who now presented herself at the door.

'What, Nelly!' cried Quilp.

'Yes,' said the child, hesitating whether to enter or retreat, for the dwarf just aroused, with his dishevelled hair hanging all about him, and a yellow handkerchief over his head, was something fearful to behold; 'it 's only me, sir.'

'Come in,' said Quilp, without getting off the desk. 'Come in. Stay. Just look out into the yard, and see whether there 's a boy standing on his head.'

'No, sir,' replied Nell. 'He 's on his feet.'

'You 're sure he is?' said Quilp. 'Well. Now come in and shut the door. What 's your message, Nelly?'

The child handed him a letter; Mr. Quilp, without changing his position otherwise than to turn over a little more on his side and rest his chin on his hand, proceeded to make himself acquainted with its contents.

CHAPTER VI

Little Nell stood timidly by, with her eyes raised to the countenance of Mr. Quilp, as he read the letter, plainly showing by her looks that while she entertained some fear and distrust of the little man, she was much inclined to laugh at his uncouth appearance and grotesque attitude. And yet, there was visible on the part of the child a painful anxiety for his reply, and a consciousness of his power to render it disagreeable or distressing, which was strongly at variance with this impulse and restrained it more effectually than she could possibly have done by any efforts of her own.

That Mr. Quilp was himself perplexed, and that in no small degree, by the contents of the letter, was sufficiently obvious. Before he had got through the first two or three lines he began to open his eyes very wide and to frown most horribly, the next two or three caused him to scratch his head in an uncommonly vicious manner, and when he came to the conclusion he gave a long dismal whistle indicative of surprise and dismay. After folding and laying it down beside him, he bit the nails of all his ten fingers with extreme voracity; and taking it up sharply, read it again. The second perusal was to all appearance as unsatisfactory as the first, and plunged him into a profound reverie from which he awakened to another assault upon his nails and a long stare at the child, who with her eyes turned towards the ground awaited his further pleasure.

'Halloa here!' he said at length, in a voice, and with a suddenness, which made the child start as though a gun had been fired off at her ear. 'Nelly!'

'Yes, sir.'

'Do you know what 's inside this letter, Nell?'

'No, sir!'

'Are you sure, quite sure, quite certain, upon your soul?'

'Quite sure, sir.'

'Do you wish you may die if you do know, hey?' said the dwarf.

'Indeed I don't know,' returned the child.

'Well!' muttered Quilp as he marked her earnest look. 'I believe you. Humph! Gone already?

Gone in four-and-twenty hours. What the devil has he done with it? That 's the mystery!'

This reflection set him scratching his head, and biting his nails, once more. While he was thus employed his features gradually relaxed into what was with him a cheerful smile, but which in any other man would have been a ghastly grin of pain; and when the child looked up again she found that he was regarding her with extraordinary favour and complacency.

'You look very pretty to-day, Nelly, charmingly pretty. Are you tired, Nelly?'

'No, sir. I 'm in a hurry to get back, for he will be anxious while I am away.'

'There 's no hurry, little Nell, no hurry at all,' said Quilp. 'How should you like to be my number two, Nelly?'

'To be what, sir?'

'My number two, Nelly; my second; my Mrs. Quilp,' said the dwarf.

The child looked frightened, but seemed not to understand him, which Mr. Quilp observing, hastened to explain his meaning more distinctly.

'To be Mrs. Quilp the second, when Mrs. Quilp the first is dead, sweet Nell,' said Quilp, wrinkling up his eyes and luring her towards him with his bent forefinger, 'to be my wife, my little cherry-cheeked, red-lipped wife. Say that Mrs. Quilp lives five years, or only four, you 'll be just the proper age for me. Ha ha! Be a good girl, Nelly, a very good girl, and see if one of these days you don't come to be Mrs. Quilp of Tower Hill.'

So far from being sustained and stimulated by this delightful prospect, the child shrunk from him, and trembled. Mr. Quilp, either because frightening anybody afforded him a constitutional delight, or because it was pleasant to contemplate the death of Mrs. Quilp number one, and the elevation of Mrs. Quilp number two to her post and title, or because he was determined for purposes of his own to be agreeable and good-humoured at that particular time, only laughed and feigned to take no heed of her alarm.

'You shall come with me to Tower Hill, and see Mrs. Quilp, that is, directly,' said the dwarf. 'She 's very fond of you, Nell, though not so fond as I am. You shall come home with me.'

'I must go back indeed,' said the child. 'He told me to return directly I had the answer.'

'But you haven't it, Nelly,' retorted the dwarf, 'and won't have it, and can't have it, until I have been home, so you see that to do your errand, you must go with me. Reach me yonder hat, my dear, and we 'll go directly.' With that, Mr. Quilp suffered himself to roll gradually off the desk until his short legs touched the ground, when he got upon them and led the way from the counting-house to the wharf outside, where the first objects that presented themselves were the boy who had stood on his head and another young gentleman of about his own stature, rolling in the mud together, locked in a tight embrace and cuffing each other with mutual heartiness.

'It 's Kit!' cried Nelly, clasping her hands, 'poor Kit who came with me! Oh pray stop them, Mr. Quilp!'

'I 'll stop 'em,' cried Quilp, diving into the little counting-house and returning with a thick stick. 'I 'll stop 'em. Now, my boys, fight away. I 'll fight you both. I 'll take both of you, both together, both together!'

With which defiances the dwarf flourished his cudgel, and dancing round the combatants and treading upon them and skipping over them, in a kind of frenzy, laid about him, now on one and now on the other, in a most desperate manner, always aiming at their heads and dealing such blows as none but the veriest little savage would have inflicted. This being warmer work than they had calculated upon, speedily cooled the courage of the belligerents, who scrambled to their feet and called for quarter.

'I 'll beat you to a pulp, you dogs,' said Quilp, vainly endeavouring to get near either of them for a parting blow. 'I 'll bruise you till you 're copper-coloured, I 'll break your faces till you haven't a profile between you, I will.'

'Come, you drop that stick or it 'll be worse for you,' said his boy, dodging round him and watching an opportunity to rush in: 'you drop that stick.'

'Come a little nearer, and I 'll drop it on your skull, you dog,' said Quilp with gleaming eyes; 'a little nearer; nearer yet.'

But the boy declined the invitation until his master was apparently a little off his guard, when he darted in and seizing the weapon tried to wrest it from his grasp. Quilp, who was as strong as a lion, easily kept his hold until the boy was tugging at it with his utmost power, when he suddenly let it go and sent him reeling backwards, so that he fell violently upon his head. The success of this manœuvre tickled Mr. Quilp beyond description, and he laughed and stamped upon the ground as at a most irresistible jest.

'Never mind,' said the boy, nodding his head and rubbing it at the same time; 'you see if ever I offer to strike anybody again because they say you 're a uglier dwarf than can be seen anywheres for a penny, that 's all.'

'Do you mean to say, I 'm not, you dog?' returned Quilp.

"I'LL BEAT YOU TO A PULP, YOU DOGS."

'No!' retorted the boy.

'Then what do you fight on my wharf for, you villain?' said Quilp.

'Because he said so,' replied the boy pointing to Kit, 'not because you an't.'

'Then why did he say,' bawled Kit, 'that Miss Nelly was ugly, and that she and my master was obliged to do whatever his master liked? Why did he say that?'

'He said what he did because he 's a fool, and you said what you did because you 're very wise and clever—almost too clever to live, unless you 're very careful of yourself, Kit,' said Quilp with great suavity in his manner, but still more of quiet malice about his eyes and mouth. 'Here 's sixpence for you, Kit. Always speak the truth. At all times, Kit, speak the truth. Lock the counting-house, you dog, and bring me the key.'

The other boy, to whom this order was addressed, did as he was told, and was rewarded for his partisanship in behalf of his master, by a dexterous rap on the nose with the key, which brought the water into his eyes. Then, Mr. Quilp departed, with the child and Kit in a boat, and the boy revenged himself by dancing on his head at intervals on the extreme verge of the wharf, during the whole time they crossed the river.

There was only Mrs. Quilp at home, and she, little expecting the return of her lord, was just composing herself for a refreshing slumber when the sound of his footsteps roused her. She had barely time to seem to be occupied in some needle-work, when he entered, accompanied by the child; having left Kit downstairs.

'Here 's Nelly Trent, dear Mrs. Quilp,' said her husband. 'A glass of wine, my dear, and a biscuit, for she has had a long walk. She 'll sit with you, my soul, while I write a letter.'

Mrs. Quilp looked tremblingly in her spouse's face to know what this unusual courtesy might portend, and obedient to the summons she saw in his gesture, followed him into the next room.

'Mind what I say to you,' whispered Quilp. 'See if you can get out of her anything about her grandfather, or what they do, or how they live, or what he tells her. I 've my reasons for knowing, if I can. You women talk more freely to one another than you do to us, and you have a soft, mild way with you that 'll win upon her. Do you hear?'

'Yes, Quilp.'

'Go, then. What 's the matter now?'

'Dear Quilp,' faltered his wife, 'I love the child—if you *could* do without making me deceive her—'

The dwarf muttering a terrible oath looked round as if for some weapon with which to inflict condign punishment upon his disobedient wife. The submissive little woman hurriedly entreated him not to be angry, and promised to do as he bade her.

'Do you hear me?' whispered Quilp, nipping and pinching her arm; 'worm yourself into her secrets; I know you can. I 'm listening, recollect. If you 're not sharp enough I 'll creak the door, and woe betide you if I have to creak it much. Go!'

Mrs. Quilp departed according to order. Her amiable husband, ensconcing himself behind the partly-opened door, and applying his ear close to it, began to listen with a face of great craftiness and attention.

Poor Mrs. Quilp was thinking, however, in what manner to begin or what kind of inquiries she could make; it was not until the door, creaking in a very urgent manner, warned her to proceed without further consideration, that the sound of her voice was heard.

'How very often you have come backwards and forwards lately to Mr. Quilp, my dear.'

'I have said so to grandfather, a hundred times,' returned Nell innocently.

'And what has he said to that?'

'Only sighed, and dropped his head, and seemed so sad and wretched that if you could have seen him I am sure you must have cried; you could not have helped it more than I, I know. How that door creaks!'

'It often does,' returned Mrs. Quilp with an uneasy glance towards it. 'But your grandfather—he used not to be so wretched?'

'Oh no!' said the child eagerly, 'so different! we were once so happy and he so cheerful and contented! You cannot think what a sad change had fallen on us, since.'

'I am very, very sorry, to hear you speak like this, my dear!' said Mrs. Quilp. And she spoke the truth.

'Thank you,' returned the child, kissing her cheek, 'you are always kind to me, and it is a pleasure to talk to you. I can speak to no one else about him, but poor Kit. I am very happy still, I ought to feel happier perhaps than I do, but you cannot think how it grieves me sometimes to see him alter so.'

'He 'll alter again, Nelly,' said Mrs. Quilp, 'and be what he was before.'

'Oh, if God would only let that come about!' said the child with streaming eyes; 'but it is a long time now, since he first began to—I thought I saw that door moving!'

'It 's the wind,' said Mrs. Quilp faintly. 'Began to—?'

'To be so thoughtful and dejected, and to forget our old way of spending the time in the long evenings,' said the child. 'I used to read to him by the fireside, and he sat listening, and when I stopped and we began to talk, he told me about my mother, and how she once looked and spoke just like me when she was a little child. Then, he used to take me on his knee, and try to make me understand that she was not lying in her grave, but had flown to a beautiful country beyond the sky, where nothing died or ever grew old—we were very happy once!'

'Nelly, Nelly!'—said the poor woman, 'I can't bear to see one as young as you, so sorrowful. Pray don't cry.'

'I do so very seldom,' said Nell, 'but I have kept this to myself a long time, and I am not quite well, I think, for the tears come into my eyes and I cannot keep them back. I don't mind telling you of my grief, for I know you will not tell it to any one again.'

Mrs. Quilp turned away her head and made no answer.

'Then,' said the child, 'we often walked in the fields and among the green trees, and when we came home at night, we liked it better for being tired, and said what a happy place it was. And if it was dark and rather dull, we used to say, what did it matter to us, for it only made us remember our last walk with greater pleasure, and look forward to our next one. But, now, we never have these walks, and though it is the same house, it is darker and much more gloomy than it used to be. Indeed!'

She paused here, but though the door creaked more than once, Mrs. Quilp said nothing.

'Mind you don't suppose,' said the child earnestly, 'that grandfather is less kind to me than he was. I think he loves me better every day, and is kinder and more affectionate than he was the day before. You do not know how fond he is of me!'

'I am sure he loves you dearly,' said Mrs. Quilp.

'Indeed, indeed he does!' cried Nell, 'as dearly as I love him. But I have not told you the greatest change of all, and this you must never breathe again to any one. He has no sleep or rest, but that which he takes by day in his easy chair; for, every night and nearly all night long, he is away from home.'

'Nelly?'

'Hush!' said the child, laying her finger on her lip and looking round. 'When he comes home in the morning, which is generally just before day, I let him in. Last night he was very late, and it was quite light. I saw that his face was deadly pale, that his eyes were bloodshot, and that his legs trembled as he walked. When I had gone to bed again, I heard him groan. I got up and ran back to him, and heard him say, before he knew that I was there, that he could not bear his life much longer, and if it was not for the child, would wish to die. What shall I do? Oh! what shall I do?'

The fountains of her heart were opened; the child, overpowered by the weight of her sorrows and anxieties, by the first confidence she had ever shown, and the sympathy with which her little tale had been received, hid her face in the arms of her helpless friend, and burst into a passion of tears.

In a few moments Mr. Quilp returned, and expressed the utmost surprise to find her in this condition, which he did very naturally and with admirable effect; for that kind of acting had been rendered familiar to him by long practice, and he was quite at home in it.

'She 's tired, you see, Mrs. Quilp,' said the dwarf,

squinting in a hideous manner to imply that his wife was to follow his lead. It 's a long way from her home to the wharf, and then she was alarmed to see a couple of young scoundrels fighting, and was timorous on the water besides. All this together, has been too much for her. Poor Nell!'

Mr. Quilp unintentionally adopted the very best means he could have devised for the recovery of his young visitor, by patting her on the head. Such an application from any other hand might not have produced a remarkable effect, but the child shrunk so quickly from his touch and felt such an instinctive desire to get out of his reach, that she rose directly and declared herself ready to return.

'But you 'd better wait, and dine with Mrs. Quilp and me,' said the dwarf.

'I have been away too long, sir, already,' returned Nell, drying her eyes.

'Well,' said Mr. Quilp, 'if you will go, you will, Nelly. Here 's the note. It 's only to say that I shall see him to-morrow, or maybe next day, and that I couldn't do that little business for him this morning. Good-bye, Nelly. Here, you sir; take care of her, d' ye hear?'

Kit, who appeared at the summons, deigned to make no reply to so needless an injunction, and after staring at Quilp in a threatening manner as if he doubted whether he might not have been the cause of Nelly shedding tears, and felt more than half-disposed to revenge the fact upon him on the mere suspicion, turned about and followed his young mistress, who had by this time taken her leave of Mrs. Quilp and departed.

'You 're a keen questioner, an't you, Mrs. Quilp?' said the dwarf, turning upon her as soon as they were left alone.

'What more could I do?' returned his wife mildly.

'What more could you do?' sneered Quilp, 'couldn't you have done something less? couldn't you have done what you had to do, without appearing in your favourite part of the crocodile, you minx?'

'I am very sorry for the child, Quilp,' said his wife. 'Surely I 've done enough. I 've led her on to tell her secret when she supposed we were alone; and you were by, God forgive me.'

'You led her on! You did a great deal truly!' said Quilp. 'What did I tell you about making me creak the door? It 's lucky for you that from what she let fall, I 've got the clue I want, for if I hadn't, I 'd have visited the failure upon you.'

Mrs. Quilp being fully persuaded of this, made no reply. Her husband added with some exultation—

'But you may thank your fortunate stars—the same stars that made you Mrs. Quilp—you may thank them that I 'm upon the old gentleman's track, and have got a new light. So let me hear no more about this matter, now, or at any other time, and don't get anything too nice for dinner, for I shan't be home to it.'

So saying, Mr. Quilp put his hat on and took himself off, and Mrs. Quilp, who was afflicted beyond measure by the recollection of the part she had just acted, shut herself up in her chamber, and smothering her head in the bedclothes bemoaned her fault more bitterly than many less tender-hearted persons would have mourned a much greater offence; for, in the majority of cases, conscience is an elastic and very flexible article, which will bear a deal of stretching and adapt itself to a great variety of circumstances. Some people by prudent management and leaving it off piece by piece, like a flannel waistcoat in warm weather, even contrive, in time, to dispense with it altogether; but there be others who can assume the garment and throw it off at pleasure; and this, being the greatest and most convenient improvement, is the one most in vogue.

CHAPTER VII

'FRED,' said Mr. Swiveller, 'remember the once-popular melody of "Begone dull care"; fan the sinking flame of hilarity with the wink of friendship; and pass the rosy wine!'

Mr. Richard Swiveller's apartments were in the neighbourhood of Drury Lane, and in addition to this conveniency of situation had the advantage of being over a tobacconist's shop, so that he was enabled to procure a refreshing sneeze at any time by merely stepping out on the staircase, and was saved the trouble and expense of maintaining a snuff-box. It was in these apartments that Mr. Swiveller made use of the expressions above recorded, for the consolation and encouragement of his desponding friend; and it may not be uninteresting or improper to remark that even these brief observations partook in a double sense of the figurative and poetical character of Mr. Swiveller's mind, as the rosy wine was in fact represented by one glass of cold gin-and-water, which was replenished, as occasion required, from a bottle and jug upon the table, and was passed from one to another, in a scarcity of tumblers which, as Mr. Swiveller's was a bachelor's establishment, may be acknowledged without a blush. By a like pleasant fiction his single chamber was always mentioned in the plural number. In its disengaged times, the tobacconist had announced it in his window as 'apartments' for a single gentleman, and Mr. Swiveller, following up the hint, never failed to speak of it as his rooms, his lodgings, or his chambers: conveying to his hearers a notion of indefinite space, and leaving their imaginations to wander through long suites of lofty halls, at pleasure.

In this flight of fancy, Mr. Swiveller was assisted by a deceptive piece of furniture, in reality a bedstead, but in semblance a bookcase, which occupied a prominent situation in his chamber and seemed to defy suspicion and challenge inquiry. There is no doubt that, by day, Mr. Swiveller firmly believed this secret convenience to be a bookcase and nothing more; that he closed his eyes to the bed, resolutely denied the existence of the blankets, and spurned the bolster from his thoughts. No word of its real use, no hint of its nightly service, no allusion to its peculiar properties, had ever passed between him and his most intimate friends. Implicit faith in the deception was the first article of his creed. To be the friend of Swiveller you must reject all circumstantial evidence, all reason, observation, and experience, and repose a blind belief in the bookcase. It was his pet weakness, and he cherished it.

'Fred!' said Mr. Swiveller, finding that his former adjuration had been productive of no effect. 'Pass the rosy!'

Young Trent, with an impatient gesture, pushed the glass towards him, and fell again into the moody attitude from which he had been unwillingly roused.

'I 'll give you, Fred,' said his friend, stirring the mixture, 'a little sentiment appropriate to the occasion. Here 's May the—'

'Pshaw!' interposed the other. 'You worry me to death with your chattering. You can be merry under any circumstances.'

'Why, Mr. Trent,' returned Dick, 'there is a proverb which talks about being merry and wise. There are some people who can be merry and can't be wise, and some who can be wise (or think they can) and can't be merry. I 'm one of the first sort. If the proverb 's a good 'un, I suppose it 's better to keep to half of it than none; at all events I 'd rather be merry and not wise, than be like you—neither one nor t 'other.'

'Bah!' muttered his friend, peevishly.

'With all my heart,' said Mr. Swiveller. 'In the polite circles I believe this sort of thing isn't usually said to a gentleman in his own apartments, but never mind that. Make yourself at home.' Adding to this retort an observation to the effect that his friend appeared to be rather 'cranky' in point of temper, Richard Swiveller finished the rosy and applied himself to the composition of another glassful, in which, after tasting it with great relish, he proposed a toast to an imaginary company.

'Gentlemen, I 'll give you, if you please, Success to the ancient family of the Swivellers, and good luck to Mr. Richard in particular—Mr. Richard, gentlemen,' said Dick with great emphasis, 'who spends all his money on his friends and is *Bah!'d* for his pains. Hear, hear!'

'Dick!' said the other, returning to his seat after having paced the room twice or thrice, 'will you talk seriously for two minutes, if I show you a way to make your fortune with very little trouble?'

'You 've shown me so many,' returned Dick; 'and nothing has come of any one of 'em but empty pockets—'

'You 'll tell a different story of this one, before a very long time is over,' said his companion drawing his chair to the table. 'You saw my sister Nell?'

'What about her?' returned Dick.

'She has a pretty face, has she not?'

'Why, certainly,' replied Dick, 'I must say for her

that there 's not any very strong family likeness between her and you.'

'Has she a pretty face?' repeated his friend impatiently.

'Yes,' said Dick, 'she has a pretty face, a very pretty face. What of that?'

'I 'll tell you,' returned his friend. 'It 's very plain that the old man and I will remain at daggers-drawn to the end of our lives, and that I have nothing to expect from him. You see that, I suppose?'

'A bat might see that, with the sun shining,' said Dick.

'It 's equally plain that the money which the old flint—rot him—first taught me to expect that I should share with her at his death, will all be hers, is it not?'

'I should say it was,' replied Dick; 'unless the way in which I put the case to him, made an impression. It may have done so. It was powerful, Fred. "Here is a jolly old grandfather"—that was strong, I thought—very friendly and natural. Did it strike you in that way?'

'It didn't strike *him*,' returned the other, 'so we needn't discuss it. Now look here. Nell is nearly fourteen.'

'Fine girl of her age, but small,' observed Richard Swiveller parenthetically.

'If I am to go on, be quiet for one minute,' returned Trent, fretting at the very slight interest the other appeared to take in the conversation. 'Now I 'm coming to the point.'

'That 's right,' said Dick.

'The girl has strong affections, and brought up as she has been, may, at her age, be easily influenced and persuaded. If I take her in hand, I will be bound by a very little coaxing and threatening to bend her to my will. Not to beat about the bush (for the advantages of the scheme would take a week to tell) what 's to prevent your marrying her?'

Richard Swiveller, who had been looking over the rim of the tumbler while his companion addressed the foregoing remarks to him with great energy and earnestness of manner, no sooner heard these words than he evinced the utmost consternation, and with difficulty ejaculated the monosyllable,

'What?'

'I say, what 's to prevent,' repeated the other, with a steadiness of manner, of the effect of which upon his companion he was well assured by long experience, 'what 's to prevent your marrying her?'

'And she "nearly fourteen!" ' cried Dick.

'I don't mean marrying her now'—returned the brother angrily; 'say in two years' time, in three, in four. Does the old man look like a long-liver?'

'He don't look like it,' said Dick shaking his head, 'but these old people—there 's no trusting 'em, Fred. There 's an aunt of mine down in Dorsetshire that was going to die when I was eight years old, and hasn't kept her word yet. They 're so aggravating, so unprincipled, so spiteful—unless there 's apoplexy in the family, Fred, you can't calculate upon 'em, and even then they deceive you just as often as not.'

'Look at the worst side of the question then,' said Trent as steadily as before, and keeping his eyes upon his friend. 'Suppose he lives.'

'To be sure,' said Dick. 'There 's the rub.'

'I say,' resumed his friend, 'suppose he lives, and I persuaded, or if the word sounds more feasible, forced, Nell to a secret marriage with you. What do you think would come of that?'

'A family and an annual income of nothing, to keep 'em on,' said Richard Swiveller after some reflection.

'I tell you,' returned the other with an increased

earnestness, which, whether it were real or assumed, had the same effect on his companion, 'that he lives for her, that his whole energies and thoughts are bound up in her, that he would no more disinherit her for an act of disobedience than he would take me into his favour again for any act of obedience or virtue that I could possibly be guilty of. He could not do it. You or any other man with eyes in his head may see that, if he chooses.'

'It seems improbable certainly,' said Dick, musing.

'It seems improbable because it is improbable,' his friend returned. 'If you would furnish him with an additional inducement to forgive you, let there be an irreconcileable breach, a most deadly quarrel, between you and me—let there be a pretence of such a thing, I mean, of course—and he 'll do so fast enough. As to Nell, constant dropping will wear away a stone; you know you may trust to me as far as she is concerned. So, whether he lives or dies, what does it come to? That you become the sole inheritor of the wealth of this rich old hunks; that you and I spend it together; and that you get, into the bargain, a beautiful young wife.'

'I suppose there 's no doubt about his being rich,' said Dick.

'Doubt! Did you hear what he let fall the other day when we were there? Doubt! What will you doubt next, Dick?'

It would be tedious to pursue the conversation through all its artful windings, or to develop the gradual approaches by which the heart of Richard Swiveller was gained. It is sufficient to know that vanity, interest, poverty, and every spendthrift consideration urged him to look upon the proposal with favour, and that where all other inducements were wanting, the habitual carelessness of his disposition stepped in and still weighed down the scale on the same side. To these impulses must be added the complete ascendancy which his friend had long been accustomed to exercise over him—an ascendancy exerted in the beginning sorely at the expense of the unfortunate Dick's purse and prospects, but still maintained without the slightest relaxation, nothwithstanding that Dick suffered for all his friend's vices and was, in nine cases out of ten, looked upon as his designing tempter when he was indeed nothing but his thoughtless light-headed tool.

The motives on the other side were something deeper than any which Richard Swiveller entertained or understood, but these being left to their own development, require no present elucidation. The negotiation was concluded very pleasantly, and Mr. Swiveller was in the act of stating in flowery terms that he had no insurmountable objection to marrying anybody plentifully endowed with money or moveables, who could be induced to take him, when he was interrupted in his observations by a knock at the door, and the consequent necessity of crying 'Come in.'

The door was opened, but nothing came in except a soapy arm and a strong gush of tobacco. The gush of tobacco came from the shop downstairs, and the soapy arm proceeded from the body of a servant girl, who being then and there engaged in cleaning the stairs had just drawn it out of a warm pail to take in a letter, which letter she now held in her hand; proclaiming aloud, with that quick perception of surnames peculiar to her class, that it was for Mister Snivelling.

Dick looked rather pale and foolish when he glanced at the direction, and still more so when he came to look at the inside; observing that this was one of the inconveniences of being a lady's man, and that it was very easy to talk as they had been talking, but he had quite forgotten her.

'*Her*. Who?' demanded Trent.

'Sophy Wackles,' said Dick.

'Who 's she?'

'She 's all my fancy painted her, sir, that 's what she is,' said Mr. Swiveller, taking a long pull at 'the rosy' and looking gravely at his friend. 'She is lovely, she 's divine. You know her.'

'I remember,' said his companion carelessly. 'What of her?'

'Why, sir,' returned Dick, 'between Miss Sophia Wackles and the humble individual who has now the honour to address you, warm and tender sentiments have been engendered—sentiments of the most honourable and inspiring kind. The Goddess Diana, sir, that calls aloud for the chase, is not more particular in her behaviour than Sophia Wackles; I can tell you that.'

'Am I to believe there 's anything real in what you say?' demanded his friend; 'you don't mean to say that any love-making has been going on?'

'Love-making, yes. Promising, no,' said Dick. 'There can be no action for breach, that 's one comfort. I 've never committed myself in writing, Fred.'

'And what 's in the letter pray?'

'A reminder, Fred, for to-night—a small party of twenty—making two hundred light fantastic toes in all, supposing every lady and gentleman to have the proper complement. I must go, if it 's only to begin breaking off the affair—I 'll do it, don't you be afraid. I should like to know whether she left this, herself. If she did, unconscious of any bar to her happiness, it 's affecting, Fred.

To solve this question, Mr. Swiveller summoned the handmaid and ascertained that Miss Sophy

Wackles had indeed left the letter with her own hands; and that she had come accompanied, for decorum's sake, no doubt, by a younger Miss Wackles; and that on learning that Mr. Swiveller was at home and being requested to walk upstairs, she was extremely shocked and professed that she would rather die. Mr. Swiveller heard this account with a degree of admiration not altogether consistent with the project in which he had just concurred, but his friend attached very little importance to his behaviour in this respect, probably because he knew that he had influence sufficient to control Richard Swiveller's proceedings in this or any other matter, whenever he deemed it necessary, for the advancement of his own purposes, to exert it.

CHAPTER VIII

Business disposed of, Mr. Swiveller was inwardly reminded of its being nigh dinner-time, and to the intent that his health might not be endangered by longer abstinence, despatched a message to the nearest eating-house requiring an immediate supply of boiled beef and greens for two. With this demand, however, the eating-house (having experience of its customer) declined to comply, churlishly sending back for answer that if Mr. Swiveller stood in need of beef perhaps he would be so obliging as to come there and eat it, bringing with him, as grace before meat, the amount of a certain small account which had been long outstanding. Not at all intimidated by this rebuff, but rather sharpened in wits and appetite, Mr. Swiveller forwarded the same message to another and more distant eating-house, adding to it by way of rider that the gentleman was induced to send so far, not only by the great fame and popularity its beef had acquired, but in consequence of the extreme toughness of the beef retailed at the obdurate cook's shop, which rendered it quite unfit not merely for gentlemanly food but for any human consumption. The good effect of this politic course was demonstrated by the speedy arrival of a small pewter pyramid, curiously constructed of platters and covers, whereof the boiled-beef-plates formed the base, and a foaming quart-pot the apex; the structure being resolved into its component parts afforded all things requisite and necessary for a hearty meal, to which Mr. Swiveller and his friend applied themselves with great keenness and enjoyment.

'May the present moment,' said Dick, sticking his fork into a large carbuncular potato, 'be the worst of our lives! I like this plan of sending 'em with the peel on; there 's a charm in drawing a potato from its native element (if I may so express it) to which the rich and powerful are strangers. Ah! "Man wants but little here below, nor wants that little long!" How true that is!—after dinner.'

'I hope the eating-house keeper will want but little and that *he* may not want that little long,' returned his companion; 'but I suspect you 've no means of paying for this!'

'I shall be passing presently, and I 'll call,' said Dick, winking his eye significantly. 'The waiter 's quite helpless. The goods are gone, Fred, and there 's an end of it.'

In point of fact, it would seem that the waiter felt this wholesome truth, for when he returned for the empty plates and dishes and was informed by Mr. Swiveller with dignified carelessness that he would call and settle when he should be passing presently, he displayed some perturbation of spirit, and muttered a few remarks about 'payment on delivery,' and 'no trust,' and other unpleasant subjects, but was fain to content himself with inquiring at what hour it was likely the gentleman would call, in order that being personally responsible for the beef, greens, and sundries, he might take care to be in the way at the time. Mr. Swiveller, after mentally calculating his engagements to a nicety, replied that he should look in at from two minutes before six to seven minutes past; and the man disappearing with this feeble consolation, Richard Swiveller took a greasy memorandum-book from his pocket and made an entry therein.

'Is that a reminder, in case yould should forget to call?' said Trent with a sneer.

'Not exactly, Fred,' replied the imperturbable Richard, continuing to write with a business-like air, 'I enter in this little book the names of the streets that I can't go down while the shops are open. This dinner to-day closes Long Acre. I bought a pair of boots in Great Queen Street last week, and made that no thoroughfare too. There 's only one avenue to the Strand left open now, and I shall have to stop up that to-night with a pair of gloves. The roads are closing so fast in every direction, that in about a month's time, unless my aunt sends me a remittance, I shall have to go three or four miles out of town to get over the way.'

'There 's no fear of her failing, in the end?' said Trent.

'Why, I hope not,' returned Mr. Swiveller, 'but the average number of letters it takes to soften her is six, and this time we have got as far as eight without any effect at all. I 'll write another to-morrow morning. I mean to blot it a good deal and shake some water over it out of the pepper-castor, to make it look penitent. "I 'm in such a state of mind that I hardly know what I write"—blot—"if you could see me at this minute shedding tears for my past misconduct"—pepper-castor—"my hand trembles when I think"—blot again—if that don't produce the effect, it 's all over.'

By this time Mr. Swiveller had finished his entry, and he now replaced his pencil in its little sheath and closed the book, in a perfectly grave and serious frame of mind. His friend discovered that it was time for him to fulfil some other engagement, and Richard Swiveller was accordingly left alone, in company with the rosy wine and his own meditations touching Miss Sophy Wackles.

'It 's rather sudden,' said Dick shaking his head with a look of infinite wisdom, and running on (as he was accustomed to do) with scraps of verse as if they were only prose in a hurry; 'when the heart of a man is depressed with fears, the mist is dispelled when Miss Wackles appears; she 's a very nice girl. She 's like the red red rose that 's newly sprung in June—there 's no denying that—she 's also like a melody that 's sweetly played in tune. It 's really very sudden. Not that there 's any need, on account of Fred 's little sister, to turn cool directly, but it 's better not to go too far. If I begin to cool at all I must begin at once, I see that. There 's the chance of an action for breach, that 's one reason. There 's the chance of Sophy's getting another husband, that 's another. There 's the chance of—no, there 's no chance of that, but it 's as well to be on the safe side.'

This undeveloped consideration was the possibility, which Richard Swiveller sought to conceal even from himself, of his not being proof against the charms of Miss Wackles, and in some unguarded moment, by linking his fortunes to her for ever, of putting it out of his own power to further the notable scheme to which he had so readily become a party. For all these reasons, he decided to pick a quarrel with Miss Wackles without delay, and casting about for a pretext determined in favour of groundless jealousy. Having made up his mind on this important point, he circulated the glass (from his right hand to his left, and back again) pretty freely, to enable him to act his part with the greater discretion, and then, after making some slight improvements in his toilet, bent his steps towards the spot hallowed by the fair object of his meditations.

This spot was at Chelsea, for there Miss Sophia Wackles resided with her widowed mother and two sisters, in conjunction with whom she maintained a very small day-school for young ladies of proportionate dimensions; a circumstance which was made known to the neighbourhood by an oval board over the front first-floor window, whereon appeared, in circumambient flourishes, the words 'Ladies' Seminary'; and which was further published and proclaimed at intervals between the hours of half-past nine and ten in the morning, by a straggling and solitary young lady of tender years standing on the scraper on the tips of her toes and making futile attempts to reach the knocker with a spelling-book. The several duties of instruction in this establishment were thus discharged. English grammar, composition, geography, and the use of the dumb bells, by Miss Melissa Wackles; writing, arithmetic, dancing, music, and general fascination, by Miss Sophy Wackles; the art of needle-work, marking, and samplery, by Miss Jane Wackles; corporal punishment, fasting, and other tortures and terrors, by Mrs. Wackles. Miss Melissa Wackles was the eldest daughter, Miss Sophy the next, and Miss Jane the youngest. Miss Melissa might have seen five-and-thirty summers or thereabouts, and verged on the autumnal; Miss Sophy was a fresh, good-humoured, buxom girl of twenty; and Miss Jane numbered scarcely sixteen years. Mrs. Wackles was an excellent, but rather venomous old lady of three-score.

To this Ladies' Seminary then, Richard Swiveller hied, with designs obnoxious to the peace of the fair Sophia, who, arrayed in virgin white, embellished by no ornament but one blushing rose, received him on his arrival, in the midst of very elegant not to say brilliant preparations; such as the embellishment of the room with the little flower-pots which always stood on the window-sill outside, save in windy weather when they blew into the area; the choice attire of the day-scholars who were allowed to grace the festival; the unwonted curls of Miss Jane Wackles who had kept her head during the whole of the preceding day screwed up tight in a yellow play-bill; and the solemn gentility and stately bearing of the old lady and her eldest daughter, which struck Mr. Swiveller as being uncommon but made no further impression upon him.

The truth is—and, as there is no accounting for tastes, even a taste so strange as this may be recorded without being looked upon as a wilful and malicious invention—the truth is, that neither Mrs. Wackles nor her eldest daughter had at any time greatly favoured the pretensions of Mr. Swiveller: they being accustomed to make slight mention of him as 'a gay young man' and to sigh and shake their heads ominously, whenever his name was mentioned. Mr. Swiveller's conduct in respect to Miss Sophy having been of that vague and dilatory kind which is usually looked upon as betokening no fixed matrimonial intentions, the young lady herself began in course of time to deem it highly desirable, that it should be brought to an issue one way or other. Hence, she had at last consented to play off, against Richard Swiveller, a stricken market-gardener known to be ready with his offer on the smallest encouragement, and hence—as this occasion had been especially assigned for the purpose—that great anxiety on her part for Richard Swiveller's presence which had occasioned her to leave the note he has been seen to receive. 'If he has any expectations at all or any means of keeping a wife well,' said Mrs. Wackles to her eldest daughter, 'he 'll state 'em to us now or never.'—'If he really cares about me,' thought Miss Sophy, 'he must tell me so, to-night.'

But all these sayings and doings and thinkings being unknown to Mr. Swiveller, affected him not in the least; he was debating in his mind how he could best turn jealous, and wishing that Sophy were, for that occasion only, far less pretty than she was, or that she were her own sister, which would have served his turn as well, when the company came, and among them the market-gardener, whose name was Cheggs. But Mr. Cheggs came not alone or unsupported, for he prudently brought along with him his sister, Miss Cheggs, who making straight to Miss Sophy and taking her by both hands, and kissing her on both cheeks, hoped in an audible whisper that they had not come too early.

'Too early? No!' replied Miss Sophy.

'Oh my dear,' rejoined Miss Cheggs in the same whisper as before, 'I 've been so tormented, so worried, that it 's a mercy we were not here at four o'clock in the afternoon. Alick has been in *such* a state of impatience to come! You 'd hardly believe that he was dressed before dinner-time and has been looking at the clock and teasing me ever since. It 's all your fault, you naughty thing.'

Miss Sophy blushed, and Mr. Cheggs (who was bashful before ladies) blushed too, and Miss Sophy's mother and sisters, to prevent Mr. Cheggs from blushing more, lavished civilities and attentions upon him, and left Richard Swiveller to take care of himself. Here was the very thing he wanted; here was good cause, reason, and foundation, for pretending to be angry; but having this cause, reason, and foundation which he had come expressly to seek, not expecting to find, Richard Swiveller was angry in sound earnest, and wondered what the devil Cheggs meant by his impudence.

However, Mr. Swiveller had Miss Sophy's hand for the first quadrille (country-dances being low, were utterly proscribed), and so gained an advantage over his rival, who sat despondingly in a corner and contemplated the glorious figure of the young lady as she moved through the mazy dance. Nor was this the only start Mr. Swiveller had of the market-gardener; for, determining to show the family what quality of man they trifled with, and influenced perhaps by his late libations, he performed such feats of agility and such spins and twirls as filled the company with astonishment, and in particular caused a very long gentleman who was dancing with a very short scholar, to stand quite transfixed by wonder and admiration. Even Mrs. Wackles forgot for the moment to snub three small young ladies who were inclined to be happy, and could not repress a rising thought that to have such a dancer as that in the family would be a pride indeed.

At this momentous crisis, Miss Cheggs proved herself a vigorous and useful ally; for, not confining herself to expressing by scornful smiles a contempt for Mr. Swiveller's accomplishments, she took every opportunity of whispering into Miss Sophy's ear expressions of condolence and sympathy on her being worried by such a ridiculous creature, declaring that she was frightened to death lest Alick should fall upon him, and beat him, in the fulness of his wrath, and entreating Miss Sophy to observe how the eyes of the said Alick gleamed with love and fury; passions, it may be observed, which being too much for his eyes rushed into his nose also, and suffused it with a crimson glow.

'You must dance with Miss Cheggs,' said Miss Sophy to Dick Swiveller, after she had herself danced twice with Mr. Cheggs and made a great show of encouraging his advances. 'She 's such a nice girl—and her brother 's quite delightful.'

'Quite delightful is he?' muttered Dick. 'Quite delighted too, I should say, from the manner in which he 's looking this way.'

Here Miss Jane (previously instructed for the purpose) interposed her many curls and whispered her sister to observe how jealous Mr. Cheggs was.

'Jealous! Like his impudence!' said Richard Swiveller.

'His impudence, Mr. Swiveller!' said Miss Jane, tossing her head. 'Take care he don't hear you, sir, or you may be sorry for it.'

'Oh pray, Jane—' said Miss Sophy.

'Nonsense!' replied her sister. 'Why shouldn't Mr. Cheggs be jealous if he likes? I like that, certainly. Mr. Cheggs has as good a right to be jealous as anybody else has, and perhaps he may have a better right soon if he hasn't already. You know best about that, Sophy!'

Though this was a concerted plot between Miss Sophy and her sister, originating in humane intentions and having for its object the inducing Mr. Swiveller to declare himself in time, it failed in its effect; for Miss Jane being one of those young ladies who are prematurely shrill and shrewish, gave such undue importance to her part that Mr. Swiveller retired in dudgeon, resigning his mistress to Mr. Cheggs and conveying a defiance into his looks which that gentleman indignantly returned.

'Did you speak to me, sir?' said Mr. Cheggs, following him into a corner.—'Have the kindness to smile, sir, in order that we may not be suspected.—Did you speak to me, sir?'

Mr. Swiveller looked with a supercilious smile at Mr. Cheggs's toes, then raised his eyes from them to his ankle, from that to his chin, from that to his knee, and so on very gradually, keeping up his right leg, until he reached his waistcoat, when he raised his eyes from button to button until he reached his chin, and travelling straight up the middle of his nose came at last to his eyes, when he said abruptly—

'No, sir, I didn't.'

'Hem!' said Mr. Cheggs, glancing over his shoulder, 'have the goodness to smile again, sir. Perhaps you wished to speak to me, sir.'

'No, sir, I didn't do that, either.'

'Perhaps you may have nothing to say to me *now*, sir,' said Mr. Cheggs fiercely.

At these words, Richard Swiveller withdrew his eyes from Mr. Cheggs's face, and travelling down the middle of his nose, and down his waistcoat, and down his right leg, reached his toes again, and carefully surveyed them; this done, he crossed over, and coming up the other leg, and thence approaching by the waistcoat as before, said when he had got to his eyes 'No, sir, I haven't.'

'Oh indeed, sir!' said Mr. Cheggs. 'I 'm glad to hear it. You know where I 'm to be found, I suppose, sir, in case you *should* have anything to say to me?'

'I can easily inquire, sir, when I want to know.'

'There 's nothing more we need say, I believe, sir?'

'Nothing more, sir,'—With that they closed the tremendous dialogue by frowning mutually. Mr. Cheggs hastened to tender his hand to Miss Sophy, and Mr. Swiveller sat himself down in a corner in a very moody state.

Hard by this corner, Mrs. Wackles and Miss Wackles were seated, looking on at the dance; and unto Mrs. and Miss Wackles, Miss Cheggs occasionally darted when her partner was occupied with his share of the figure, and made some remark or other which was gall and wormwood to Richard Swiveller's soul. Looking into the eyes of Mrs. and Miss Wackles for encouragement, and sitting very upright and uncomfortable on a couple of hard stools, were two of the day-scholars; and when Miss Wackles smiled, and Mrs. Wackles smiled, the two little girls on the stools sought to curry favour by smiling likewise, in gracious acknowledgment of which attention the old lady frowned them down instantly, and said that if they dared to be guilty of such an impertinence again, they should be sent under convoy to their respective homes. This threat caused one of the young ladies, she being of a weak and trembling temperament, to shed tears, and for this offence they were both filed off immediately, with a dreadful promptitude that struck terror into the souls of all the pupils.

'I 've got such news for you,' said Miss Cheggs approaching once more. 'Alick has been saying such things to Sophy. Upon my word, you know, it 's quite serious and in earnest, that 's clear.'

'What 's he been saying, my dear?' demanded Mrs. Wackles.

'All manner of things,' replied Miss Cheggs, 'you can't think how out he has been speaking!'

Richard Swiveller considered it advisable to hear no more, but taking advantage of a pause in the dancing, and the approach of Mr. Cheggs to pay his court to the old lady, swaggered with an extremely careful assumption of extreme carelessness towards the door, passing on the way Miss Jane Wackles, who in all the glory of her curls was holding a flirtation (as good practice when no better was to be had) with a feeble old gentleman who lodged in the parlour. Near the door sat Miss Sophy, still fluttered and confused by the attentions of Mr. Cheggs, and by her side Richard Swiveller lingered for a moment to exchange a few parting words.

'My boat is on the shore and my bark is on the sea, but before I pass this door I will say farewell to thee,' murmured Dick, looking gloomily upon her.

'Are you going?' said Miss Sophy, whose heart sunk within her at the result of her stratagem, but who affected a light indifference notwithstanding.

'Am I going?' echoed Dick bitterly. 'Yes, I am. What then?'

'Nothing, except that it's very early,' said Miss Sophy; 'but you are your own master of course.'

'I would that I had been my own mistress too,' said Dick, 'before I had ever entertained a thought of you. Miss Wackles, I believed you true, and I was blest in so believing, but now I mourn that e'er I knew, a girl so fair yet so deceiving.'

Miss Sophy bit her lip and affected to look with great interest after Mr. Cheggs, who was quaffing lemonade in the distance.

'I came here,' said Dick, rather oblivious of the purpose with which he had really come, 'with my bosom expanded, my heart dilated, and my sentiments of a corresponding description. I go away with feelings that may be conceived, but cannot be described: feeling within myself the desolating truth that my best affections have experienced, this night, a stifler!'

'I am sure I don't know what you mean, Mr. Swiveller,' said Miss Sophy with downcast eyes. 'I 'm very sorry if—'

'Sorry, ma'am!' said Dick, 'sorry in the possession of a Cheggs! But I wish you a very good-night; concluding with this light remark, that there is a young lady growing up at this present moment for me, who has not only great personal attractions but great wealth, and who has requested her next of kin to propose for my hand, which, having a regard for some members of her family, I have consented to promise. It 's a gratifying circumstance which you 'll be glad to hear, that a young and lovely girl is growing into a woman expressly on my account, and is now saving up for me. I thought I 'd mention it. I have now merely to apologise for trespassing so long upon your attention. Good-night!'

'There 's one good thing springs out of all this,' said Richard Swiveller to himself when he had reached home and was hanging over the candle with the extinguisher in his hand, 'which is, that I now go heart and soul, neck and heels, with Fred in all his scheme about little Nelly, and right glad he 'll be to find me so strong upon it. He shall know all about that to-morrow, and in the meantime, as it 's rather late, I 'll try and get a wink or two of the balmy.'

'The balmy' came almost as soon as it was courted. In a very few minutes Mr. Swiveller was fast asleep, dreaming that he had married Nelly Trent and come into the property, and that his first act of power was to lay waste the market-garden of Mr. Cheggs and turn it into a brick-field.

CHAPTER IX

THE child, in her confidence with Mrs. Quilp, had but feebly described the sadness and sorrow of her thoughts, or the heaviness of the cloud which overhung her home, and cast dark shadows on its hearth. Besides that it was very difficult to impart to any person not intimately acquainted with the life she led, an adequate sense of its gloom and loneliness, a constant fear of in some way committing or injuring the old man to whom she was so tenderly attached, had restrained her, even in the midst of her heart's overflowing, and made her timid of allusion to the main cause of her anxiety and distress.

For, it was not the monotonous days unchequered by variety and uncheered by pleasant companionship, it was not the dark dreary evenings or the long solitary nights, it was not the absence of every slight and easy pleasure for which young hearts beat high, or the knowing nothing of childhood but its weakness and its easily wounded spirit, that had wrung such tears from Nell. To see the old man struck down beneath the pressure of some hidden grief, to mark his wavering and unsettled state, to be agitated at times with a dreadful fear that his mind was wandering, and to trace in his words and looks the dawning of despondent madness; to watch and wait and listen for confirmation of these things day after day, and to feel and know that, come what might, they were alone in the world with no one to help or advise or care about them—these were causes of depression and anxiety that might have sat heavily on an older breast with many influences at work to cheer and gladden it, but how heavily on the mind of a young child to whom they were ever present, and who was constantly surrounded by all that could keep such thoughts in restless action!

And yet, to the old man's vision, Nell was still the same. When he could, for a moment, disengage his mind from the phantom that haunted and brooded on it always, there was his young companion with the same smile for him, the same earnest words, the same merry laugh, the same love and care that, sinking deep into his soul, seemed to have been present to him through his whole life. And so he went on, content to read the book of her heart from the page first presented to him, little dreaming of the story that lay hidden in its other leaves, and murmuring within himself that at least the child was happy.

She had been once. She had gone singing through the dim rooms, and moving with gay and lightsome step among their dusty treasures, making them older by her young life, and sterner and more grim by her gay and cheerful presence. But, now, the chambers were cold and gloomy, and when she left her own little room to while away the tedious hours, and sat in one of them, she was still and motionless as their inanimate occupants, and had no heart to startle the echoes —hoarse from their long silence—with her voice.

In one of these rooms, was a window looking into the street, where the child sat, many and many a long evening, and often far into the night, alone and thoughtful. None are so anxious as those who watch and wait; at these times, mournful fancies came flocking on her mind, in crowds.

She would take her station here, at dusk, and watch the people as they passed up and down the street, or appeared at the windows of the opposite houses; wondering whether those rooms were as lonesome as that in which she sat, and whether those people felt it company to see her sitting there, as she did only to see them look out and draw in their heads again. There was a crooked stack of chimneys on one of the roofs, in which, by often looking at them, she had fancied ugly faces that were frowning over at her and trying to peer into the room; and she felt glad when it grew too dark to make them out, though she was sorry to, when the man came to light the lamps in the street—for it made it late, and very dull inside. Then, she would draw in her head to look round the room and see that everything was in its place and hadn't moved; and looking out into the street again, would perhaps see a man passing with a coffin on his back, and two or three others silently following him to a house where somebody lay dead; which made her shudder and think of such things until they suggested afresh the old man's altered face and manner, and a new train of fears and speculations. If he were to die—if sudden illness had happened to him, and he were never to come home again, alive—if, one night, he should come home, and kiss and bless her as usual, and after she had gone to bed and had fallen asleep and was perhaps dreaming pleasantly, and smiling in her sleep, he should kill himself and his blood come creeping, creeping, on the ground to her own bedroom door! These thoughts were too terrible to dwell upon, and again she would have recourse to the street, now trodden by fewer feet, and darker and more silent than before. The shops were closing fast, and lights began to shine from the upper windows, as the neighbours went to bed. By degrees, these dwindled away and disappeared, or were replaced, here and there, by a feeble rush-candle which was to burn all night. Still, there was one late shop at no great distance which sent forth a ruddy glare upon the pavement even yet, and looked bright and companionable. But, in a little time, this closed, the light was extinguished, and all was gloomy and quiet, except when some stray foot-step sounded on the pavement, or a neighbour, out later than his wont, knocked lustily at his house-door to rouse the sleeping inmates.

When the night had worn away thus far (and seldom now until it had) the child would close the window, and steal softly downstairs, thinking as she went that if one of those hideous faces below, which often mingled with her dreams, were to meet her by the way, rendering itself visible by some strange light of its own, how terrified she would be. But these fears vanished before a well-trimmed lamp and the familiar aspect of her own room. After praying fervently, and with many bursting tears, for the old man, and the restoration of his peace of mind and the happiness they had once enjoyed, she would lay her head upon the pillow and sob herself to sleep: often starting up again, before the daylight came, to listen for the bell, and respond to the imaginary summons which had roused her from her slumber.

One night, the third after Nelly's interview with Mrs. Quilp, the old man, who had been weak and ill all day, said he should not leave home. The child's eyes sparkled at the intelligence, but her joy subsided when they reverted to his worn and sickly face.

'Two days,' he said, 'two whole, clear, days have passed, and there is no reply. What *did* he tell thee, Nell?'

'Exactly what I told you, dear grandfather, indeed.'

'True,' said the old man, faintly. 'Yes. But tell me again, Nell. My head fails me. What was it that he told thee? Nothing more than that he would see me to-morrow or next day? That was in the note.'

'Nothing more,' said the child. 'Shall I go to him

again to-morrow, dear grandfather? Very early? I will be there and back, before breakfast.'

The old man shook his head, and sighing mournfully, drew her towards him.

''Twould be of no use, my dear, no earthly use. But if he deserts me, Nell, at this moment—if he deserts me now, when I should, with his assistance, be recompensed for all the time and money I have lost, and all the agony of mind I have undergone, which makes me what you see, I am ruined, and—worse, far worse than that—have ruined thee, for whom I ventured all. If we are beggars—!'

'What if we are?' said the child boldly. 'Let us be beggars, and be happy.'

'Beggars—and happy!' said the old man. 'Poor child!'

'Dear grandfather,' cried the girl with an energy which shone in her flushed face, trembling voice, and impassioned gesture, 'I am not a child in that, I think, but even if I am, oh hear me pray that we may beg, or work in open roads or fields, to earn a scanty living, rather than live as we do now.'

'Nelly!' said the old man.

'Yes, yes, rather than live as we do now,' the child repeated, more earnestly than before. 'If you are sorrowful, let me know why and be sorrowful too; if you waste away and are paler and weaker every day, let me be your nurse and try to comfort you. If you are poor, let us be poor together; but let me be with you, do let me be with you; do not let me see such change and not know why, or I shall break my heart and die. Dear grandfather, let us leave this sad place to-morrow, and beg our way from door to door.'

The old man covered his face with his hands, and hid it in the pillow of the couch on which he lay.

'Let us be beggars,' said the child passing an arm round his neck, 'I have no fear but we shall have enough, I am sure we shall. Let us walk through country places, and sleep in fields and under trees, and never think of money again, or anything that can make you sad, but rest at nights, and have the sun and wind upon our faces in the day, and thank God together! Let us never set foot in dark rooms or melancholy houses, any more, but wander up and down wherever we like to go; and when you are tired, you shall stop to rest in the pleasantest place that we can find, and I will go and beg for both.'

The child's voice was lost in sobs as she dropped upon the old man's neck; nor did she weep alone.

These were not words for other ears, nor was it a scene for other eyes. And yet other ears and eyes were there and greedily taking in all that passed, and moreover they were the ears and eyes of no less a person than Mr. Daniel Quilp, who, having entered unseen when the child first placed herself at the old man's side, refrained—actuated, no doubt, by motives of the purest delicacy—from interrupting the conversation, and stood looking on with his accustomed grin. Standing, however, being a tiresome attitude to a gentleman already fatigued with walking, and the dwarf being one of that kind of persons who usually make themselves at home, he soon cast his eyes upon a chair, into which he skipped with uncommon agility, and perching himself on the back with his feet upon the seat, was thus enabled to look on and listen with greater comfort to himself, besides gratifying at the same time that taste for doing something fantastic and monkey-like, which on all occasions had strong possession of him. Here, then, he sat, one leg cocked carelessly over the other, his chin resting on the palm of his hand, his head turned a little on one side, and his ugly features twisted into a complacent grimace. And in this position the old man, happening in course of time to look that way, at length chanced to see him: to his unbounded astonishment.

The child uttered a suppressed shriek on beholding this agreeable figure; in their first surprise both she and the old man, not knowing what to say, and half doubting its reality, looked shrinkingly at it. Not at all disconcerted by this reception, Daniel Quilp preserved the same attitude, merely nodding twice or thrice with great condescension. At length, the old man pronounced his name, and inquired how he came there.

'Through the door,' said Quilp pointing over his shoulder with his thumb. 'I 'm not quite small enough to get through key-holes. I wish I was. I want to have some talk with you, particularly, and in private. With nobody present, neighbour. Good-bye, little Nelly.'

Nell looked at the old man, who nodded to her to retire, and kissed her cheek.

'Ah!' said the dwarf, smacking his lips, 'what a nice kiss that was—just upon the rosy part. What a capital kiss!'

Nell was none the slower in going away, for this remark. Quilp looked after her with an admiring leer, and when she had closed the door, fell to complimenting the old man upon her charms.

'Such a fresh, blooming, modest little bud, neighbour,' said Quilp, nursing his short leg, and making his eyes twinkle very much; 'such a chubby, rosy, cosy, little Nell!'

The old man answered by a forced smile, and was plainly struggling with a feeling of the keenest and most exquisite impatience. It was not lost upon Quilp, who delighted in torturing him, or indeed anybody else, when he could.

'She 's so,' said Quilp, speaking very slowly, and feigning to be quite absorbed in the subject, 'so small, so compact, so beautifully modelled, so fair, with such blue veins and such a transparent skin, and such little feet, and such winning ways—but bless me, you 're nervous! Why, neighbour, what 's the matter? I swear to you,' continued the dwarf dismounting from the chair and sitting down in it, with a careful slowness of gesture very different from the rapidity with which he had sprung up unheard, 'I swear to you that I had no idea old blood ran so fast or kept so warm. I thought it was sluggish in its course, and cool, quite cool. I am pretty sure it ought to be. Yours must be out of order, neighbour.'

'I believe it is,' groaned the old man, clasping his head with both hands. 'There 's burning fever here, and something now and then to which I fear to give a name.'

The dwarf said never a word, but watched his companion as he paced restlessly up and down the room, and presently returned to his seat. Here he remained, with his head bowed upon his breast for some time, and then suddenly raising it, said—

'Once, and once for all, have you brought me any money?'

'No!' returned Quilp.

'Then,' said the old man, clenching his hands desperately, and looking upward, 'the child and I are lost!'

'Neighbour,' said Quilp glancing sternly at him, and beating his hand twice or thrice upon the table to attract his wandering attention, 'let me be plain with you, and play a fairer game than when you held all the cards, and I saw but the backs and nothing more. You have no secret from me now.'

The old man looked up, trembling.

'You are surprised,' said Quilp. 'Well, perhaps that 's natural. You have no secret from me now, I say; no, not one. For now, I know, that all those sums of money, that all those loans, advances, and supplies that you have had from me, have found their way to—shall I say the word?'

'Ay!' replied the old man, 'say it, if you will.'

'To the gaming-table,' rejoined Quilp, 'your nightly haunt. This was the precious scheme to make your fortune, was it; this was the secret certain source of wealth in which I was to have sunk my money (if I had been the fool you took me for); this was your inexhaustible mine of gold, your El Dorado, eh?'

'Yes,' cried the old man, turning upon him with gleaming eyes, 'it was. It is. It will be, till I die.'

'That I should have been blinded,' said Quilp, looking contemptuously at him, 'by a mere shallow gambler!'

'I am no gambler,' cried the old man fiercely. 'I call Heaven to witness that I never played for gain of mine, or love of play; that at every piece I staked, I whispered to myself that orphan's name and called on Heaven to bless the venture;—which it never did. Whom did it prosper? Who were those with whom I played? Men who lived by plunder, profligacy, and riot; squandering their gold in doing ill, and propagating vice and evil. My winnings would have been from them, my winnings would have been bestowed to the last farthing on a young sinless child whose life they would have sweetened and made happy. What would they have contracted? The means of corruption, wretchedness, and misery. Who would not have hoped in such a cause? Tell me that! Who would not have hoped as I did?'

'When did you first begin this mad career?' asked Quilp, his taunting inclination subdued, for a moment, by the old man's grief and wildness.

'When did I first begin?' he rejoined, passing his hand across his brow. 'When *was* it, that I first began? When should it be, but when I began to think how little I had saved, how long a time it took to save at all, how short a time I might have at my age to live, and how she would be left to the rough mercies of the world, with barely enough to keep her from the sorrows that wait on poverty; then it was, that I began to think about it.'

'After you first came to me to get your precious grandson packed off to sea?' said Quilp.

'Shortly after that,' replied the old man. 'I thought of it a long time, and had it in my sleep for months. Then I began. I found no pleasure in it, I expected none. What has it ever brought me but anxious days and sleepless nights; but loss of health and peace of mind, and gain of feebleness and sorrow!'

'You lost what money you had laid by, first, and then came to me. While I thought you were making your fortune (as you said you were) you were making yourself a beggar, eh? Dear me! And so it comes to pass that I hold every security you could scrape together, and a bill of sale upon the—upon the stock and property,' said Quilp standing up and looking about him, as if to assure himself that none of it had been taken away. 'But did you never win?'

'Never!' groaned the old man. 'Never won back my loss!'

'I thought,' sneered the dwarf, 'that if a man played

long enough he was sure to win at last, or, at the worst, not to come off a loser.'

'And so he is,' cried the old man, suddenly rousing himself from his state of despondency, and lashed into the most violent excitement, 'so he is; I have felt that from the first, I have always known it, I've seen it, I never felt it half so strongly as I feel it now. Quilp, I have dreamed, three nights, of winning the same large sum, I never could dream that dream before, though I have often tried. Do not desert me, now I have this chance. I have no resource but you, give me some help, let me try this one last hope.'

The dwarf shrugged his shoulders and shook his head.

'See, Quilp, good tender-hearted Quilp,' said the old man, drawing some scraps of paper from his pocket with a trembling hand, and clasping the dwarf's arm, 'only see here. Look at these figures, the result of long calculation, and painful and hard experience. I *must* win. I only want a little help once more, a few pounds, but two score pounds, dear Quilp.'

'The last advance was seventy,' said the dwarf; 'and it went in one night.'

'I know it did,' answered the old man, 'but that was the very worst fortune of all, and the time had not come then. Quilp, consider, consider,' the old man cried, trembling so much the while, that the papers in his hand fluttered as if they were shaken by the wind, 'that orphan child! If I were alone, I could die with gladness—perhaps even anticipate that doom which is dealt out so unequally: coming, as it does, on the proud and happy in their strength, and shunning the needy and afflicted, and all who court it in their despair—but what I have done, has been for her. Help me for her sake I implore you; not for mine; for hers!'

'I 'm sorry I 've got an appointment in the City,' said Quilp, looking at his watch with perfect self-possession, 'or I should have been very glad to have spent half an hour with you while you composed yourself, very glad.'

'Nay, Quilp, good Quilp,' gasped the old man, catching at his skirts, 'you and I have talked together, more than once, of her poor mother's story. The fear of her coming to poverty has perhaps been bred in me by that. Do not be hard upon me, but take that into account. You are a great gainer by me. Oh spare me the money for this one last hope!'

'I couldn't do it really,' said Quilp with unusual politeness, 'though I tell you what—and this is a circumstance worth bearing in mind as showing how the sharpest among us may be taken in sometimes—I was so deceived by the penurious way in which you lived, alone with Nelly—'

'All done to save money for tempting fortune, and to make her triumph greater,' cried the old man.

'Yes yes, I understand that now,' said Quilp; 'but I was going to say, I was so deceived by that, your miserly way, the reputation you had among those who knew you of being rich, and your repeated assurances that you would make of my advances treble and quadruple the interest you paid me, that I 'd have advanced you, even now, what you want, on your simple note of hand, if I hadn't unexpectedly become acquainted with your secret way of life.'

'Who is it,' retorted the old man desperately, 'that notwithstanding all my caution, told you? Come. Let me know the name—the person.'

The crafty dwarf, bethinking himself that his giving up the child would lead to the disclosure of the artifice he had employed, which, as nothing was to be gained by it, it was well to conceal, stopped short in his answer and said, 'Now, who do you think?'

'It was Kit, it must have been the boy; he played the spy, and you tampered with him?' said the old man.

'How came you to think of him?' said the dwarf in a tone of great commiseration. 'Yes, it was Kit. Poor Kit!'

So saying, he nodded in a friendly manner, and took his leave: stopping when he had passed the outer door a little distance, and grinning with extraordinary delight.

'Poor Kit!' muttered Quilp. 'I think it was Kit who said I was an uglier dwarf than could be seen anywhere for a penny, wasn't it? Ha ha ha! Poor Kit!'

And with that he went his way, still chuckling as he went.

CHAPTER X

DANIEL QUILP neither entered nor left the old man's house, unobserved. In the shadow of an archway nearly opposite, leading to one of the many passages which diverged from the main street, there lingered one, who, having taken up his position when the twilight first came on, still maintained it with undiminished patience, and leaning against the wall with the manner of a person who had a long time to wait, and being well used to it was quite resigned, scarcely changed his attitude for the hour together.

This patient lounger attracted little attention from any of those who passed, and bestowed as little upon them. His eyes were constantly directed towards one object; the window at which the child was accustomed to sit. If he withdrew them for a moment, it was only to glance at a clock in some neighbouring shop, and then to strain his sight once more in the old quarter with increased earnestness and attention.

It had been remarked that this personage evinced no weariness in his place of concealment; nor did he, long as his waiting was. But as the time went on, he manifested some anxiety and surprise, glancing at the clock more frequently and at the window less hopefully than before. At length, the clock was hidden from his sight by some envious shutters, then the church-steeples proclaimed eleven at night, then quarter past, and then the conviction seemed to obtrude itself on his mind that it was of no use tarrying there any longer.

That the conviction was an unwelcome one, and that he was by no means willing to yield to it, was apparent from his reluctance to quit the spot; from the tardy steps with which he often left it, still looking over his shoulder at the same window; and from the precipitation with which he as often returned, when a fancied noise or the changing and imperfect light induced him to suppose it had been softly raised. At length, he gave the matter up, as hopeless for that night, and suddenly breaking into a run as though to force himself away, scampered off at his utmost speed, nor once ventured to look behind him lest he should be tempted back again.

Without relaxing his pace, or stopping to take breath, this mysterious individual dashed on through a great many alleys and narrow ways until he at length arrived in a square paved court, when he subsided into a walk, and making for a small house from the window of which a light was shining, lifted the latch of the door and passed in.

'Bless us!' cried a woman turning sharply round, 'who 's that? Oh! It 's you, Kit!'

'Yes, mother, it 's me.'

'Why, how tired you look, my dear!'

'Old master an't gone out to-night,' said Kit; 'and so she hasn't been at the window at all.' With which words, he sat down by the fire and looked very mournful and discontented.

The room in which Kit sat himself down, in this condition, was an extremely poor and homely place, but with that air of comfort about it, nevertheless, which—or the spot must be a wretched one indeed—cleanliness and order can always impart in some degree. Late as the Dutch clock showed it to be, the poor woman was still hard at work at an ironing-table; a young child lay sleeping in a cradle near the fire; and another, a sturdy boy of two or three years old, very wide awake, with a very tight night-cap on his head, and a night-gown very much too small for him on his body, was sitting bolt upright in a clothes-basket, staring over the rim with his great round eyes, and looking as if he had thoroughly made up his mind never to go to sleep any more; which, as he had already declined to take his natural rest and had been brought out of bed in consequence, opened a cheerful prospect for his relations and friends. It was rather a queer-looking family: Kit, his mother, and the children, being all strongly alike.

Kit was disposed to be out of temper, as the best of us are too often—but he looked at the youngest child who was sleeping soundly, and from him to his other brother in the clothes-basket, and from him to their mother, who had been at work without complaint since morning, and thought it would be a better and kinder thing to be good-humoured. So he rocked the cradle with his foot: made a face at the rebel in the clothes-basket, which put him in high good-humour directly; and stoutly determined to be talkative and make himself agreeable.

'Ah mother!' said Kit, taking out his clasp-knife and falling upon a great piece of bread and meat which she had had ready for him, hours before, 'what a one you are! There an't many such as you, *I* know.'

'I hope there are many a great deal better, Kit,' said Mrs. Nubbles; 'and that there are, or ought to be, accordin' to what the parson at chapel says.'

'Much *he* knows about it,' returned Kit contemptuously. 'Wait till he 's a widder and works like you do, and gets as little, and does as much, and keeps his spirit up the same, and then I 'll ask him what 's o'clock and trust him for being right to half a second.'

'Well,' said Mrs. Nubbles, evading the point, 'your beer 's down there by the fender, Kit.'

'I see,' replied her son, taking up the porter-pot, 'my love to you, mother. And the parson's health too if you like. I don't bear him any malice, not I!'

'Did you tell me, just now, that your master hadn't gone out to-night?' inquired Mrs. Nubbles.

'Yes,' said Kit, 'worse luck!'

'You should say better luck, I think,' returned his mother, 'because Miss Nelly won't have been left alone.'

'Ah!' said Kit, 'I forgot that. I said worse luck, because I 've been watching ever since eight o'clock, and seen nothing of her.'

'I wonder what she 'd say,' cried his mother, stopping in her work and looking round, 'if she knew that every night, when she—poor thing—is sitting alone at that window, you are watching in the open street for fear any harm should come to her, and that you never leave the place or come home to your bed though you 're ever so tired, till such time as you think she 's safe in hers.'

'Never mind what she 'd say,' replied Kit, with something like a blush on his uncouth face; 'she 'll never know nothing, and consequently she 'll never say nothing.'

Mrs. Nubbles ironed away in silence for a minute or two, and coming to the fireplace for another iron, glanced stealthily at Kit while she rubbed it on a board and dusted it with a duster, but said nothing until she had returned to her table again: when, holding the iron at an alarmingly short distance from her cheek, to test its temperature, and looking round with a smile, she observed—

'I know what some people would say, Kit—'

'Nonsense,' interposed Kit with a perfect apprehension of what was to follow.

'No, but they would indeed. Some people would say that you 'd fallen in love with her, I know they would.'

To this, Kit only replied by bashfully bidding his mother 'get out,' and forming sundry strange figures with his legs and arms, accompanied by sympathetic contortions of his face. Not deriving from these means the relief which he sought, he bit off an immense mouthful from the bread and meat, and took a quick drink of the porter; by which artificial aids he choked himself and effected a diversion of the subject.

'Speaking seriously though, Kit,' said his mother taking up the theme afresh, after a time, 'for of course I was only in joke just now, it 's very good and thoughtful, and like you, to do this, and never let anybody know it, though some day I hope she may come to know it, for I 'm sure she would be very grateful to you and feel it very much. It 's a cruel thing to keep the dear child shut up there. I don't wonder that the old gentleman wants to keep it from you.'

'He don't think it 's cruel, bless you,' said Kit, 'and don't mean it to be so, or he wouldn't do it—I do consider, mother, that he wouldn't do it for all the gold and silver in the world. No, no, that he wouldn't. I know him better than that.'

'Then what does he do it for, and why does he keep it so close from you?' said Mrs. Nubbles.

'That I don't know,' returned her son. 'If he hadn't tried to keep it so close though, I should never have found it out, for it was getting me away at night and sending me off so much earlier than he used to, that first made me curious to know what was going on. Hark! what 's that?'

'It 's only somebody outside.'

'It 's somebody crossing over here,' said Kit, standing up to listen, 'and coming very fast too. He can't have gone out after I left, and the house caught fire, mother!'

The boy stood for a moment, really bereft, by the apprehension he had conjured up, of the power to move. The footsteps drew nearer, the door was opened with a hasty hand, and the child herself, pale and breathless, and hastily wrapped in a few disordered garments, hurried into the room.

'Miss Nelly! What is the matter?' cried mother and son together.

'I must not stay a moment,' she returned, 'grandfather has been taken very ill. I found him in a fit upon the floor—'

'I 'll run for a doctor'—said Kit, seizing his brimless hat. 'I 'll be there directly, I 'll—'

'No, no,' cried Nell, 'there is one there, you 're not

wanted, you—you—must never come near us any more!'

'What?' roared Kit.

'Never again,' said the child. 'Don't ask me why, for I don't know. Pray don't ask me why, pray don't be sorry, pray don't be vexed with me! I have nothing to do with it indeed!'

Kit looked at her with his eyes stretched wide; and opened and shut his mouth a great many times; but couldn't get out one word.

'He complains and raves of you,' said the child, 'I don't know what you have done, but I hope it 's nothing very bad.'

'*I* done!' roared Kit.

'He cries that you 're the cause of all his misery,' returned the child with tearful eyes; 'he screamed and called for you; they say you must not come near him or he will die. You must not return to us any more. I came to tell you. I thought it would be better that I should come than somebody quite strange. Oh, Kit, what *have* you done? You, in whom I trusted so much, and who were almost the only friend I had!'

The unfortunate Kit looked at his young mistress harder and harder, and with eyes growing wider and wider, but was perfectly motionless and silent.

'I have brought his money for the week,' said the child, looking to the woman and laying it on the table—'and—and—a little more, for he was always good and kind to me. I hope he will be sorry and do well somewhere else and not take this to heart too much. It grieves me very much to part with him like this, but there is no help. It must be done. Good night!'

With the tears streaming down her face, and her slight figure trembling with the agitation of the scene she had left, the shock she had received, the errand she had just discharged, and a thousand painful and affectionate feelings, the child hastened to the door, and disappeared as rapidly as she had come.

The poor woman, who had no cause to doubt her son, but every reason for relying on his honesty and truth, was staggered, notwithstanding, by his not having advanced one word in his defence. Visions of gallantry, knavery, robbery; and of the nightly absences from home for which he had accounted so strangely, having been occasioned by some unlawful pursuit; flocked into her brain and rendered her afraid to question him. She rocked herself upon a chair, wringing her hands and weeping bitterly, but Kit made no attempt to comfort her and remained quite bewildered. The baby in the cradle woke up and cried; the boy in the clothes-basket fell over on his back with the basket upon him, and was seen no more; the mother wept louder yet and rocked faster; but Kit, insensible to all the din and tumult, remained in a state of utter stupefaction.

CHAPTER XI

QUIET and solitude were destined to hold uninterrupted rule no longer, beneath the roof that sheltered the child. Next morning, the old man was in a raging fever accompanied with delirium; and sinking under the influence of this disorder he lay for many weeks in imminent peril of his life. There was watching enough, now, but it was the watching of strangers who made a greedy trade of it, and who, in the intervals of their attendance upon the sick man huddled together with a ghastly good-fellowship, and ate and drank and made merry; for disease and death were their ordinary household gods.

Yet, in all the hurry and crowding of such a time, the child was more alone than she had ever been before; alone in spirit, alone in her devotion to him who was wasting away upon his burning bed; alone in her unfeigned sorrow, and her unpurchased sympathy. Day after day, and night after night, found her still by the pillow of the unconscious sufferer, still anticipating his every want, still listening to those repetitions of her name and those anxieties and cares for her, which were ever uppermost among his feverish wanderings.

The house was no longer theirs. Even the sick chamber seemed to be retained, on the uncertain tenure of Mr. Quilp's favour. The old man's illness had not lasted many days when he took formal possession of the premises and all upon them, in virtue of certain legal powers to that effect, which few understood and none presumed to call in question. This important step secured, with the assistance of a man of law whom he brought with him for the purpose, the dwarf proceeded to establish himself and his coadjutor in the house, as an assertion of his claim against all comers; and then set about making his quarters comfortable, after his own fashion.

To this end, Mr. Quilp encamped in the back-parlour, having first put an effectual stop to any further business by shutting up the shop. Having looked out, from among the old furniture, the handsomest and most commodious chair he could possibly find (which he reserved for his own use) and an especially hideous and uncomfortable one (which he considerately appropriated to the accommodation of his friend) he caused them to be carried into this room, and took up his position in great state. The apartment was very far removed from the old man's chamber, but Mr. Quilp deemed it prudent, as a precaution against infection from fever, and a means of wholesome fumigation, not only to smoke, himself, without cessation, but to insist upon it that his legal friend did the like. Moreover, he sent an express to the wharf for the tumbling boy, who arriving with all despatch was enjoined, to sit himself down in another chair just inside the door, continually to smoke a great pipe which the dwarf had provided for the purpose, and to take it from his lips under any pretence whatever, were it only for one minute at a time, if he dared. These arrangements completed, Mr. Quilp looked round him with chuckling satisfaction, and remarked that he called that comfort.

The legal gentleman, whose melodious name was Brass, might have called it comfort also but for two drawbacks: one was, that he could by no exertion sit easy in his chair, the seat of which was very hard, angular, slippery, and sloping; the other, that tobacco-smoke always caused him great internal discomposure and annoyance. But as he was quite a creature of Mr. Quilp's and had a thousand reasons for conciliating his good opinion, he tried to smile, and nodded his acquiescence with the best grace he could assume.

This Brass was an attorney of no very good repute, from Bevis Marks in the City of London; he was a tall, meagre man, with a nose like a wen, a protruding forehead, retreating eyes, and hair of a deep red. He wore a long black surtout reaching nearly to his ankles, short black trousers, high shoes, and cotton stockings of a bluish-grey. He had a cringing manner, but a very harsh voice; and his blandest smiles were so extremely forbidding, that to have had his company under the least repulsive circumstances, one would have wished him to be out of temper that he might only scowl.

Quilp looked at his legal adviser, and seeing that

"IS IT GOOD, BRASS, IS IT FRAGRANT?"

he was winking very much in the anguish of his pipe, that he sometimes shuddered when he happened to inhale its full flavour, and that he constantly fanned the smoke from him, was quite overjoyed and rubbed his hands with glee.

'Smoke away, you dog,' said Quilp turning to the boy; 'fill your pipe again and smoke it fast, down to the last whiff, or I 'll put the sealing-waxed end of it in the fire and rub it red-hot upon your tongue.'

Luckily the boy was case-hardened, and would have smoked a small lime-kiln if anybody had treated him with it. Wherefore, he only muttered a brief defiance of his master, and did as he was ordered.

'Is it good, Brass, is it nice, is it fragrant, do you feel like the Grand Turk?' said Quilp.

Mr. Brass thought that if he did, the Grand Turk's feelings were by no means to be envied, but he said it was famous, and he had no doubt he felt very like that Potentate.

'This is the way to keep off fever,' said Quilp, 'this is the way to keep off every calamity of life! We 'll never leave off, all the time we stop here—smoke away, you dog, or you shall swallow the pipe!'

'Shall we stop here long, Mr. Quilp?' inquired his legal friend, when the dwarf had given his boy this gentle admonition.

'We must stop, I suppose, till the old gentleman upstairs is dead,' returned Quilp.

'He he he!' laughed Mr. Brass, 'oh! very good!'

'Smoke away!' cried Quilp. 'Never stop! you can talk as you smoke. Don't lose time.'

'He he he!' cried Brass faintly, as he again applied himself to the odious pipe. 'But if he should get better, Mr. Quilp?'

'Then we shall stop till he does, and no longer,' returned the dwarf.

'How kind it is of you, sir, to wait till then!' said Brass. 'Some people, sir, would have sold or removed the goods—oh dear, the very instant the law allowed 'em. Some people, sir, would have been all flintiness and granite. Some people, sir, would have—'

'Some people would have spared themselves the jabbering of such a parrot as you,' interposed the dwarf.

'He he he!' cried Brass. 'You have *such* spirits!'

The smoking sentinel at the door interposed in this place, and without taking his pipe from his lips, growled—

'Here 's the gal a comin' down.'

'The what, you dog?' said Quilp.

'The gal,' returned the boy. 'Are you deaf?'

'Oh!' said Quilp, drawing in his breath with great relish as if he were taking soup, 'you and I will have such a settling presently; there 's such a scratching and bruising in store for you, my dear young friend! Aha! Nelly! How is he now, my duck of diamonds?'

'He 's very bad,' replied the weeping child.

'What a pretty little Nell!' cried Quilp.

'Oh beautiful, sir, beautiful indeed,' said Brass. 'Quite charming!'

'Has she come to sit upon Quilp's knee,' said the dwarf, in what he meant to be a soothing tone, 'or is she going to bed in her own little room inside here? Which is poor Nelly going to do?'

'What a remarkably pleasant way he has with children!' muttered Brass, as if in confidence between himself and the ceiling; 'upon my word it 's quite a treat to hear him.'

'I 'm not going to stay at all,' faltered Nell. 'I want a few things out of that room, and then I—I—won't come down here any more.'

'And a very nice little room it is!' said the dwarf

looking into it as the child entered. 'Quite a bower! You 're sure you 're not going to use it; you 're sure you 're not coming back, Nelly?'

'No,' replied the child, hurrying away, with the few articles of dress she had come to remove; 'never again! Never again.'

'She 's very sensitive,' said Quilp, looking after her. 'Very sensitive; that 's a pity. The bedstead is much about my size. I think I shall make it *my* little room.'

Mr. Brass encouraging this idea, as he would have encouraged any other emanating from the same source, the dwarf walked in to try the effect. This he did, by throwing himself on his back upon the bed with his pipe in his mouth, and then kicking up his legs and smoking violently. Mr. Brass applauding this picture very much, and the bed being soft and comfortable, Mr. Quilp determined to use it, both as a sleeping place by night and as a kind of Divan by day; and in order that it might be converted to the latter purpose at once, remained where he was, and smoked his pipe out. The legal gentleman being by this time rather giddy and perplexed in his ideas (for this was one of the operations of tobacco on his nervous system), took the opportunity of slinking away into the open air, where, in course of time, he recovered sufficiently to return with a countenance of tolerable composure. He was soon led on by the malicious dwarf to smoke himself into a relapse, and in that state stumbled upon a settee where he slept till morning.

Such were Mr. Quilp's first proceedings on entering upon his new property. He was, for some days, restrained by business from performing any particular pranks, as his time was pretty well occupied between taking, with the assistance of Mr. Brass, a minute inventory of all the goods in the place, and going abroad upon his other concerns which happily engaged him for several hours at a time. His avarice and caution being, now, thoroughly awakened, however, he was never absent from the house one night; and his eagerness for some termination, good or bad, to the old man's disorder, increasing rapidly, as the time passed by, soon began to vent itself in open murmurs and exclamations of impatience.

Nell shrunk timidly from all the dwarf's advances towards conversation, and fled from the very sound of his voice; nor were the lawyer's smiles less terrible to her than Quilp's grimaces. She lived in such continual dread and apprehension of meeting one or other of them on the stairs or in the passages if she stirred from her grandfather's chamber, that she seldom left it, for a moment, until late at night, when the silence encouraged her to venture forth and breathe the purer air of some empty room.

One night, she had stolen to her usual window, and was sitting there very sorrowfully—for the old man had been worse that day—when she thought she heard her name pronounced by a voice in the street. Looking down, she recognised Kit, whose endeavours to attract her attention had roused her from her sad reflections.

'Miss Nell!' said the boy in a low voice.

'Yes,' replied the child, doubtful whether she ought to hold any communication with the supposed culprit, but inclining to her old favourite still; 'what do you want?'

'I have wanted to say a word to you, for a long time,' the boy replied, 'but the people below have driven me away and wouldn't let me see you. You don't believe—I hope you don't really believe—that I deserve to be cast off as I have been; do you, miss?'

'I must believe it,' returned the child. 'Or why would grandfather have been so angry with you?'

'I don't know,' replied Kit. 'I 'm sure I never deserved it from him, no, nor from you. I can say that, with a true and honest heart any way. And then to be driven from the door, when I only came to ask how old master was—!'

'They never told me that,' said the child. 'I didn't know it indeed. I wouldn't have had them do it for the world.'

'Thank 'ee, miss,' returned Kit, 'it 's comfortable to hear you say that. I said I never would believe that it was your doing.'

'That was right!' said the child eagerly.

'Miss Nell,' cried the boy coming under the window, and speaking in a lower tone, 'there are new masters downstairs. It 's a change for you.'

'It is indeed,' replied the child.

'And so it will be for him when he gets better,' said the boy, pointing towards the sick-room.

'—If he ever does,' added the child, unable to restrain her tears.

'Oh, he 'll do that, he 'll do that,' said Kit, 'I 'm sure he will. You mustn't be cast down, Miss Nell. Now don't be, pray!'

These words of encouragement and consolation were few and roughly said, but they affected the child and made her, for the moment, weep the more.

'He 'll be sure to get better now,' said the boy anxiously, 'if you don't give way to low spirits and turn ill yourself, which would make him worse and throw him back, just as he was recovering. When he does, say a good word—say a kind word for me, Miss Nell!'

'They tell me I must not even mention your name to him for a long, long time,' rejoined the child, 'I dare not; and even if I might, what good would a kind word do you, Kit? We shall be very poor. We shall scarcely have bread to eat.'

'It 's not that I may be taken back,' said the boy, 'that I ask the favour of you. It isn't for the sake of food and wages that I 've been waiting about, so long, in hopes to see you. Don't think that I 'd come in a time of trouble to talk of such things as them.'

The child looked gratefully and kindly at him, but waited that he might speak again.

'No, it 's not that,' said Kit hesitating, 'it 's something very different from that. I haven't got much sense I know, but if he could be brought to believe that I 'd been a faithful servant to him, doing the best I could and never meaning harm, perhaps he mightn't—'

Here Kit faltered so long that the child entreated him to speak out, and quickly, for it was very late, and time to shut the window.

'Perhaps he mightn't think it over-venturesome of me to say—well then, to say this,' cried Kit with sudden boldness. 'This home is gone from you and him. Mother and I have got a poor one, but that 's better than this with all these people here; and why not come there, till he 's had time to look about, and find a better?'

The child did not speak. Kit, in the relief of having made his proposition, found his tongue loosened, and spoke out in its favour with his utmost eloquence.

'You think,' said the boy, 'that it 's very small and inconvenient. So it is, but it 's very clean. Perhaps you think it would be noisy, but there 's not a quieter court than ours in all the town. Don't be afraid of the children; the baby hardly ever cries, and the other one is very good—besides, *I* 'd mind 'em. They wouldn't vex you much, I 'm sure. Do try, Miss

Nell, do try. The little front-room upstairs is very pleasant. You can see a piece of the church-clock, through the chimneys, and almost tell the time; mother says it would be just the thing for you, and so it would, and you 'd have her to wait upon you both, and me to run of errands. We don't mean money, bless you; you 're not to think of that! Will you try him, Miss Nell? Only say you 'll try him. Do try to make old master come, and ask him first what I have done. Will you only promise that, Miss Nell?'

Before the child could reply to this earnest solicitation, the street-door opened, and Mr. Brass thrusting out his night-capped head called in a surly voice, 'Who 's there?' Kit immediately glided away, and Nell, closing the window softly, drew back into the room.

Before Mr. Brass had repeated his inquiry many times, Mr. Quilp, also embellished with a night-cap, emerged from the same door and looked carefully up and down the street, and up at all the windows of the house, from the opposite side. Finding that there was nobody in sight, he presently returned into the house with his legal friend, protesting (as the child heard from the staircase), that there was a league and plot against him; that he was in danger of being robbed and plundered by a band of conspirators who prowled about the house at all seasons; and that he would delay no longer but take immediate steps for disposing of the property and returning to his own peaceful roof. Having growled forth these, and a great many other threats of the same nature, he coiled himself once more in the child's little bed, and Nell crept softly up the stairs.

It was natural enough that her short and unfinished dialogue with Kit should leave a strong impression on her mind, and influence her dreams that night and her recollections for a long, long time. Surrounded by unfeeling creditors, and mercenary attendants upon the sick, and meeting in the height of her anxiety and sorrow with little regard or sympathy even from the women about her, it is not surprising that the affectionate heart of the child should have been touched to the quick by one kind and generous spirit, however uncouth the temple in which it dwelt. Thank Heaven that the temples of such spirits are not made with hands, and that they may be even more worthily hung with poor patchwork than with purple and fine linen!

CHAPTER XII

At length, the crisis of the old man's disorder was past, and he began to mend. By very slow and feeble degrees his consciousness came back; but the mind was weakened and its functions were impaired. He was patient, and quiet; often sat brooding, but not despondently, for a long space; was easily amused, even by a sunbeam on the wall or ceiling; made no complaint that the days were long, or the nights tedious; and appeared indeed to have lost all count of time, and every sense of care or weariness. He would sit, for hours together, with Nell's small hand in his, playing with the fingers and stopping sometimes to smooth her hair or kiss her brow; and, when he saw that tears were glistening in her eyes, would look, amazed, about him for the cause, and forget his wonder even while he looked.

The child and he rode out: the old man propped up with pillows, and the child beside him. They were hand in hand as usual. The noise and motion in the streets fatigued his brain at first, but he was not surprised, or curious, or pleased, or irritated. He was asked if he remembered this, or that. 'Oh yes,' he said, 'quite well—why not?' Sometimes he turned his head, and looked, with earnest gaze and outstretched neck, after some stranger in the crowd, until he disappeared from sight; but, to the question why he did this, he answered not a word.

He was sitting in his easy-chair one day, and Nell upon a stool beside him, when a man outside the door inquired if he might enter. 'Yes,' he said without emotion, 'it was Quilp he knew. Quilp was master there. Of course he might come in.' And so he did.

'I 'm glad to see you well again at last, neighbour,' said the dwarf, sitting down opposite to him. 'You 're quite strong now?'

'Yes,' said the old man feebly, 'yes.'

'I don't want to hurry you, you know, neighbour,' said the dwarf, raising his voice, for the old man's senses were duller than they had been; 'but as soon as you *can* arrange your future proceedings, the better.'

'Surely,' said the old man. 'The better for all parties.'

'You see,' pursued Quilp after a short pause, 'the goods being once removed, this house would be uncomfortable; uninhabitable in fact.'

'You say true,' returned the old man. 'Poor Nell too, what would *she* do?'

'Exactly,' bawled the dwarf nodding his head; 'that 's very well observed. Then will you consider about it, neighbour?'

'I will, certainly,' replied the old man. 'We shall not stop here.'

'So I supposed,' said the dwarf. 'I have sold the things. They have not yielded quite as much as they might have done, but pretty well—pretty well. To-day 's Tuesday. When shall they be moved? There 's no hurry—shall we say this afternoon?'

'Say Friday morning,' returned the old man.

'Very good,' said the dwarf. 'So be it,—with the understanding that I can't go beyond that day, neighbour, on any account.'

'Good,' returned the old man. 'I shall remember it.'

Mr. Quilp seemed rather puzzled by the strange, even spiritless way in which all this was said; but as the old man nodded his head and repeated 'on Friday morning. I shall remember it,' he had no excuse for dwelling on the subject any further, and so took a friendly leave with many expressions of good-will and many compliments to his friend on his looking so remarkably well; and went below-stairs to report progress to Mr. Brass.

All that day, and all the next, the old man remained in this state. He wandered up and down the house and into and out of the various rooms, as if with some vague intent of bidding them adieu, but he referred neither by direct allusions nor in any other manner to the interview of the morning or the necessity of finding some other shelter. An indistinct idea he had, that the child was desolate and in want of help; for he often drew her to his bosom and bade her be of good cheer, saying that they would not desert each other; but he seemed unable to contemplate their real position more distinctly, and was still the listless, passionless creature, that suffering of mind and body had left him.

We call this a state of childishness, but it is the same poor hollow mockery of it, that death is of sleep. Where, in the dull eyes of doting men, are the laughing light and life of childhood, the gaiety that has known no check, the frankness that has felt no chill, the hope that has never withered, the joys that fade in blossoming? Where, in the sharp lineaments of rigid and unsightly death, is the calm beauty of slumber, telling of rest for the waking hours that are past, and gentle hopes and loves for those which are to come? Lay death and sleep down, side by side, and say who shall find the two akin. Send forth the child and childish man together, and blush for the pride that libels our own old happy state, and gives its title to an ugly and distorted image.

Thursday arrived, and there was no alteration in the old man. But, a change came upon him that evening, as he and the child sat silently together.

In a small dull yard below his window, there was a tree—green and flourishing enough, for such a place—and as the air stirred among its leaves, it threw a rippling shadow on the white wall. The old man sat watching the shadows as they trembled in this patch of light, until the sun went down; and when it was night, and the moon was slowly rising, he still sat in the same spot.

To one who had been tossing on a restless bed so long, even these few green leaves and this tranquil light, although it languished among chimneys and house-tops, were pleasant things. They suggested quiet places afar off, and rest, and peace.

The child thought, more than once, that he was moved: and had forborne to speak. But, now, he shed tears—tears that it lightened her aching heart to see—and making as though he would fall upon his knees, besought her to forgive him.

'Forgive you—what?' said Nell, interposing to prevent his purpose. 'Oh grandfather, what should *I* forgive?'

'All that is past, all that has come upon thee, Nell,

all that was done in that uneasy dream,' returned the old man.

'Do not talk so,' said the child. 'Pray do not. Let us speak of something else.'

'Yes, yes, we will,' he rejoined. 'And it shall be of what we talked of long ago—many months—months is it, or weeks, or days? which is it, Nell?'

'I do not understand you,' said the child.

'It has come back upon me to-day, it has all come back since we have been sitting here. I bless thee for it, Nell!'

'For what, dear grandfather?'

'For what you said when we were first made beggars, Nell. Let us speak softly. Hush! for if they knew our purpose downstairs, they would cry that I was mad and take thee from me. We will not stop here, another day. We will go far away from here.'

'Yes, let us go,' said the child earnestly. 'Let us begone from this place, and never turn back or think of it again. Let us wander barefoot through the world, rather than linger here.'

'We will,' answered the old man, 'we will travel afoot through the fields and woods, and by the side of rivers, and trust ourselves to God in the places where He dwells. It is far better to lie down at night beneath an open sky like that yonder—see how bright it is!—than to rest in close rooms which are always full of care and weary dreams. Thou and I together, Nell, may be cheerful and happy yet, and learn to forget this time, as if it had never been.'

'We will be happy,' cried the child. 'We never can be here.'

'No, we never can again—never again—that 's truly said,' rejoined the old man. 'Let us steal away to-morrow morning—early and softly, that we may not be seen or heard—and leave no trace or track for them to follow by. Poor Nell! Thy cheek is pale, and thy eyes are heavy with watching and weeping for me—I know—for me; but thou wilt be well again, and merry too, when we are far away. To-morrow morning, dear, we 'll turn our faces from this scene of sorrow, and be as free and happy as the birds.'

And then, the old man clasped his hands above her head, and said, in a few broken words, that from that time forth they would wander up and down together, and never part more until Death took one or other of the twain.

The child's heart beat high with hope and confidence. She had no thought of hunger, or cold, or thirst, or suffering. She saw in this, but a return of the simple pleasures they had once enjoyed, a relief from the gloomy solitude in which she had lived, an escape from the heartless people by whom she had been surrounded in her late time of trial, the restoration of the old man's health and peace, and a life of tranquil happiness. Sun, and stream, and meadow, and summer days, shone brightly in her view, and there was no dark tint in all the sparkling picture.

The old man had slept, for some hours, soundly in his bed, and she was yet busily engaged in preparing for their flight. There were a few articles of clothing for herself to carry, and a few for him; old garments, such as became their fallen fortunes, laid out to wear; and a staff to support his feeble steps, put ready for his use. But this was not all her task; for now she must visit the old rooms for the last time.

And how different the parting with them was, from any she had expected, and most of all from that which she had oftenest pictured to herself. How could she ever have thought of bidding them farewell in triumph, when the recollection of the many hours she had passed among them rose to her swelling heart, and made her feel the wish a cruelty: lonely and sad though many of those hours had been! She sat down at the window where she had spent so many evenings —darker far than this—and every thought of hope or cheerfulness that had occurred to her in that place came vividly upon her mind, and blotted out all its dull and mournful associations in an instant.

Her own little room too, where she had so often knelt down and prayed at night—prayed for the time which she hoped was dawning now—the little room where she had slept so peacefully, and dreamed such pleasant dreams! It was hard not to be able to glance round it once more, and to be forced to leave it without one kind look or grateful tear. There were some trifles there—poor useless things— that she would have liked to take away; but that was impossible.

This brought to mind her bird, her poor bird, who hung there yet. She wept bitterly for the loss of this little creature—until the idea occurred to her—she did not know how, or why, it came into her head— that it might, by some means, fall into the hands of Kit who would keep it for her sake, and think, perhaps, that she had left it behind in the hope that he might have it, and as an assurance that she was grateful to him. She was calmed and comforted by the thought, and went to rest with a lighter heart.

From many dreams of rambling through light and sunny places, but with some vague object unattained which ran indistinctly through them all, she awoke to find that it was yet night, and that the stars were shining brightly in the sky. At length, the day began to glimmer, and the stars to grow pale and dim. As soon as she was sure of this, she arose, and dressed herself for the journey.

The old man was yet asleep, and as she was unwilling to disturb him, she left him to slumber on, until the sun rose. He was anxious that they should leave the house without a minute's loss of time, and was soon ready.

The child then took him by the hand, and they trod lightly and cautiously down the stairs, trembling whenever a board creaked, and often stopping to listen. The old man had forgotten a kind of wallet which contained the light burden he had to carry; and the going back a few steps to fetch it, seemed an interminable delay.

At last, they reached the passage on the ground-floor, where the snoring of Mr. Quilp and his legal friend sounded more terrible in their ears than the roars of lions. The bolts of the door were rusty, and difficult to unfasten without noise. When they were all drawn back, it was found to be locked, and worst of all, the key was gone. Then the child remembered, for the first time, one of the nurses having told her that Quilp always locked both the house-doors at night, and kept the keys on the table in his bedroom.

It was not without great fear and trepidation, that little Nell slipped off her shoes and gliding through the store-room of old curiosities, where Mr. Brass—the ugliest piece of goods in all the stock—lay sleeping on a mattress, passed into her own little chamber.

Here she stood, for a few moments, quite transfixed with terror at the sight of Mr. Quilp, who was hanging so far out of bed that he almost seemed to be standing on his head, and who, either from the uneasiness of this posture, or in one of his agreeable habits, was gasping and growling with his mouth wide open, and the whites (or rather the dirty yellows) of his eyes distinctly visible. It was no time, however, to ask whether anything ailed him; so, possessing herself of the key after one hasty glance about the room, and repassing the prostrate Mr. Brass, she rejoined the old man in safety. They got the door open without noise, and passing into the street, stood still.

'Which way?' said the child.

The old man looked, irresolutely and helplessly, first at her, then to the right and left, then at her again, and shook his head. It was plain that she was thenceforth his guide and leader. The child felt it, but had no doubts or misgiving, and putting her hand in his, led him gently away.

It was the beginning of a day in June; the deep blue sky unsullied by a cloud, and teeming with brilliant light. The streets were, as yet, nearly free from passengers, the houses and shops were closed, and the healthy air of morning fell like breath from angels, on the sleeping town.

The old man and the child passed on through the glad silence, elate with hope and pleasure. They were alone together, once again; every object was bright and fresh; nothing reminded them, otherwise than by contrast, of the monotony and constraint they had left behind; church towers and steeples, frowning and dark at other times, now shone in the sun; each humble nook and corner rejoiced in light; and the sky, dimmed only by excessive distance, shed its placid smile on everything beneath.

Forth from the city, while it yet slumbered, went the two poor adventurers, wandering they knew not whither.

CHAPTER XIII

Daniel Quilp of Tower Hill, and Sampson Brass of Bevis Marks in the City of London, Gentleman, one of her Majesty's attorneys of the Courts of King's Bench and Common Pleas at Westminster and a solicitor of the High Court of Chancery, slumbered on, unconscious and unsuspicious of any mischance until a knocking at the street-door, often repeated and gradually mounting up from a modest single rap to a perfect battery of knocks, fired in long discharges with a very short interval between, caused the said Daniel Quilp to struggle into a horizontal position, and to stare at the ceiling with a drowsy indifference, betokening that he heard the noise and rather wondered at the same, and couldn't be at the trouble of bestowing any further thought upon the subject.

As the knocking, however, instead of accommodating itself to his lazy state, increased in vigour and became more importunate, as if in earnest remonstrance against his falling asleep again, now that he had once opened his eyes, Daniel Quilp began by degrees to comprehend the possibility of there being somebody at the door; and thus he gradually came to recollect that it was Friday morning, and he had ordered Mrs. Quilp to be in waiting upon him at an early hour.

Mr. Brass, after writhing about, in a great many strange attitudes, and often twisting his face and eyes into an expression like that which is usually produced by eating gooseberries very early in the season, was by this time awake also. Seeing that Mr. Quilp invested himself in his every-day garments, he hastened to do the like, putting on his shoes before his stockings, and thrusting his legs into his coat-sleeves, and making such other small mistakes in his toilet as are not uncommon to those who dress in a hurry, and labour under the agitation of having been suddenly roused.

While the attorney was thus engaged, the dwarf was groping under the table, muttering desperate imprecations on himself, and mankind in general, and all inanimate objects to boot, which suggested to Mr. Brass the question, 'what 's the matter?'

'The key,' said the dwarf, looking viciously at him, 'the door-key,—that 's the matter. D' ye know anything of it?'

'How should I know anything of it, sir?' returned Mr. Brass.

'How should you?' repeated Quilp with a sneer. 'You 're a nice lawyer, an't you? Ugh, you idiot!'

Not caring to represent to the dwarf in his present humour, that the loss of a key by another person could scarcely be said to affect his (Brass's) legal knowledge in any material degree, Mr. Brass humbly suggested that it must have been forgotten overnight, and was, doubtless, at that moment, in its native key-hole. Notwithstanding that Mr. Quilp had a strong conviction to the contrary, founded on his recollection of having carefully taken it out, he was fain to admit that this was possible, and therefore went grumbling to the door, where, sure enough, he found it.

Now, just as Mr. Quilp laid his hand upon the lock, and saw with great astonishment that the fastenings were undone, the knocking came again with most irritating violence, and the daylight which had been shining through the key-hole was intercepted on the outside by a human eye. The dwarf was very much exasperated, and wanting somebody to wreak his ill-humour upon, determined to dart out suddenly, and favour Mrs. Quilp with a gentle acknowledgment of her attention in making that hideous uproar.

With this view, he drew back the lock very silently and softly, and opening the door all at once, pounced out upon the person on the other side, who had at that moment raised the knocker for another application, and at whom the dwarf ran head first: throwing out his hands and feet together, and biting the air in the fulness of his malice.

So far, however, from rushing upon somebody who offered no resistance and implored his mercy, Mr. Quilp was no sooner in the arms of the individual whom he had taken for his wife than he found himself complimented with two staggering blows on the head, and two more, of the same quality, in the chest; and closing with his assailant, such a shower of buffets rained down upon his person as sufficed to convince him that he was in skilful and experienced hands. Nothing daunted by this reception, he clung tight to his opponent, and bit and hammered away with such good-will and heartiness, that it was at least a couple of minutes before he was dislodged. Then, and not until then, Daniel Quilp found himself, all flushed and dishevelled, in the middle of the street, with Mr. Richard Swiveller performing a kind of dance round him and requiring to know 'whether he wanted any more?'

'There 's plenty more of it at the same shop,' said Mr. Swiveller, by turns advancing and retreating in a threatening attitude, 'a large and extensive assortment always on hand—country orders executed with promptitude and despatch—will you have a little more, sir—don't say no, if you 'd rather not.'

'I thought it was somebody else,' said Quilp rubbing his shoulders, 'why didn't you say who you were?'

'Why didn't you say who *you* were?' returned Dick, 'instead of flying out of the house like a Bedlamite?'

'It was you that—that knocked,' said the dwarf, getting up with a short groan, 'was it?'

'Yes, I am the man,' replied Dick. 'That lady had begun when I came, but she knocked too soft, so I relieved her.' As he said this, he pointed towards Mrs. Quilp, who stood trembling at a little distance.

'Humph!' muttered the dwarf, darting an angry look at his wife, 'I thought it was your fault! And you, sir,—don't you know there has been somebody ill here, that you knock as if you 'd beat the door down?'

'Damme!' answered Dick, 'that 's why I did it. I thought there was somebody dead here.'

'You came for some purpose, I suppose,' said Quilp. 'What is it you want?'

'I want to know how the old gentleman is,' rejoined Mr. Swiveller, 'and to hear from Nell herself, with whom I should like to have a little talk. I 'm a friend of the family, sir,—at least I 'm the friend of one of the family, and that 's the same thing.'

'You 'd better walk in then,' said the dwarf. 'Go on, sir, go on. Now, Mrs. Quilp—after you, ma'am.'

Mrs. Quilp hesitated, but Mr. Quilp insisted. And it was not a contest of politeness, or by any means a matter of form, for she knew very well that her husband wished to enter the house in this order, that he might have a favourable opportunity of inflicting a few pinches on her arms, which were seldom free from impressions of his fingers in black and blue colours. Mr. Swiveller, who was not in the secret, was a little surprised to hear a suppressed scream, and, looking round, to see Mrs. Quilp following him with a sudden jerk; but he did not remark on these appearances, and soon forgot them.

'Now, Mrs. Quilp,' said the dwarf when they had entered the shop, 'go you upstairs, if you please, to Nelly's room, and tell her that she 's wanted.'

'You seem to make yourself at home here,' said Dick, who was unacquainted with Mr. Quilp's authority.

'I *am* at home, young gentleman,' returned the dwarf.

Dick was pondering what these words might mean, and still more what the presence of Mr. Brass might mean, when Mrs. Quilp came hurrying downstairs, declaring that the rooms above were empty.

'Empty, you fool!' said the dwarf.

'I give you my word, Quilp,' answered his trembling wife, 'that I have been into every room and there 's not a soul in any of them.'

'And that,' said Mr. Brass, clapping his hands once, with an emphasis, 'explains the mystery of the key!'

Quilp looked frowningly at him, and frowningly at his wife, and frowningly at Richard Swiveller; but, receiving no enlightenment from any of them, hurried upstairs, whence he soon hurried down again, confirming the report which had been already made.

'It 's a strange way of going,' he said, glancing at Swiveller: 'very strange not to communicate with me who am such a close and intimate friend of his! Ah! he 'll write to me no doubt, or he 'll bid Nelly write—yes, yes, that 's what he 'll do. Nelly's very fond of me. Pretty Nell!'

Mr. Swiveller looked, as he was, all open-mouthed astonishment. Still glancing furtively at him, Quilp turned to Mr. Brass and observed, with assumed carelessness, that this need not interfere with the removal of the goods.

'For indeed,' he added, 'we knew that they 'd go

away to-day, but not that they 'd go so early, or so quietly. But they have their reasons, they have their reasons.'

'Where in the devil's name are they gone?' said the wondering Dick.

Quilp shook his head, and pursed up his lips, in a manner which implied that he knew very well, but was not at liberty to say.

'And what,' said Dick, looking at the confusion about him, 'what do you mean by moving the goods?'

'That I have bought 'em, sir,' rejoined Quilp. 'Eh? What then?'

'Has the sly old fox made his fortune then, and gone to live in a tranquil cot in a pleasant spot with a distant view of the changing sea?' said Dick, in great bewilderment.

'Keeping his place of retirement very close, that he may not be visited too often by affectionate grandsons and their devoted friends, eh?' added the dwarf, rubbing his hands hard: '*I* say nothing, but is that your meaning?'

Richard Swiveller was utterly aghast at this unexpected alteration of circumstances, which threatened the complete overthrow of the project in which he bore so conspicuous a part, and seemed to nip his prospects in the bud. Having only received from Frederick Trent, late on the previous night, information of the old man's illness, he had come upon a visit of condolence and inquiry to Nell, prepared with the first instalment of that long train of fascinations which was to fire her heart at last. And here, when he had been thinking of all kinds of graceful and insinuating approaches, and meditating on the fearful retaliation which was slowly working against Sophy Wackles—here were Nell, the old man, and all the money gone, melted away, decamped he knew not whither, as if with a foreknowledge of the scheme and a resolution to defeat it in the very outset, before a step was taken.

In his secret heart, Daniel Quilp was both surprised and troubled by the flight which had been made. It had not escaped his keen eye that some indispensable articles of clothing were gone with the fugitives, and knowing the old man's weak state of mind, he marvelled what that course of proceeding might be in which he had so readily procured the concurrence of the child. It must not be supposed (or it would be a gross injustice to Mr. Quilp) that he was tortured by any disinterested anxiety on behalf of either. His uneasiness arose from a misgiving that the old man had some secret store of money which he had not suspected; and the idea of its escaping his clutches, overwhelmed him with mortification and self-reproach.

In this frame of mind, it was some consolation to him to find that Richard Swiveller was, for different reasons, evidently irritated and disappointed by the same cause. It was plain, thought the dwarf, that he had come there, on behalf of his friend, to cajole or frighten the old man out of some small fraction of that wealth of which they supposed him to have an abundance. Therefore, it was a relief to vex his heart with a picture of the riches the old man hoarded, and to expatiate on his cunning in removing himself even beyond the reach of importunity.

'Well,' said Dick, with a blank look, 'I suppose it 's of no use my staying here.'

'Not the least in the world,' rejoined the dwarf.

'You 'll mention that I called, perhaps?' said Dick.

Mr. Quilp nodded, and said he certainly would, the very first time he saw them.

'And say,' added Mr. Swiveller, 'say, sir, that I

was wafted here upon the pinions of concord; that I came to remove, with the rake of friendship, the seeds of mutual wiolence and heart-burning, and to sow in their place, the germs of social harmony. Will you have the goodness to charge yourself with that commission, sir?'

'Certainly!' rejoined Quilp.

'Will you be kind enough to add to it, sir,' said Dick, producing a very small limp card, 'that *that* is my address, and that I am to be found at home every morning. Two distinct knocks, sir, will produce the slavey at any time. My particular friends, sir, are accustomed to sneeze when the door is opened, to give her to understand that they *are* my friends and have no interested motives in asking if I 'm at home. I beg your pardon; will you allow me to look at that card again?'

'Oh! by all means,' rejoined Quilp.

'By a slight and not unnatural mistake, sir,' said Dick, substituting another in its stead, 'I had handed you the pass-ticket of a select convivial circle called the Glorious Apollers, of which I have the honour to be Perpetual Grand. *That* is the proper document, sir. Good-morning.'

Quilp bade him good-day; the perpetual Grand Master of the Glorious Apollers, elevating his hat in honour of Mrs. Quilp, dropped it carelessly on the side of his head again, and disappeared with a flourish.

By this time, certain vans had arrived for the conveyance of the goods, and divers strong men in caps were balancing chests of drawers and other trifles of that nature upon their heads, and performing muscular feats which heightened their complexions considerably. Not to be behindhand in the bustle, Mr. Quilp went to work with surprising vigour; hustling

MR. QUILP WENT TO WORK WITH SURPRISING VIGOUR.

and driving the people about, like an evil spirit; setting Mrs. Quilp upon all kinds of arduous and impracticable tasks; carrying great weights up and down, with no apparent effort; kicking the boy from the wharf, whenever he could get near him; and inflicting, with his loads, a great many sly bumps and blows on the shoulders of Mr. Brass, as he stood upon the door-steps to answer all the inquiries of curious neighbours: which was his department. His presence and example diffused such alacrity among the persons employed, that, in a few hours, the house was emptied of everything, but pieces of matting, empty porter-pots, and scattered fragments of straw.

Seated, like an African chief, on one of these pieces of matting, the dwarf was regaling himself in the parlour, with bread and cheese and beer, when he observed without appearing to do so, that a boy was prying in at the outer door. Assured that it was Kit, though he saw little more than his nose, Mr. Quilp hailed him by his name; whereupon Kit came in and demanded what he wanted.

'Come here, you sir,' said the dwarf. 'Well, so your old master and young mistress have gone?'

'Where?' rejoined Kit, looking round.

'Do you mean to say you don't know where?' answered Quilp sharply. 'Where have they gonc, eh?'

'I don't know,' said Kit.

'Come,' retorted Quilp, 'let 's have no more of this! Do you mean to say that you don't know they went away by stealth, as soon as it was light this morning?'

'No,' said the boy, in evident surprise.

'You don't know that?' cried Quilp. 'Don't I know that you were hanging about the house the other night, like a thief, eh? Weren't you told then?'

'No,' replied the boy.

'You were not?' said Quilp. 'What were you told then; what were you talking about?'

Kit, who knew no particular reason why he should keep the matter secret now, related the purpose for which he had come on that occasion, and the proposal he had made.

'Oh!' said the dwarf after a little consideration. 'Then, I think they 'll come to you yet.'

'Do you think they will?' cried Kit eagerly.

'Ay, I think they will,' returned the dwarf. 'Now, when they do, let me know; d' ye hear? Let me know, and I 'll give you something. I want to do 'em a kindness, and I can't do 'em a kindness unless I know where they are. You hear what I say?'

Kit might have returned some answer which would not have been agreeable to his irascible questioner, if the boy from the wharf, who had been skulking about the room in search of anything that might have been left about by accident, had not happened to cry, 'Here 's a bird! What 's to be done with this?'

'Wring its neck,' rejoined Quilp.

'Oh no, don't do that,' said Kit, stepping forward. 'Give it to me.'

'Oh yes, I dare say,' cried the other boy. 'Come! You let the cage alone, and let me wring its neck will you? He said I was to do it. You let the cage alone, will you?'

'Give it here, give it to me, you dogs,' roared Quilp. 'Fight for it, you dogs, or I 'll wring its neck myself!'

Without further persuasion, the two boys fell upon each other, tooth and nail, while Quilp, holding up the cage in one hand, and chopping the ground with his knife in an ecstasy, urged them on by his taunts and cries to fight more fiercely. They were a pretty equal match, and rolled about together, exchanging blows which were by no means child's play, until at length Kit, planting a well-directed hit in his adversary's chest, disengaged himself, sprung nimbly up, and snatching the cage from Quilp's hands made off with his prize.

He did not stop once, until he reached home, where his bleeding face occasioned great consternation, and caused the elder child to howl dreadfully.

'Goodness gracious, Kit, what is the matter, what have you been doing?' cried Mrs. Nubbles.

'Never you mind, mother,' answered her son, wiping his face on the jack-towel behind the door. 'I 'm not hurt, don't you be afraid for me. I 've been a fightin' for a bird and won him, that 's all. Hold your noise, little Jacob. I never see such a naughty boy in all my days!'

'You have been a fighting for a bird!' exclaimed his mother.

'Ah! Fightin' for a bird!' replied Kit, 'and here he is—Miss Nelly's bird, mother, that they was a goin' to wring the neck of! I stopped that though—ha ha ha! They wouldn't wring his neck and me by, no no. It wouldn't do, mother, it wouldn't do at all. Ha ha ha!'

Kit laughing so heartily, with his swoln and bruised face looking out of the towel, made little Jacob laugh, and then his mother laughed, and then the baby crowed and kicked with great glee, and then they all laughed in concert: partly because of Kit's triumph, and partly because they were very fond of each other. When this fit was over, Kit exhibited the bird to both children, as a great and precious rarity—it was only a poor linnet—and looking about the wall for an old nail, made a scaffolding of a chair and table and twisted it out with great exultation.

'Let me see,' said the boy, 'I think I 'll hang him

in the winder, because it 's more light and cheerful, and he can see the sky there, if he looks up very much. He 's such a one to sing, I can tell you!'

So, the scaffolding was made again, and Kit, climbing up with the poker for a hammer, knocked in the nail and hung up the cage, to the immeasurable delight of the whole family. When it had been adjusted and straightened a great many times, and he had walked backwards into the fireplace in his admiration of it, the arrangement was pronounced to be perfect.

'And now, mother,' said the boy, 'before I rest any more, I 'll go out and see if I can find a horse to hold, and then I can buy some birdseed, and a bit of something nice for you, into the bargain.'

CHAPTER XIV

As it was very easy for Kit to persuade himself that the old house was in his way, his way being anywhere, he tried to look upon his passing it at once more as a matter of imperative and disagreeable necessity, quite apart from any desire of his own, to which he could not choose but yield. It is not uncommon for people who are much better fed and taught than Christopher Nubbles had ever been, to make duties of their inclinations in matters of more doubtful propriety, and to take great credit for the self-denial with which they gratify themselves.

There was no need of any caution this time, and no fear of being detained by having to play out a return match with Daniel Quilp's boy. The place was entirely deserted, and looked as dusty and dingy as if it had been so for months. A rusty padlock was fastened on the door, ends of discoloured blinds and curtains flapped drearily against the half-opened upper windows, and the crooked holes cut in the closed shutters below, were black with the darkness of the inside. Some of the glass in the window he had so often watched, had been broken in the rough hurry of the morning, and that room looked more deserted and dull than any. A group of idle urchins had taken possession of the door-steps; some were plying the knocker and listening with delighted dread to the hollow sounds it spread through the dismantled house; others were clustered about the key-hole, watching half in jest and half in earnest for 'the ghost,' which an hour's gloom, added to the mystery that hung about the late inhabitants, had already raised. Standing all alone in the midst of the business and bustle of the street, the house looked a picture of cold desolation; and Kit, who remembered the cheerful fire that used to burn there on a winter's night and the no less cheerful laugh that made the small room ring, turned quite mournfully away.

It must be especially observed in justice to poor Kit that he was by no means of a sentimental turn, and perhaps had never heard that adjective in all his life. He was only a soft-hearted grateful fellow, and had nothing genteel or polite about him; consequently, instead of going home again, in his grief, to kick the children and abuse his mother (for, when your finely-strung people are out of sorts, they must have everybody else unhappy likewise), he turned his thoughts to the vulgar expedient of making them more comfortable if he could.

Bless us, what a number of gentlemen on horseback there were riding up and down, and how few of them wanted their horses held! A good city speculator or a parliamentary commissioner could have told to a fraction, from the crowds that were cantering about, what sum of money was realised in London, in the course of a year, by holding horses alone. And undoubtedly it would have been a very large one, if only a twentieth part of the gentlemen without grooms had had occasion to alight; but they had not; and it is often an ill-natured circumstance like this, which spoils the most ingenious estimate in the world.

Kit walked about, now with quick steps and now with slow; now lingering as some rider slackened his horse's pace and looked about him; and now darting at full speed up a by-street as he caught a glimpse of some distant horseman going lazily up the shady side of the road, and promising to stop, at every door. But on they all went, one after another, and there was not a penny stirring. 'I wonder,' thought the boy, 'if one of these gentlemen knew there was nothing in the cupboard at home, whether he 'd stop on purpose, and make believe that he wanted to call somewhere, that I might earn a trifle?'

He was quite tired out with pacing the streets, to say nothing of repeated disappointments, and was sitting down upon a step to rest, when there approached towards him a little clattering jingling four-wheeled chaise, drawn by a little obstinate-looking rough-coated pony, and driven by a little fat placid-faced old gentleman. Beside the little old gentleman sat a little old lady, plump and placid like himself, and the pony was coming along at his own pace and doing exactly as he pleased with the whole concern. If the old gentleman remonstrated by shaking the reins, the pony replied by shaking his head. It was plain that the utmost the pony would consent to do, was to go in his own way up any street that the old gentleman particularly wished to traverse, but that it was an understanding between them that he must do this after his own fashion or not at all.

As they passed where he sat, Kit looked so wistfully at the little turn-out, that the old gentleman looked at him. Kit rising and putting his hand to his hat, the old gentleman intimated to the pony that he wished to stop, to which proposal the pony (who seldom objected to that part of his duty) graciously acceded.

'I beg your pardon, sir,' said Kit. 'I 'm sorry you stopped, sir. I only meant did you want your horse minded.'

'I 'm going to get down in the next street,' returned the old gentleman. 'If you like to come on after us, you may have the job.'

Kit thanked him, and joyfully obeyed. The pony ran off at a sharp angle to inspect a lamp-post on the opposite side of the way, and then went off at a tangent to another lamp-post on the other side. Having satisfied himself that they were of the same pattern and materials, he came to a stop apparently absorbed in meditation.

'Will you go on, sir,' said the old gentleman, gravely, 'or are we to wait here for you till it 's too late for our appointment?'

The pony remained immovable.

'Oh you naughty Whisker,' said the old lady. 'Fie upon you! I 'm ashamed of such conduct.'

The pony appeared to be touched by this appeal to his feelings, for he trotted on directly, though in a sulky manner, and stopped no more until he came to a door whereon was a brass plate with the words 'Witherden—Notary.' Here the old gentleman got out and helped out the old lady, and then took from under the seat a nosegay resembling in shape and dimensions a full-sized warming-pan with the handle cut short off. This, the old lady carried into the house with a staid and stately air, and the old gentleman (who had a club-foot) followed close upon her.

They went, as it was easy to tell from the sound of their voices, into the front-parlour, which seemed to be a kind of office. The day being very warm and the street a quiet one, the windows were wide open; and it was easy to hear through the Venetian blinds all that passed inside.

At first there was a great shaking of hands and shuffling of feet, succeeded by the presentation of the nosegay; for a voice, supposed by the listener to be that of Mr. Witherden, the notary, was heard to exclaim a great many times, 'oh, delicious!' 'oh, fragrant, indeed!' and a nose, also supposed to be the property of that gentleman, was heard to inhale the scent with a snuffle of exceeding pleasure.

'I brought it in honour of the occasion, sir,' said the old lady.

'Ah! an occasion indeed, ma'am; an occasion which does honour to me, ma'am, honour to me,' rejoined Mr. Witherden, the notary. 'I have had many a gentleman articled to me, ma'am, many a one. Some of them are now rolling in riches, unmindful of their old companion and friend, ma'am, others are in the habit of calling upon me to this day and saying, "Mr. Witherden, some of the pleasantest hours I ever spent in my life were spent in this office—were spent, sir, upon this very stool"; but there was never one among the number, ma'am, attached as I have been to many of them, of whom I augured such bright things as I do of your only son.'

'Oh dear!' said the old lady. 'How happy you do make us when you tell us that, to be sure!'

'I tell you, ma'am,' said Mr. Witherden, 'what I think as an honest man, which, as the poet observes, is the noblest work of God. I agree with the poet in every particular, ma'am. The mountainous Alps on the one hand, or a humming-bird on the other, is nothing, in point of workmanship, to an honest man —or woman—or woman.'

'Anything that Mr. Witherden can say of me,' observed a small quiet voice, 'I can say, with interest, of him, I am sure.'

'It 's a happy circumstance, a truly happy circumstance,' said the notary, 'to happen too upon his eight-and-twentieth birthday, and I hope I know how to appreciate it. I trust, Mr. Garland, my dear sir, that we may mutually congratulate each other upon this auspicious occasion.'

To this the old gentleman replied that he felt assured they might. There appeared to be another shaking of hands in consequence, and when it was over, the old gentleman said that, though he said it who should not, he believed no son had ever been a greater comfort to his parents than Abel Garland had been to his.

'Marrying as his mother and I did, late in life, sir, after waiting for a great many years, until we were well enough off—coming together when we were no longer young and then being blessed with one child who has always been dutiful and affectionate—why, it 's a source of great happiness to us both, sir.'

'Of course it is, I have no doubt of it,' returned the notary in a sympathising voice. 'It 's the contemplation of this sort of thing, that makes me deplore my fate in being a bachelor. There was a young lady once, sir, the daughter of an outfitting warehouse of the first respectability—but that 's a weakness. Chuckster, bring in Mr. Abel's articles.'

'You see, Mr. Witherden,' said the old lady, 'that Abel has not been brought up like the run of young men. He has always had a pleasure in our society, and always been with us. Abel has never been absent from us, for a day; has he, my dear?'

'Never, my dear,' returned the old gentleman, 'except when he went to Margate one Saturday with Mr. Tomkinley that had been a teacher at that school he went to, and came back upon the Monday; but he was very ill after that, you remember, my dear; it was quite a dissipation.'

'He was not used to it, you know,' said the old lady, 'and he couldn't bear it, that 's the truth. Besides, he had no comfort in being there without us, and had nobody to talk to or enjoy himself with.'

'That was it, you know,' interposed the same small quiet voice that had spoken once before. 'I was quite abroad, mother, quite desolate, and to think that the sea was between us—oh, I never shall forget what I felt when I first thought that the sea was between us!'

'Very natural under the circumstances,' observed the notary. 'Mr. Abel's feelings did credit to his nature, and credit to your nature, ma'am, and his father's nature, and human nature. I trace the same current now, flowing through all his quiet and unobtrusive proceedings.—I am about to sign my name, you observe, at the foot of the articles which Mr. Chuckster will witness; and placing my finger upon this blue wafer with the vandyked corners, I am constrained to remark in a distinct tone of voice—don't be alarmed, ma'am, it is merely a form of law—that I deliver this, as my act and deed. Mr. Abel will place his name against the other wafer, repeating the same cabalistic words, and the business is over. Ha, ha, ha! You see how easily these things are done!'

There was a short silence, apparently, while Mr. Abel went through the prescribed form, and then the shaking of hands and shuffling of feet were renewed, and shortly afterwards there was a clinking of wineglasses and a great talkativeness on the part of everybody. In about a quarter of an hour Mr. Chuckster (with a pen behind his ear and his face inflamed with wine) appeared at the door, and condescending to address Kit by the jocose appellation of 'Young Snob,' informed him that the visitors were coming out.

Out they came forthwith; Mr. Witherden, who was short, chubby, fresh-coloured, brisk, and pompous, leading the old lady with extreme politeness, and the father and son following them, arm-in-arm. Mr. Abel, who had a quaint old-fashioned air about him, looked nearly of the same age as his father, and bore a wonderful resemblance to him in face and figure, though wanting something of his full, round, cheerfulness, and substituting in its place, a timid reserve. In all other respects, in the neatness of the dress, and even in the club-foot, he and the old gentleman were precisely alike.

Having seen the old lady safely in her seat, and assisted in the arrangement of her cloak and a small basket which formed an indispensable portion of her equipage, Mr. Abel got into a little box behind which had evidently been made for his express accommodation, and smiled at everybody present by turns, beginning with his mother and ending with the pony. There was then a great to-do to make the pony hold up his head that the bearing-rein might be fastened; at last even this was effected; and the old gentleman, taking his seat and the reins, put his hand in his pocket to find a sixpence for Kit.

He had no sixpences, neither had the old lady, nor Mr. Abel, nor the notary, nor Mr. Chuckster. The old gentleman thought a shilling too much, but there was no shop in the street to get change at, so he gave it to the boy.

'There,' he said jokingly, 'I 'm coming here again next Monday at the same time, and mind you 're here, my lad, to work it out.'

'Thank you, sir,' said Kit. 'I 'll be sure to be here.'

He was quite serious, but they all laughed heartily at his saying so, especially Mr. Chuckster, who roared outright and appeared to relish the joke amazingly. As the pony, with a presentiment that he was going home, or a determination that he would not go anywhere else (which was the same thing) trotted away pretty nimbly, Kit had no time to justify himself, and went his way also. Having expended his treasure in such purchases as he knew would be most acceptable at home, not forgetting some seed for the wonderful bird, he hastened back as fast as he could, so elated with his success and great good-fortune, that he more than half expected Nell and the old man would have arrived before him.

CHAPTER XV

OFTEN, while they were yet pacing the silent streets of the town on the morning of their departure, the child trembled with a mingled sensation of hope and fear as in some far-off figure imperfectly seen in the clear distance, her fancy traced a likeness to honest Kit. But although she would gladly have given him her hand and thanked him for what he had said at their last meeting, it was always a relief to find, when they came nearer to each other, that the person who approached was not he, but a stranger; for even if she had not dreaded the effect which the sight of him might have wrought upon her fellow-traveller, she felt that to bid farewell to anybody now, and most of all to him who had been so faithful and so true, was more than she could bear. It was enough to leave dumb things behind, and objects that were insensible both to her love and sorrow. To have parted from her only other friend upon the threshold of that wild journey, would have wrung her heart indeed.

Why is it that we can better bear to part in spirit than in body, and while we have the fortitude to act farewell have not the nerve to say it? On the eve of long voyages or an absence of many years, friends who are tenderly attached will separate with the usual look, the usual pressure of the hand, planning one final interview for the morrow, while each well knows that it is but a poor feint to save the pain of uttering that one word, and that the meeting will never be. Should possibilities be worse to bear than certainties? We do not shun our dying friends; the not having distinctly taken leave of one among them, whom we left in all kindness and affection, will often embitter the whole remainder of a life.

The town was glad with morning light; places that had shown ugly and distrustful all night long, now wore a smile; and sparkling sunbeams dancing on chamber windows, and twinkling through blind and curtain before sleepers' eyes, shed light even into dreams, and chased away the shadows of the night. Birds in hot rooms, covered up close and dark, felt it was morning, and chafed and grew restless in their little cells; bright-eyed mice crept back to their tiny homes and nestled timidly together; the sleek house-cat, forgetful of her prey, sat winking at the rays of sun starting through key-hole and cranny in the door, and longed for her stealthy run and warm sleek bask outside. The nobler beasts confined in dens, stood motionless behind their bars, and gazed on fluttering boughs, and sunshine peeping through some little window, with eyes in which old forests gleamed—then trod impatiently the track their prisoned feet had worn—and stopped and gazed again. Men in their dungeons stretched their cramped cold limbs and cursed the stone that no bright sky could warm. The flowers that sleep by night, opened their gentle eyes, and turned them to the day. The light, creation's mind, was everywhere, and all things owned its power.

The two pilgrims, often pressing each other's hands, or exchanging a smile or cheerful look, pursued their way in silence. Bright and happy as it was, there was something solemn in the long, deserted streets, from which, like bodies without souls, all habitual character and expression had departed, leaving but one dead uniform repose, that made them all alike. All was so still at that early hour, that the few pale people whom they met seemed as much unsuited to the scene, as the sickly lamp which had been here and there left burning, was powerless and faint in the full glory of the sun.

Before they had penetrated very far into the labyrinth of men's abodes which yet lay between them and the outskirts, this aspect began to melt away, and noise and bustle to usurp its place. Some straggling carts and coaches rumbling by, first broke the charm, then others came, then others yet more active, then a crowd. The wonder was, at first, to see a tradesman's room-window open, but it was a rare thing, to see one closed; then, smoke rose slowly from the chimneys, and sashes were thrown up to let in air, and doors opened, and servant-girls, looking lazily in all directions but their brooms, scattered brown clouds of dust into the eyes of shrinking passengers, or listened disconsolately to milkmen who spoke of country fairs, and told of waggons in the mews, with awnings and all things complete, and gallant swains to boot, which another hour would see upon their journey.

This quarter passed, they came upon the haunts of commerce and great traffic, where many people were resorting, and business was already rife. The old man looked about him with a startled and bewildered gaze, for these were places that he hoped to shun. He pressed his finger on his lip, and drew the child along by narrow courts and winding ways, nor did he seem at ease until they had left it far behind, often casting a backward look towards it, murmuring that ruin and self-murder were crouching in every street, and would follow if they scented them; and that they could not fly too fast.

Again this quarter passed, they came upon a straggling neighbourhood, where the mean houses parcelled off in rooms, and windows patched with rags and paper, told of the populous poverty that sheltered there. The shops sold goods that only poverty could buy, and sellers and buyers were pinched and griped alike. Here were poor streets where faded gentility essayed with scanty space and shipwrecked means to make its last feeble stand, but tax-gatherer and creditor came there as elsewhere, and the poverty that yet faintly struggled was hardly less squalid and manifest than that which had long ago submitted and given up the game.

This was a wide, wide track—for the humble followers of the camp of wealth pitch their tents round about it for many a mile—but its character was still the same. Damp rotten houses, many to let, many yet building, many half-built and mouldering away—lodgings, where it would be hard to tell which needed pity most, those who let or those who came to take—children, scantily fed and clothed, spread over every street, and sprawling in the dust—scolding mothers, stamping their slipshod feet with noisy threats upon the pavement—shabby fathers, hurrying with dispirited looks to the occupation which brought them 'daily bread' and little more—mangling-women, washerwomen, cobblers, tailors, chandlers, driving their trades in parlours and kitchens and back rooms and garrets, and sometimes all of them under the same roof—brick-fields skirting gardens paled with staves of old casks, or timber pillaged from houses burnt down, and blackened and blistered by the flames—mounds of dock-weed, nettles, coarse grass and oyster-shells, heaped in rank confusion—small dissenting chapels to teach, with no lack of illustration, the miseries of Earth, and plenty of new churches, erected with a little superfluous wealth, to show the way to Heaven.

At length these streets becoming more straggling yet, dwindled and dwindled away, until there were only small garden patches bordering the road, with many a summer-house innocent of paint and built of old timber or some fragments of a boat, green as the tough cabbage-stalks that grew about it, and grottoed at the seams with toad-stools and tight-sticking snails. To these succeeded pert cottages, two and two with plots of ground in front, laid out in angular beds with stiff box borders and narrow paths between, where footstep never strayed to make the gravel rough. Then came the public-house, freshly painted in green and white, with tea-gardens and a bowling-green, spurning its old neighbour with the horse-trough where the waggons stopped; then, fields; and then, some houses, one by one, of goodly size with awns, some even with a lodge where dwelt a porter and his wife. Then, came a turnpike; then fields again with trees and hay-stacks; then, a hill; and on the top of that, the traveller might stop, and—looking back at old Saint Paul's looming through the smoke, its cross peeping above the cloud (if the day were clear), and glittering in the sun; and casting his eyes upon the Babel out of which it grew until he traced it down to the furthest outposts of the invading army of bricks and mortar whose station lay for the present nearly at his feet—might feel at last that he was clear of London.

Near such a spot as this, and in a pleasant field, the old man and his little guide (if guide she were, who knew not whither they were bound) sat down to rest. She had had the precaution to furnish her basket with some slices of bread and meat, and here they made their frugal breakfast.

The freshness of the day, the singing of the birds, the beauty of the waving grass, the deep green leaves, the wild flowers, and the thousand exquisite scents and sounds that floated in the air,—deep joys to most of us, but most of all to those whose life is in a crowd or who live solitarily in great cities as in the bucket of a human well,—sunk into their breasts and made them very glad. The child had repeated her artless prayers once that morning, more earnestly perhaps than she had ever done in all her life, but as she felt all this, they rose to her lips again. The old man took off his hat—he had no memory for the words—but he said amen, and that they were very good.

There had been an old copy of the Pilgrim's Progress, with strange plates, upon a shelf at home, over which she had often pored whole evenings, wondering whether it was true in every word, and where those distant countries with the curious names might be. As she looked back upon the place they had left, one part of it came strongly on her mind.

'Dear grandfather,' she said, 'only that this place is prettier and a great deal better than the real one, if that in the book is like it, I feel as if we were both Christian, and laid down on this grass all the cares and troubles we brought with us; never to take them up again.'

'No—never to return—never to return'—replied the old man, waving his hand towards the city. 'Thou and I are free of it now, Nell. They shall never lure us back.'

'Are you tired?' said the child, 'are you sure you don't feel ill from this long walk?'

'I shall never feel ill again, now that we are once away,' was the reply. 'Let us be stirring, Nell. We must be further away—a long, long way further. We are too near to stop, and be at rest. Come!'

There was a pool of clear water in the field, in which the child laved her hands and face, and cooled her feet before setting forth to walk again. She would have the old man refresh himself in this way, too, and making him sit down upon the grass, cast the water on him with her hands, and dried it with her simple dress.

'I can do nothing for myself, my darling,' said the grandfather; 'I don't know how it is, I could once, but the time 's gone. Don't leave me, Nell; say that thou 'lt not leave me. I loved thee all the while, indeed I did. If I lose thee too, my dear, I must die!'

He laid his head upon her shoulder and moaned piteously. The time had been, and a very few days before, when the child could not have restrained her tears and must have wept with him. But now she soothed him with gentle and tender words, smiled at his thinking they could ever part, and rallied him cheerfully upon the jest. He was soon calmed and fell asleep, singing to himself in a low voice, like a little child.

He awoke refreshed, and they continued their journey. The road was pleasant, lying between beautiful pastures and fields of corn, above which, poised high in the clear blue sky, the lark trilled out her happy song. The air came laden with the fragrance it caught upon its way, and the bees, upborne upon its scented breath, hummed forth their drowsy satisfaction as they floated by.

They were now in the open country; the houses were very few and scattered at long intervals, often miles apart. Occasionally they came upon a cluster of poor cottages, some with a chair or low board put across the open door to keep the scrambling children from the road, others shut up close while all the family were working in the fields. These were often the commencement of a little village: and after an interval came a wheelwright's shed or perhaps a blacksmith's forge; then a thriving farm with sleepy cows lying about the yard, and horses peering over the low wall and scampering away when harnessed horses passed upon the road, as though in triumph at their freedom. There were dull pigs too, turning up the ground in search of dainty food, and grunting their monotonous grumblings as they prowled about, or crossed each other in their quest; plump pigeons skimming round the roof or strutting on the eaves; and ducks and geese, far more graceful in their own conceit, waddling awkwardly about the edges of the pond or sailing glibly on its surface. The farm-yard passed, then came the little inn; the humbler beer-shop; and the village tradesman's; then the lawyer's and the parson's, at whose dread names the beer-shop trembled; the church then peeped out modestly from a clump of trees; then there were a few more cottages; then the cage, and pound, and not unfrequently, on a bank by the wayside, a deep old dusty well. Then came the trim-hedged fields on either hand, and the open road again.

They walked all day, and slept that night at a small

cottage where beds were let to travellers. Next morning they were afoot again, and though jaded at first, and very tired, recovered before long and proceeded briskly forward.

They often stopped to rest, but only for a short space at a time, and still kept on, having had but slight refreshment since the morning. It was nearly five o'clock in the afternoon, when drawing near another cluster of labourers' huts, the child looked wistfully in each, doubtful at which to ask for permission to rest awhile, and buy a draught of milk.

It was not easy to determine, for she was timid and fearful of being repulsed. Here was a crying child, and there a noisy wife. In this, the people seemed too poor; in that, too many. At length she stopped at one where the family were seated round the table—chiefly because there was an old man sitting in a cushioned chair beside the hearth, and she thought he was a grandfather and would feel for hers.

There were besides, the cottager and his wife, and three young sturdy children, brown as berries. The request was no sooner preferred, than granted. The eldest boy ran out to fetch some milk, the second dragged two stools towards the door, and the youngest crept to his mother's gown, and looked at the strangers from beneath his sun-burnt hand.

'God save you, master,' said the old cottager in a thin piping voice; 'are you travelling far?'

'Yes, sir, a long way'—replied the child; for her grandfather appealed to her.

'From London?' inquired the old man.

The child said yes.

Ah! He had been in London many a time—used to go there often once, with waggons. It was nigh two-and-thirty year since he had been there last, and he did hear say there were great changes. Like enough! He had changed himself since then. Two-and-thirty year was a long time and eighty-four a great age, though there was some he had known that had lived to very hard upon a hundred—and not so hearty as he, neither—no, nothing like it.

'Sit thee down, master, in the elbow-chair,' said the old man, knocking his stick upon the brick floor, and trying to do so sharply. 'Take a pinch out o' that box; I don't take much myself, for it comes dear, but I find it wakes me up sometimes, and ye 're but a boy to me. I should have a son pretty nigh as old as you if he 'd lived, but they 'listed him for a so'ger—he come back home though, for all he had but one poor leg. He always said he 'd be buried near the sun-dial he used to climb upon when he was a baby, did my poor boy, and his words come true—you can see the place with your own eyes; we 've kept the turf up, ever since.'

He shook his head, and looking at his daughter with watery eyes, said she needn't be afraid that he was going to talk about that, any more. He didn't wish to trouble nobody, and if he had troubled anybody by what he said, he asked pardon, that was all.

The milk arrived, and the child producing her little basket, and selecting its best fragments for her grandfather, they made a hearty meal. The furniture of the room was very homely of course—a few rough chairs and a table, a corner cupboard with their little stock of crockery and delf, a gaudy tea-tray, representing a lady in bright red, walking out with a very blue parasol, a few common, coloured scripture subjects in frames upon the wall and chimney, an old dwarf clothes-press and an eight-day clock, with a few bright saucepans and a kettle, comprised the whole. But everything was clean and neat, and as the child glanced round, she felt a tranquil air of comfort and content to which she had long been unaccustomed.

'How far is it to any town or village?' she asked of the husband.

'A matter of good five mile, my dear,' was the reply, 'but you 're not going on to-night?'

'Yes, yes, Nell,' said the old man hastily, urging her too by signs. 'Further on, further on, darling, further away if we walk till midnight.'

'There 's a good barn hard by, master,' said the man, 'or there 's travellers' lodging, I know, at the Plow an' Harrer. Excuse me, but you do seem a little tired, and unless you 're very anxious to get on—'

'Yes, yes, we are,' returned the old man fretfully. 'Further away, dear Nell, pray further away.'

'We must go on, indeed,' said the child, yielding to his restless wish. 'We thank you very much, but we cannot stop so soon. I 'm quite ready, grandfather.'

But the woman had observed, from the young wanderer's gait, that one of her little feet was blistered and sore, and being a woman and a mother too, she would not suffer her to go until she had washed the place and applied some simple remedy, which she did so carefully and with such a gentle hand—rough-grained and hard though it was, with work—that the child's heart was too full to admit of her saying more than a fervent 'God bless you!' nor could she look back nor trust herself to speak, until they had left the cottage some distance behind. When she turned her head, she saw that the whole family, even the old grandfather, were standing in the road watching them as they went, and so, with many waves of the hand, and cheering nods, and on one side at least not without tears, they parted company.

They trudged forward, more slowly and painfully

than they had done yet, for another mile or thereabouts, when they heard the sound of wheels behind them, and looking round observed an empty cart approaching pretty briskly. The driver on coming up to them stopped his horse and looked earnestly at Nell.

'Didn't you stop to rest at a cottage yonder?' he said.

'Yes, sir,' replied the child.

'Ah! They asked me to look out for you,' said the man. 'I 'm going your way. Give me your hand—jump up, master.'

This was a great relief, for they were very much fatigued and could scarcely crawl along. To them the jolting cart was a luxurious carriage, and the ride the most delicious in the world. Nell had scarcely settled herself on a little heap of straw in one corner, when she fell asleep, for the first time that day.

She was awakened by the stopping of the cart, which was about to turn up a by-lane. The driver kindly got down to help her out, and pointing to some trees at a very short distance before them, said that the town lay there, and that they had better take the path which they would see leading through the churchyard. Accordingly, towards this spot, they directed their weary steps.

CHAPTER XVI

THE sun was setting when they reached the wicket-gate at which the path began, and, as the rain falls upon the just and unjust alike, it shed its warm tint even upon the resting-places of the dead, and bade them be of good hope for its rising on the morrow. The church was old and grey, with ivy clinging to the walls, and round the porch. Shunning the tombs, it crept about the mounds, beneath which slept poor humble men: twining for them the first wreaths they had ever won, but wreaths less liable to wither and far more lasting in their kind, than some which were graven deep in stone and marble, and told in pompous terms of virtues meekly hidden for many a year, and only revealed at last to executors and mourning legatees.

The clergyman's horse, stumbling with a dull blunt sound among the graves, was cropping the grass; at once deriving orthodox consolation from the dead parishioners, and enforcing last Sunday's text that this was what all flesh came to; a lean ass who had sought to expound it also, without being qualified and ordained, was pricking his ears in an empty pound hard by, and looking with hungry eyes upon his priestly neighbour.

The old man and the child quitted the gravel-path, and strayed among the tombs; for there the ground was soft, and easy to their tired feet. As they passed behind the church, they heard voices near at hand, and presently came on those who had spoken.

They were two men who were seated in easy attitudes upon the grass, and so busily engaged as to be at first unconscious of intruders. It was not difficult to divine that they were of a class of itinerant showmen—exhibitors of the freaks of Punch—for, perched cross-legged upon a tombstone behind them, was a figure of that hero himself, his nose and chin as hooked and his face as beaming as usual. Perhaps his imperturbable character was never more strikingly developed, for he preserved his usual equable smile notwithstanding that his body was dangling in a most uncomfortable position, all loose and limp and shapeless, while his long peaked cap, unequally balanced against his exceedingly slight legs, threatened every instant to bring him toppling down.

In part scattered upon the ground at the feet of the two men, and in part jumbled together in a long flat box, were the other persons of the drama. The hero's wife and one child, the hobby-horse, the doctor, the foreign gentleman who not being familiar with the language is unable in the representation to express his ideas otherwise than by the utterance of the word 'Shallabalah' three distinct times, the radical neighbour who will by no means admit that a tin bell is an organ, the executioner, and the devil, were all here. Their owners had evidently come to that spot to make some needful repairs in the stage arrangements, for one of them was engaged in binding together a small gallows with thread, while the other was intent upon fixing a new black wig, with the aid of a small hammer and some tacks, upon the head of the radical neighbour, who had been beaten bald.

They raised their eyes when the old man and his young companion were close upon them, and pausing in their work, returned their looks of curiosity. One of them, the actual exhibitor no doubt, was a little merry-faced man with a twinkling eye and a red nose, who seemed to have unconsciously imbibed something of his hero's character. The other—that was he who took the money—had rather a careful and cautious look, which was perhaps inseparable from his occupation also.

The merry man was the first to greet the strangers with a nod; and following the old man's eyes, he observed that perhaps that was the first time he had ever seen a Punch off the stage. (Punch, it may be remarked, seemed to be pointing with the tip of his cap to a most flourishing epitaph, and to be chuckling over it with all his heart.)

'Why do you come here to do this?' said the old man, sitting down beside them, and looking at the figures with extreme delight.

'Why you see,' rejoined the little man, 'we 're putting up for to-night at the public-house yonder, and it wouldn't do to let 'em see the present company undergoing repair.'

'No?' cried the old man, making signs to Nell to listen, 'why not, eh? why not?'

'Because it would destroy all the delusion, and take away all the interest, wouldn't it?' replied the little man. 'Would you care a ha'penny for the Lord Chancellor if you know'd him in private and without his wig?—certainly not.'

'Good!' said the old man, venturing to touch one of the puppets, and drawing away his hand with a shrill laugh. 'Are you going to show 'em to-night? are you?'

'That is the intention, governor,' replied the other, 'and unless I 'm much mistaken, Tommy Codlin is a calculating at this minute what we 've lost through your coming upon us. Cheer up, Tommy, it can't be much.'

The little man accompanied these latter words with a wink, expressive of the estimate he had formed of the travellers' finances.

To this Mr. Codlin, who had a surly, grumbling manner, replied, as he twitched Punch off the tombstone and flung him into the box—

'I don't care if we haven't lost a farden, but you 're too free. If you stood in front of the curtain and see the public's faces as I do, you 'd know human natur' better.'

'Ah! it 's been the spoiling of you, Tommy, your taking to that branch,' rejoined his companion. 'When you played the ghost in the reg'lar drama in the fairs, you believed in everything—except ghosts. But now you 're a universal mistruster. *I* never see a man so changed.'

'Never mind,' said Mr. Codlin, with the air of a discontented philosopher. 'I know better now, and p'raps I 'm sorry for it.'

Turning over the figures in the box like one who knew and despised them, Mr. Codlin drew one forth and held it up for the inspection of his friend.

'Look here; here 's all this Judy's clothes falling to pieces again. You haven't got a needle and thread I suppose?'

The little man shook his head, and scratched it ruefully as he contemplated this severe indisposition of a principal performer. Seeing that they were at a loss, the child said timidly—

'I have a needle, sir, in my basket, and thread too. Will you let me try to mend it for you? I think I could do it neater than you could.'

Even Mr. Codlin had nothing to urge against a proposal so seasonable. Nelly, kneeling down beside the box, was soon busily engaged in her task, and accomplishing it to a miracle.

While she was thus engaged, the merry little man looked at her with an interest which did not appear to be diminished when he glanced at her helpless companion. When she had finished her work he thanked her, and inquired whither they were travelling.

'N—no further to-night, I think,' said the child, looking towards her grandfather.

'If you 're wanting a place to stop at,' the man remarked, 'I should advise you to take up at the same house with us. That 's it. The long, low, white house there. It 's very cheap.'

The old man, notwithstanding his fatigue, would have remained in the churchyard all night if his new acquaintances had remained there too. As he yielded to this suggestion a ready and rapturous assent, they all rose and walked away together; he keeping close to the box of puppets in which he was quite absorbed, the merry little man carrying it slung over his arm by a strap attached to it for the purpose, Nelly having hold of her grandfather's hand, and Mr. Codlin sauntering slowly behind, casting up at the church-tower and neighbouring trees such looks as he was accustomed in town-practice to direct to drawing-room and nursery windows, when seeking for a profitable spot on which to plant the show.

The public-house was kept by a fat old landlord and landlady who made no objection to receiving their new guests, but praised Nelly's beauty and were at once prepossessed in her behalf. There was no other company in the kitchen but the two showmen, and the child felt very thankful that they had fallen upon such good quarters. The landlady was very much astonished to learn that they had come all the way from London, and appeared to have no little curiosity touching their farther destination. The child parried her inquiries as well as she could, and with no great trouble, for finding that they appeared to give her pain, the old lady desisted.

'These two gentlemen have ordered supper in an hour's time,' she said, taking her into the bar; 'and your best plan will be to sup with them. Meanwhile you shall have a little taste of something that 'll do you good, for I 'm sure you must want it after all you 've gone through to-day. Now, don't look after the old gentleman, because when you 've drank that, he shall have some too.'

As nothing could induce the child to leave him alone, however, or to touch anything in which he was not the first and greatest sharer, the old lady was obliged to help him first. When they had been thus refreshed, the whole house hurried away into an empty stable where the show stood, and where, by the light of a few flaring candles stuck round a hoop which hung by a line from the ceiling, it was to be forthwith exhibited.

And now Mr. Thomas Codlin, the misanthrope, after blowing away at the Pan's pipes until he was intensely wretched, took his station on one side of the checked drapery which concealed the mover of the figures, and putting his hands in his pockets prepared to reply to all questions and remarks of Punch, and to make a dismal feint of being his most intimate private friend, of believing in him to the fullest and most unlimited extent, of knowing that he enjoyed day and night a merry and glorious existence in that temple, and that he was at all times and under every circumstance the same intelligent and joyful person that the spectators then beheld him. All this Mr. Codlin did with the air of a man who has made up his mind for the worst and was quite resigned; his eye slowly wandering about during the briskest repartee to observe the effect upon the audience, and particularly the impression made upon the landlord and landlady, which might be productive of very important results in connection with the supper.

Upon this head, however, he had no cause for any anxiety, for the whole performance was applauded to the echo, and voluntary contributions were showered in with a liberality which testified yet more strongly to the general delight. Among the laughter none was more loud and frequent than the old man's. Nell's was unheard, for she, poor child, with her head drooping on his shoulder, had fallen asleep, and slept too soundly to be roused by any of his efforts to awaken her to a participation in his glee.

The supper was very good, but she was too tired to eat, and yet would not leave the old man until she had kissed him in his bed. He, happily insensible to every care and anxiety, sat listening with a vacant smile and admiring face to all that his new friends said; and it was not until they retired yawning to their room, that he followed the child upstairs.

It was but a loft partitioned into two compartments, where they were to rest, but they were well pleased with their lodging and had hoped for none so good. The old man was uneasy when he had lain down, and begged that Nell would come and sit at his bedside as she had done for so many nights. She hastened to him, and sat there till he slept.

There was a little window, hardly more than a chink in the wall, in her room, and when she left him, she opened it, quite wondering at the silence. The sight of the old church and the graves about it in the moonlight, and the dark trees whispering among themselves, made her more thoughtful than before. She closed the window again, and sitting down upon the bed, thought of the life that was before them.

She had a little money, but it was very little, and when that was gone, they must begin to beg. There was one piece of gold among it, and an emergency might come when its worth to them would be increased a hundred-fold. It would be best to hide this coin, and never produce it unless their case was absolutely desperate, and no other resource was left them.

Her resolution taken, she sewed the piece of gold into her dress, and going to bed with a lighter heart sunk into a deep slumber.

CHAPTER XVII

Another bright day shining in through the small casement, and claiming fellowship with the kindred eyes of the child, awoke her. At sight of the strange room and its unaccustomed objects she started up in alarm, wondering how she had been moved from the familiar chamber in which she seemed to have fallen asleep last night, and whither she had been conveyed. But, another glance around called to her mind all that had lately passed, and she sprung from her bed, hoping and trustful.

It was yet early, and the old man being still asleep, she walked out into the churchyard, brushing the dew from the long grass with her feet, and often turning aside into places where it grew longer than in others, that she might not tread upon the graves. She felt a curious kind of pleasure in lingering among these houses of the dead, and read the inscriptions on the tombs of the good people (a great number of good people were buried there), passing on from one to another with increasing interest.

It was a very quiet place, as such a place should be, save for the cawing of the rooks who had built their nests among the branches of some tall old trees, and were calling to one another, high up in the air. First, one sleek bird, hovering near his ragged house as it swung and dangled in the wind, uttered his hoarse cry, quite by chance as it would seem, and in a sober tone as though he were but talking to himself. Another answered, and he called again, but louder than before; then another spoke and then another; and each time the first, aggravated by contradiction, insisted on his case more strongly. Other voices, silent till now, struck in from boughs lower down and higher up and midway, and to the right and left, and from the tree-tops; and others, arriving hastily from the grey church turrets and old belfry window, joined the clamour which rose and fell, and swelled and dropped again, and still went on; and all this noisy contention amidst a skimming to and fro, and lighting on fresh branches, and frequent change of place, which satirised the old restlessness of those who lay so still beneath the moss and turf below, and the strife in which they had worn away their lives.

Frequently raising her eyes to the trees whence these sounds came down, and feeling as though they made the place more quiet than perfect silence would have done, the child loitered from grave to grave, now stopping to replace with careful hands the bramble which had started from some green mound it helped to keep in shape and now peeping through one of the low latticed windows into the church, with its worm-eaten books upon the desks, and baize of whitened-green mouldering from the pew sides and leaving the naked wood to view. There were the seats where the poor old people sat, worn, spare, and yellow like themselves; the rugged font where children had their names, the homely altar where they knelt in after-life, the plain black tressels that bore their weight on their last visit to the cool old shady church. Everything told of long use and quiet slow decay; the very bell-rope in the porch was frayed into a fringe, and hoary with old age.

She was looking at a humble stone which told of a young man who had died at twenty-three years old, fifty-five years ago, when she heard a faltering step approaching, and looking round saw a feeble woman bent with the weight of years, who tottered to the foot of that same grave and asked her to read the writing on the stone. The old woman thanked her when she had done, saying that she had had the words by heart for many a long, long year, but could not see them now.

'Were you his mother?' said the child.

'I was his wife, my dear.'

She the wife of a young man of three-and-twenty! Ah, true! It was fifty-five years ago.

'You wonder to hear me say that,' remarked the old woman, shaking her head. 'You 're not the first. Older folk than you have wondered at the same thing before now. Yes, I was his wife. Death doesn't change us more than life, my dear.'

'Do you come here often?' asked the child.

'I sit here very often in the summer time,' she answered, 'I used to come here once to cry and mourn, but that was a weary while ago, bless God!'

'I pluck the daisies as they grow, and take them home,' said the old woman after a short silence. 'I like no flowers so well as these, and haven't for five-and-fifty years. It 's a long time, and I 'm getting very old!'

Then growing garrulous upon a theme which was new to one listener though it were but a child, she told her how she had wept and moaned and prayed to die herself, when this happened; and how when she first came to that place, a young creature strong in love and grief, she had hoped that her heart was breaking as it seemed to be. But that time passed by, and although she continued to be sad when she came there, still she could bear to come, and so went on until it was pain no longer, but a solemn pleasure, and a duty she had learned to like. And now that five-and-fifty years were gone, she spoke of the dead man as if he had been her son or grandson, with a kind of pity for his youth, growing out of her own old age, and an exalting of his strength and manly beauty as compared with her own weakness and decay; and yet she spoke about him as her husband too, and thinking of herself in connection with him, as she used to be and not as she was now, talked of their meeting in another world, as if he were dead but yesterday, and she, separated from her former self, were thinking of the happiness of that comely girl who seemed to have died with him.

The child left her gathering the flowers that grew upon the grave, and thoughtfully retraced her steps.

The old man was by this time up and dressed. Mr. Codlin, still doomed to contemplate the harsh realities of existence, was packing among his linen the candle-ends which had been saved from the previous night's performance; while his companion received the compliments of all the loungers in the stable-yard, who, unable to separate him from the master-mind of Punch, set him down as next in importance to that merry outlaw, and loved him scarcely less. When he had sufficiently acknowledged his popularity he came in to breakfast, at which meal they all sat down together.

'And where are you going to-day?' said the little man, addressing himself to Nell.

'Indeed I hardly know,—we have not determined yet,' replied the child.

'We 're going on to the races,' said the little man. 'If that 's your way and you like to have us for company, let us travel together. If you prefer going alone, only say the word and you 'll find that we shan't trouble you.'

'We 'll go with you,' said the old man. 'Nell,—with them, with them.'

The child considered for a moment, and reflecting that she must shortly beg, and could scarcely hope to do so at a better place than where crowds of rich ladies and gentlemen were assembled together for purposes of enjoyment and festivity, determined to accompany these men so far. She therefore thanked the little man for his offer, and said, glancing timidly towards his friend, that if there was no objection to their accompanying them as far as the race-town—

'Objection!' said the little man. 'Now be gracious for once, Tommy, and say that you 'd rather they went with us. I know you would. Be gracious, Tommy.'

'Trotters,' said Mr. Codlin, who talked very slowly and eat very greedily, as is not uncommon with philosophers and misanthropes; 'you 're too free.'

'Why what harm can it do?' urged the other.

'No harm at all in this particular case, perhaps,' replied Mr. Codlin; 'but the principle 's a dangerous one, and you 're too free I tell you.'

'Well, are they to go with us or not?'

'Yes, they are,' said Mr. Codlin; 'but you might have made a favour of it, mightn't you?'

The real name of the little man was Harris, but it had gradually merged into the less euphonious one of Trotters, which, with the prefatory adjective, Short, had been conferred upon him by reason of the small size of his legs. Short Trotters, however, being a compound name, inconvenient of use in friendly dialogue, the gentleman on whom it had been bestowed was known among his intimates either as 'Short,' or 'Trotters,' and was seldom accosted at full length as Short Trotters, except in formal conversations and on occasions of ceremony.

Short, then, or Trotters, as the reader pleases, returned unto the remonstrance of his friend Mr. Thomas Codlin a jocose answer calculated to turn aside his discontent; and applying himself with great relish to the cold boiled beef, and tea, and bread-and-butter, strongly impressed upon his companions that they should do the like. Mr. Codlin indeed required no such persuasion, as he had already eat as much as he could possibly carry and was now moistening his clay with strong ale, whereof he took deep draughts with a silent relish and invited nobody to partake,—thus again strongly indicating his misanthropical turn of mind.

Breakfast being at length over, Mr. Codlin called the bill, and charging the ale to the company generally (a practice also savouring of misanthropy) divided the sum-total into two fair and equal parts, assigning one moiety to himself and friend, and the other to Nelly and her grandfather. These being duly discharged and all things ready for their departure, they took farewell of the landlord and landlady and resumed their journey.

And here Mr. Codlin's false position in society and the effect it wrought upon his wounded spirit, were strongly illustrated; for whereas he had been last night accosted by Mr. Punch as 'master,' and had by inference left the audience to understand that he maintained that individual for his own luxurious entertainment and delight, here he was, now, painfully walking beneath the burden of that same Punch's temple, and bearing it bodily upon his shoulders on a sultry day and along a dusty road. In place of enlivening his patron with a constant fire of wit or the cheerful rattle of his quarter-staff on the heads of his relations and acquaintance, here was that beaming Punch utterly devoid of spine, all slack and drooping in a dark box, with his legs doubled up round his neck, and not one of his social qualities remaining.

Mr. Codlin trudged heavily on, exchanging a word or two at intervals with Short, and stopping to rest and growl occasionally. Short led the way; with the flat box, the private luggage (which was not extensive) tied up in a bundle, and a brazen trumpet slung from his shoulder-blade. Nell and her grandfather walked next him on either hand, and Thomas Codlin brought up the rear.

When they came to any town or village, or even to a detached house of good appearance, Short blew a blast upon the brazen trumpet and carolled a fragment of a song in that hilarious tone common to Punches, and their consorts. If people hurried to the windows, Mr. Codlin pitched the temple, and hastily unfurling the drapery and concealing Short therewith, flourished hysterically on the pipes and performed an air. Then the entertainment began as soon as might be; Mr. Codlin having the responsibility of deciding on its length and of protracting or expediting the time for the hero's final triumph over the enemy of mankind, according as he judged that the after-crop of halfpence would be plentiful or scant. When it had been gathered in to the last farthing, he resumed his load and on they went again.

Sometimes they played out the toll across a bridge or ferry, and once exhibited by particular desire at a turnpike, where the collector, being drunk in his solitude, paid down a shilling to have it to himself. There was one small place of rich promise in which their hopes were blighted, for a favourite character in the play having gold-lace upon his coat and being a meddling wooden-headed fellow was held to be a libel on the beadle, for which reason the authorities enforced a quick retreat; but they were generally well received, and seldom left a town without a troop of ragged children shouting at their heels.

They made a long day's journey, despite these interruptions, and were yet upon the road when the moon was shining in the sky. Short beguiled the time with songs and jests, and made the best of everything that happened. Mr. Codlin on the other hand, cursed his fate, and all the hollow things of earth (but Punch especially), and limped along with the theatre on his back, a prey to the bitterest chagrin.

They had stopped to rest beneath a finger-post where four roads met, and Mr. Codlin in his deep misanthropy had let down the drapery and seated himself in the bottom of the show, invisible to mortal eyes and disdainful of the company of his fellow-creatures, when two monstrous shadows were seen stalking towards them from a turning in the road by which they had come. The child was at first quite terrified by the sight of these gaunt giants—for such they looked as they advanced with lofty strides beneath the shadow of the trees—but Short, telling her there was nothing to fear, blew a blast upon the trumpet, which was answered by a cheerful shout.

'It 's Grinder's lot, an't it?' cried Mr. Short in a loud key.

'Yes,' replied a couple of shrill voices.

'Come on then,' said Short. 'Let 's have a look at you. I thought it was you.'

Thus invited, 'Grinder's lot' approached with redoubled speed and soon came up with the little party.

Mr. Grinder's company, familiarly termed a lot, consisted of a young gentleman and a young lady on stilts, and Mr. Grinder himself, who used his natural legs for pedestrian purposes and carried at his back a drum. The public costume of the young people was of the Highland kind, but the night being damp and cold, the young gentleman wore over his kilt a man's pea-jacket reaching to his ankles, and a glazed hat; the young lady too was muffled in an old cloth pelisse and had a handkerchief tied about her head. Their Scotch bonnets, ornamented with plumes of jet-black feathers, Mr. Grinder carried on his instrument.

'Bound for the races, I see,' said Mr. Grinder coming up out of breath. 'So are we. How are you, Short?' With that they shook hands in a very friendly manner. The young people being too high up for the ordinary salutations, saluted Short after their own fashion. The young gentleman twisted up his right stilt and patted him on the shoulder, and the young lady rattled her tambourine.

'Practice?' said Short, pointing to the stilts.

'No,' returned Grinder. 'It comes either to walkin' in 'em or carryin' of 'em, and they like walkin' in 'em best. It 's wery pleasant for the prospects. Which road are you takin'? We go the nighest.'

'Why, the fact is,' said Short, 'that we are going the longest way, because then we could stop for the night, a mile and a half on. But three or four mile gained to-night is so many saved to-morrow, and if you keep on, I think our best way is to do the same.'

'Where 's your partner?' inquired Grinder.

'Here he is,' cried Mr. Thomas Codlin, presenting his head and face in the proscenium of the stage, and exhibiting an expression of countenance not often seen there; 'and he 'll see *his* partner boiled alive before he 'll go on to-night. That 's what *he* says.'

'Well, don't say such things as them, in a spear which is dewoted to something pleasanter,' urged Short. 'Respect associations, Tommy, even if you do cut up rough.'

'Rough or smooth,' said Mr. Codlin, beating his hand on the little footboard where Punch, when suddenly struck with the symmetry of his legs and their capacity for silk stockings, is accustomed to exhibit them to popular admiration, 'rough or smooth, I won't go further than the mile and a half to-night. I put up at the Jolly Sandboys and nowhere else. If you like to come there, come there. If you like to go on by yourself, go on by yourself, and do without me if you can.'

So saying, Mr. Codlin disappeared from the scene and immediately presented himself outside the theatre, took it on his shoulders at a jerk, and made off with most remarkable agility.

Any further controversy being now out of the question, Short was fain to part with Mr. Grinder and his pupils and to follow his morose companion. After lingering at the finger-post for a few minutes to see the stilts frisking away in the moonlight and the bearer of the drum toiling slowly after them, he blew a few notes upon the trumpet as a parting salute, and hastened with all speed to follow Mr. Codlin. With this view he gave his unoccupied hand to Nell, and bidding her be of good cheer as they would soon be at the end of their journey for that night, and stimulating the old man with a similar assurance, led them at a pretty swift pace towards their destination, which he was the less unwilling to make for, as the moon was now overcast and the clouds were threatening rain.

CHAPTER XVIII

THE Jolly Sandboys was a small roadside inn of pretty ancient date, with a sign, representing three Sandboys increasing their jollity with as many jugs of ale and bags of gold, creaking and swinging on its post on the opposite side of the road. As the travellers had observed that day many indications of their drawing nearer and nearer to the race-town, such as gipsy camps, carts laden with gambling booths and their appurtenances, itinerant showmen of various kinds, and beggars and trampers of every degree, all wending their way in the same direction, Mr. Codlin was fearful of finding the accommodations forestalled; this fear increasing as he diminished the distance between himself and the hostelry, he quickened his pace, and notwithstanding the burden he had to carry, maintained a round trot until he reached the threshold. Here he had the gratification of finding that his fears were without foundation, for the landlord was leaning against the door-post looking lazily at the rain, which had by this time begun to descend heavily, and no tinkling of cracked bell, nor boisterous shout, nor noisy chorus, gave note of company within.

'All alone?' said Mr. Codlin, putting down his burden and wiping his forehead.

'All alone as yet,' rejoined the landlord, glancing at the sky, 'but we shall have more company to-night I expect. Here one of you boys, carry that show into the barn. Make haste in out of the wet, Tom; when it came on to rain I told 'em to make the fire up, and there 's a glorious blaze in the kitchen, I can tell you.'

Mr. Codlin followed with a willing mind, and soon found that the landlord had not commended his preparations without good reason. A mighty fire was blazing on the hearth and roaring up the wide chimney with a cheerful sound, which a large iron cauldron, bubbling and simmering in the heat, lent its pleasant aid to swell. There was a deep red ruddy blush upon the room, and when the landlord stirred the fire, sending the flames skipping and leaping up—when he took off the lid of the iron pot and there rushed out a savoury smell, while the bubbling sound grew deeper and more rich, and an unctuous steam came floating out, hanging in a delicious mist above their heads—when he did this, Mr. Codlin's heart was touched. He sat down in the chimney-corner and smiled.

Mr. Codlin sat smiling in the chimney-corner, eyeing the landlord as with a roguish look he held the cover in his hand, and, feigning that his doing so was needful to the welfare of the cookery, suffered the delightful steam to tickle the nostrils of his guest. The glow of the fire was upon the landlord's bald head, and upon his twinkling eye, and upon his watering mouth, and upon his pimpled face, and upon his round fat figure. Mr. Codlin drew his sleeve across his lips, and said in a murmuring voice, 'What is it?'

'It 's a stew of tripe,' said the landlord smacking his lips, 'and cow-heel,' smacking them again, 'and bacon,' smacking them once more, 'and steak,' smacking them for the fourth time, 'and peas, cauliflowers, new potatoes, and sparrow-grass, all working up together in one delicious gravy.' Having come to the climax, he smacked his lips a great many times, and taking a long hearty sniff of the fragrance that was hovering about, put on the cover again with the air of one whose toils on earth were over.

'At what time will it be ready?' asked Mr. Codlin faintly.

'It 'll be done to a turn,' said the landlord looking up at the clock—and the very clock had a colour in its fat white face, and looked a clock for Jolly Sandboys to consult—'it 'll be done to a turn at twenty-two minutes before eleven.'

'Then,' said Mr. Codlin, 'fetch me a pint of warm ale, and don't let nobody bring into the room even so much as a biscuit till the time arrives.'

Nodding his approval of this decisive and manly course of procedure, the landlord retired to draw the beer, and presently returning with it, applied himself to warm the same in a small tin-vessel shaped funnel-wise, for the convenience of sticking it far down in the fire and getting at the bright places. This was soon done, and he handed it over to Mr. Codlin with that creamy froth upon the surface which is one of the happy circumstances attendant on mulled malt.

Greatly softened by this soothing beverage, Mr. Codlin now bethought him of his companions, and acquainted mine host of the Sandboys that their arrival might be shortly looked for. The rain was rattling against the windows and pouring down in torrents, and such was Mr. Codlin's extreme amiability of mind, that he more than once expressed his earnest hope that they would not be so foolish as to get wet.

At length they arrived, drenched with the rain and presenting a most miserable appearance, notwithstanding that Short had sheltered the child as well as he could under the skirts of his own coat, and they were nearly breathless from the haste they had made. But their steps were no sooner heard upon the road than the landlord, who had been at the outer door anxiously watching for their coming, rushed into the kitchen and took the cover off. The effect was electrical. They all came in with smiling faces though the wet was dripping from their clothes upon the floor, and Short's first remark was, 'What a delicious smell!'

It is not very difficult to forget rain and mud by the side of a cheerful fire, and in a bright room. They were furnished with slippers and such dry garments as the house or their own bundles afforded, and ensconcing themselves, as Mr. Codlin had already done, in the warm chimney-corner, soon forgot their late troubles or only remembered them as enhancing the delights of the present time. Overpowered by the warmth and comfort and the fatigue they had undergone, Nelly and the old man had not long taken their seats here, when they fell asleep.

'Who are they?' whispered the landlord.

Short shook his head, and wished he knew himself.

'Don't *you* know?' asked the host, turning to Mr. Codlin.

'Not I,' he replied. 'They 're no good, I suppose.'

'They 're no harm,' said Short. 'Depend upon that. I tell you what—it 's plain that the old man an't in his right mind—'

'If you haven't got anything newer than that to say,' growled Mr. Codlin, glancing at the clock, 'you 'd better let us fix our minds upon the supper, and not disturb us.'

'Hear me out, won't you?' retorted his friend. 'It 's very plain to me, besides, that they 're not used to this way of life. Don't tell me that that handsome child has been in the habit of prowling about as she 's done these last two or three days. I know better.'

'Well, who *does* tell you she has?' growled Mr. Codlin, again glancing at the clock and from it to the cauldron, 'can't you think of anything more suitable to present circumstances than saying things and then contradicting 'em?'

'I wish somebody would give you your supper,' returned Short, 'for there 'll be no peace till you 've got it. Have you seen how anxious the old man is to get on—always wanting to be furder away—furder away? Have you seen that?'

'Ah! what then?' muttered Thomas Codlin.

'This, then,' said Short. 'He has given his friends the slip. Mind what I say,—he has given his friends the slip, and persuaded this delicate young creetur all along of her fondness for him to be his guide and travelling companion—where to, he knows no more than the man in the moon. Now I 'm not a going to stand that.'

'*You 're* not a going to stand that!' cried Mr. Codlin, glancing at the clock again and pulling his hair with both hands in a kind of frenzy, but whether occasioned by his companion's observation or the tardy pace of Time, it was difficult to determine. 'Here 's a world to live in!'

'I,' repeated Short emphatically and slowly, 'am not a going to stand it. I am not a going to see this fair young child a falling into bad hands, and getting among people that she 's no more fit for, than they are to get among angels as their ordinary chums. Therefore when they dewelope an intention of parting company from us, I shall take measures for detaining of 'em, and restoring 'em to their friends, who I dare say have had their disconsolation pasted up on every wall in London by this time.'

'Short,' said Mr. Codlin, who with his head upon his hands, and his elbows on his knees, had been shaking himself impatiently from side to side up to this point and occasionally stamping on the ground, but who now looked up with eager eyes; 'it 's possible that there may be uncommon good sense in what you 've said. If there is, and there should be a reward, Short, remember that we 're partners in everything!'

His companion had only time to nod a brief assent to this position, for the child awoke at the instant. They had drawn close together during the previous whispering, and now hastily separated and were rather awkwardly endeavouring to exchange some casual remarks in their usual tone, when strange footsteps were heard without, and fresh company entered.

These were no other than four very dismal dogs, who came pattering in one after the other, headed by an old bandy dog of particularly mournful aspect, who stopping when the last of his followers had got as far as the door, erected himself upon his hind-legs and looked round at his companions, who immediately stood upon their hind-legs, in a grave and melancholy row. Nor was this the only remarkable circumstance about these dogs, for each of them wore a kind of little coat of some gaudy colour trimmed with tarnished spangles, and one of them had a cap upon his head, tied very carefully under his chin, which had fallen down upon his nose and completely obscured one eye; add to this, that the gaudy coats were all wet through and discoloured with rain, and that the wearers were splashed and dirty, and some idea may be formed of the unusual appearance of these new visitors to the Jolly Sandboys.

Neither Short nor the landlord nor Thomas Codlin, however, was in the least surprised, merely remarking that these were Jerry's dogs and that Jerry could not be far behind. So there the dogs stood, patiently winking and gaping and looking extremely hard at the boiling pot, until Jerry himself appeared, when they all dropped down at once and walked about the room in their natural manner. This posture it must be confessed did not much improve their appearance, as their own personal tails and their coat tails—both capital things in their way—did not agree together.

Jerry, the manager of these dancing dogs, was a tall black-whiskered man in a velveteen coat, who seemed well known to the landlord and his guests and accosted them with great cordiality. Disencumbering himself of a barrel organ which he placed upon a chair, and retaining in his hand a small whip wherewith to awe his company of comedians, he came up to the fire to dry himself, and entered into conversation.

'Your people don't usually travel in character, do

they?' said Short, pointing to the dresses of the dogs. 'It must come expensive if they do.'

'No,' replied Jerry, 'no, it 's not the custom with us. But we 've been playing a little on the road to-day, and we come out with a new wardrobe at the races, so I didn't think it worth while to stop to undress. Down, Pedro!'

This was addressed to the dog with the cap on, who being a new member of the company, and not quite certain of his duty, kept his unobscured eye anxiously on his master, and was perpetually starting upon his hind-legs when there was no occasion, and falling down again.

'I 've got a animal here,' said Jerry, putting his hand into the capacious pocket of his coat, and diving into one corner as if he were feeling for a small orange or an apple or some such article, 'a animal here, wot I think you know something of, Short.'

'Ah!' cried Short, 'let 's have a look at him.'

'Here he is,' said Jerry, producing a little terrier from his pocket. 'He was once a Toby of yours, warn't he?'

In some versions of the great drama of Punch there is a small dog—a modern innovation—supposed to be the property of that gentleman, whose name is always Toby. This Toby has been stolen in youth from another gentleman and fraudulently sold to the confiding hero, who having no guile himself has no suspicion that it lurks in others; but Toby, entertaining a grateful recollection of his old master, and scorning to attach himself to any new patrons, not only refuses to smoke a pipe at the bidding of Punch, but to mark his old fidelity more strongly, seizes him by the nose and wrings the same with violence, at which instance of canine attachment the spectators are deeply affected. This was the character which the little terrier in question had once sustained; if there had been any doubt upon the subject he would speedily have resolved it by his conduct; for not only did he, on seeing Short, give the strongest tokens of recognition, but catching sight of the flat box he barked so furiously at the pasteboard nose which he knew was inside, that his master was obliged to gather him up and put him into his pocket again, to the great relief of the whole company.

The landlord now busied himself in laying the cloth, in which process Mr. Codlin obligingly assisted by setting forth his own knife and fork in the most convenient place and establishing himself behind them. When everything was ready, the landlord took off the cover for the last time, and then indeed there burst forth such a goodly promise of supper, that if he had offered to put it on again or had hinted at postponement, he would certainly have been sacrificed on his own hearth.

However, he did nothing of the kind, but instead thereof assisted a stout servant-girl in turning the contents of the cauldron into a large tureen; a proceeding which the dogs, proof against various hot splashes which fell upon their noses, watched with terrible eagerness. At length the dish was lifted on the table, and mugs of ale having been previously set round, little Nell ventured to say grace, and supper began.

At this juncture the poor dogs were standing on their hind-legs quite surprisingly; and the child, having pity on them, was about to cast some morsels of food to them before she tasted it herself, hungry though she was, when their master interposed.

'No, my dear, no, not an atom from anybody's hand but mine if you please. That dog,' said Jerry, pointing out the old leader of the troop, and speaking in a terrible voice, 'lost a halfpenny to-day. *He* goes without his supper.'

The unfortunate creature dropped upon his fore-legs directly, wagged his tail, and looked imploringly at his master.

'You must be more careful, sir,' said Jerry, walking coolly to the chair where he had placed the organ, and setting the stop. 'Come here. Now, sir, you play away at that, while we have supper, and leave off if you dare.'

The dog immediately began to grind most mournful music. His master having shown him the whip resumed his seat and called up the others, who, at his directions, formed in a row, standing upright as a file of soldiers.

'Now, gentlemen,' said Jerry, looking at them attentively. 'The dog whose name 's called, eats. The dogs whose names an't called, keep quiet. Carlo!'

The lucky individual whose name was called, snapped up the morsel thrown towards him, but none of the others moved a muscle. In this manner they were fed at the discretion of their master. Meanwhile the dog in disgrace ground hard at the organ, sometimes in quick time, sometimes in slow, but never leaving off for an instant. When the knives and forks rattled very much, or any of his fellows got an unusually large piece of fat, he accompanied the music with a short howl, but he immediately checked it on his master looking round, and applied himself with increased diligence to the Old Hundredth.

CHAPTER XIX

Supper was not yet over, when there arrived at the Jolly Sandboys two more travellers bound for the same haven as the rest, who had been walking in the rain for some hours, and came in shining and heavy with water. One of these was the proprietor of a giant, and a little lady without legs or arms, who had jogged forward in a van; the other, a silent gentleman who earned his living by showing tricks upon the cards, and who had rather deranged the natural expression of his countenance by putting small leaden lozenges into his eyes and bringing them out at his mouth, which was one of his professional accomplishments. The name of the first of these new comers was Vuffin; the other, probably, as a pleasant satire upon his ugliness, was called Sweet William. To render them as comfortable as he could, the landlord bestirred himself nimbly, and in a very short time both gentlemen were perfectly at their ease.

'How 's the Giant?' said Short, when they all sat smoking round the fire.

'Rather weak upon his legs,' returned Mr. Vuffin. 'I begin to be afraid he 's going at the knees.'

'That 's a bad look-out,' said Short.

'Aye! Bad indeed,' replied Mr. Vuffin, contemplating the fire with a sigh. 'Once get a giant shaky on his legs, and the public care no more about him than they do for a dead cabbage-stalk.'

'What becomes of the old giants?' said Short, turning to him again after a little reflection.

'They 're usually kept in carawans to wait upon the dwarfs,' said Mr. Vuffin.

'The maintaining of 'em must come expensive, when

they can't be shown, eh?' remarked Short, eyeing him doubtfully.

'It 's better that, than letting 'em go upon the parish or about the streets,' said Mr. Vuffin. 'Once make a giant common and giants will never draw again. Look at wooden legs. If there was only one man with a wooden leg what a property *he* 'd be!'

'So he would!' observed the landlord and Short both together. 'That 's very true.'

'Instead of which,' pursued Mr. Vuffin, 'if you was to advertise Shakespeare played entirely by wooden legs, it 's my belief you wouldn't draw a sixpence.'

'I don't suppose you would,' said Short. And the landlord said so too.

'This shows, you see,' said Mr. Vuffin, waving his pipe with an argumentative air, 'this shows the policy of keeping the used-up giants still in the carawans, where they get food and lodging for nothing, all their lives, and in general very glad they are to stop there. There was one giant—a black 'un—as left his carawan some year ago and took to carrying coach-bills about London, making himself as cheap as crossing-sweepers. He died. I make no insinuation against anybody in particular,' said Mr. Vuffin, looking solemnly round, 'but he was ruining the trade;—and he died.'

The landlord drew his breath hard, and looked at the owner of the dogs, who nodded and said gruffly that *he* remembered.

'I know you do, Jerry,' said Mr. Vuffin with profound meaning. 'I know you remember it, Jerry, and the universal opinion was, that it served him right. Why, I remember the time when old Maunders as had three-and-twenty wans—I remember the time when old Maunders had in his cottage in Spa Fields in the winter time, when the season was over, eight male and female dwarfs setting down to dinner every day, who was waited on by eight old giants in green coats, red smalls, blue cotton stockings, and high-lows: and there was one dwarf as had grown elderly and wicious who whenever his giant wasn't quick enough to please him, used to stick pins in his legs, not being able to reach up any higher. I know that 's a fact, for Maunders told it me himself.'

'What about the dwarfs when *they* get old?' inquired the landlord.

'The older a dwarf is, the better worth he is,' returned Mr. Vuffin; 'a grey-headed dwarf, well wrinkled, is beyond all suspicion. But a giant weak in the legs and not standing upright!—keep him in the carawan, but never show him, never show him, for any persuasion that can be offered.'

While Mr. Vuffin and his two friends smoked their pipes and beguiled the time with such conversation as this, the silent gentleman sat in a warm corner, swallowing, or seeming to swallow, sixpennyworth of halfpence for practice, balancing a feather upon his nose, and rehearsing other feats of dexterity of that kind, without paying any regard whatever to the company, who in their turn left him utterly unnoticed. At length the weary child prevailed upon her grandfather to retire, and they withdrew, leaving the company yet seated round the fire, and the dogs fast asleep at a humble distance.

After bidding the old man good-night, Nell retired to her poor garret, but had scarcely closed the door, when it was gently tapped at. She opened it directly, and was a little startled by the sight of Mr. Thomas Codlin, whom she had left, to all appearance, fast asleep downstairs.

'What is the matter?' said the child.

'Nothing 's the matter, my dear,' returned her visitor. 'I 'm your friend. Perhaps you haven't thought so, but it 's me that 's your friend—not him.'

'Not who?' the child inquired.

'Short, my dear. I 'll tell you what,' said Codlin, 'for all his having a kind of way with him that you 'd be very apt to like, I 'm the real open-hearted man. I mayn't look it, but I am indeed.'

The child began to be alarmed, considering that the ale had taken effect upon Mr. Codlin, and that this commendation of himself was the consequence.

'Short 's very well, and seems kind,' resumed the misanthrope, 'but he overdoes it. Now I don't.'

Certainly if there were any fault in Mr. Codlin's usual deportment, it was that he rather underdid his kindness to those about him, than overdid it. But the child was puzzled, and could not tell what to say.

'Take my advice,' said Codlin: 'don't ask me why, but take it. As long as you travel with us, keep as near me as you can. Don't offer to leave us—not on any account—but always stick to me and say that I 'm your friend. Will you bear that in mind, my dear, and always say that it was me that was your friend?'

'Say so where,—and when?' inquired the child innocently.

'O, nowhere in particular,' replied Codlin a little put out as it seemed by the question; 'I 'm only anxious that you should think me so, and do me justice. You can't think what an interest I have in you. Why didn't you tell me your little history—that about you and the poor old gentleman? I 'm the best adviser that ever was, and *so* interested in you—so much more interested than Short. I think they 're breaking up downstairs; you needn't tell Short, you know, that we 've had this little talk together. God bless you. Recollect the friend. Codlin 's the friend, not Short. Short 's very well as far as he goes, but the real friend is Codlin—not Short.'

Eking out these professions with a number of benevolent and protecting looks and great fervour of manner, Thomas Codlin stole away on tip-toe, leaving the child in a state of extreme surprise. She was still ruminating upon his curious behaviour, when the floor of the crazy stairs and landing cracked beneath the tread of the other travellers who were passing to their beds. When they had all passed, and the sound of their footsteps had died away, one of them returned, and after a little hesitation and rustling in the passage, as if he were doubtful what door to knock at, knocked at hers.

'Yes,' said the child from within.

'It 's me—Short'—a voice called through the keyhole. 'I only wanted to say that we must be off early to-morrow morning, my dear, because unless we get the start of the dogs and the conjuror, the villages won't be worth a penny. You 'll be sure to be stirring early and go with us? I 'll call you.'

The child answered in the affirmative, and returning his 'good-night' heard him creep away. She felt some uneasiness at the anxiety of these men, increased by the recollection of their whispering together downstairs and their slight confusion when she awoke, nor was she quite free from a misgiving that they were not the fittest companions she could have stumbled on. Her uneasiness, however, was nothing, weighed against her fatigue; and she soon forgot it in sleep.

Very early next morning, Short fulfilled his promise, and knocking softly at her door, entreated that she would get up directly, as the proprietor of the dogs was still snoring, and if they lost no time they might get a good deal in advance both of him and the conjuror, who was talking in his sleep, and from what he could be heard to say, appeared to be balancing a donkey in his dreams. She started from her bed without delay, and roused the old man with so much expedition that they were both ready as soon as Short himself, to that gentleman's unspeakable gratification and relief.

After a very unceremonious and scrambling breakfast, of which the staple commodities were bacon and bread, and beer, they took leave of the landlord and issued from the door of the Jolly Sandboys. The morning was fine and warm, the ground cool to the feet after the late rain, the hedges gayer and more green, the air clear, and everything fresh and healthful. Surrounded by these influences, they walked on pleasantly enough.

They had not gone very far, when the child was again struck by the altered behaviour of Mr. Thomas Codlin, who instead of plodding on sulkily by himself as he had heretofore done, kept close to her, and when he had an opportunity of looking at her unseen by his companion, warned her by certain wry faces and jerks of the head not to put any trust in Short, but to reserve all confidences for Codlin. Neither did he confine himself to looks and gestures, for when she and her grandfather were walking on beside the aforesaid Short, and that little man was talking with his accustomed cheerfulness on a variety of indifferent subjects, Thomas Codlin testified his jealousy and distrust by following close at her heels, and occasionally admonishing her ankles with the legs of the theatre in a very abrupt and painful manner.

All these proceedings naturally made the child more watchful and suspicious, and she soon observed that whenever they halted to perform outside a village ale-house or other place, Mr. Codlin while he went through his share of the entertainments kept his eyes steadily upon her and the old man, or with a show of great friendship and consideration invited the latter to lean upon his arm, and so held him tight until the representation was over and they again went forward. Even Short seemed to change in this respect, and to mingle with his good-nature something of a desire to keep them in safe custody. This increased the child's misgivings, and made her yet more anxious and uneasy.

Meanwhile, they were drawing near the town where the races were to begin next day; for, from passing numerous groups of gipsies and trampers on the road, wending their way towards it, and straggling out from every by-way and cross-country lane, they gradually fell into a stream of people, some walking by the side of covered carts, others with horses, others with donkeys, others toiling on with heavy loads upon their backs, but all tending to the same point. The public-houses by the wayside, from being empty and noiseless as those in the remoter parts had been, now sent out boisterous shouts and clouds of smoke; and, from the misty windows, clusters of broad red faces looked down upon the road. On every piece of waste or common ground, some small gambler drove his noisy trade, and bellowed to the idle passers-by to stop and try their chance; the crowd grew thicker and more noisy; gilt gingerbread in blanket-stalls exposed its glories to the dust; and often a four-horse carriage, dashing by, obscured all objects in the gritty cloud it raised, and left them, stunned and blinded, far behind.

It was dark before they reached the town itself, and long indeed the last few miles had been. Here all was tumult and confusion; the streets were filled with throngs of people—many strangers were there, it seemed, by the looks they cast about—the church-bells rang out their noisy peals, and flags streamed from windows and house-tops. In the large inn-yards waiters flitted to and fro and ran against each other, horses clattered on the uneven stones, carriage steps fell rattling down, and sickening smells from many dinners came in a heavy lukewarm breath upon the sense. In the smaller public-houses, fiddles with all their might and main were squeaking out the tune to staggering feet; drunken men, oblivious of the burden of their song, joined in a senseless howl, which drowned the tinkling of the feeble bell and made them savage for their drink; vagabond groups assembled round the doors to see the stroller woman dance, and add their uproar to the shrill flageolet and deafening drum.

Through this delirious scene, the child, frightened and repelled by all she saw, led on her bewildered charge, clinging close to her conductor, and trembling lest in the press she should be separated from him and left to find her way alone. Quickening their steps to get clear of all the roar and riot, they at length passed through the town and made for the race-course, which was upon an open heath, situated on an eminence, a full mile distant from its furthest bounds.

Although there were many people here, none of the best favoured or best clad, busily erecting tents and driving stakes in the ground, and hurrying to and fro with dusty feet and many a grumbled oath—although there were tired children cradled on heaps of straw between the wheels of carts, crying themselves to sleep—and poor lean horses and donkeys just turned loose, grazing among the men and women, and pots and kettles, and half-lighted fires, and ends of candles flaring and wasting in the air—for all this, the child felt it an escape from the town and drew her breath more freely. After a scanty supper, the purchase of which reduced her little stock so low, that she had only a few halfpence with which to buy a breakfast on the morrow, she and the old man lay down to rest in a corner of a tent, and slept, despite the busy preparations that were going on around them all night long.

And now they had come to the time when they must beg their bread. Soon after sunrise in the morning she stole out from the tent, and rambling into some fields at a short distance, plucked a few wild roses and such humble flowers, purposing to make them into little nosegays and offer them to the ladies in the carriages when the company arrived. Her thoughts were not idle while she was thus employed; when she returned and was seated beside the old man in one corner of the tent, tying her flowers together, while the two men lay dozing in another corner, she plucked him by the sleeve, and slightly glancing towards them, said, in a low voice—

'Grandfather, don't look at those I talk of, and don't seem as if I spoke of anything but what I am about. What was that you told me before we left the old house? That if they knew what we were going to do, they would say that you were mad, and part us?'

The old man turned to her with an aspect of wild terror; but she checked him by a look, and bidding him hold some flowers while she tied them up, and so bringing her lips closer to his ear, said—

'I know that was what you told me. You needn't speak, dear. I recollect it very well. It was not likely that I should forget it. Grandfather, these men suspect that we have secretly left our friends, and mean to carry us before some gentleman and have us taken care of and sent back. If you let your hand tremble so, we can never get away from them, but if you 're only quiet now, we shall do so easily.'

'How?' muttered the old man. 'Dear Nelly, how? They will shut me up in a stone room, dark and cold, and chain me up to the wall, Nell—flog me with whips, and never let me see thee more!'

'You 're trembling again,' said the child. 'Keep close to me all day. Never mind them, don't look at them, but me. I shall find a time when we can steal away. When I do, mind you come with me, and do not stop or speak a word. Hush! That 's all.'

'Halloa! what are you up to, my dear?' said Mr. Codlin, raising his head, and yawning. Then observing that his companion was fast asleep, he added in an earnest whisper, 'Codlin 's the friend, remember —not Short.'

'Making some nosegays,' the child replied; 'I am going to try and sell some, these three days of the races. Will you have one—as a present I mean?'

Mr. Codlin would have risen to receive it, but the child hurried towards him and placed it in his hand. He stuck it in his buttonhole with an air of ineffable complacency for a misanthrope, and leering exultingly at the unconscious Short, muttered, as he laid himself down again, 'Tom Codlin 's the friend by G—!'

As the morning wore on, the tents assumed a gayer and more brilliant appearance, and long lines of carriages came rolling softly on the turf. Men who had lounged about all night in smock-frocks and leather leggings, came out in silken vests and hats and plumes, as jugglers or mountebanks; or in gorgeous liveries as soft-spoken servants at gambling booths; or in sturdy yeoman dress as decoys at unlawful games. Black-eyed gipsy girls, hooded in showy handkerchiefs, sallied forth to tell fortunes, and pale slender women with consumptive faces lingered upon the footsteps of ventriloquists and conjurors, and counted the sixpences with anxious eyes long before they were gained. As many of the children as could be kept within bounds, were stowed away, with all the other signs of dirt and poverty, among the donkeys, carts, and horses; and as many as could not be thus disposed of ran in and out in all intricate spots, crept between people's legs and carriage-wheels, and came forth unharmed from under horses' hoofs. The dancing-dogs, the stilts, the little lady and the tall man, and all the other attractions, with organs out of number and bands innumerable, emerged from the holes and corners in which they had passed the night, and flourished boldly in the sun.

Along the uncleared course, Short led his party, sounding the brazen trumpet and revelling in the voice of Punch; and at his heels went Thomas Codlin, bearing the show as usual, and keeping his eye on Nelly and her grandfather, as they rather lingered in the rear. The child bore upon her arm the little basket with her flowers, and sometimes stopped, with timid and modest looks, to offer them at some gay carriage; but alas! there were many bolder beggars there, gipsies who promised husbands, and other adepts in their trade, and although some ladies smiled gently, as they shook their heads, and others cried to the gentlemen beside them 'See, what a pretty face!' they let the pretty face pass on, and never thought that it looked tired or hungry.

There was but one lady who seemed to understand the child, and she was one who sat alone in a handsome carriage, while two young men in dashing clothes, who had just dismounted from it, talked and laughed loudly at a little distance, appearing to forget her, quite. Therc were many ladies all around, but they turned their backs or looked another way, or at the two young men (not unfavourably at *them*), and left her to herself. She motioned away a gipsy woman urgent to tell her fortune, saying that it was told already and had been for some years, but called the child towards her, and taking her flowers put money into her trembling hand, and bade her go home and keep at home for God's sake.

Many a time they went up and down those long, long lines, seeing everything but the horses and the race; when the bell rung to clear the course, going back to rest among the carts and donkeys, and not coming out again until the heat was over. Many a time, too, was Punch displayed in the full zenith of his humour, but all this while the eye of Thomas Codlin was upon them, and to escape without notice was impracticable.

At length, late in the day, Mr. Codlin pitched the show in a convenient spot, and the spectators were soon in the very triumph of the scene. The child, sitting down with the old man close behind it, had been thinking how strange it was that horses who were such fine honest creatures should seem to make vagabonds of all the men they drew about them, when a loud laugh at some extemporaneous witticism of Mr. Short's, having allusion to the circumstances of the day, roused her from her meditation and caused her to look around.

If they were ever to get away unseen, that was the very moment. Short was plying the quarter-staves vigorously and knocking the characters in the fury of the combat against the sides of the show, the people were looking on with laughing faces, and Mr. Codlin had relaxed into a grim smile as his roving eye detected hands going into waistcoat-pockets and groping secretly for sixpences. If they were ever to get away unseen, that was the very moment. They seized it, and fled.

They made a path through booths and carriages and throngs of people, and never once stopped to look behind. The bell was ringing and the course was cleared by the time they reached the ropes, but they dashed across it insensible to the shouts and screeching that assailed them for breaking in upon its sanctity, and creeping under the brow of the hill at a quick pace, made for the open fields.

CHAPTER XX

Day after day as he bent his steps homeward, returning from some new effort to procure employment, Kit raised his eyes to the window of the little room he had so much commended to the child, and hoped to see some indication of her presence. His own earnest wish, coupled with the assurance he had received from Quilp, filled him with the belief that she would yet arrive to claim the humble shelter he had offered, and from the death of each day's hope, another hope sprung up to live to-morrow.

'I think they must certainly come to-morrow, eh, mother?' said Kit, laying aside his hat with a weary air and sighing as he spoke. 'They have been gone a week. They surely couldn't stop away more than a week, could they now?'

The mother shook her head, and reminded him how often he had been disappointed already.

'For the matter of that,' said Kit, 'you speak true and sensible enough, as you always do, mother. Still, I do consider that a week is quite long enough for 'em to be rambling about; don't you say so?'

'Quite long enough, Kit, longer than enough, but they may not come back for all that.'

Kit was for a moment disposed to be vexed by this contradiction, and not the less so from having anticipated it in his own mind and knowing how just it was. But the impulse was only momentary, and the vexed look became a kind one before it had crossed the room.

'Then what do you think, mother, has become of 'em? You don't think they 've gone to sea, anyhow?'

'Not gone for sailors, certainly,' returned the mother with a smile. 'But I can't help thinking that they have gone to some foreign country.'

'I say,' cried Kit with a rueful face, 'don't talk like that, mother.'

'I am afraid they have, and that 's the truth,' she said. 'It 's the talk of all the neighbours, and there are some even that know of their having been seen on board ship, and can tell you the name of the place they 've gone to, which is more than I can, my dear, for it 's a very hard one.'

'I don't believe it,' said Kit. 'Not a word of it. A set of idle chatterboxes, how should they know!'

'They may be wrong of course,' returned the mother, 'I can't tell about that, though I don't think it 's at all unlikely that they 're in the right, for the talk is that the old gentleman had put by a little money that nobody knew of, not even that ugly little man you talk to me about—what 's his name—Quilp; and that he and Miss Nell have gone to live abroad where it can't be taken from them, and they will never be disturbed. That don't seem very far out of the way now, do it?'

Kit scratched his head mournfully, in reluctant admission that it did not, and clambering up to the old nail took down the cage and set himself to clean it and to feed the bird. His thoughts reverting from this occupation to the little old gentleman who had given him the shilling, he suddenly recollected that that was the very day—nay, nearly the very hour—at which the little old gentleman had said he should be at the notary's house again. He no sooner remembered this, than he hung up the cage with great precipitation, and hastily explaining the nature of his errand, went off at full speed to the appointed place.

It was some two minutes after the time when he reached the spot, which was a considerable distance from his home, but by great good luck the little old gentleman had not yet arrived; at least there was no pony-chaise to be seen, and it was not likely that he had come and gone again in so short a space. Greatly relieved to find that he was not too late, Kit leant against a lamp-post to take breath, and waited the advent of the pony and his charge.

Sure enough, before long the pony came trotting round the corner of the street, looking as obstinate as pony might, and picking his steps as if he were spying about for the cleanest places, and would by no means dirty his feet or hurry himself inconveniently. Behind the pony sat the little old gentleman, and by the old gentleman's side sat the little old lady, carrying just such a nosegay as she had brought before.

The old gentleman, the old lady, the pony, and the chaise, came up the street in perfect unanimity, until they arrived within some half a dozen doors of the notary's house, when the pony, deceived by a brass plate beneath a tailor's knocker, came to a halt, and maintained by a sturdy silence, that that was the house they wanted.

'Now, sir, will you have the goodness to go on; this is *not* the place,' said the old gentleman.

The pony looked with great attention into a fire-plug which was near him, and appeared to be quite absorbed in contemplating it.

'Oh dear, such a naughty Whisker!' cried the old lady. 'After being so good too, and coming along so well! I am quite ashamed of him. I don't know what we are to do with him, I really don't.'

The pony having thoroughly satisfied himself as to the nature and properties of the fire-plug, looked into the air after his old enemies the flies, and as there happened to be one of them tickling his ear at that moment he shook his head and whisked his tail, after which he appeared full of thought but quite comfortable and collected. The old gentleman having exhausted his powers of persuasion, alighted to lead him; whereupon the pony, perhaps because he held this to be a sufficient concession, perhaps because he happened to catch sight of the other brass plate, or perhaps because he was in a spiteful humour, darted off with the old lady and stopped at the right house, leaving the old gentleman to come panting on behind.

It was then that Kit presented himself at the pony's head, and touched his hat with a smile.

'Why, bless me,' cried the old gentleman, 'the lad *is* here! My dear, do you see?'

'I said I 'd be here, sir,' said Kit, patting Whisker's neck. 'I hope you 've had a pleasant ride, sir. He 's a very nice little pony.'

'My dear,' said the old gentleman. 'This is an uncommon lad; a good lad, I 'm sure.'

'I 'm sure he is,' rejoined the old lady. 'A very good lad, and I am sure he is a good son.'

Kit acknowledged these expressions of confidence by touching his hat again and blushing very much. The old gentleman then handed the old lady out, and after looking at him with an approving smile, they went into the house—talking about him as they went, Kit could not help feeling. Presently Mr. Witherden, smelling very hard at the nosegay, came to the window and looked at him, and after that Mr. Abel came and looked at him, and after that the old gentleman and lady came and looked at him again, and after that they all came and looked at him together, which Kit, feeling very much embarrassed by, made a pretence of not observing. Therefore he patted the pony more and more; and this liberty the pony most handsomely permitted.

The faces had not disappeared from the window many moments, when Mr. Chuckster in his official coat, and with his hat hanging on his head just as it happened to fall from its peg, appeared upon the pavement, and telling him he was wanted inside, bade him go in and he would mind the chaise the while. In giving him this direction Mr. Chuckster remarked that he wished that he might be blessed if he could make out whether he (Kit) was 'precious raw' or 'precious deep,' but intimated by a distrustful shake of the head, that he inclined to the latter opinion.

Kit entered the office in a great tremor, for he was not used to going among strange ladies and gentlemen, and the tin boxes and bundles of dusty papers had in his eyes an awful and venerable air. Mr. Witherden too was a bustling gentleman who talked loud and fast, and all eyes were upon him, and he was very shabby.

'Well, boy,' said Mr. Witherden, 'you came to work out that shilling;—not to get another, hey?'

'No indeed, sir,' replied Kit, taking courage to look up. 'I never thought of such a thing.'

'Father alive?' said the notary.

'Dead, sir.

'Mother?'

'Yes, sir.'

'Married again—eh?'

Kit made answer, not without some indignation, that she was a widow with three children, and that as to her marrying again, if the gentleman knew her he wouldn't think of such a thing. At this reply Mr. Witherden buried his nose in the flowers again, and whispered behind the nosegay to the old gentleman that he believed the lad was as honest a lad as need be.

'Now,' said Mr. Garland when they had made some further inquiries of him, 'I am not going to give you anything—'

'Thank you, sir,' Kit replied; and quite seriously too, for this announcement seemed to free him from the suspicion which the notary had hinted.

'—But,' resumed the old gentleman, 'perhaps I may want to know something more about you, so tell me where you live, and I 'll put it down in my pocket-book.'

Kit told him, and the old gentleman wrote down the address with his pencil. He had scarcely done so, when there was a great uproar in the street, and the old lady hurrying to the window cried that Whisker had run away, upon which Kit darted out to the rescue, and the others followed.

It seemed that Mr. Chuckster had been standing with his hands in his pockets looking carelessly at the pony, and occasionally insulting him with such admonitions as 'Stand still,'—'Be quiet,'—'Wo-a-a,' and the like, which by a pony of spirit cannot be borne. Consequently, the pony being deterred by no considerations of duty or obedience, and not having before him the slightest fear of the human eye, had at length started off, and was at that moment rattling down the street,—Mr. Chuckster, with his hat off and a pen behind his ear, hanging on in the rear of the chaise and making futile attempts to draw it the other way, to the unspeakable admiration of all beholders. Even in running away, however, Whisker was perverse, for he had not gone very far when he suddenly stopped, and before assistance could be rendered, commenced backing at nearly as quick a pace as he had gone forward. By these means Mr. Chuckster was pushed and hustled to the office again, in the most inglorious manner, and arrived in a state of great exhaustion and discomfiture.

The old lady then stepped into her seat, and Mr. Abel (whom they had come to fetch) into his. The old gentleman, after reasoning with the pony on the extreme impropriety of his conduct, and making the best amends in his power to Mr. Chuckster, took his place also, and they drove away, waving a farewell to the notary and his clerk, and more than once turning to nod kindly to Kit as he watched them from the road.

CHAPTER XXI

Kit turned away and very soon forgot the pony, and the chaise, and the little old lady, and the little old gentleman, and the little young gentleman to boot, in thinking what could have become of his late master and his lovely grandchild, who were the fountain-head of all his meditations. Still casting about for some plausible means of accounting for their non-appearance, and of persuading himself that they must soon return, he bent his steps towards home, intending to finish the task which the sudden recollection of his contract had interrupted, and then to sally forth once more to seek his fortune for the day.

When he came to the corner of the court in which

he lived, lo and behold there was the pony again! Yes, there he was, looking more obstinate than ever; and alone in the chaise, keeping a steady watch upon his every wink, sat Mr. Abel, who, lifting up his eyes by chance and seeing Kit pass by, nodded to him as though he would have nodded his head off.

Kit wondered to see the pony again, so near his own home, too, but it never occurred to him for what purpose the pony might have come there, or where the old lady and the old gentleman had gone, until he lifted the latch of the door, and walking in, found them seated in the room in conversation with his mother, at which unexpected sight he pulled off his hat and made his best bow in some confusion.

'We are here before you, you see, Christopher,' said Mr. Garland smiling.

'Yes, sir,' said Kit; and as he said it, he looked towards his mother for an explanation of the visit.

'The gentleman 's been kind enough, my dear,' said she, in reply to this mute interrogation, 'to ask me whether you were in a good place, or in any place at all, and when I told him no, you were not in any, he was so good as to say that—'

'That we wanted a good lad in our house,' said the old gentleman and the old lady both together, 'and that perhaps we might think of it, if we found everything as we would wish it to be.'

As this thinking of it, plainly meant the thinking of engaging Kit, he immediately partook of his mother's anxiety and fell into a great flutter; for the little old couple were very methodical and cautious, and asked so many questions that he began to be afraid there was no chance of his success.

'You see, my good woman,' said Mrs. Garland to Kit's mother, 'that it 's necessary to be very careful and particular in such a matter as this, for we 're only three in family, and are very quiet regular folks, and it would be a sad thing if we made any kind of mistake, and found things different from what we hoped and expected.'

To this, Kit's mother replied, that certainly it was quite true, and quite right, and quite proper, and Heaven forbid that she should shrink, or have cause to shrink, from any inquiry into her character or that of her son, who was a very good son though she was his mother, in which respect, she was bold to say, he took after his father, who was not only a good son to *his* mother, but the best of husbands and the best of fathers besides, which Kit could and would corroborate she knew, and so would little Jacob and the baby likewise if they were old enough, which unfortunately they were not, though as they didn't know what a loss they had had, perhaps it was a great deal better that they should be as young as they were; and so Kit's mother wound up a long story by wiping her eyes with her apron, and patting little Jacob's head, who was rocking the cradle and staring with all his might at the strange lady and gentleman.

When Kit's mother had done speaking, the old lady struck in again, and said that she was quite sure she was a very honest and very respectable person or she never would have expressed herself in that manner, and that certainly the appearance of the children and the cleanliness of the house deserved great praise and did her the utmost credit, whereat Kit's mother dropped a curtsey and became consoled. Then the good woman entered into a long and minute account of Kit's life and history from the earliest period down to that time, not omitting to make mention of his miraculous fall out of a back-parlour window when an infant of tender years, or his uncommon sufferings in a state of measles, which were illustrated by correct imitations of the plaintive manner in which he called for toast and water, day and night, and said, 'don't cry, mother, I shall soon be better'; for proof of which statements reference was made to Mrs. Green, lodger, at the cheesemonger's round the corner, and divers other ladies and gentlemen in various parts of England and Wales, (and one Mr. Brown, who was supposed to be then a corporal in the East Indies, and who could of course be found with very little trouble), within whose personal knowledge the circumstances had occurred. This narration ended, Mr. Garland put some questions to Kit respecting his qualifications and general acquirements, while Mrs. Garland noticed the children, and hearing from Kit's mother certain remarkable circumstances which had attended the birth of each, related certain other remarkable circumstances which had attended the birth of her own son, Mr. Abel, from which it appeared that both Kit's mother and herself had been, above and beyond all other women of what condition or age soever, peculiarly hemmed in with perils and dangers. Lastly, inquiry was made into the nature and extent of Kit's wardrobe, and a small advance being made to improve the same, he was formally hired at an annual income of Six Pounds, over and above his board and lodging, by Mr. and Mrs. Garland, of Abel Cottage, Finchley.

It would be difficult to say which party appeared most pleased with this arrangement, the conclusion of which was hailed with nothing but pleasant looks and cheerful smiles on both sides. It was settled that Kit should repair to his new abode on the next day but one, in the morning; and finally, the little old couple, after bestowing a bright half-crown on little Jacob and another on the baby, took their leaves; being escorted as far as the street by their new attendant, who held the obdurate pony by the bridle while they took their seats, and saw them drive away with a lightened heart.

'Well, mother,' said Kit, hurrying back into the house, 'I think my fortune 's about made now.'

'I should think it was indeed, Kit,' rejoined his mother. 'Six pound a year! Only think!'

'Ah!' said Kit, trying to maintain the gravity which the consideration of such a sum demanded, but grinning with delight in spite of himself. 'There 's a property!'

Kit drew a long breath when he had said this, and putting his hands deep into his pockets as if there were one year's wages at least in each, looked at his mother, as though he saw through her, and down an immense perspective of sovereigns beyond.

'Please God we 'll make such a lady of you for Sundays, mother! such a scholar of Jacob, such a child of the baby, such a room of the one upstairs! Six pound a year!'

'Hem!' croaked a strange voice. 'What 's that about six pound a year? What about six pounds a year?' And as the voice made this inquiry, Daniel Quilp walked in with Richard Swiveller at his heels.

'Who said he was to have six pound a year?' said Quilp, looking sharply round. 'Did the old man say it, or did little Nell say it? And what 's he to have it for, and where are they, eh!'

The good woman was so much alarmed by the sudden apparition of this unknown piece of ugliness, that she hastily caught the baby from its cradle and retreated into the furthest corner of the room; while little Jacob, sitting upon his stool with his hands on his knees, looked full at him in a species of fascination, roaring lustily all the time. Richard Swiveller took an easy observation of the family over Mr.

Quilp's head, and Quilp himself, with his hands in his pockets, smiled in an exquisite enjoyment of the commotion he occasioned.

'Don't be frightened, mistress,' said Quilp, after a pause. 'Your son knows me; I don't eat babies; I don't like 'em. It will be as well to stop that young screamer though, in case I should be tempted to do him a mischief. Halloa, sir! Will you be quiet?'

Little Jacob stemmed the course of two tears which he was squeezing out of his eyes, and instantly subsided into a silent horror.

'Mind you don't break out again, you villain,' said Quilp, looking sternly at him, 'or I 'll make faces at you and throw you into fits, I will. Now you, sir, why haven't you been to me as you promised?'

'What should I come for?' retorted Kit. 'I hadn't any business with you, no more than you had with me.'

'Here, mistress,' said Quilp, turning quickly away, and appealing from Kit to his mother. 'When did his old master come or send here last? Is he here now? If not, where 's he gone?'

'He has not been here at all,' she replied. 'I wish we knew where they have gone, for it would make my son a good deal easier in his mind, and me too. If you 're the gentleman named Mr. Quilp, I should have thought you 'd have known, and so I told him only this very day.'

'Humph!' muttered Quilp, evidently disappointed to believe that this was true. 'That 's what you tell this gentleman too, is it?'

'If the gentleman comes to ask the same question, I can't tell him anything else, sir; and I only wish I could for our own sakes,' was the reply.

Quilp glanced at Richard Swiveller, and observed that having met him on the threshold, he assumed that he had come in search of some intelligence of the fugitives. He supposed he was right?

'Yes,' said Dick, 'that was the object of the present expedition. I fancied it possible—but let us go ring fancy's knell. *I'll* begin it.'

'You seem disappointed,' observed Quilp.

'A baffler, sir, a baffler, that 's all,' returned Dick. 'I have entered upon a speculation which has proved a baffler; and a Being of brightness and beauty will be offered up a sacrifice at Cheggs's altar. That 's all, sir.'

The dwarf eyed Richard with a sarcastic smile, but Richard, who had been taking a rather strong lunch with a friend, observed him not, and continued to deplore his fate with mournful and despondent looks. Quilp plainly discerned that there was some secret reason for this visit and his uncommon disappointment, and, in the hope that there might be means of mischief lurking beneath it, resolved to worm it out. He had no sooner adopted this resolution, than he conveyed as much honesty into his face as it was capable of expressing, and sympathised with Mr. Swiveller exceedingly.

'I am disappointed myself,' said Quilp, 'out of mere friendly feeling for them; but you have real reasons, private reasons I have no doubt, for your disappointment, and therefore it comes heavier than mine.'

'Why, of course it does,' Dick observed, testily.

'Upon my word, I 'm very sorry, very sorry. I 'm rather cast down myself. As we are companions in adversity, shall we be companions in the surest way of forgetting it? If you had no particular business, now, to lead you in another direction,' urged Quilp, plucking him by the sleeve and looking slyly up into his face out of the corners of his eyes, 'there is a house by the waterside where they have some of the noblest Schiedam—reputed to be smuggled, but that 's between ourselves—that can be got in all the world. The landlord knows me. There 's a little summer-house overlooking the river, where we might take a glass of this delicious liquor with a whiff of the best tobacco—it 's in this case, and of the rarest quality, to my certain knowledge—and be perfectly snug and happy, could we possibly contrive it; or is there any very particular engagement that peremptorily takes you another way, Mr. Swiveller, eh?'

As the dwarf spoke, Dick's face relaxed into a compliant smile, and his brows slowly unbent. By the time he had finished, Dick was looking down at Quilp in the same sly manner as Quilp was looking up at him, and there remained nothing more to be done but to set out for the house in question. This they did, straightway. The moment their backs were turned, little Jacob thawed, and resumed his crying from the point where Quilp had frozen him.

The summer-house of which Mr. Quilp had spoken was a rugged wooden box, rotten and bare to see, which overhung the river's mud, and threatened to slide down into it. The tavern to which it belonged was a crazy building, sapped and undermined by the rats, and only upheld by great bars of wood which were reared against its walls, and had propped it up so long that even they were decaying and yielding with their load, and of a windy night might be heard to creak and crack as if the whole fabric were about to come toppling down. The house stood—if anything so old and feeble could be said to stand—on a piece of waste ground, blighted with the unwholesome smoke of factory chimneys, and echoing the clank of iron wheels and rush of troubled water. Its internal accommodations amply fulfilled the promise of the outside. The rooms were low and damp, the clammy walls were pierced with chinks and holes, the rotten floors had sunk from their level, the very beams started from their places and warned the timid stranger from their neighbourhood.

To this inviting spot, entreating him to observe its beauties as they passed along, Mr. Quilp led Richard Swiveller, and on the table of the summer-house, scored deep with many a gallows and initial letter, there soon appeared a wooden keg, full of the vaunted liquor. Drawing it off into the glasses with the skill of a practised hand, and mixing it with about a third part of water, Mr. Quilp assigned to Richard Swiveller his portion, and lighting his pipe from an end of a candle in a very old and battered lantern, drew himself together upon a seat and puffed away.

'Is it good?' said Quilp, as Richard Swiveller smacked his lips, 'is it strong and fiery? Does it make you wink, and choke, and your eyes water, and your breath come short—does it?'

'Does it?' cried Dick, throwing away part of the contents of his glass, and filling it up with water, 'why, man, you don't mean to tell me that you drink such fire as this?'

'No!' rejoined Quilp, 'not drink it! Look here. And here. And here again. Not drink it!'

As he spoke, Daniel Quilp drew off and drank three small glassfuls of the raw spirit, and then with a horrible grimace took a great many pulls at his pipe, and swallowing the smoke, discharged it in a heavy cloud from his nose. This feat accomplished he drew himself together in his former position, and laughed excessively.

'Give us a toast!' cried Quilp, rattling on the table in a dexterous manner with his fist and elbow alternately, in a kind of tune, 'a woman, a beauty. Let 's have a beauty for our toast and empty our glasses to the last drop. Her name, come!'

'If you want a name,' said Dick, 'here 's Sophy Wackles.'

'Sophy Wackles,' screamed the dwarf, 'Miss Sophy Wackles that is—Mrs. Richard Swiveller that shall be—that shall be—ha ha ha!'

'Ah!' said Dick, 'you might have said that a few weeks ago, but it won't do now, my buck. Immolating herself upon the shrine of Cheggs—'

'Poison Cheggs, cut Cheggs's ears off,' rejoined Quilp. 'I won't hear of Cheggs. Her name is Swiveller or nothing. I 'll drink her health again, and her father's, and her mother's; and to all her sisters and brothers—the glorious family of the Wackleses—all the Wackleses in one glass—down with it to the dregs!'

'Well,' said Richard Swiveller, stopping short in the act of raising the glass to his lips and looking at the dwarf in a species of stupor as he flourished his arms and legs about: 'you 're a jolly fellow, but of all the jolly fellows I ever saw or heard of, you have the queerest and most extraordinary way with you, upon my life you have.'

This candid declaration tended rather to increase than restrain Mr. Quilp's eccentricities, and Richard Swiveller, astonished to see him in such a roystering vein, and drinking not a little himself, for company, —began imperceptibly to become more companionable and confiding, so that, being judiciously led on by Mr. Quilp, he grew at last very confiding indeed. Having once got him into this mood, and knowing now the key-note to strike whenever he was at a loss, Daniel Quilp's task was comparatively an easy one, and he was soon in possession of the whole details of the scheme contrived between the easy Dick and his more designing friend.

'Stop!' said Quilp. 'That 's the thing, that 's the thing. It can be brought about, it shall be brought about. There 's my hand upon it; I am your friend from this minute.'

'What? do you think there 's still a chance?' inquired Dick, in surprise at this encouragement.

'A chance!' echoed the dwarf, 'a certainty! Sophy Wackles may become a Cheggs or anything else she likes, but not a Swiveller. Oh you lucky dog! He 's richer than any Jew alive; you 're a made man. I see in you now nothing but Nelly's husband, rolling in gold and silver. I 'll help you. It shall be done. Mind my words, it shall be done.'

'But how?' said Dick.

'There 's plenty of time,' rejoined the dwarf, 'and it shall be done. We 'll sit down and talk it over again all the way through. Fill your glass while I 'm gone. I shall be back directly—directly.'

With these hasty words, Daniel Quilp withdrew into a dismantled skittle-ground behind the public-house, and, throwing himself upon the ground, actually screamed and rolled about in uncontrollable delight.

'Here 's sport!' he cried, 'sport ready to my hand, all invented and arranged, and only to be enjoyed. It was this shallow-pated fellow who made my bones ache t' other day, was it? It was his friend and fellow-plotter, Mr. Trent, that once made eyes at Mrs. Quilp, and leered and looked, was it? After labouring for two or three years in their precious scheme, to find that they 've got a beggar at last, and one of them tied for life. Ha ha ha! He shall marry Nell. He shall have her, and I 'll be the first man, when the knot 's tied hard and fast, to tell 'em what they 've gained and what I 've helped 'em to. Here will be a clearing of old scores, here will be a time to remind 'em what a capital friend I was, and how I helped them to the heiress. Ha ha ha!'

In the height of his ecstasy, Mr. Quilp had like to have met with a disagreeable check, for rolling very near a broken dog-kennel, there leapt forth a large fierce dog, who, but that his chain was of the shortest, would have given him a disagreeable salute. As it was, the dwarf remained upon his back in perfect safety, taunting the dog with hideous faces, and triumphing over him in his inability to advance another inch, though there was not a couple of feet between them.

'Why don't you come and bite me, why don't you come and tear me to pieces, you coward?' said Quilp, hissing and worrying the animal till he was nearly mad. 'You 're afraid, you bully, you 're afraid, you know you are.'

The dog tore and strained at his chain with starting eyes and furious bark, but there the dwarf lay, snapping his fingers with gestures of defiance and contempt. When he had sufficiently recovered from his delight, he rose, and with his arms akimbo, achieved a kind of demon-dance round the kennel, just without the limits of the chain, driving the dog quite wild. Having by this means composed his spirits and put himself in a pleasant train, he returned to his unsuspicious companion, whom he found looking at the tide with exceeding gravity, and thinking of that same gold and silver which Mr. Quilp had mentioned.

CHAPTER XXII

THE remainder of that day and the whole of the next were a busy time for the Nubbles family, to whom everything connected with Kit's outfit and departure was matter of as great moment as if he had been about to penetrate into the interior of Africa, or to take a cruise round the world. It would be difficult to suppose that there ever was a box which was opened and shut so many times within four-and-twenty hours, as that which contained his wardrobe and necessaries; and certainly there never was one which to two small eyes presented such a mine of clothing, as this mighty chest with its three shirts and proportionate allowance of stockings and pocket-handkerchiefs, disclosed to the astonished vision of little Jacob. At last it was conveyed to the carrier's, at whose house at Finchley Kit was to find it next day; and the box being gone, there remained but two questions for consideration: firstly, whether the carrier would lose, or dishonestly feign to lose, the box upon the road; secondly, whether Kit's mother perfectly understood how to take care of herself in the absence of her son.

'I don't think there 's hardly a chance of his really losing it, but carriers are under great temptation to pretend they lose things, no doubt,' said Mrs. Nubbles apprehensively, in reference to the first point.

'No doubt about it,' returned Kit, with a serious look; 'upon my word, mother, I don't think it was right to trust it to itself. Somebody ought to have gone with it, I 'm afraid.'

'We can't help it now,' said his mother; 'but it was foolish and wrong. People oughtn't to be tempted.'

Kit inwardly resolved that he would never tempt a carrier any more, save with an empty box; and having formed this Christian determination, he turned his thoughts to the second question.

'You know you must keep up your spirits, mother, and not be lonesome because I 'm not at home. I shall very often be able to look in when I come into town I dare say, and I shall send you a letter sometimes, and when the quarter comes round, I can get a holiday of course; and then see if we don't take little Jacob to the play, and let him know what oysters means.'

'I hope plays mayn't be sinful, Kit, but I 'm a'most afraid,' said Mrs. Nubbles.

'I know who has been putting that in your head,' rejoined her son disconsolately; 'that 's Little Bethel again. Now I say, mother, pray don't take to going there regularly, for if I was to see your good-humoured face that has always made home cheerful, turned into a grievous one, and the baby trained to look grievous too, and to call itself a young sinner (bless its heart) and a child of the devil (which is calling its dead father names); if I was to see this, and see little Jacob looking grievous likewise, I should so take it to heart that I 'm sure I should go and 'list for a soldier, and run my head on purpose against the first cannon-ball I saw coming my way.'

'Oh, Kit, don't talk like that.'

'I would, indeed, mother, and unless you want to make me feel very wretched and uncomfortable, you 'll keep that bow on your bonnet which you 'd more than half a mind to pull off last week. Can you suppose there 's any harm in looking as cheerful and being as cheerful as our poor circumstances will permit? Do I see anything in the way I 'm made, which calls upon me to be a snivelling, solemn, whispering chap, sneaking about as if I couldn't help it, and expressing myself in a most unpleasant snuffle? on the contrairy, don't I see every reason why I shouldn't? Just hear this! Ha ha ha! An't that as nat'ral as walking, and as good for the health? Ha ha ha! An't that as nat'ral as a sheep's bleating, or a pig's grunting, or a horse's neighing, or a bird's singing? Ha ha ha! Isn't it, mother?'

There was something contagious in Kit's laugh, for his mother, who had looked grave before, first subsided into a smile, and then fell to joining in it heartily, which occasioned Kit to say that he knew it was natural, and to laugh the more. Kit and his mother, laughing together in a pretty loud key, woke the baby, who, finding that there was something very jovial and agreeable in progress, was no sooner in its mother's arms than it began to kick and laugh, most vigorously. This new illustration of his argument so tickled Kit, that he fell backward in his chair in a state of exhaustion, pointing at the baby and shaking his sides till he rocked again. After recovering twice or thrice, and as often relapsing, he wiped his eyes and said grace; and a very cheerful meal their scanty supper was.

With more kisses, and hugs, and tears, than many young gentlemen who start upon their travels, and leave well-stocked homes behind them, would deem within the bounds of probability (if matter so low could be herein set down), Kit left the house at an early hour next morning, and set out to walk to Finchley; feeling a sufficient pride in his appearance to have warranted his excommunication from Little Bethel from that time forth, if he had ever been one of that mournful congregation.

Lest anybody should feel a curiosity to know how Kit was clad, it may be briefly remarked that he wore no livery, but was dressed in a coat of pepper-and-salt with waistcoat of canary colour, and nether garments of iron-grey; besides these glories, he shone in the lustre of a new pair of boots and an extremely stiff and shiny hat, which on being struck anywhere with the knuckles, sounded like a drum. And in this attire, rather wondering that he attracted so little attention, and attributing the circumstance to the insensibility of those who got up early, he made his way towards Abel Cottage.

Without encountering any more remarkable adventure on the road, than meeting a lad in a brimless hat, the exact counterpart of his old one, on whom he bestowed half the sixpence he possessed, Kit arrived in course of time at the carrier's house, where, to the lasting honour of human nature, he found the box in safety. Receiving from the wife of this immaculate man, a direction to Mr. Garland's, he took the box upon his shoulder and repaired thither directly.

To be sure, it was a beautiful little cottage with a thatched roof and little spires at the gable-ends, and pieces of stained glass in some of the windows, almost as large as pocket-books. On one side of the house was a little stable, just the size for the pony, with a little room over it, just the size for Kit. White curtains were fluttering, and birds in cages that looked as bright as if they were made of gold, were singing at the windows; plants were arranged on either side of the path, and clustered about the door; and the garden was bright with flowers in full bloom, which shed a sweet odour all round, and had a charming and elegant appearance. Everything within the house and without, seemed to be the perfection of neatness and order. In the garden there was not a weed to be seen, and to judge from some dapper gardening-tools, a basket, and a pair of gloves which were lying in one of the walks, old Mr. Garland had been at work in it that very morning.

Kit looked about him, and admired, and looked again, and this a great many times before he could make up his mind to turn his head another way and ring the bell. There was abundance of time to look about him again though, when he had rung it, for nobody came, so after ringing it twice or thrice he sat down upon his box, and waited.

He rung the bell a great many times, and yet nobody came. But at last, as he was sitting upon the box thinking about giants' castles, and princesses tied up to pegs by the hair of their heads, and dragons bursting out from behind gates, and other incidents of the like nature, common in story-books to youths of low degree on their first visit to strange houses, the door was gently opened, and a little servant-girl, very tidy, modest, and demure, but very pretty too, appeared.

'I suppose you 're Christopher, sir,' said the servant-girl.

Kit got off the box, and said yes, he was.

'I 'm afraid you 've rung a good many times, perhaps,' she rejoined, 'but we couldn't hear you, because we 've been catching the pony.'

Kit rather wondered what this meant, but as he couldn't stop there, asking questions, he shouldered the box again and followed the girl into the hall, where through a back-door he descried Mr. Garland leading Whisker in triumph up the garden, after that self-willed pony had (as he afterwards learned) dodged the family round a small paddock in the rear, for one hour and three-quarters.

The old gentleman received him very kindly, and so did the old lady, whose previous good opinion of him was greatly enhanced by his wiping his boots on the mat until the soles of his feet burnt again. He was then taken into the parlour to be inspected in his new clothes; and when he had been surveyed several times, and had afforded by his appearance unlimited satisfaction, he was taken into the stable (where the pony received him with uncommon complaisance); and thence into the little chamber he had already observed, which was very clean and comfortable: and thence into the garden, in which the old gentleman told him he would be taught to employ himself, and where he told him, besides, what great things he meant to do to make him comfortable, and happy, if he found he deserved it. All these kindnesses, Kit acknowledged with various expressions of gratitude, and so many touches of the new hat, that the brim suffered considerably. When the old gentleman had said all he had to say in the way of promise and advice, and Kit had said all he had to say in the way of assurance and thankfulness, he was handed over again to the old lady, who, summoning the little servant-girl (whose name was Barbara) instructed her to take him downstairs and give him something to eat and drink, after his walk.

Downstairs, therefore, Kit went; and at the bottom of the stairs there was such a kitchen as was never before seen or heard of out of a toy-shop window, with everything in it as bright and glowing, and as precisely ordered too, as Barbara herself. And in this kitchen, Kit sat himself down at a table as white as a table-cloth, to eat cold meat, and drink small ale, and use his knife and fork the more awkwardly, because there was an unknown Barbara looking on and observing him.

It did not appear, however, that there was anything remarkably tremendous about this strange Barbara, who having lived a very quiet life, blushed very much and was quite as embarrassed and uncertain what she ought to say or do, as Kit could possibly be. When he had sat for some little time, attentive to the ticking of the sober clock, he ventured to glance curiously at the dresser, and there, among the plates and dishes, were Barbara's little work-box with a sliding lid to shut in the balls of cotton, and Barbara's prayer-book, and Barbara's hymn-book, and Barbara's Bible. Barbara's little looking-glass hung in a good light near the window, and Barbara's bonnet was on a nail behind the door. From all these mute signs and tokens of her presence, he naturally glanced at Barbara herself, who sat as mute as they, shelling peas into a dish; and just when Kit was looking at her eyelashes and wondering—quite in the simplicity of his heart—what colour her eyes might be, it perversely happened that Barbara raised her head a little to look at him, when both pair of eyes were hastily withdrawn, and Kit leant over his plate, and Barbara over her pea-shells, each in extreme confusion as having been detected by the other.

CHAPTER XXIII

Mr. Richard Swiveller wending homeward from the Wilderness (for such was the appropriate name of Quilp's choice retreat), after a sinuous and corkscrew fashion, with many checks and stumbles; after stopping suddenly and staring about him, then as suddenly running forward for a few paces, and as suddenly halting again and shaking his head; doing everything with a jerk and nothing by premeditation;—Mr. Richard Swiveller wending his way homeward after this fashion, which is considered by evil-minded men to be symbolical of intoxication, and is not held by such persons to denote that state of deep wisdom and reflection in which the actor knows himself to be, began to think that possibly he had misplaced his confidence and that the dwarf might not be precisely the sort of person to whom to entrust a secret of such delicacy and importance. And being led and tempted on by this remorseful thought into a condition which the evil-minded class before referred to would term the maudlin state or stage of drunkenness, it occurred to Mr. Swiveller to cast his hat upon the ground, and moan, crying aloud that he was an unhappy orphan, and that if he had not been an unhappy orphan things had never come to this.

'Left an infant by my parents, at an early age,' said Mr. Swiveller, bewailing his hard lot, 'cast upon the world in my tenderest period, and thrown upon the mercies of a deluding dwarf, who can wonder at my weakness? Here's a miserable orphan for you. Here,' said Mr. Swiveller, raising his voice to a high pitch, and looking sleepily round, 'is a miserable orphan!'

'Then,' said somebody hard by, 'let me be a father to you.'

Mr. Swiveller swayed himself to and fro to preserve his balance, and, looking into a kind of haze which seemed to surround him, at last perceived two eyes dimly twinkling through the mist, which he observed after a short time were in the neighbourhood of a nose and mouth. Casting his eyes down towards that quarter in which, with reference to a man's face, his legs are usually to be found, he observed that the face had a body attached; and when he looked more intently he was satisfied that the person was Mr.

Quilp, who indeed had been in his company all the time, but whom he had some vague idea of having left a mile or two behind.

'You have deceived an orphan, sir,' said Mr. Swiveller solemnly.

'I! I 'm a second father to you,' replied Quilp.

'You my father, sir!' retorted Dick. 'Being all right myself, sir, I request to be left alone—instantly, sir.'

'What a funny fellow you are!' cried Quilp.

'Go, sir,' returned Dick, leaning against a post and waving his hand. 'Go, deceiver, go, some day, sir, p'r'aps you 'll waken, from pleasure's dream to know the grief of orphans forsaken. Will you go, sir?'

The dwarf taking no heed of this adjuration, Mr. Swiveller advanced with the view of inflicting upon him condign chastisement. But forgetting his purpose or changing his mind before he came close to him, he seized his hand and vowed eternal friendship, declaring with an agreeable frankness that from that time forth they were brothers in everything but personal appearance. Then he told his secret over again, with the addition of being pathetic on the subject of Miss Wackles, who, he gave Mr. Quilp to understand, was the occasion of any slight incoherency he might observe in his speech at that moment, which was attributable solely to the strength of his affection and not to rosy wine or other fermented liquor. And then they went on arm-in-arm, very lovingly together.

'I 'm as sharp,' said Quilp to him, at parting, 'as sharp as a ferret, and as cunning as a weazel. You bring Trent to me; assure him that I 'm his friend though I fear he a little distrusts me (I don't know why, I have not deserved it); and you 've both of you made your fortunes—in perspective.'

AND THEN THEY WENT ON ARM-IN-ARM.

'That 's the worst of it,' returned Dick. 'These fortunes in perspective look such a long way off.'

'But they look smaller than they really are, on that account,' said Quilp pressing his arm. 'You 'll have no conception of the value of your prize until you draw close to it. Mark that.'

'D' ye think not?' said Dick.

'Aye, I do; and I am certain of what I say, that 's better,' returned the dwarf. 'You bring Trent to me. Tell him I am his friend and yours—why shouldn't I be?'

'There 's no reason why you shouldn't certainly,' replied Dick, 'and perhaps there are a great many why you should—at least there would be nothing strange in your wanting to be my friend, if you were a choice spirit, but then you know you 're *not* a choice spirit.'

'I not a choice spirit?' cried Quilp.

'Devil a bit, sir,' returned Dick. 'A man of your appearance couldn't be. If you 're any spirit at all, sir, you 're an evil spirit. Choice spirits,' added Dick, smiting himself on the breast, 'are quite a different-looking sort of people, you may take your oath of that, sir.'

Quilp glanced at his free-spoken friend with a mingled expression of cunning and dislike, and wringing his hand almost at the same moment, declared that he was an uncommon character and had his warmest esteem. With that they parted; Mr. Swiveller to make the best of his way home and sleep himself sober; and Quilp to cogitate upon the discovery he had made, and exult in the prospect of the rich field of enjoyment and reprisal it opened to him.

It was not without great reluctance and misgiving that Mr. Swiveller, next morning, his head racked by the fumes of the renowned Schiedam, repaired to the lodging of his friend Trent (which was in the roof of an old house in an old ghostly inn), and recounted by very slow degrees what had yesterday taken place between him and Quilp. Nor was it without great surprise and much speculation on Quilp's probable motives, nor without many bitter comments on Dick Swiveller's folly, that his friend received the tale.

'I don't defend myself, Fred,' said the penitent Richard; 'but the fellow has such a queer way with him and is such an artful dog, that first of all he set me upon thinking whether there was any harm in telling him, and while I was thinking, screwed it out of me. If you had seen him drink and smoke, as I did, you couldn't have kept anything from him. He 's a Salamander you know, that 's what *he* is.'

Without inquiring whether Salamanders were of necessity good confidential agents, or whether a fireproof man was as a matter of course trustworthy, Frederick Trent threw himself into a chair, and, burying his head in his hands, endeavoured to fathom the motives which had led Quilp to insinuate himself into Richard Swiveller's confidence;—for that the discourse was of his seeking, and had not been spontaneously revealed by Dick, was sufficiently plain from Quilp's seeking his company and enticing him away.

The dwarf had twice encountered him when he was endeavouring to obtain intelligence of the fugitives. This, perhaps, as he had not shown any previous anxiety about them, was enough to awaken suspicion in the breast of a creature so jealous and distrustful by nature, setting aside any additional impulse to curiosity that he might have derived from Dick's incautious manner. But knowing the scheme they had planned, why should he offer to assist it? This was a question more difficult of solution; but as knaves generally over-reach themselves by imputing their own designs to others, the idea immediately presented itself that some circumstances of irritation between Quilp and the old man, arising out of their secret transactions and not unconnected perhaps with his sudden disappearance, now rendered the former desirous of revenging himself upon him by seeking to entrap the sole object of his love and anxiety into a connection of which he knew he had a dread and hatred. As Frederick Trent himself, utterly regardless of his sister, had this object at heart, only second to the hope of gain, it seemed to him the more likely to be Quilp's main principle of action. Once investing the dwarf with a design of his own in abetting them, which the attainment of their purpose would serve, it was easy to believe him sincere and hearty in the cause; and as there could be no doubt of his proving a powerful and useful auxiliary, Trent determined to accept his invitation and go to his house that night, and if what he said and did confirmed him in the impression he had formed, to let him share the labour of their plan, but not the profit.

Having revolved these things in his mind and arrived at this conclusion, he communicated to Mr. Swiveller as much of his meditations as he thought proper (Dick would have been perfectly satisfied with less), and giving him the day to recover himself from his late salamandering, accompanied him at evening to Mr. Quilp's house.

Mightily glad Mr. Quilp was to see him, or mightily glad he seemed to be; and fearfully polite Mr. Quilp was to Mrs. Quilp and Mrs. Jiniwin; and very sharp was the look he cast on his wife to observe how she was affected by the recognition of young Trent. Mrs. Quilp was as innocent as her own mother of any emotion, painful or pleasant, which the sight of him awakened, but as her husband's glance made her timid and confused, and uncertain what to do or what was required of her, Mr. Quilp did not fail to assign her embarrassment to the cause he had in his mind, and while he chuckled at his penetration was secretly exasperated by his jealousy.

Nothing of this appeared, however. On the contrary, Mr. Quilp was all blandness and suavity, and presided over the case-bottle of rum with extraordinary open-heartedness.

'Why, let me see,' said Quilp. 'It must be a matter of nearly two years since we were first acquainted.'

'Nearer three, I think,' said Trent.

'Nearer three!' cried Quilp. 'How fast time flies. Does it seem as long as that to you, Mrs. Quilp?'

'Yes, I think it seems full three years, Quilp,' was the unfortunate reply.

'Oh indeed, ma'am,' thought Quilp, 'you have been pining, have you? Very good, ma'am.'

'It seems to me but yesterday that you went out to Demerara in the Mary Anne,' said Quilp; 'but yesterday, I declare. Well, I like a little wildness. I was wild myself once.'

Mr. Quilp accompanied this admission with such an awful wink, indicative of old rovings and backslidings, that Mrs. Jiniwin was indignant, and could not forbear from remarking under her breath that he might at least put off his confessions until his wife was absent; for which act of boldness and insubordination Mr. Quilp first stared her out of countenance and then drank her health ceremoniously.

'I thought you 'd come back directly, Fred. I always thought that,' said Quilp setting down his glass. 'And when the Mary Anne returned with you on board, instead of a letter to say what a contrite heart you had, and how happy you were in the situation that had been provided for you, I was amused—exceedingly amused. Ha ha ha!'

The young man smiled, but not as though the theme was the most agreeable one that could have been selected for his entertainment; and for that reason Quilp pursued it.

'I always will say,' he resumed, 'that when a rich relation having two young people—sisters or brothers, or brother and sister—dependent on him, attaches himself exclusively to one, and casts off the other, he does wrong.'

The young man made a movement of impatience, but Quilp went on as calmly as if he were discussing some abstract question in which nobody present had the slightest personal interest.

'It 's very true,' said Quilp, 'that your grandfather urged repeated forgiveness, ingratitude, riot, and extravagance, and all that; but as I told him "these are common faults." "But he 's a scoundrel," said he. "Granting that," said I (for the sake of argument of course), "a great many young noblemen and gentlemen are scoundrels too!" But he wouldn't be convinced.'

'I wonder at that, Mr. Quilp,' said the young man sarcastically.

'Well, so did I at the time,' returned Quilp, 'but he was always obstinate. He was in a manner a friend of mine, but he was always obstinate and wrongheaded. Little Nell is a nice girl, a charming girl, but you 're her brother, Frederick. You 're her brother after all; as you told him the last time you met, he can't alter that.'

'He would if he could, confound him for that and

all other kindnesses,' said the young man impatiently. 'But nothing can come of this subject now, and let us have done with it in the Devil's name.'

'Agreed,' returned Quilp, 'agreed on my part readily. Why have I alluded to it? Just to show you, Frederick, that I have always stood your friend. You little knew who was your friend, and who your foe; now did you? You thought I was against you, and so there has been a coolness between us; but it was all on your side, entirely on your side. Let 's shake hands again, Fred.'

With his head sunk down between his shoulders, and a hideous grin overspreading his face, the dwarf stood up and stretched his short arm across the table. After a moment's hesitation, the young man stretched out his to meet it; Quilp clutched his fingers in a grip that for the moment stopped the current of the blood within them, and pressing his other hand upon his lip and frowning towards the unsuspicious Richard, released them and sat down.

This action was not lost upon Trent, who, knowing that Richard Swiveller was a mere tool in his hands and knew no more of his designs than he thought proper to communicate, saw that the dwarf perfectly understood their relative position, and fully entered into the character of his friend. It is something to be appreciated, even in knavery. This silent homage to his superior abilities, no less than a sense of the power with which the dwarf's quick perception had already invested him, inclined the young man towards that ugly worthy, and determined him to profit by his aid.

It being now Mr. Quilp's cue to change the subject with all convenient expedition, lest Richard Swiveller in his heedlessness should reveal anything which it was inexpedient for the women to know, he proposed a game at four-handed cribbage; and partners being cut for, Mrs. Quilp fell to Frederick Trent, and Dick himself to Quilp. Mrs. Jiniwin being very fond of cards was carefully excluded by her son-in-law from any participation in the game, and had assigned to her the duty of occasionally replenishing the glasses from the case-bottle; Mr. Quilp from that moment keeping one eye constantly upon her, lest she should by any means procure a taste of the same, and thereby tantalising the wretched old lady (who was as much attached to the case-bottle as the cards) in a double degree and most ingenious manner.

But it was not to Mrs. Jiniwin alone that Mr. Quilp's attention was restricted, as several other matters required his constant vigilance. Among his various eccentric habits he had a humorous one of always cheating at cards, which rendered necessary on his part, not only a close observance of the game, and a sleight-of-hand in counting and scoring, but also involved the constant correction, by looks, and frowns, and kicks under the table, of Richard Swiveller, who being bewildered by the rapidity with which his cards were told, and the rate at which the pegs travelled down the board, could not be prevented from sometimes expressing his surprise and incredulity. Mrs. Quilp too was the partner of young Trent, and for every look that passed between them, and every word they spoke, and every card they played, the dwarf had eyes and ears; not occupied alone with what was passing above the table, but with signals that might be exchanging beneath it, which he laid all kinds of traps to detect; besides often treading on his wife's toes to see whether she cried out or remained silent under the infliction, in which latter case it would have been quite clear that Trent had been treading on her toes before. Yet, in the most of all these distractions, the one eye was upon the old lady always, and if she so much as stealthily advanced a tea-spoon towards a neighbouring glass (which she often did), for the purpose of abstracting but one sup of its sweet contents, Quilp's hand would overset it in the very moment of her triumph, and Quilp's mocking voice implore her to regard her precious health. And in any one of these many cares, from first to last, Quilp never flagged nor faltered.

At length, when they had played a great many rubbers and drawn pretty freely upon the case-bottle, Mr. Quilp warned his lady to retire to rest, and that submissive wife complying, and being followed by her indignant mother, Mr. Swiveller fell asleep. The dwarf beckoning his remaining companion to the other end of the room, held a short conference with him in whispers.

'It 's as well not to say more than one can help before our worthy friend,' said Quilp, making a grimace towards the slumbering Dick. 'Is it a bargain between us, Fred? Shall he marry little rosy Nell by-and-by?'

'You have some end of your own to answer, of course,' returned the other.

'Of course I have, dear Fred,' said Quilp, grinning to think how little he suspected what the real end was. 'It 's retaliation perhaps; perhaps whim. I have influence, Fred, to help or oppose. Which way shall I use it? There are a pair of scales, and it goes into one.'

'Throw it into mine then,' said Trent.

'It 's done, Fred,' rejoined Quilp, stretching out his clenched hand and opening it as if he had let some weight fall out. 'It 's in the scale from this time, and turns it, Fred. Mind that.'

'Where have they gone?' asked Trent.

Quilp shook his head, and said that point remained to be discovered, which it might be, easily. When it was, they would begin their preliminary advances. He would visit the old man, or even Richard Swiveller might visit him, and by affecting a deep concern in his behalf, and imploring him to settle in some worthy home, lead to the child's remembering him with gratitude and favour. Once impressed to this extent, it would be easy, he said, to win her in a year or two, for she supposed the old man to be poor, as it was a part of his jealous policy (in common with many other misers) to feign to be so, to those about him.

'He has feigned it often enough to me, of late,' said Trent.

'Oh! and to me too!' replied the dwarf. 'Which is more extraordinary, as I know how rich he really is.'

'I suppose you should,' said Trent.

'I think I should indeed,' rejoined the dwarf; and in that, at least, he spoke the truth.

After a few more whispered words, they returned to the table, and the young man rousing Richard Swiveller informed him that he was waiting to depart. This was welcome news to Dick, who started up directly. After a few words of confidence in the result of their project had been exchanged, they bade the grinning Quilp good-night.

Quilp crept to the window as they passed in the street below, and listened. Trent was pronouncing an encomium upon his wife, and they were both wondering by what enchantment she had been brought to marry such a misshapen wretch as he. The dwarf after watching their retreating shadows with a wider grin than his face had yet displayed, stole softly in the dark to bed.

In this hatching of their scheme, neither Trent nor Quilp had had one thought about the happiness or misery of poor innocent Nell. It would have been strange if the careless profligate, who was the butt of both, had been harassed by any such consideration; for his high opinion of his own merits and deserts rendered the project rather a laudable one than otherwise; and if he had been visited by so unwonted a guest as a reflection, he would—being a brute only in the gratification of his appetites—have soothed his conscience with the plea that he did not mean to beat or kill his wife, and would therefore, after all said and done, be a very tolerable, average husband.

CHAPTER XXIV

IT was not until they were quite exhausted and could no longer maintain the pace at which they had fled from the race-ground, that the old man and the child ventured to stop, and sit down to rest upon the borders of a little wood. Here, though the course was hidden from their view, they could yet faintly distinguish the noise of distant shouts, the hum of voices, and the beating of drums. Climbing the eminence which lay between them and the spot they had left, the child could even discern the fluttering flags and white tops of booths; but no person was approaching towards them, and their resting-place was solitary and still.

Some time elapsed before she could reassure her trembling companion, or restore him to a state of moderate tranquillity. His disordered imagination represented to him a crowd of persons stealing towards them beneath the cover of the bushes, lurking in every ditch, and peeping from the boughs of every rustling tree. He was haunted by apprehensions of being led captive to some gloomy place where he would be chained and scourged, and worse than all, where Nell could never come to see him, save through iron bars and gratings in the wall. His terrors affected the child. Separation from her grandfather was the greatest evil she could dread; and feeling for the time as though, go where they would, they were to be hunted down, and could never be safe but in hiding, her heart failed her, and her courage drooped.

In one so young, and so unused to the scencs in which she had lately moved, this sinking of the spirit was not surprising. But, Nature often enshrines gallant and noble hearts in weak bosoms—oftenest, God bless her, in female breasts—and when the child, casting her tearful eyes upon the old man, remembered how weak he was, and how destitute and helpless he would be if she failed him, her heart swelled within her, and animated her with new strength and fortitude.

'We are quite safe now, and have nothing to fear indeed, dear grandfather,' she said.

'Nothing to fear!' returned the old man. 'Nothing to fear if they took me from thee! Nothing to fear if they parted us! Nobody is true to me. No, not one. Not even Nell!'

'Oh! do not say that,' replied the child, 'for if ever anybody was true at heart, and earnest, I am. I am sure you know I am.'

'Then how,' said the old man, looking fearfully round, 'how can you bear to think that we are safe, when they are searching for me everywhere, and may come here, and steal upon us, even while we 're talking?'

'Because I 'm sure we have not been followed,' said the child. 'Judge for yourself, dear grandfather; look round, and see how quiet and still it is. We are alone together, and may ramble where we like. Not safe! Could I feel easy—did I feel at ease—when any danger threatened you?'

'True, too,' he answered, pressing her hand, but still looking anxiously about. 'What noise was that?'

'A bird,' said the child, 'flying into the wood, and leading the way for us to follow. You remember that we said we would walk in woods and fields, and by the side of rivers, and how happy we would be—you remember that? But here, while the sun shines above our heads, and everything is bright and happy, we are sitting sadly down, and losing time. See what a pleasant path; and there 's the bird—the same bird—now he flies to another tree, and stays to sing. Come!'

When they rose up from the ground, and took the shady track which led them through the wood, she bounded on before, printing her tiny footsteps in the moss, which rose elastic from so light a pressure and gave it back as mirrors throw off breath; and thus she lured the old man on, with many a backward look and merry beck, now pointing stealthily to some lone bird as it perched and twittered on a branch that strayed across their path, now stopping to listen to the songs that broke the happy silence, or watch the sun as it trembled through the leaves, and stealing in among the ivied trunks of stout old trees, opened long paths of light. As they passed onward, parting the boughs that clustered in their way, the serenity which the child had first assumed, stole into her breast in earnest; the old man cast no longer fearful looks behind, but felt at ease and cheerful, for the further they passed into the deep green shade, the more they felt that the tranquil mind of God was there, and shed its peace on them.

At length the path becoming clearer and less intricate, brought them to the end of the wood, and into a public road. Taking their way along it for a short distance, they came to a lane, so shaded by the trees on either hand that they met together overhead, and arched the narrow way. A broken finger-post announced that this led to a village three miles off; and thither they resolved to bend their steps.

The miles appeared so long that they sometimes thought they must have missed their road. But at last, to their great joy, it led downwards in a steep descent, with overhanging banks over which the footpaths led; and the clustered houses of the village peeped from the woody hollow below.

It was a very small place. The men and boys were playing at cricket on the green; and as other folks were looking on, they wandered up and down, uncertain where to seek a humble lodging. There was but one old man in the little garden before his cottage, and him they were timid of approaching, for he was the schoolmaster, and had 'School' written up over his window in black letters on a white board. He was a pale, simple-looking man, of a spare and meagre habit, and sat among his flowers and beehives, smoking his pipe, in the little porch before his door.

'Speak to him, dear,' the old man whispered.

'I am almost afraid to disturb him,' said the child timidly. 'He does not seem to see us. Perhaps if we wait a little, he may look this way.'

They waited, but the schoolmaster cast no look towards them, and still sat, thoughtful and silent, in the little porch. He had a kind face. In his plain old suit of black, he looked pale and meagre. They fancied, too, a lonely air about him and his house, but perhaps that was because the other people formed a merry company upon the green, and he seemed the only solitary man in all the place.

They were very tired, and the child would have been bold enough to address even a schoolmaster, but for something in his manner which seemed to denote that he was uneasy or distressed. As they stood hesitating at a little distance, they saw that he sat for a few minutes at a time like one in a brown study, then laid aside his pipe and took a few turns in his garden, then approached the gate and looked towards the green, then took up his pipe again with a sigh, and sat down thoughtfully as before.

As nobody else appeared and it would soon be dark, Nell at length took courage, and when he had resumed his pipe and seat, ventured to draw near, leading her grandfather by the hand. The slight noise they made in raising the latch of the wicket-gate, caught his attention. He looked at them kindly but seemed disappointed too, and slightly shook his head.

Nell dropped a curtsey, and told him they were poor travellers who sought a shelter for the night which they would gladly pay for, so far as their means allowed. The schoolmaster looked earnestly at her as she spoke, laid aside his pipe, and rose up directly.

'If you could direct us anywhere, sir,' said the child, 'we should take it very kindly.'

'You have been walking a long way,' said the schoolmaster.

'A long way, sir,' the child replied.

'You 're a young traveller, my child,' he said, laying his hand gently on her head. 'Your grandchild, friend?'

'Aye, sir,' cried the old man, 'and the stay and comfort of my life.'

'Come in,' said the schoolmaster.

Without further preface he conducted them into his little schoolroom, which was parlour and kitchen likewise, and told them that they were welcome to remain under his roof until morning. Before they had done thanking him, he spread a coarse white cloth upon the table, with knives and platters; and bringing out some bread and cold meat and a jug of beer, besought them to eat and drink.

The child looked round the room as she took her seat. There were a couple of forms, notched and cut and inked all over; a small deal desk perched on four legs, at which no doubt the master sat; a few dog's-eared books upon a high shelf; and beside them a motley collection of peg-tops, balls, kites, fishing-lines, marbles, half-eaten apples, and other confiscated property of idle urchins. Displayed on hooks upon the wall in all their terrors, were the cane and ruler; and near them, on a small shelf of its own, the dunce's cap, made of old newspapers and decorated with glaring wafers of the largest size. But, the great ornaments of the walls were certain moral sentences fairly copied in good round text, and well-worked sums in simple addition and multiplication, evidently achieved by the same hand, which were plentifully pasted all round the room: for the double purpose, as it seemed, of bearing testimony to the excellence of the school, and kindling a worthy emulation in the bosoms of the scholars.

'Yes,' said the old schoolmaster, observing that her attention was caught by these latter specimens. 'That 's beautiful writing, my dear.'

'Very, sir,' replied the child modestly, 'is it yours?'

'Mine!' he returned, taking out his spectacles and putting them on, to have a better view of the triumphs so dear to his heart. '*I* couldn't write like that, nowadays. No. They 're all done by one hand; a little hand it is, not so old as yours, but a very clever one.'

As the schoolmaster said this, he saw that a small blot of ink had been thrown on one of the copies, so he took a penknife from his pocket, and going up to the wall, carefully scraped it out. When he had finished, he walked slowly backward from the writing, admiring it as one might contemplate a beautiful picture, but with something of sadness in his voice and manner which quite touched the child, though she was unacquainted with its cause.

'A little hand indeed,' said the poor schoolmaster. 'Far beyond all his companions, in his learning and his sports too, how did he ever come to be so fond of me! That I should love him is no wonder, but that he should love me—' and there the schoolmaster stopped, and took off his spectacles to wipe them, as though they had grown dim.

'I hope there is nothing the matter, sir,' said Nell anxiously.

'Not much, my dear,' returned the schoolmaster. 'I hoped to have seen him on the green to-night. He was always foremost among them. But he 'll be here to-morrow.'

'Has he been ill?' asked the child, with a child's quick sympathy.

'Not very. They said he was wandering in his head yesterday, dear boy, and so they said the day before. But that 's a part of that kind of disorder; it 's not a bad sign—not at all a bad sign.'

The child was silent. He walked to the door, and looked wistfully out. The shadows of night were gathering, and all was still.

'If he could lean upon anybody's arm, he would come to me, I know,' he said, returning into the room. 'He always came into the garden to say good-night. But perhaps his illness has only just taken a favourable turn, and it 's too late for him to come out, for it 's very damp and there 's a heavy dew. It 's much better he shouldn't come to-night.'

The schoolmaster lighted a candle, fastened the window-shutter, and closed the door. But after he had done this, and sat silent a little time, he took down his hat, and said he would go and satisfy himself, if Nell would sit up till he returned. The child readily complied, and he went out.

She sat there half an hour or more, feeling the place very strange and lonely, for she had prevailed upon the old man to go to bed, and there was nothing to be heard but the ticking of an old clock, and the whistling of the wind among the trees. When he returned, he took his seat in the chimney corner, but remained silent for a long time. At length he turned to her, and speaking very gently, hoped she would say a prayer that night for a sick child.

'My favourite scholar!' said the poor schoolmaster, smoking a pipe he had forgotten to light, and looking mournfully round upon the walls. 'It is a little hand to have done all that, and waste away with sickness. It is a very, very little hand!'

CHAPTER XXV

After a sound night's rest in a chamber in the thatched roof, in which it seemed the sexton had for some years been a lodger, but which he had lately deserted for a wife and a cottage of his own, the child rose early in the morning and descended to the room where she had supped last night. As the schoolmaster had already left his bed and gone out, she bestirred herself to make it neat and comfortable, and had just finished its arrangement when the kind host returned.

He thanked her many times, and said that the old dame who usually did such offices for him had gone to nurse the little scholar he had told her of. The child asked how he was, and hoped he was better.

'No,' rejoined the schoolmaster shaking his head

sorrowfully, 'no better. They even say he is worse.'

'I am very sorry for that, sir,' said the child.

The poor schoolmaster appeared to be gratified by her earnest manner, but yet rendered more uneasy by it, for he added hastily that anxious people often magnified an evil and thought it greater than it was; 'for my part,' he said, in his quiet, patient way, 'I hope it 's not so. I don't think he can be worse.'

The child asked his leave to prepare breakfast, and her grandfather coming downstairs, they all three partook of it together. While the meal was in progress, their host remarked that the old man seemed much fatigued, and evidently stood in need of rest.

'If the journey you have before you is a long one,' he said, 'and don't press you for one day, you 're very welcome to pass another night here. I should really be glad if you would, friend.'

He saw that the old man looked at Nell, uncertain whether to accept or decline his offer; and added—

'I shall be glad to have your young companion with me for one day. If you can do a charity to a lone man, and rest yourself at the same time, do so. If you must proceed upon your journey, I wish you well through it, and will walk a little way with you before school begins.'

'What are we to do, Nell?' said the old man irresolutely, 'say what we 're to do.'

It required no great persuasion to induce the child to answer that they had better accept the invitation and remain. She was happy to show her gratitude to the kind schoolmaster by busying herself in the performance of such household duties as his little cottage stood in need of. When these were done, she took some needlework from her basket, and sat herself down upon a stool beside the lattice, where the honeysuckle and woodbine entwined their tender stems, and stealing into the room filled it with their delicious breath. Her grandfather was basking in the sun outside, breathing the perfume of the flowers, and idly watching the clouds as they floated on before the light summer wind.

As the schoolmaster, after arranging the two forms in due order, took his seat behind his desk and made other preparations for school, the child was apprehensive that she might be in the way, and offered to withdraw to her little bedroom. But this he would not allow, and as he seemed pleased to have her there, she remained, busying herself with her work.

'Have you many scholars, sir?'

The poor schoolmaster shook his head, and said that they barely filled the two forms.

'Are the others clever, sir?' asked the child, glancing at the trophies on the wall.

'Good boys,' returned the schoolmaster, 'good boys enough, my dear, but they 'll never do like that.'

A small white-headed boy with a sunburnt face appeared at the door while he was speaking, and stopping there to make a rustic bow, came in and took his seat upon one of the forms. The white-headed boy then put an open book, astonishingly dog's-eared upon his knees, and thrusting his hands into his pockets began counting the marbles with which they were filled; displaying in the expression of his face a remarkable capacity of totally abstracting his mind from the spelling on which his eyes were fixed. Soon afterwards another white-headed little boy came straggling in, and after him a red-headed lad, and after him two more with white heads, and then one with a flaxen poll, and so on until the forms were occupied by a dozen boys or thereabouts, with heads of every colour but grey, and ranging in their ages from four years old to fourteen years or more; for the legs of the youngest were a long way from the floor when he sat upon the form, and the eldest was a heavy good-tempered foolish fellow, about half a head taller than the schoolmaster.

At the top of the first form—the post of honour in the school—was the vacant place of the little sick scholar, and at the head of the row of pegs on which those who came in hats or caps were wont to hang them up, one was left empty. No boy attempted to violate the sanctity of seat or peg, but many a one looked from the empty spaces to the schoolmaster, and whispered his idle neighbour behind his hand.

Then began the hum of conning over lessons and getting them by heart, the whispered jest and stealthy game, and all the noise and drawl of school; and in the midst of the din sat the poor schoolmaster, the very image of meekness and simplicity, vainly attempting to fix his mind upon the duties of the day, and to forget his little friend. But the tedium of his office reminded him more strongly of the willing scholar, and his thoughts were rambling from his pupils—it was plain.

None knew this better than the idlest boys, who, growing bolder with impunity, waxed louder and more daring; playing odd-or-even under the master's eye, eating apples openly and without rebuke, pinching each other in sport or malice without the least reserve, and cutting their autographs in the very legs of his desk. The puzzled dunce, who stood beside it to say his lesson out of book, looked no longer at the ceiling for forgotten words, but drew closer to the master's elbow and boldly cast his eye upon the page; the wag of the little troop squinted and made grimaces (at the smallest boy of course), holding no book before his face, and his approving audience knew no constraint in their delight. If the master did chance to rouse himself and seem alive to what was going on, the noise subsided for a moment and no eyes met his but wore a studious and a deeply humble look; but the instant he relapsed again, it broke out afresh, and ten times louder than before.

Oh! how some of those idle fellows longed to be outside, and how they looked at the open door and window, as if they half meditated rushing violently out, plunging into the woods, and being wild boys and savages from that time forth. What rebellious thoughts of the cool river, and some shady bathing-place beneath willow-trees with branches dipping in the water, kept tempting and urging that sturdy boy, who, with his shirt-collar unbuttoned and flung back as far as it could go, sat fanning his flushed face with a spelling-book, wishing himself a whale, or a tittle-bat, or a fly, or anything but a boy at school on that hot, broiling day! Heat! ask that other boy, whose seat being nearest to the door gave him opportunities of gliding out into the garden and driving his companions to madness by dipping his face into the bucket of the well and then rolling on the grass—ask him if there were ever such a day as that, when even the bees were diving deep down into the cups of flowers and stopping there, as if they had made up their minds to retire from business and be manufacturers of honey no more. The day was made for laziness, and lying on one's back in green places, and staring at the sky till its brightness forced one to shut one's eyes and go to sleep; and was this a time to be poring over musty books in a dark room, slighted by the very sun itself? Monstrous!

Nell sat by the window occupied with her work, but attentive still to all that passed, though sometimes rather timid of the boisterous boys. The lessons over, writing time began; and there being but one desk and that the master's, each boy sat at it in turn and laboured at his crooked copy, while the master walked about. This was a quieter time; for he would come and look over the writer's shoulder, and tell him mildly to observe how such a letter was turned in such a copy on the wall, praise such an up-stroke here and such a down-stroke there, and bid him take it for his model. Then he would stop and tell them what the sick child had said last night, and how he had longed to be among them once again; and such was the poor schoolmaster's gentle and affectionate manner, that the boys seemed quite remorseful that they had worried him so much, and were absolutely quiet; eating no apples, cutting no names, inflicting no pinches, and making no grimaces, for full two minutes afterwards.

'I think, boys,' said the schoolmaster when the clock struck twelve, 'that I shall give an extra half-holiday this afternoon.'

At this intelligence, the boys, led on and headed by the tall boy, raised a great shout, in the midst of which the master was seen to speak, but could not be heard. As he held up his hand, however, in token of his wish that they should be silent, they were considerate enough to leave off, as soon as the longest-winded among them were quite out of breath.

'You must promise me first,' said the schoolmaster, 'that you 'll not be noisy, or at least, if you are, that you 'll go away and be so—away out of the village I mean. I 'm sure you wouldn't disturb your old playmate and companion.'

There was a general murmur (and perhaps a very sincere one, for they were but boys) in the negative; and the tall boy, perhaps as sincerely as any of them, called those about him to witness that he had only shouted in a whisper.

'Then pray don't forget, there 's my dear scholars,'

said the schoolmaster, 'what I have asked you, and do it as a favour to me. Be as happy as you can, and don't be unmindful that you are blessed with health. Good-bye all!'

'Thank 'ee, sir,' and 'good-bye, sir,' were said a good many times in a variety of voices, and the boys went out very slowly and softly. But there was the sun shining and there were the birds singing as the sun only shines and the birds only sing on holidays and half-holidays; there were the trees waving to all free boys to climb and nestle among their leafy branches; the hay, entreating them to come and scatter it to the pure air; the green corn, gently beckoning towards wood and stream; the smooth ground, rendered smoother still by blending lights and shadows, inviting to runs and leaps, and long walks God knows whither. It was more than boy could bear, and with a joyous whoop the whole cluster took to their heels and spread themselves about, shouting and laughing as they went.

'It 's natural, thank Heaven!' said the poor schoolmaster looking after them. 'I 'm very glad they didn't mind me!'

It is difficult, however, to please everybody, as most of us would have discovered, even without the fable which bears that moral; and in the course of the afternoon several mothers and aunts of pupils looked in to express their entire disapproval of the schoolmaster's proceeding. A few confined themselves to hints, such as politely inquiring what red-letter day or saint's day the almanack said it was; a few (these were the profound village politicians) argued that it was a slight to the throne and an affront to church and state, and savoured of revolutionary principles, to grant a half-holiday upon any lighter occasion than the birthday of the Monarch; but the majority expressed their displeasure on private grounds and in plain terms, arguing that to put the pupils on this short allowance of learning was nothing but an act of downright robbery and fraud: and one old lady, finding that she could not inflame or irritate the peaceable schoolmaster by talking to him, bounced out of his house and talked at him for half an hour outside his own window, to another old lady, saying that of course he would deduct this half-holiday from his weekly charge, or of course he would naturally expect to have an opposition started against him; there was no want of idle chaps in that neighbourhood (here the old lady raised her voice), and some chaps who were too idle even to be schoolmasters, might soon find that there were other chaps put over their heads, and so she would have them take care, and look pretty sharp about them. But all these taunts and vexations failed to elicit one word from the meek schoolmaster, who sat with the child by his side,—a little more dejected perhaps, but quite silent and uncomplaining.

Towards night an old woman came tottering up the garden as speedily as she could, and meeting the schoolmaster at the door, said he was to go to Dame West's directly, and had best run on before her. He and the child were on the point of going out together for a walk, and without relinquishing her hand, the schoolmaster hurried away, leaving the messenger to follow as she might.

They stopped at a cottage-door, and the schoolmaster knocked softly at it with his hand. It was opened without loss of time. They entered a room where a little group of women were gathered about one, older than the rest, who was crying very bitterly, and sat wringing her hands and rocking herself to and fro.

'Oh dame!' said the schoolmaster, drawing near her chair, 'is it so bad as this?'

'He 's going fast,' cried the old woman; 'my grandson 's dying. It 's all along of you. You shouldn't see him now, but for his being so earnest on it. This is what his learning has brought him to. Oh dear, dear, dear, what can I do?'

'Do not say that I am in any fault,' urged the gentle schoolmaster. 'I am not hurt, dame. No, no. You are in great distress of mind, and don't mean what you say. I am sure you don't.'

'I do,' returned the old woman. 'I mean it all. If he hadn't been poring over his books out of fear of you, he would have been well and merry now, I know he would.'

The schoolmaster looked round upon the other women as if to entreat some one among them to say a kind word for him, but they shook their heads, and murmured to each other that they never thought there was much good in learning, and that this convinced them. Without saying a word in reply, or giving them a look of reproach, he followed the old woman who had summoned him (and who had now rejoined them) into another room, where his infant friend, half-dressed, lay stretched upon a bed.

He was a very young boy; quite a little child. His hair still hung in curls about his face, and his eyes were very bright; but their light was of Heaven, not earth. The schoolmaster took a seat beside him, and stooping over the pillow, whispered his name. The boy sprung up, stroked his face with his hand, and threw his wasted arms round his neck, crying out that he was his dear friend.

'I hope I always was. I meant to be, God knows,' said the poor schoolmaster.

'Who is that?' said the boy, seeing Nell. 'I am afraid to kiss her lest I should make her ill. Ask her to shake hands with me.'

The sobbing child came closer up, and took the little languid hand in hers. Releasing his again after a time, the sick boy laid him gently down.

'You remember the garden, Harry,' whispered the schoolmaster, anxious to rouse him, for a dulness seemed gathering upon the child, 'and how pleasant it used to be in the evening time? You must make haste to visit it again, for I think the very flowers have missed you, and are less gay than they used to be. You will come soon, my dear, very soon now,—won't you?'

The boy smiled faintly—so very, very faintly—and put his hand upon his friend's grey head. He moved his lips too, but no voice came from them; no, not a sound.

In the silence that ensued, the hum of distant voices borne upon the evening air came floating through the open window. 'What's that?' said the sick child, opening his eyes.

'The boys at play upon the green.'

He took a handkerchief from his pillow, and tried to wave it above his head. But the feeble arm dropped powerless down.

'Shall I do it?' said the schoolmaster.

'Please wave it at the window,' was the faint reply. 'Tie it to the lattice. Some of them may see it there. Perhaps they'll think of me and look this way.'

He raised his head, and glanced from the fluttering signal to his idle bat, that lay with slate and book and other boyish property upon a table in the room. And then he laid him softly down once more, and asked if the little girl were there, for he could not see her.

She stepped forward, and pressed the passive hand that lay upon the coverlet. The two old friends and companions—for such they were, though they were man and child—held each other in a long embrace, and then the little scholar turned his face towards the wall, and fell asleep.

The poor schoolmaster sat in the same place, holding the small cold hand in his, and chafing it. It was but the hand of a dead child. He felt that; and yet he chafed it still, and could not lay it down.

CHAPTER XXVI

ALMOST broken-hearted, Nell withdrew with the schoolmaster from the bedside and returned to his cottage. In the midst of her grief and tears she was yet careful to conceal their real cause from the old man, for the dead boy had been a grandchild, and left but one aged relative to mourn his premature decay.

She stole away to bed as quickly as she could, and when she was alone, gave free vent to the sorrow with which her breast was overcharged. But the sad scene she had witnessed, was not without its lesson of content and gratitude; of content with the lot which left her health and freedom; and gratitude that she was spared to the one relative and friend she loved, and to live and move in a beautiful world, when so many young creatures—as young and full of hope as she—were stricken down and gathered to their graves. How many of the mounds in that old churchyard where she had lately strayed, grew green above the graves of children! And though she thought as a child herself, and did not perhaps sufficiently consider to what a bright and happy existence those who die young are borne, and how in death they lose the pain of seeing others die around them, bearing to the tomb some strong affection of their hearts (which makes the old die many times in one long life), still she thought wisely enough, to draw a plain and easy moral from what she had seen that night, and to store it, deep in her mind.

Her dreams were of the little scholar: not coffined and covered up, but mingling with angels, and smiling happily. The sun darting his cheerful rays into the room, awoke her; and now there remained but to take leave of the poor schoolmaster and wander forth once more.

By the time they were ready to depart, school had begun. In the darkened room, the din of yesterday was going on again: a little sobered and softened down, perhaps, but only a very little, if at all. The schoolmaster rose from his desk and walked with them to the gate.

It was with a trembling and reluctant hand, that the child held out to him the money which the lady had given her at the races for her flowers: faltering in her thanks as she thought how small the sum was, and blushing as she offered it. But he bade her put it up, and stooping to kiss her cheek, turned back into his house.

They had not gone half a dozen paces when he was at the door again; the old man retraced his steps to shake hands, and the child did the same.

'Good fortune and happiness go with you!' said the poor schoolmaster. 'I am quite a solitary man now. If you ever pass this way again, you 'll not forget the little village-school.'

'We shall never forget it, sir,' rejoined Nell; 'nor ever forget to be grateful to you for your kindness to us.'

'I have heard such words from the lips of children very often,' said the schoolmaster, shaking his head, and smiling thoughtfully, 'but they were soon forgotten. I had attached one young friend to me, the better friend for being young—but that 's over—God bless you!'

They bade him farewell very many times, and turned away, walking slowly and often looking back, until they could see him no more. At length they had left the village far behind, and even lost sight of the smoke among the trees. They trudged onward now, at a quicker pace, resolving to keep the main road, and go wherever it might lead them.

But main roads stretch a long, long way. With the exception of two or three inconsiderable clusters of cottages which they passed, without stopping, and one lonely roadside public-house where they had some bread and cheese, this highway had led them to nothing—late in the afternoon—and still lengthened out, far in the distance, the same dull, tedious, winding course, that they had been pursuing all day. As they had no resource, however, but to go forward, they still kept on, though at a much slower pace, being very weary and fatigued.

The afternoon had worn away into a beautiful evening, when they arrived at a point where the road made a sharp turn and struck across a common. On the border of this common, and close to the hedge which divided it from the cultivated fields, a caravan was drawn up to rest; upon which, by reason of its situation, they came so suddenly that they could not have avoided it if they would.

It was not a shabby, dingy, dusty cart, but a smart little house upon wheels, with white dimity curtains festooning the windows, and window-shutters of green picked out with panels of a staring red, in which happily-contrasted colours the whole concern shone brilliant. Neither was it a poor caravan drawn by a single donkey or emaciated horse, for a pair of horses in pretty good condition were released from the shafts and grazing on the frouzy grass. Neither was it a gipsy caravan, for at the open door (graced with a bright brass knocker) sat a Christian lady, stout and comfortable to look upon, who wore a large bonnet trembling with bows. And that it was not an unprovided or destitute caravan was clear from this lady's occupation, which was the very pleasant and refreshing one of taking tea. The tea-things, including a bottle of rather suspicious character and a cold knuckle of ham, were set forth upon a drum, covered with a white napkin; and there, as if at the most convenient round-table in all the world, sat this roving lady, taking her tea and enjoying the prospect.

It happened that at that moment the lady of the caravan had her cup (which, that everything about her might be of a stout and comfortable kind, was a breakfast cup) to her lips, and that having her eyes lifted to the sky in her enjoyment of the full flavour of the tea, not unmingled possibly with just the slightest dash or gleam of something out of the suspicious bottle—but this is mere speculation and not distinct matter of history—it happened that being thus agreeably engaged, she did not see the travellers when they first came up. It was not until she was in the act of setting down the cup, and drawing a long breath after the exertion of causing its contents to disappear, that the lady of the caravan beheld an old man and a young child walking slowly by, and glancing at her proceedings with eyes of modest but hungry admiration.

'Hey!' cried the lady of the caravan, scooping the crumbs out of her lap and swallowing the same before wiping her lips. 'Yes, to be sure—Who won the Helter-Skelter Plate, child?'

'Won what, ma'am?' asked Nell.

'The Helter-Skelter Plate at the races, child—the plate that was run for on the second day.'

'On the second day, ma'am?'

'Second day! Yes, second day,' repeated the lady with an air of impatience. 'Can't you say who won the Helter-Skelter Plate when you 're asked the question civilly?'

'I don't know, ma'am.'

'Don't know!' repeated the lady of the caravan; 'why, you were there. I saw you with my own eyes.'

Nell was not a little alarmed to hear this, supposing that the lady might be intimately acquainted with the firm of Short and Codlin; but what followed tended to reassure her.

'And very sorry I was,' said the lady of the caravan, 'to see you in company with a Punch; a low, practical, wulger wretch, that people should scorn to look at.'

'I was not there by choice,' returned the child; 'we didn't know our way, and the two men were very kind to us, and let us travel with them. Do you—do you know them, ma'am?'

'Know 'em, child!' cried the lady of the caravan in a sort of shriek. 'Know *them*! But you' re young and inexperienced, and that 's your excuse for asking sich a question. Do I look as if I know'd 'em, does the caravan look as if *it* know'd 'em?'

'No, ma'am, no,' said the child, fearing she had committed some grievous fault. 'I beg your pardon.'

It was granted immediately, though the lady still appeared much ruffled and discomposed by the degrading supposition. The child then explained that they had left the races on the first day, and were travelling to the next town on that road, where they purposed to spend the night. As the countenance of the stout lady began to clear up, she ventured to inquire how far it was. The reply—which the stout lady did not come to, until she had thoroughly explained that she went to the races on the first day in a gig, and as an expedition of pleasure, and that her presence there had no connection with any matters of business or profit—was, that the town was eight miles off.

This discouraging information a little dashed the child, who could scarcely repress a tear as she glanced along the darkening road. Her grandfather made no complaint, but he sighed heavily as he leaned upon his staff, and vainly tried to pierce the dusty distance.

The lady of the caravan was in the act of gathering her tea equipage together preparatory to clearing the table, but noting the child's anxious manner she hesitated and stopped. The child curtsied, thanked her for her information, and giving her hand to the old man had already got some fifty yards or so, away, when the lady of the caravan called her to return.

'Come nearer, nearer still'—said she, beckoning to her to ascend the steps. 'Are you hungry, child?'

'Not very, but we are tired, and it 's—it *is* a long way—'

'Well, hungry or not, you had better have some tea,' rejoined her new acquaintance. 'I suppose you are agreeable to that, old gentleman?'

The grandfather humbly pulled off his hat and thanked her. The lady of the caravan then bade him come up the steps likewise, but the drum proving an inconvenient table for two, they descended again, and sat upon the grass, where she handed down to them the tea-tray, the bread and butter, the knuckle of ham, and in short everything of which she had partaken herself, except the bottle which she had already embraced an opportunity of slipping into her pocket.

'Set 'em out near the hind-wheels, child, that 's the best place'—said their friend, superintending the arrangements from above. 'Now hand up the tea-pot for a little more hot water, and a pinch of fresh tea, and then both of you eat and drink as much as you can, and don't spare anything; that 's all I ask of you.'

They might perhaps have carried out the lady's wish, if it had been less freely expressed, or even if it had not been expressed at all. But as this direction relieved them from any shadow of delicacy or uneasiness, they made a hearty meal and enjoyed it to the utmost.

While they were thus engaged, the lady of the caravan alighted on the earth, and with her hands clasped behind her, and her large bonnet trembling excessively, walked up and down in a measured tread and very stately manner, surveying the caravan from time to time with an air of calm delight, and deriving particular gratification from the red panels and the brass knocker. When she had taken this gentle exercise for some time, she sat down upon the steps and called 'George'; whereupon a man in a carter's frock, who had been so shrouded in a hedge up to this time as to see everything that passed without being seen himself, parted the twigs that concealed him, and appeared in a sitting attitude, supporting on his legs a baking-dish and a half-gallon stone bottle, and bearing in his right-hand a knife, and in his left a fork.

'Yes, missus'—said George.

'How did you find the cold pie, George?'

'It warn't amiss, mum.'

'And the beer,' said the lady of the caravan, with an appearance of being more interested in this question than the last; 'is it passable, George?'

'It 's more flatterer than it might be,' George returned, 'but it ain't so bad for all that.'

To set the mind of his mistress at rest, he took a sip (amounting in quantity to a pint or thereabouts) from the stone bottle, and then smacked his lips, winked his eye, and nodded his head. No doubt with the same amiable desire, he immediately resumed his knife and fork, as a practical assurance that the beer had wrought no bad effect upon his appetite.

The lady of the caravan looked on approvingly for some time, and then said—

'Have you nearly finished?'

'Wery nigh, mum.' And indeed, after scraping the dish all round with his knife and carrying the choice brown morsels to his mouth, and after taking such a scientific pull at the stone bottle that, by degrees almost imperceptible to the sight, his head went further and further back until he lay nearly at his full length upon the ground, this gentleman declared himself quite disengaged, and came forth from his retreat.

'I hope I haven't hurried you, George,' said his mistress, who appeared to have a great sympathy with his late pursuit.

'If you have,' returned the follower, wisely reserving himself for any favourable contingency that might occur, 'we must make up for it next time, that 's all.'

'We are not a heavy load, George?'

'That 's always what the ladies say,' replied the man, looking a long way round, as if he were appealing to Nature in general against such monstrous propositions. 'If you see a woman a driving, you 'll always perceive that she never will keep her whip still; the horse can't go fast enough for her. If cattle have got their proper load, you never can persuade a woman that they 'll not bear something more. What is the cause of this here?'

'Would these two travellers make much difference to the horses, if we took them with us?' asked his mistress, offering no reply to the philosophical inquiry, and pointing to Nell and the old man, who were painfully preparing to resume their journey on foot.

'They 'd make a difference in course,' said George doggedly.

'Would they make much difference?' repeated his mistress. 'They can't be very heavy.'

'The weight o' the pair, mum,' said George, eyeing them with the look of a man who was calculating within half an ounce or so, 'would be a trifle under that of Oliver Cromwell.'

Nell was very much surprised that the man should be so accurately acquainted with the weight of one whom she had read of in books as having lived considerably before their time, but speedily forgot the subject in the joy of hearing that they were to go forward in the caravan, for which she thanked its lady with unaffected earnestness. She helped with great readiness and alacrity to put away the tea-things and other matters that were lying about, and, the horses being by that time harnessed, mounted into the vehicle, followed by her delighted grandfather. Their patroness then shut the door and sat herself down by her drum at an open window; and, the steps being struck by George and stowed under the carriage, away they went, with a great noise of flapping and creaking and straining, and the bright brass knocker, which nobody ever knocked at, knocking one perpetual double-knock of its own accord as they jolted heavily along.

CHAPTER XXVII

WHEN they had travelled slowly forward for some short distance, Nell ventured to steal a look round the caravan and observe it more closely. One half of it—that moiety in which the comfortable proprietress was then seated—was carpeted, and so partitioned off at the further end as to accommodate a sleeping-place, constructed after the fashion of a berth on board ship, which was shaded, like the little windows, with fair white curtains, and looked comfortable enough, though by what kind of gymnastic exercise the lady of the caravan ever contrived to get into it, was an unfathomable mystery. The other half served for a kitchen, and was fitted up with a stove whose small chimney passed through the roof. It held also a closet or larder, several chests, a great pitcher of water, and a few cooking-utensils and articles of crockery. These latter necessaries hung upon the walls, which, in that portion of the establishment devoted to the lady of the caravan, were ornamented with such gayer and lighter decorations as a triangle and a couple of well-thumbed tambourines.

The lady of the caravan sat at one window in all the pride and poetry of the musical instruments, and little Nell and her grandfather sat at the other in all the humility of the kettle and saucepans, while the machine jogged on and shifted the darkening prospect very slowly. At first the two travellers spoke little, and only in whispers, but as they grew more familiar with the place they ventured to converse with greater freedom, and talked about the country through which they were passing, and the different objects that presented themselves, until the old man fell asleep; which the lady of the caravan observing invited Nell to come and sit beside her.

'Well, child,' she said, 'how do you like this way of travelling?'

Nell replied that she thought it was very pleasant indeed, to which the lady assented in the case of people who had their spirits. For herself, she said, she was troubled with a lowness in that respect which required a constant stimulant; though whether the aforesaid stimulant was derived from the suspicious bottle of which mention has been already made or from other sources, she did not say.

'That 's the happiness of you young people,' she continued. 'You don't know what it is to be low in your feelings. You always have your appetites too, and what a comfort that is.'

Nell thought that she could sometimes dispense with her own appetite very conveniently; and thought, moreover, that there was nothing either in the lady's personal appearance or in her manner of taking tea, to lead to the conclusion that her natural relish for meat and drink had at all failed her. She silently assented, however, as in duty bound, to what the lady had said, and waited until she should speak again.

Instead of speaking, however, she sat looking at the child for a long time in silence, and then getting up, brought out from a corner a large roll of canvas about a yard in width, which she laid upon the floor and spread open with her foot until it nearly reached from one end of the caravan to the other.

'There, child,' she said, 'read that.'

Nell walked down it, and read aloud, in enormous black letters, the inscription, 'JARLEY'S WAX-WORK.'

'Read it again,' said the lady, complacently.

'Jarley's Wax-Work,' repeated Nell.

'That 's me,' said the lady. 'I am Mrs. Jarley.'

Giving the child an encouraging look, intended to reassure her and let her know, that, although she stood in the presence of the original Jarley, she must not allow herself to be utterly overwhelmed and borne down, the lady of the caravan unfolded another scroll, whereon was the inscription, 'One hundred figures the full size of life,' and then another scroll, on which was written, 'The only stupendous collection of real wax-work in the world,' and then several smaller scrolls with such inscriptions as 'Now exhibiting within'—'The genuine and only Jarley'—'Jarley's unrivalled collection'—'Jarley is the delight of the Nobility and Gentry'—'The Royal Family are the patrons of Jarley.' When she had exhibited these leviathans of public announcement to the astonished child, she brought forth specimens of the lesser fry in the shape of handbills, some of which were couched in the form of parodies on popular melodies, as 'Believe me if all Jarley's wax-work so rare'—'I saw thy show in youthful prime'—'Over the water to Jarley'; while, to consult all tastes, others were composed with a view to the lighter and more facetious spirits, as a parody on the favourite air of 'If I had a donkey,' beginning

> 'If I know'd a donkey wot wouldn't go
> To see Mrs. Jarley's wax-work show,
> Do you think I 'd acknowledge him?
> Oh no no!
> Then run to Jarley's—'

—besides several compositions in prose, purporting to be dialogues between the Emperor of China and an oyster, or the Archbishop of Canterbury and a dissenter on the subject of church-rates, but all having the same moral, namely, that the reader must make haste to Jarley's, and that children and servants were admitted at half-price. When she had brought all these testimonials of her important position in society to bear upon her young companion, Mrs. Jarley rolled them up, and having put them carefully away, sat down again, and looked at the child in triumph.

'Never go into the company of a filthy Punch any more,' said Mrs. Jarley, 'after this.'

'I never saw any wax-work, ma'am,' said Nell. 'Is it funnier than Punch?'

'Funnier!' said Mrs. Jarley in a shrill voice. 'It is not funny at all.'

'Oh!' said Nell, with all possible humility.

'It isn't funny at all,' repeated Mrs. Jarley. 'It 's calm and—what 's that word again—critical?—no—classical, that 's it—it 's calm and classical. No low beatings and knockings about, no jokings and squeakings like your precious Punches, but always the same, with a constantly unchanging air of coldness and gentility; and so like life, that if wax-work only spoke and walked about, you 'd hardly know the difference. I won't go so far as to say, that, as it is, I 've seen wax-work quite like life, but I 've certainly seen some life that was exactly like wax-work.'

'Is it here, ma'am?' asked Nell, whose curiosity was awakened by this description.

'Is what here, child?'

'The wax-work, ma'am.'

'Why, bless you, child, what are you thinking of? How could such a collection be here, where you see everything except the inside of one little cupboard and a few boxes? It 's gone on in the other wans to the assembly-rooms, and there it 'll be exhibited the day after to-morrow. You are going to the same town, and you 'll see it I dare say. It 's natural to expect that you 'll see it, and I 've no doubt you will. I suppose you couldn't stop away if you was to try ever so much.'

'I shall not be in the town, I think, ma'am,' said the child.

'Not there?' cried Mrs. Jarley. 'Then where will you be?'

'I—I—don't quite know. I am not certain.'

'You don't mean to say that you 're travelling about the country without knowing where you 're going to?' said the lady of the caravan. 'What curious people you are! What line are you in? You looked to me at the races, child, as if you were quite out of your element, and had got there by accident.'

'We were there quite by accident,' returned Nell, confused by this abrupt questioning. 'We are poor people, ma'am, and are only wandering about. We have nothing to do;—I wish we had.'

'You amaze me more and more,' said Mrs. Jarley, after remaining for some time as mute as one of her own figures. 'Why, what do you call yourselves? Not beggars?'

'Indeed, ma'am, I don't know what else we are,' returned the child.

'Lord bless me,' said the lady of the caravan. 'I never heard of such a thing. Who 'd have thought it!'

She remained so long silent after this exclamation, that Nell feared she felt her having been induced to bestow her protection and conversation upon one so poor, to be an outrage upon her dignity that nothing could repair. This persuasion was rather confirmed than otherwise by the tone in which she at length broke silence and said—

'And yet you can read. And write too, I shouldn't wonder?'

'Yes, ma'am,' said the child, fearful of giving new offence by the confession.

'Well, and what a thing that is,' returned Mrs. Jarley. 'I can't!'

Nell said 'indeed' in a tone which might imply, either that she was reasonably surprised to find the genuine and only Jarley, who was the delight of the Nobility and Gentry and the peculiar pet of the Royal Family, destitute of these familiar arts; or that she presumed so great a lady could scarcely stand in need of such ordinary accomplishments. In whatever way Mrs. Jarley received the response, it did not provoke her to further questioning, or tempt her into any more remarks at the time, for she relapsed into a thoughtful silence, and remained in that state so long that Nell withdrew to the other window and rejoined her grandfather, who was now awake.

At length the lady of the caravan shook off her fit of meditation, and, summoning the driver to come under the window at which she was seated, held a long conversation with him in a low tone of voice, as if she were asking his advice on an important point, and discussing the pros and cons of some very weighty matter. This conference at length concluded, she drew in her head again, and beckoned Nell to approach.

'And the old gentleman too,' said Mrs. Jarley; 'for I want to have a word with him. Do you want a good situation for your grand-daughter, master? If you do, I can put her in the way of getting one. What do you say?'

'I can't leave her,' answered the old man. 'We can't separate. What would become of me without her?'

'I should have thought you were old enough to take

care of yourself, if you ever will be,' retorted Mrs. Jarley sharply.

'But he never will be,' said the child in an earnest whisper. 'I fear he never will be again. Pray do not speak harshly to him. We are very thankful to you,' she added aloud; 'but neither of us could part from the other if all the wealth of the world were halved between us.'

Mrs. Jarley was a little disconcerted by this reception of her proposal, and looked at the old man, who tenderly took Nell's hand and detained it in his own, as if she could have very well dispensed with his company or even his earthly existence. After an awkward pause, she thrust her head out of the window again, and had another conference with the driver upon some point on which they did not seem to agree quite so readily as on their former topic of discussion; but they concluded at last, and she addressed the grandfather again.

'If you 're really disposed to employ yourself,' said Mrs. Jarley, 'there would be plenty for you to do in the way of helping to dust the figures, and take the checks, and so forth. What I want your granddaughter for, is to point 'em out to the company; they would be soon learnt, and she has a way with her that people wouldn't think unpleasant, though she *does* come after me; for I 've been always accustomed to go round with visitors myself, which I should keep on doing now, only that my spirits make a little ease absolutely necessary. It 's not a common offer, bear in mind,' said the lady, rising into the tone and manner in which she was accustomed to address her audiences; 'it 's Jarley's wax-work, remember. The duty 's very light and genteel, the company particularly select, the exhibition takes place in assembly-rooms, town-halls, large rooms at inns, or auction galleries. There is none of your open-air wagrancy at Jarley's, recollect; there is no tarpaulin and sawdust at Jarley's, remember. Every expectation held out in the handbills is realised to the utmost, and the whole forms an effect of imposing brilliancy hitherto unrivalled in this kingdom. Remember that the price of admission is only sixpence, and that this is an opportunity which may never occur again!'

Descending from the sublime when she had reached this point, to the details of common life, Mrs. Jarley remarked that with reference to salary she could pledge herself to no specific sum until she had sufficiently tested Nell's abilities, and narrowly watched her in the performance of her duties. But board and lodging, both for her and her grandfather, she bound herself to provide, and she furthermore passed her word that the board should always be good in quality, and in quantity plentiful.

Nell and her grandfather consulted together, and while they were so engaged, Mrs. Jarley with her hands behind her walked up and down the caravan, as she had walked after tea on the dull earth, with uncommon dignity and self-esteem. Nor will this appear so slight a circumstance as to be unworthy of mention, when it is remembered that the caravan was in uneasy motion all the time, and that none but a person of great natural stateliness and acquired grace could have forborne to stagger.

'Now, child?' cried Mrs. Jarley, coming to a halt as Nell turned towards her.

'We are very much obliged to you, ma'am,' said Nell, 'and thankfully accept your offer.'

'And you 'll never be sorry for it,' returned Mrs. Jarley. 'I'm pretty sure of that. So as that 's all settled, let us have a bit of supper.'

In the meanwhile, the caravan blundered on as if

it too had been drinking strong beer and was drowsy, and came at last upon the paved streets of a town which were clear of passengers, and quiet, for it was by this time near midnight, and the townspeople were all abed. As it was too late an hour to repair to the exhibition-room, they turned aside into a piece of waste ground that lay just within the old town-gate, and drew up there for the night, near to another caravan, which notwithstanding that it bore on the lawful panel the great name of Jarley, and was employed besides in conveying from place to place the waxwork which was its country's pride, was designated by a grovelling stamp-office as a 'Common Stage Waggon,' and numbered too—seven thousand odd hundred—as though its precious freight were mere flour or coals!

This ill-used machine being empty (for it had deposited its burden at the place of exhibition, and lingered here until its services were again required) was assigned to the old man as his sleeping-place for the night; and within its wooden walls, Nell made him up the best bed she could, from the materials at hand. For herself, she was to sleep in Mrs. Jarley's own travelling-carriage, as a signal mark of that lady's favour and confidence.

She had taken leave of her grandfather and was returning to the other waggon, when she was tempted by the pleasant coolness of the night to linger for a little while in the air. The moon was shining down upon the old gateway of the town, leaving the low archway very black and dark; and with a mingled sensation of curiosity and fear, she slowly approached the gate, and stood still to look up at it, wondering to see how dark, and grim, and old, and cold, it looked.

There was an empty niche from which some old statue had fallen or been carried away hundreds of years ago, and she was thinking what strange people it must have looked down upon when it stood there, and how many hard struggles might have taken place, and how many murders might have been done, upon that silent spot, when there suddenly emerged from the black shade of the arch, a man. The instant he appeared, she recognised him—Who could have failed to recognise, in that instant, the ugly mis-shapen Quilp?

The street beyond was so narrow and the shadow of the houses on one side of the way so deep, that he seemed to have risen out of the earth. But there he was. The child withdrew into a dark corner, and saw him pass close to her. He had a stick in his hand, and, when he had got clear of the shadow of the gateway, he leant upon it, looked back—directly, as it seemed, towards where she stood—and beckoned.

To her? oh no, thank God, not to her; for as she stood, in an extremity of fear, hesitating whether to scream for help, or come from her hiding-place and fly, before he should draw nearer, there issued slowly forth from the arch another figure—that of a boy—who carried on his back a trunk.

'Faster, sirrah!' cried Quilp, looking up at the old gateway, and showing in the moonlight like some monstrous image that had come down from its niche and was casting a backward glance at its old house, 'faster!'

'It 's a dreadful heavy load, sir,' the boy pleaded. 'I 've come on very fast, considering.'

'*You* have come fast, considering!' retorted Quilp; 'you creep, you dog, you crawl, you measure distance like a worm. There are the chimes now, half-past twelve.'

He stopped to listen, and then turning upon the boy with a suddenness and ferocity that made him start, asked at what hour that London coach passed the corner of the road. The boy replied, at one.

'Come on then,' said Quilp, 'or I shall be too late. Faster—do you hear me? Faster.'

The boy made all the speed he could, and Quilp led onward, constantly turning back to threaten him, and urge him to greater haste. Nell did not dare to move until they were out of sight and hearing, and then hurried to where she had left her grandfather, feeling as if the very passing of the dwarf so near him must have filled him with alarm and terror. But he was sleeping soundly, and she softly withdrew.

As she was making her way to her own bed, she determined to say nothing of this adventure, as upon whatever errand the dwarf had come (and she feared it must have been in search of them) it was clear by his inquiry about the London coach that he was on his way homeward, and as he had passed through that place, it was but reasonable to suppose that they were safer from his inquiries there, than they could be elsewhere. These reflections did not remove her own alarm, for she had been too much terrified to be easily composed, and felt as if she were hemmed in by a legion of Quilps, and the very air itself were filled with them.

The delight of the Nobility and Gentry and the patronised of Royalty had, by some process of self-abridgment known only to herself, got into her travelling bed, where she was snoring peacefully, while the large bonnet, carefully disposed upon the drum, was revealing its glories by the light of a dim lamp that swung from the roof. The child's bed was already made upon the floor, and it was a great comfort to her to hear the steps removed as soon as she had entered, and to know that all easy communication between persons outside and the brass knocker was by this means effectually prevented. Certain guttural sounds, too, which from time to time ascended through the floor of the caravan, and a rustling of straw in the same direction, apprised her that the driver was couched upon the ground beneath, and gave her an additional feeling of security.

Notwithstanding these protections, she could get none but broken sleep by fits and starts all night, for fear of Quilp, who throughout her uneasy dreams was somehow connected with the wax-work, or was wax-work himself, or was Mrs. Jarley and wax-work too, or was himself, Mrs. Jarley, wax-work, and a barrel-organ all in one, and yet not exactly any of them either. At length, towards break of day, that deep sleep came upon her which succeeds to weariness and over-watching, and which has no consciousness but one of overpowering and irresistible enjoyment.

CHAPTER XXVIII

SLEEP hung upon the eye-lids of the child so long, that, when she awoke, Mrs. Jarley was already decorated with her large bonnet, and actively engaged in preparing breakfast. She received Nell's apology for being so late with perfect good-humour, and said that she should not have aroused her if she had slept on until noon.

'Because it does you good,' said the lady of the caravan, 'when you 're tired, to sleep as long as ever you can, and get the fatigue quite off; and that 's another blessing of your time of life—you can sleep so very sound.'

'Have you had a bad night, ma'am?' asked Nell.

'I seldom have anything else, child,' replied Mrs.

Jarley, with the air of a martyr. 'I sometimes wonder how I bear it.'

Remembering the snores which had proceeded from that cleft in the caravan in which the proprietress of the wax-work passed the night, Nell rather thought she must have been dreaming of lying awake. However, she expressed herself very sorry to hear such a dismal account of her state of health, and shortly afterwards sat down with her grandfather and Mrs. Jarley to breakfast. The meal finished, Nell assisted to wash the cups and saucers, and put them in their proper places, and these household duties performed, Mrs. Jarley arrayed herself in an exceedingly bright shawl for the purpose of making a progress through the streets of the town.

'The wan will come on to bring the boxes,' said Mrs. Jarley, 'and you had better come in it, child. I am obliged to walk, very much against my will; but the people expect it of me, and public characters can't be their own masters and mistresses in such matters as these. How do I look, child?'

Nell returned a satisfactory reply, and Mrs. Jarley, after sticking a great many pins into various parts of her figure, and making several abortive attempts to obtain a full view of her own back, was at last satisfied with her appearance, and went forth majestically.

The caravan followed at no great distance. As it went jolting through the streets, Nell peeped from the window, curious to see in what kind of place they were, and yet fearful of encountering at every turn the dreaded face of Quilp. It was a pretty large town, with an open square which they were crawling slowly across, and in the middle of which was the Town Hall, with a clock-tower and a weathercock. There were houses of stone, houses of red brick, houses of yellow brick, houses of lath and plaster; and houses of wood, many of them very old, with withered faces carved upon the beams, and staring down into the street. These had very little winking windows, and low-arched doors, and in some of the narrower ways, quite overhung the pavement. The streets were very clean, very sunny, very empty, and very dull. A few idle men lounged about the two inns, and the empty market-place, and the tradesmen's doors, and some old people were dozing in chairs outside an alms-house wall; but scarcely any passengers who seemed bent on going anywhere, or to have any object in view, went by; and if perchance some straggler did, his footsteps echoed on the hot bright pavement for minutes afterwards. Nothing seemed to be going on but the clocks, and they had such drowsy faces, such heavy lazy hands, and such cracked voices that they surely must have been too slow. The very dogs were all asleep, and the flies, drunk with moist sugar in the grocer's shop, forgot their wings and briskness, and baked to death in dusty corners of the window.

Rumbling along with most unwonted noise, the caravan stopped at last at the place of exhibition, where Nell dismounted amidst an admiring group of children, who evidently supposed her to be an important item of the curiosities, and were fully impressed with the belief that her grandfather was a cunning device in wax. The chests were taken out with all convenient despatch, and taken in to be unlocked by Mrs. Jarley, who, attended by George and another man in velveteen shorts and a drab hat ornamented with turnpike tickets, were waiting to dispose their contents (consisting of red festoons and other ornamental devices in upholstery work) to the best advantage in the decoration of the room.

They all got to work without loss of time, and very busy they were. As the stupendous collection were yet concealed by cloths, lest the envious dust should injure their complexions, Nell bestirred herself to assist in the embellishment of the room, in which her grandfather also was of great service. The two men being well used to it, did a great deal in a short time; and Mrs. Jarley served out the tin tacks from a linen pocket like a toll-collector's which she wore for the purpose, and encouraged her assistants to renewed exertion.

While they were thus employed, a tallish gentleman with a hook nose and black hair, dressed in a military surtout very short and tight in the sleeves, and which had once been frogged and braided all over, but was now sadly shorn of its garniture and quite threadbare—dressed too in ancient grey pantaloons fitting tight to the leg, and a pair of pumps in the winter of their existence—looked in at the door and smiled affably. Mrs. Jarley's back being then towards him, the military gentleman shook his forefinger as a sign that her myrmidons were not to apprise her of his presence, and stealing up close behind her, tapped her on the neck, and cried playfully 'Boh!'

'What, Mr. Slum!' cried the lady of the wax-work. 'Lor! who 'd have thought of seeing you here?'

' 'Pon my soul and honour,' said Mr. Slum, 'that 's a good remark. 'Pon my soul and honour that 's a wise remark. Who *would* have thought it? George, my faithful feller, how are you?'

George received this advance with a surly indifference, observing that he was well enough for the matter of that, and hammering lustily all the time.

'I came here,' said the military gentleman, turning to Mrs. Jarley,—' 'pon my soul and honour I hardly know what I came here for. It would puzzle me to tell you, it would by Gad. I wanted a little inspiration, a little freshening up, a little change of ideas, and—'Pon my soul and honour,' said the military gentleman, checking himself and looking round the room 'what a devilish classical thing this is! By Gad, it 's quite Minervian!'

'It 'll look well enough when it comes to be finished,' observed Mrs. Jarley.

'Well enough!' said Mr. Slum. 'Will you believe me when I say it 's the delight of my life to have dabbled in poetry, when I think I 've exercised my pen upon this charming theme? By the way—any orders? Is there any little thing I can do for you?'

'It comes so very expensive, sir,' replied Mrs. Jarley, 'and I really don't think it does much good.'

'Hush! No, no!' returned Mr. Slum, elevating his hand. 'No fibs. I 'll not hear it. Don't say it don't do good. Don't say it. I know better!'

'I don't think it does,' said Mrs. Jarley.

'Ha, ha!' cried Mr. Slum, 'you 're giving way, you 're coming down. Ask the perfumers, ask the blacking-makers, ask the hatters, ask the old lottery-office-keepers—ask any man among 'em what my poetry has done for him, and mark my words, he blesses the name of Slum. If he 's an honest man, he raises his eyes to heaven, and blesses the name of Slum—mark that! You are acquainted with Westminster Abbey, Mrs. Jarley?'

'Yes, surely.'

'Then upon my soul and honour, ma'am, you 'll find in a certain angle of that dreary pile, called Poets' Corner, a few smaller names than Slum,' retorted that gentleman, tapping himself expressively on the forehead to imply that there was some slight quantity of brain behind it. 'I 've got a little trifle here, now,' said

Mr. Slum, taking off his hat which was full of scraps of paper, 'a little trifle here, thrown off in the heat of the moment, which I should say was exactly the thing you wanted to set this place on fire with. It 's an acrostic—the name at this moment is Warren, but the idea 's a convertible one, and a positive inspiration for Jarley. Have the acrostic.'

'I suppose it 's very dear,' said Mrs. Jarley.

'Five shillings,' returned Mr. Slum, using his pencil as a tooth-pick. 'Cheaper than any prose.'

'I couldn't give more than three,' said Mrs. Jarley.

'—And six,' retorted Slum. 'Come. Three-and-six.'

Mrs. Jarley was not proof against the poet's insinuating manner, and Mr. Slum entered the order in a small note-book as a three-and-sixpenny one. Mr. Slum then withdrew to alter the acrostic, after taking a most affectionate leave of his patroness, and promising to return, as soon as he possibly could, with a fair copy for the printer.

As his presence had not interfered with or interrupted the preparations, they were now far advanced, and were completed shortly after his departure. When the festoons were all put up as tastily as they might be, the stupendous collection was uncovered, and there were displayed, on a raised platform some two feet from the floor, running round the room and parted from the rude public by a crimson rope breast-high, divers sprightly effigies of celebrated characters, singly and in groups, clad in glittering dresses of various climes and times, and standing more or less unsteadily upon their legs, with their eyes very wide open, and their nostrils very much inflated, and the muscles of their legs and arms very strongly developed, and all their countenances expressing great surprise. All the gentlemen were very pigeon-breasted and very blue about the beards; and all the ladies were miraculous figures; and all the ladies and all the gentlemen were looking intensely nowhere, and staring with extraordinary earnestness at nothing.

When Nell had exhausted her first raptures at this glorious sight, Mrs. Jarley ordered the room to be cleared of all but herself and the child, and, sitting herself down in an arm-chair in the centre, formally invested Nell with a willow wand, long used by herself for pointing out the characters, and was at great pains to instruct her in her duty.

'That,' said Mrs. Jarley in her exhibition tone, as Nell touched a figure at the beginning of the platform, 'is an unfortunate Maid of Honour in the Time of Queen Elizabeth, who died from pricking her finger in consequence of working upon a Sunday. Observe the blood which is trickling from her finger; also the gold-eyed needle of the period, with which she is at work.'

All this, Nell repeated twice or thrice: pointing to the finger and the needle at the right times: and then passed on to the next.

'That, ladies and gentlemen,' said Mrs. Jarley, 'is Jasper Packlemerton of atrocious memory, who courted and married fourteen wives, and destroyed them all, by tickling the soles of their feet when they were sleeping in the consciousness of innocence and virtue. On being brought to the scaffold and asked if he was sorry for what he had done, he replied yes, he was sorry for having let 'em off so easy, and hoped all Christian husbands would pardon him the offence. Let this be a warning to all young ladies to be particular in the character of the gentlemen of their choice. Observe that his fingers are curled as if in the act of tickling, and that his face is represented with a wink, as he appeared when committing his barbarous murders.'

When Nell knew all about Mr. Packlemerton, and could say it without faltering, Mrs. Jarley passed on to the fat man, and then to the thin man, the tall man, the short man, the old lady who died of dancing at a hundred and thirty-two, the wild boy of the woods, the woman who poisoned fourteen families with pickled walnuts, and other historical characters and interesting but misguided individuals. And so well did Nell profit by her instructions, and so apt was she to remember them, that by the time they had been shut up together for a couple of hours, she was in full possession of the history of the whole establishment, and perfectly competent to the enlightenment of visitors.

Mrs. Jarley was not slow to express her admiration at this happy result, and carried her young friend and pupil to inspect the remaining arrangements within doors, by virtue of which the passage had been already converted into a grove of green-baize hung with the inscriptions she had already seen (Mr. Slum's productions), and a highly ornamented table placed at the upper end for Mrs. Jarley herself, at which she was to preside and take the money, in company with his Majesty King George the Third, Mr. Grimaldi as clown, Mary Queen of Scots, an anonymous gentleman of the Quaker persuasion, and Mr. Pitt holding in his hand a correct model of the bill for the imposition of the window duty. The preparations without doors had not been neglected either; a nun of great personal attractions was telling her beads on the little portico over the door; and a brigand with the blackest possible head of hair, and the clearest possible complexion, was at that moment going round the town in a cart, consulting the miniature of a lady.

It now only remained that Mr. Slum's compositions should be judiciously distributed; that the pathetic effusions should find their way to all private houses and tradespeople; and that the parody commencing 'If I know'd a donkey,' should be confined to the taverns, and circulated only among the lawyers' clerks and choice spirits of the place. When this had been done, and Mrs. Jarley had waited upon the boarding-schools in person, with a handbill composed expressly for them, in which it was distinctly proved that wax-work refined the mind, cultivated the taste, and enlarged the sphere of the human understanding, that indefatigable lady sat down to dinner, and drank out of the suspicious bottle to a flourishing campaign.

CHAPTER XXIX

UNQUESTIONABLY Mrs. Jarley had an inventive genius. In the midst of the various devices for attracting visitors to the exhibition, little Nell was not forgotten. The light cart in which the Brigand usually made his perambulations being gaily dressed with flags and streamers, and the Brigand placed therein, contemplating the miniature of his beloved as usual, Nell was accommodated with a seat beside him, decorated with artificial flowers, and in this state and ceremony rode slowly through the town every morning, dispersing handbills from a basket, to the sound of drum and trumpet. The beauty of the child, coupled with her gentle and timid bearing, produced quite a sensation in the little country place. The Brigand, heretofore a source of exclusive interest in the streets, became a mere secondary consideration, and to be important only as a part of the show of which she was the chief attraction. Grown-up folks began to be interested in the bright-eyed girl, and some score of little boys fell desperately in love, and constantly left inclosures of nuts and apples, directed in small-text, at the wax-work door.

This desirable impression was not lost on Mrs. Jarley, who, lest Nell should become too cheap, soon sent the Brigand out alone again, and kept her in the exhibition-room, where she described the figures every half-hour to the great satisfaction of admiring audiences. And these audiences were of a very superior description, including a great many young ladies' boarding-schools, whose favour Mrs. Jarley had been at great pains to conciliate, by altering the face and costume of Mr. Grimaldi as clown to represent Mr. Lindley Murray as he appeared when engaged in the composition of his English Grammar, and turning a murderess of great renown into Mrs. Hannah More—both of which likenesses were admitted by Miss Monflathers, who was at the head of the head Boarding and Day Establishment in the town, and who condescended to take a Private View with eight chosen young ladies, to be quite startling from their extreme correctness. Mr. Pitt in a nightcap and bedgown, and without his boots, represented the poet Cowper with perfect exactness; and Mary Queen of Scots in a dark wig, white shirt-collar, and male attire, was such a complete image of Lord Byron that the young ladies quite screamed when they saw it. Miss Monflathers, however, rebuked this enthusiasm, and took occasion to reprove Mrs. Jarley for not keeping her collection more select: observing that His Lordship had held certain opinions quite incompatible with wax-work honours, and adding something about a Dean and Chapter, which Mrs. Jarley did not understand.

Although her duties were sufficiently laborious, Nell found in the lady of the caravan a very kind and considerate person, who had not only a peculiar relish for being comfortable herself, but for making everybody about her comfortable also; which latter taste, it may be remarked, is, even in persons who live in much finer places than caravans, a far more rare and uncommon one than the first, and is not by any means its necessary consequence. As her popularity procured her various little fees from the visitors on which her patroness never demanded any toll, and as her grandfather too was well-treated and useful, she had no cause of anxiety in connection with the wax-work, beyond that which sprung from her recollection of Quilp, and her fears that he might return and one day suddenly encounter them.

Quilp indeed was a perpetual night-mare to the child, who was constantly haunted by a vision of his ugly face and stunted figure. She slept, for their better security, in the room where the wax-work figures were, and she never retired to this place at night but she tortured herself—she could not help it—with imagining a resemblance, in some one or other of their deathlike faces, to the dwarf, and this fancy would sometimes so gain upon her that she would almost believe he had removed the figure and stood within the clothes. Then there were so many of them with their great glassy eyes—and, as they stood one behind the other all about her bed, they looked so like living creatures, and yet so unlike in their grim stillness and silence, that she had a kind of terror of them for their own sakes, and would often lie watching their dusky figures until she was obliged to rise and light a candle, or go and sit at the open window and feel a companionship in the bright stars. At these times, she would recall the old house and the window at which she used to sit alone; and then she would think of poor Kit and all his kindness, until the tears came into her eyes, and she would weep and smile together.

Often and anxiously at this silent hour, her thoughts reverted to her grandfather, and she would wonder how much he remembered of their former life, and whether he was ever really mindful of the change in their condition and of their late helplessness and destitution. When they were wandering about, she seldom thought of this, but now she could not help considering what would become of them if he fell sick or her own strength were to fail her. He was very patient and willing, happy to execute any little task, and glad to be of use; but he was in the same listless state, with no prospect of improvement—a mere child—a poor thoughtless, vacant creature—a harmless fond old man, susceptible of tender love and regard for her, and of pleasant and painful impressions, but alive to nothing more. It made her very sad to know that this was so—so sad to see it that sometimes when he sat idly by, smiling and nodding to her when she looked round, or when he caressed some little child and carried it to and fro, as he was fond of doing by the hour together, perplexed by its simple questions, yet patient under his own infirmity, and seeming almost conscious of it too, and humbled even before the mind of an infant—so sad it made her to see him thus, that she would burst into tears, and, withdrawing into some secret place, fall down upon her knees and pray that he might be restored.

But, the bitterness of her grief was not in beholding him in this condition, when he was at least content and tranquil, nor in her solitary meditations on his altered state, though these were trials for a young heart. Cause for deeper and heavier sorrow was yet to come.

One evening, a holiday night with them, Nell and her grandfather went out to walk. They had been rather closely confined for some days, and the weather being warm, they strolled a long distance. Clear of the town, they took a footpath which struck through some pleasant fields, judging that it would terminate in the road they quitted and enable them to return that way. It made, however, a much wider circuit than they had supposed, and thus they were tempted onward until sunset, when they reached the track of which they were in search, and stopped to rest.

It had been gradually getting overcast, and now the sky was dark and lowering, save where the glory of the departing sun piled up masses of gold and burning fire, decaying embers of which gleamed here and there through the black veil, and shone redly down upon the earth. The wind began to moan in hollow murmurs, as the sun went down carrying glad day elsewhere; and a train of dull clouds coming up against it, menaced thunder and lightning. Large drops of rain soon began to fall, and, as the storm clouds came sailing onward, others supplied the void they left behind and spread over all the sky. Then was heard the low rumbling of distant thunder, then the lightning quivered, and then the darkness of an hour seemed to have gathered in an instant.

Fearful of taking shelter beneath a tree or hedge, the old man and the child hurried along the high road, hoping to find some house in which they could seek a refuge from the storm, which had now burst forth in earnest, and every moment increased in violence. Drenched with the pelting rain, confused by the deafening thunder, and bewildered by the glare of the forked lightning, they would have passed a solitary house without being aware of its vicinity, had not a man, who was standing at the door, called lustily to them to enter.

'Your ears ought to be better than other folks' at any rate, if you make so little of the chance of being struck blind,' he said, retreating from the door and shading his eyes with his hands as the jagged lightning came again. 'What are you going past for, eh?' he added, as he closed the door and led the way along a passage to a room behind.

'We didn't see the house, sir, till we heard you calling,' Nell replied.

'No wonder,' said the man, 'with this lightning in one's eyes, by the bye. You had better stand by the fire here, and dry yourselves a bit. You can call for what you like if you want anything. If you don't want anything, you are not obliged to give an order. Don't be afraid of that. This is a public-house, that 's all. The Valiant Soldier is pretty well known hereabouts.'

'Is this house called the Valiant Soldier, sir?' asked Nell.

'I thought everybody knew that,' replied the landlord. 'Where have you come from, if you don't know the Valiant Soldier as well as the church catechism? This is the Valiant Soldier, by James Groves, —Jem Groves—honest Jem Groves, as is a man of unblemished moral character, and has a good dry skittle-ground. If any man has got anything to say again Jem Groves, let him say it *to* Jem Groves, and Jem Groves can accommodate him with a customer on any terms from four pound a side to forty.'

With these words, the speaker tapped himself on the waistcoat to intimate that he was the Jem Groves so highly eulogised; sparred scientifically at a counterfeit Jem Groves, who was sparring at society in general from a black frame over the chimney-piece; and, applying a half-emptied glass of spirits-and-water to his lips, drank Jem Groves's health.

The night being warm, there was a large screen drawn across the room, for a barrier against the heat of the fire. It seemed as if somebody on the other side of this screen had been insinuating doubts of Mr. Groves's prowess, and had thereby given rise to these egotistical expressions, for Mr. Groves wound up his defiance by giving a loud knock upon it with his knuckles and pausing for a reply from the other side.

'There an't many men,' said Mr. Groves, no answer being returned, 'who would ventur' to cross Jem Groves under his own roof. There 's only one man, I know, that has nerve enough for that, and that man 's not a hundred mile from here neither. But he 's worth a dozen men, and I let him say of me whatever he likes in consequence—he knows that.'

In return for this complimentary address, a very gruff hoarse voice bade Mr. Groves 'hold his noise and light a candle.' And the same voice remarked that the same gentleman 'needn't waste his breath in brag, for most people knew pretty well what sort of stuff he was made of.'

'Nell, they 're—they 're playing cards,' whispered the old man, suddenly interested. 'Don't you hear them?'

'Look sharp with that candle,' said the voice; 'it 's as much as I can do to see the pips on the cards as it is; and get this shutter closed as quick as you can, will you? Your beer will be the worse for to-night's thunder I expect.—Game! Seven-and-sixpence to me, old Isaac. Hand over.'

'Do you hear, Nell, do you hear them?' whispered the old man again, with increased earnestness, as the money chinked upon the table.

'I haven't seen such a storm as this,' said a sharp cracked voice of most disagreeable quality, when a tremendous peal of thunder had died away, 'since the night when old Luke Withers won thirteen times running on the red. We all said he had the Devil's luck and his own, and as it was the kind of night for the Devil to be out and busy, I suppose he *was* looking over his shoulder, if anybody could have seen him.'

'Ah!' returned the gruff voice; 'for all old Luke's winning through thick and thin of late years, I remember the time when he was the unluckiest and unfortunatest of men. He never took a dice-box in his hand, or held a card, but he was plucked, pigeoned, and cleaned out completely.'

'Do you hear what he says?' whispered the old man. 'Do you hear that, Nell?'

The child saw with astonishment and alarm that his whole appearance had undergone a complete change. His face was flushed and eager, his eyes were strained, his teeth set, his breath came short and thick, and the hand he laid upon her arm trembled so violently that she shook beneath its grasp.

'Bear witness,' he muttered, looking upward, 'that I always said it; that I knew it, dreamed of it, felt it was the truth, and that it must be so! What money have we, Nell? Come! I saw you with money yesterday. What money have we? Give it to me.'

'No, no, let me keep it, grandfather,' said the

frightened child. 'Let us go away from here. Do not mind the rain. Pray let us go.'

'Give it to me, I say,' returned the old man fiercely. 'Hush, hush, don't cry, Nell. If I spoke sharply, dear, I didn't mean it. It 's for thy good. I have wronged thee, Nell, but I will right thee yet, I will indeed. Where is the money?'

'Do not take it,' said the child. 'Pray do not take it, dear. For both our sakes let me keep it, or let me throw it away—better let me throw it away, than you take it now. Let us go; do let us go.'

'Give me the money,' returned the old man, 'I must have it. There—there—that 's my dear Nell. I 'll right thee one day, child, I 'll right thee, never fear!'

She took from her pocket a little purse. He seized it with the same rapid impatience which had characterised his speech, and hastily made his way to the other side of the screen. It was impossible to restrain him, and the trembling child followed close behind.

The landlord had placed a light upon the table, and was engaged in drawing the curtain of the window. The speakers whom they had heard were two men, who had a pack of cards and some silver money between them, while upon the screen itself the games they had played were scored in chalk. The man with the rough voice was a burly fellow of middle age, with large black whiskers, broad cheeks, a coarse wide mouth, and bull neck, which was pretty freely displayed as his shirt-collar was only confined by a loose red neckerchief. He wore his hat, which was of a brownish-white, and had beside him a thick knotted stick. The other man, whom his companion had called Isaac, was of a more slender figure—stooping, and high in the shoulders—with a very ill-favoured face, and a most sinister and villainous squint.

'Now, old gentleman,' said Isaac, looking round. 'Do you know either of us? This side of the screen is private, sir.'

'No offence, I hope,' returned the old man.

'But by G—, sir, there *is* offence,' said the other, interrupting him, 'when you intrude yourself upon a couple of gentlemen who are particularly engaged.'

'I had no intention to offend,' said the old man, looking anxiously at the cards. 'I thought that—'

'But you had no right to think, sir,' retorted the other. 'What the devil has a man at your time of life to do with thinking?'

'Now bully boy,' said the stout man, raising his eyes from his cards for the first time, 'can't you let him speak?'

The landlord, who had apparently resolved to remain neutral until he knew which side of the question the stout man would espouse, chimed in at this place with 'Ah, to be sure, can't you let him speak, Isaac List?'

'Can't I let him speak,' sneered Isaac in reply, mimicking as nearly as he could, in his shrill voice, the tones of the landlord. 'Yes, I can let him speak, Jemmy Groves.'

'Well then, do it, will you?' said the landlord.

Mr. List's squint assumed a portentous character, which seemed to threaten a prolongation of this controversy, when his companion, who had been looking sharply at the old man, put a timely stop to it.

'Who knows,' said he, with a cunning look, 'but the gentleman may have civilly meant to ask if he might have the honour to take a hand with us?'

'I did mean it,' cried the old man. 'That is what I mean. That is what I want now!'

'I thought so,' returned the same man. 'Then who knows but the gentleman, anticipating our objection to play for love, civilly desired to play for money?'

The old man replied by shaking the little purse in his eager hand, and then throwing it down upon the table, and gathering up the cards as a miser would clutch at gold.

'Oh! That indeed—' said Isaac; 'if that 's what the gentleman meant, I beg the gentleman's pardon. Is this the gentleman's little purse? A very pretty little purse. Rather a light purse,' added Isaac, throwing it into the air and catching it dexterously, 'but enough to amuse a gentleman for half an hour or so.'

'We 'll make a four-handed game of it, and take in Groves,' said the stout man. 'Come, Jemmy.'

The landlord, who conducted himself like one who was well used to such little parties, approached the table and took his seat. The child, in a perfect agony, drew her grandfather aside, and implored him, even then, to come away.

'Come; and we may be so happy,' said the child.

'We *will* be happy,' replied the old man hastily. 'Let me go, Nell. The means of happiness are on the cards and on the dice. We must rise from little winnings to great. There 's little to be won here; but great will come in time. I shall but win back my own, and it 's all for thee, my darling.'

'God help us!' cried the child. 'Oh! what hard fortune brought us here?'

'Hush!' rejoined the old man laying his hand upon her mouth, 'Fortune will not bear chiding. We must not reproach her, or she shuns us; I have found that out.'

'Now, mister,' said the stout man. 'If you 're not coming yourself, give us the cards, will you?'

'I am coming,' cried the old man. 'Sit thee down, Nell, sit thee down and look on. Be of good heart, it 's all for thee—all—every penny. I don't tell them, no, no, or else they wouldn't play, dreading the chance that such a cause must give me. Look at them. See what they are and what thou art. Who doubts that we must win?'

'The gentleman has thought better of it, and isn't coming,' said Isaac, making as though he would rise from the table. 'I 'm sorry the gentleman 's daunted —nothing venture, nothing have—but the gentleman knows best.'

'Why I am ready. You have all been slow but me,' said the old man. 'I wonder who is more anxious to begin than I.'

As he spoke he drew a chair to the table; and the other three closing round it at the same time, the game commenced.

The child sat by, and watched its progress with a troubled mind. Regardless of the run of luck, and mindful only of the desperate passion which had its hold upon her grandfather, losses and gains were to her alike. Exulting in some brief triumph, or cast down by a defeat, there he sat so wild and restless, so feverishly and intensely anxious, so terribly eager, so ravenous for the paltry stakes, that she could have almost better borne to see him dead. And yet she was the innocent cause of all this torture, and he, gambling with such a savage thirst for gain as the most insatiable gambler never felt, had not one selfish thought!

On the contrary, the other three—knaves and gamesters by their trade—while intent upon their game, were yet as cool and quiet as if every virtue had been centred in their breasts. Sometimes one would look up to smile to another, or to snuff the feeble candle, or to glance at the lightning as it shot through the open window and fluttering curtain, or to listen to some louder peal of thunder than the rest, with a kind of momentary impatience, as if it put him out; but there they sat, with a calm indifference to everything but their cards, perfect philosophers in appearance, and with no greater show of passion or excitement than if they had been made of stone.

The storm had raged for full three hours; the lightning had grown fainter and less frequent; the thunder, from seeming to roll and break above their heads, had gradually died away into a deep hoarse distance; and still the game went on, and still the anxious child was quite forgotten.

CHAPTER XXX

At length the play came to an end, and Mr. Isaac List rose the only winner. Mat and the landlord bore their losses with professional fortitude. Isaac pocketed his gains with the air of a man who had quite made up his mind to win, all along, and was neither surprised nor pleased.

Nell's little purse was exhausted; but although it lay empty by his side, and the other players had now risen from the table, the old man sat pouring over the cards, dealing them as they had been dealt before, and turning up the different hands to see what each man would have held if they had still been playing. He was quite absorbed in this occupation, when the child drew near and laid her hand upon his shoulder, telling him it was near midnight.

'See the curse of poverty, Nell,' he said, pointing to the packs he had spread out upon the table. 'If I could have gone on a little longer, only a little longer, the luck would have turned on my side. Yes, it 's as plain as the marks upon the cards. See here —and there—and here again.'

'Put them away,' urged the child. 'Try to forget them.'

'Try to forget them!' he rejoined, raising his haggard face to hers, and regarding her with an incredulous stare. 'To forget them! How are we ever to grow rich if I forget them?'

The child could only shake her head.

'No, no, Nell,' said the old man, patting her cheek; 'they must not be forgotten. We must make amends for this as soon as we can. Patience—patience, and we 'll right thee yet, I promise thee. Lose to-day, win to-morrow. And nothing can be won without anxiety and care—nothing. Come, I am ready.'

'Do you know what the time is?' said Mr. Groves, who was smoking with his friends. 'Past twelve o'clock—'

'—And a rainy night,' added the stout man.

'The Valiant Soldier, by James Groves. Good beds. Cheap entertainment for man and beast,' said Mr. Groves, quoting his sign-board. 'Half-past twelve o'clock.'

'It 's very late,' said the uneasy child. 'I wish we had gone before. What will they think of us! It will be two o'clock by the time we get back. What would it cost, sir, if we stopped here?'

'Two good beds, one-and-sixpence; supper and beer one shilling; total two shillings and sixpence,' replied the Valiant Soldier.

Now, Nell had still the piece of gold sewn in her dress; and when she came to consider the lateness of the hour, and the somnolent habits of Mrs. Jarley, and to imagine the state of consternation in which they would certainly throw that good lady by knocking her up in the middle of the night—and when she reflected, on the other hand, that if they remained where they were, and rose early in the morning, they might get back before she awoke, and could plead the violence of the storm by which they had been overtaken, as a good apology for their absence—she decided, after a great deal of hesitation, to remain. She therefore took her grandfather aside, and telling him that she had still enough left to defray the cost of their lodging, proposed that they should stay there for the night.

'If I had had but that money before—If I had only known of it a few minutes ago!' muttered the old man.

'We will decide to stop here if you please,' said Nell, turning hastily to the landlord.

'I think that 's prudent,' returned Mr. Groves. 'You shall have your suppers directly.'

Accordingly, when Mr. Groves had smoked his pipe out, knocked out the ashes, and placed it carefully in a corner of the fireplace, with the bowl downwards, he brought in the bread and cheese and beer, with many high encomiums upon their excellence, and bade his guests fall to and make themselves at home. Nell and her grandfather ate sparingly, for both were occupied with their own reflections; the other gentlemen, for whose constitutions beer was too weak and tame a liquid, consoled themselves with spirits and tobacco.

As they would leave the house very early in the morning, the child was anxious to pay for their entertainment before they retired to bed. But as she felt the necessity of concealing her little hoard from her grandfather, and had to change the piece of gold, she took it secretly from its place of concealment, and embraced an opportunity of following the landlord when he went out of the room, and tendered it to him in the little bar.

'Will you give me the change here, if you please?' said the child.

Mr. James Groves was evidently surprised, and looked at the money, and rang it, and looked at the child, and at the money again, as though he had a mind to inquire how she came by it. The coin being genuine, however, and changed at his house, he probably felt, like a wise landlord, that it was no business of his. At any rate, he counted out the change, and gave it her. The child was returning to the room where they had passed the evening, when she fancied she saw a figure just gliding in at the door. There was nothing but a long dark passage between this door and the place where she had changed the money, and, being very certain that no person had passed in or out while she stood there, the thought struck her that she had been watched.

But by whom? When she re-entered the room, she found its inmates exactly as she had left them. The stout fellow lay upon two chairs, resting his head on his hand, and the squinting man reposed in a similar attitude on the opposite side of the table. Between them sat her grandfather, looking intently at the winner with a kind of hungry admiration, and hanging upon his words as if he were some superior being. She was puzzled for a moment, and looked round to see if any one else were there. No. Then she asked her grandfather in a whisper whether anybody had left the room while she was absent. 'No,' he said, 'nobody.'

It must have been her fancy then; and yet it was strange, that, without anything in her previous thoughts to lead to it, she should have imagined this figure so very distinctly. She was still wondering and thinking of it, when a girl came to light her to bed.

The old man took leave of the company at the same time, and they went upstairs together. It was a great, rambling house, with dull corridors and wide staircases which the flaring candles seemed to make more gloomy. She left her grandfather in his chamber, and followed her guide to another, which was at the end of a passage, and approached by some half-dozen crazy steps. This was prepared for her. The girl lingered a little while to talk, and tell her grievances. She had not a good place, she said; the wages were low, and the work was hard. She was going to leave it in a fortnight; the child couldn't recommend her to another, she supposed? Indeed she was afraid another would be difficult to get after living there, for the house had a very indifferent character; there was far too much card-playing, and such like. She was very much mistaken if some of the people who came there oftenest were quite as honest as they might be, but she wouldn't have it known that she had said so, for the world. Then there were some rambling allusions to a rejected sweetheart, who had threatened to go a soldiering—a final promise of knocking at the door early in the morning—and 'Good-night.'

The child did not feel comfortable when she was left alone. She could not help thinking of the figure stealing through the passage downstairs; and what the girl had said did not tend to reassure her. The men were very ill-looking. They might get their living by robbing and murdering travellers. Who could tell?

Reasoning herself out of these fears, or losing sight of them for a little while, there came the anxiety to which the adventures of the night gave rise. Here was the old passion awakened again in her grandfather's breast, and to what further distraction it might tempt him Heaven only knew. What fears their absence might have occasioned already! Persons might be seeking for them even then. Would they be forgiven in the morning, or turned adrift again? Oh! why had they stopped in that strange place? It would have been better, under any circumstances to have gone on!

At last, sleep gradually stole upon her—a broken, fitful sleep, troubled by dreams of falling from high towers, and waking with a start and in great terror. A deeper slumber followed this—and then—What? That figure in the room.

A figure was there. Yes, she had drawn up the blind to admit the light when it should be dawn, and there, between the foot of the bed and the dark casement, it crouched and slunk along, groping its way with noiseless hands, and stealing round the bed. She had no voice to cry for help, no power to move, but lay still, watching it.

On it came—on, silently and stealthily, to the bed's head. The breath so near her pillow, that she shrunk back into it, lest those wandering hands should light upon her face. Back again it stole to the window—then turned its head towards her.

The dark form was a mere blot upon the lighter darkness of the room, but she saw the turning of the head, and felt and knew how the eyes looked and the ears listened. There it remained, motionless as she. At length, still keeping the face towards her, it busied its hands in something, and she heard the chink of money.

Then, on it came again, silent and stealthy as before, and replacing the garments it had taken from the bedside, dropped upon its hands and knees, and crawled away. How slowly it seemed to move, now that she could hear but not see it, creeping along the floor! It reached the door at last, and stood upon its feet. The steps creaked beneath its noiseless tread, and it was gone.

The first impulse of the child was to fly from the terror of being by herself in that room—to have somebody by—not to be alone—and then her power of speech would be restored. With no consciousness of having moved, she gained the door.

There was the dreadful shadow, pausing at the bottom of the steps.

She could not pass it; she might have done so, perhaps, in the darkness without being seized, but her blood curdled at the thought. The figure stood quite still, and so did she; not boldly, but of necessity; for going back into the room was hardly less terrible than going on.

The rain beat fast and furiously without, and ran down in plashing streams from the thatched roof. Some summer insect, with no escape into the air, flew blindly to and fro, beating its body against the walls and ceiling, and filling the silent place with murmurs. The figure moved again. The child involuntarily did the same. Once in her grandfather's room, she would be safe.

It crept along the passage until it came to the very door she longed so ardently to reach. The child, in the agony of being so near, had almost darted forward with the design of bursting into the room and closing it behind her, when the figure stopped again.

The idea flashed suddenly upon her—what if it entered there, and had a design upon the old man's life! She turned faint and sick. It did. It went in. There was a light inside. The figure was now within the chamber, and she, still dumb—quite dumb, and almost senseless—stood looking on.

The door was partly open. Not knowing what she meant to do, but meaning to preserve him or be killed herself, she staggered forward and looked in.

What sight was that which met her view!

The bed had not been lain on, but was smooth and empty. And at a table sat the old man himself; the only living creature there; his white face pinched and sharpened by the greediness which made his eyes unnaturally bright—counting the money of which his hands had robbed her.

CHAPTER XXXI

WITH steps more faltering and unsteady than those with which she had approached the room, the child withdrew from the door, and groped her way back to her own chamber. The terror she had lately felt was nothing compared with that which now oppressed her. No strange robber, no treacherous host conniving at the plunder of his guests, or stealing to their beds to kill them in their sleep, no nightly prowler, however terrible and cruel, could have awakened in her bosom half the dread which the recognition of her silent visitor inspired. The grey-headed old man gliding like a ghost into her room and acting the thief while he supposed her fast asleep, then bearing off his prize and hanging over it with the ghastly exultation she had witnessed, was worse—immeasurably worse, and far more dreadful, for the moment, to reflect upon—than anything her wildest fancy could have suggested. If he should return—there was no lock or bolt upon the door, and if, distrustful of having left some money yet behind, he should come back to seek for more—a vague awe and horror surrounded the idea of his slinking in again with stealthy tread, and turning his face toward the empty bed, while she shrank down close at his feet to avoid his touch, which was almost insupportable. She sat and listened. Hark! A footstep on the stairs, and now the door was slowly opening. It was but imagination, yet imagination had all the terrors of reality; nay, it was worse, for the reality would have come and gone, and there an end, but in imagination it was always coming and never went away.

The feeling which beset the child was one of dim uncertain horror. She had no fear of the dear old grandfather, in whose love for her this disease of the brain had been engendered; but the man she had seen that night, wrapt in the game of chance, lurking in her room, and counting the money by the glimmering light, seemed like another creature in his shape, a monstrous distortion of his image, a something to recoil from, and be the more afraid of, because it bore a likeness to him, and kept close about her, as he did. She could scarcely connect her own affectionate companion, save by his loss, with this old man, so like yet so unlike him. She had wept to see him dull and quiet. How much greater cause she had for weeping now!

The child sat watching and thinking of these things, until the phantom in her mind so increased in gloom and terror, that she felt it would be a relief to hear the old man's voice, or, if he were asleep, even to see him, and banish some of the fears that clustered round his image. She stole down the stairs and passage again. The door was still ajar as she had left it, and the candle burning as before.

She had her own candle in her hand, prepared to

say, if he were waking, that she was uneasy and could not rest, and had come to see if his were still alight. Looking into the room, she saw him lying calmly on his bed, and soon took courage to enter.

Fast asleep. No passion in the face, no avarice, no anxiety, no wild desire; all gentle, tranquil, and at peace. This was not the gambler, or the shadow in her room; this was not even the worn and jaded man whose face had so often met her own in the grey morning light; this was her dear old friend, her harmless fellow-traveller, her good, kind grandfather.

She had no fear as she looked upon his slumbering features, but she had a deep and weighty sorrow, and it found its relief in tears.

'God bless him!' said the child, stooping softly to kiss his placid cheek. 'I see too well now, that they would indeed part us if they found us out, and shut him up from the light of the sun and sky. He has only me to help him. God bless us both!'

Lighting her candle, she retreated as silently as she had come, and, gaining her own room once more, sat up during the remainder of that long, long, miserable night.

At last the day turned her waning candle pale, and she fell asleep. She was quickly roused by the girl who had shown her up to bed; and, as soon as she was dressed, prepared to go down to her grandfather. But first she searched her pocket, and found that her money was all gone—not a sixpence remained.

The old man was ready, and in a few seconds they were on their road. The child thought he rather avoided her eye, and appeared to expect that she would tell him of her loss. She felt she must do that, or he might suspect the truth.

'Grandfather,' she said in a tremulous voice, after

they had walked about a mile in silence, 'do you think they are honest people at the house yonder?'

'Why?' returned the old man trembling. 'Do I think them honest—yes, they played honestly.'

'I 'll tell you why I ask,' rejoined Nell. 'I lost some money last night—out of my bedroom I am sure. Unless it was taken by somebody in jest—only in jest, dear grandfather, which would make me laugh heartily if I could but know it—'

'Who would take money in jest?' returned the old man in a hurried manner. 'Those who take money, take it to keep. Don't talk of jest.'

'Then it was stolen out of my room, dear,' said the child, whose last hope was destroyed by the manner of this reply.

'But is there no more, Nell?' said the old man; 'no more anywhere? Was it all taken—every farthing of it—was there nothing left?'

'Nothing,' replied the child.

'We must get more,' said the old man, 'we must earn it, Nell, hoard it up, scrape it together, come by it somehow. Never mind this loss. Tell nobody of it, and perhaps we may regain it. Don't ask how;—we may regain it, and a great deal more;—but tell nobody, or trouble may come of it. And so they took it out of thy room, when thou wert asleep!' he added in a compassionate tone, very different from the secret, cunning way in which he had spoken until now. 'Poor Nell, poor little Nell!'

The child hung down her head and wept. The sympathising tone in which he spoke, was quite sincere; she was sure of that. It was not the lightest part of her sorrow to know that this was done for her.

'Not a word about it to any one but me,' said the old man, 'no, not even to me,' he added hastily, 'for it can do no good. All the losses that ever were, are not worth tears from thy eyes, darling. Why should they be, when we will win them back?'

'Let them go,' said the child looking up. 'Let them go, once and for ever, and I would never shed another tear if every penny had been a thousand pounds.'

'Well, well,' returned the old man, checking himself as some impetuous answer rose to his lips, 'she knows no better. I ought to be thankful for it.'

'But listen to me,' said the child earnestly, 'will you listen to me?'

'Aye, aye, I 'll listen,' returned the old man, still without looking at her; 'a pretty voice. It has always a sweet sound to me. It always had when it was her mother's, poor child.'

'Let me persuade you, then—oh, do let me persuade you,' said the child, 'to think no more of gains or losses, and to try no fortune but the fortune we pursue together.'

'We pursue this aim together,' retorted her grandfather, still looking away and seeming to confer with himself. 'Whose image sanctifies the game?'

'Have we been worse off,' resumed the child, 'since you forgot these cares, and we have been travelling on together? Have we not been much better and happier without a home to shelter us, than ever we were in that unhappy house, when they were on your mind?'

'She speaks the truth,' murmured the old man in the same tone as before. 'It must not turn me, but it is the truth; no doubt it is.'

'Only remember what we have been since that bright morning when we turned our backs upon it for the last time,' said Nell, 'only remember what we have been since we have been free of all those miseries—what peaceful days and quiet nights we have had—what pleasant times we have known—what happiness we have enjoyed. If we have been tired or hungry, we have been soon refreshed, and slept the sounder for it. Think what beautiful things we have seen, and how contented we have felt. And why was this blessed change?'

He stopped her with a motion of his hand, and bade her talk to him no more just then, for he was busy. After a time he kissed her cheek, still motioning her to silence, and walked on, looking far before him, and sometimes stopping and gazing with a puckered brow upon the ground, as if he were painfully trying to collect his disordered thoughts. Once she saw tears in his eyes. When he had gone on thus for some time, he took her hand in his as he was accustomed to do, with nothing of the violence or animation of his late manner; and so, by degrees so fine that the child could not trace them, he settled down into his usual quiet way, and suffered her to lead him where she would.

When they presented themselves in the midst of the stupendous collection, they found, as Nell had anticipated, that Mrs. Jarley was not yet out of bed, and that, although she had suffered some uneasiness on their account overnight, and had indeed sat up for them until past eleven o'clock, she had retired in the persuasion, that, being overtaken by storm at some distance from home, they had sought the nearest shelter, and would not return before morning. Nell immediately applied herself with great assiduity to the decoration and preparation of the room, and had the satisfaction of completing her task, and dressing herself neatly, before the beloved of the Royal Family came down to breakfast.

'We haven't had,' said Mrs. Jarley when the meal

was over, 'more than eight of Miss Monflather's young ladies all the time we 've been here, and there 's twenty-six of 'em, as I was told by the cook when I asked her a question or two and put her on the free-list. We must try 'em with a parcel of new bills, and you shall take it, my dear, and see what effect that has upon 'em.'

The proposed expedition being one of paramount importance, Mrs. Jarley adjusted Nell's bonnet with her own hands, and declaring that she certainly did look very pretty, and reflected credit on the establishment, dismissed her with many commendations, and certain needful directions as to the turnings on the right which she was to take, and the turnings on the left which she was to avoid. Thus instructed, Nell had no difficulty in finding out Miss Monflathers's Boarding and Day Establishment, which was a large house, with a high wall, and a large garden-gate with a large brass plate, and a small grating through which Miss Monflathers's parlour-maid inspected all visitors before admitting them; for nothing in the shape of a man—no, not even a milkman—was suffered, without special licence, to pass that gate. Even the tax-gatherer, who was stout, and wore spectacles and a broad-brimmed hat, had the taxes handed through the grating. More obdurate than gate of adamant or brass, this gate of Miss Monflathers's frowned on all mankind. The very butcher respected it as a gate of mystery, and left off whistling when he rang the bell.

As Nell approached the awful door, it turned slowly upon its hinges with a creaking noise, and, forth from the solemn grove beyond, came a long file of young ladies, two and two, all with open books in their hands, and some with parasols likewise. And last of the goodly procession came Miss Monflathers, bearing herself a parasol of lilac silk, and supported by two smiling teachers, each mortally envious of the other, and devoted unto Miss Monflathers.

Confused by the looks and whispers of the girls, Nell stood with downcast eyes and suffered the procession to pass on, until Miss Monflathers, bringing up the rear, approached her, when she curtsied and presented her little packet; on receipt whereof Miss Monflathers commanded that the line should halt.

'You 're the wax-work child, are you not?' said Miss Monflathers.

'Yes, ma'am,' replied Nell, colouring deeply, for the young ladies had collected about her, and she was the centre on which all eyes were fixed.

'And don't you think you must be a very wicked little child,' said Miss Monflathers, who was of rather uncertain temper, and lost no opportunity of impressing moral truths upon the tender minds of the young ladies, 'to be a wax-work child at all?'

Poor Nell had never viewed her position in this light, and not knowing what to say, remained silent, blushing more deeply than before.

'Don't you know,' said Miss Monflathers, 'that it 's very naughty and unfeminine, and a perversion of the properties wisely and benignantly transmitted to us, with expansive powers to be roused from their dormant state through the medium of cultivation?'

The two teachers murmured their respectful approval of this home-thrust, and looked at Nell as though they would have said that there indeed Miss Monflathers had hit her very hard. Then they smiled and glanced at Miss Monflathers and then, their eyes meeting, they exchanged looks which plainly said that each considered herself smiler in ordinary to Miss

Monflathers, and regarded the other as having no right to smile, and that her so doing was an act of presumption and impertinence.

'Don't you feel how naughty it is of you,' resumed Miss Monflathers, 'to be a wax-work child, when you might have the proud consciousness of assisting, to the extent of your infant powers, the manufactures of your country; of improving your mind by the constant contemplation of the steam-engine; and of earning a comfortable and independent subsistence of from two-and-ninepence to three shillings per week? Don't you know that the harder you are at work, the happier you are?'

'"How doth the little—"' murmured one of the teachers, in quotation from Doctor Watts.

'Eh?' said Miss Monflathers, turning smartly round. 'Who said that?'

Of course the teacher who had not said it, indicated the rival who had, whom Miss Monflathers frowningly requested to hold her peace; by that means throwing the informing teacher into raptures of joy.

'The little busy bee,' said Miss Monflathers, drawing herself up, 'is applicable only to genteel children.

'"In books, or work, or healthful play"

is quite right as far as they are concerned; and the work means painting on velvet, fancy needlework, or embroidery. In such cases as these,' pointing to Nell, with her parasol, 'and in the case of all poor people's children, we should read it thus—

'"In work, work, work. In work alway
Let my first years be past,
That I may give for ev'ry day
Some good account at last."'

A deep hum of applause rose not only from the two

teachers, but from all the pupils, who were equally astonished to hear Miss Monflathers improvising after this brilliant style; for although she had been long known as a politician, she had never appeared before as an original poet. Just then somebody happened to discover that Nell was crying, and all eyes were again turned towards her.

There were indeed tears in her eyes, and drawing out her handkerchief to brush them away, she happened to let it fall. Before she could stoop to pick it up, one young lady of about fifteen or sixteen, who had been standing a little apart from the others, as though she had no recognised place among them, sprang forward and put it in her hand. She was gliding timidly away again, when she was arrested by the governess.

'It was Miss Edwards who did that, I *know,*' said Miss Monflathers predictively. 'Now I am sure that was Miss Edwards.'

It was Miss Edwards, and everybody said it was Miss Edwards, and Miss Edwards herself admitted that it was.

'Is it not,' said Miss Monflathers, putting down her parasol to take a severer view of the offender, 'a most remarkable thing, Miss Edwards, that you have an attachment to the lower classes which always draws you to their sides; or, rather, is it not a most extraordinary thing that all I say and do will not wean you from propensities which your original station in life have unhappily rendered habitual to you, you extremely vulgar-minded girl?'

'I really intended no harm, ma'am,' said a sweet voice. 'It was a momentary impulse, indeed.'

'An impulse!' repeated Miss Monflathers scornfully. 'I wonder that you presume to speak of impulses to me'—both the teachers assented—'I am astonished'—both the teachers were astonished—'I suppose it is an impulse which induces you to take the part of every grovelling and debased person that comes in your way'—both the teachers supposed so too.

'But I would have you know, Miss Edwards,' resumed the governess in a tone of increased severity, 'that you cannot be permitted—if it be only for the sake of preserving a proper example and decorum in this establishment—that you cannot be permitted, and that you shall not be permitted, to fly in the face of your superiors in this exceedingly gross manner. If *you* have no reason to feel a becoming pride before wax-work children, there are young ladies here who have, and you must either defer to those young ladies or leave the establishment, Miss Edwards.'

This young lady, being motherless and poor, was apprenticed at the school—taught for nothing—teaching others what she learnt, for nothing—boarded for nothing—lodged for nothing—and set down and rated as something immeasurably less than nothing, by all the dwellers in the house. The servant-maids felt her inferiority, for they were better treated; free to come and go, and regarded in their stations with much more respect. The teachers were infinitely superior, for they had paid to go to school in their time, and were paid now. The pupils cared little for a companion who had no grand stories to tell about home; no friends to come with post-horses, and be received in all humility, with cake and wine, by the governess; no deferential servant to attend and bear her home for the holidays; nothing genteel to talk about, and nothing to display. But why was Miss Monflathers always vexed and irritated with the poor apprentice—how did that come to pass?

Why, the gayest feather in Miss Monflathers's cap, and the brightest glory of Miss Monflathers's school, was a baronet's daughter—the real live daughter of a real live baronet—who, by some extraordinary reversal of the Laws of Nature, was not only plain in features but dull in intellect, while the poor apprentice had both a ready wit and a handsome face and figure. It seems incredible. Here was Miss Edwards, who only paid a small premium which had been spent long ago, every day outshining and excelling the baronet's daughter, who learned all the extras (or was taught them all) and whose half-yearly bill came to double that of any other young lady's in the school, making no account of the honour and reputation of her pupilage. Therefore, and because she was a dependent, Miss Monflathers had a great dislike to Miss Edwards, and was spiteful to her, and aggravated by her, and, when she had compassion on little Nell, verbally fell upon and maltreated her as we have already seen.

'You will not take the air to-day, Miss Edwards,' said Miss Monflathers. 'Have the goodness to retire to your own room and not to leave it without permission.'

The poor girl was moving hastily away when she was suddenly, in nautical phrase, 'brought to' by a subdued shriek from Miss Monflathers.

'She has passed me without any salute!' cried the governess, raising her eyes to the sky. 'She has actually passed me without the slightest acknowledgment of my presence!'

The young lady turned and curtsied. Nell could see that she raised her dark eyes to the face of her superior, and that their expression, and that of her whole attitude for the instant, was one of mute but most touching appeal against this ungenerous usage. Miss Monflathers only tossed her head in reply, and the great gate closed upon a bursting heart.

'As for you, you wicked child,' said Miss Monflathers, turning to Nell, 'tell your mistress that if she presumes to take the liberty of sending to me any more, I will write to the legislative authorities and have her put in the stocks, or compelled to do penance in a white sheet; and you may depend upon it that you shall certainly experience the treadmill if you dare to come here again. Now, ladies, on.'

The procession filed off, two and two, with the books and parasols, and Miss Monflathers, calling the baronet's daughter to walk with her and smooth her ruffled feelings, discarded the two teachers—who by this time had exchanged their smiles for looks of sympathy—and left them to bring up the rear, and hate each other a little more for being obliged to walk together.

CHAPTER XXXII

Mrs. Jarley's wrath on first learning that she had been threatened with the indignity of Stocks and Penance, passed all description. The genuine and only Jarley exposed to public scorn, jeered by children and flouted by beadles! The delight of the Nobility and Gentry shorn of a bonnet which a Lady Mayoress might have sighed to wear, and arrayed in a white sheet as a spectacle of mortification and humility! And Miss Monflathers, the audacious creature who presumed, even in the dimmest and remotest distance of her imagination, to conjure up the degrading picture, 'I am a'most inclined,' said Mrs. Jarley, bursting with the fulness of her anger and the weakness of her means of revenge, 'to turn atheist when I think of it!'

But instead of adopting this course of retaliation, Mrs. Jarley, on second thoughts, brought out the suspicious bottle, and ordering glasses to be set forth upon her favourite drum, and sinking into a chair behind it, called her satellites about her, and to them several times recounted, word for word, the affronts she had received. This done, she begged them in a kind of deep despair to drink; then laughed, then cried, then took a little sip herself, then laughed and cried again, and took a little more; and so, by degrees, the worthy lady went on, increasing in smiles and decreasing in tears, until at last she could not laugh enough at Miss Monflathers, who, from being an object of dire vexation, became one of sheer ridicule and absurdity.

'For which of us is best off, I wonder,' quoth Mrs. Jarley, 'she or me? It 's only talking, when all is said and done, and if she talks of me in the stocks, why I can talk of her in the stocks, which is a good deal funnier if we come to that. Lord, what *does* it matter, after all?'

Having arrived at this comfortable frame of mind (to which she had been greatly assisted by certain short interjectional remarks of the philosophical George), Mrs. Jarley consoled Nell with many kind words, and requested as a personal favour that whenever she thought of Miss Monflathers, she would do nothing else but laugh at her, all the days of her life.

So ended Mrs. Jarley's wrath, which subsided long before the going-down of the sun. Nell's anxieties, however, were of a deeper kind, and the checks they imposed upon her cheerfulness were not so easily removed.

That evening, as she had dreaded, her grandfather stole away, and did not come back until the night was far spent. Worn out as she was, and fatigued in mind and body, she sat up alone, counting the minutes, until he returned—penniless, broken-spirited, and wretched, but still hotly bent upon his infatuation.

'Get me money,' he said wildly, as they parted for the night. 'I must have money, Nell. It shall be paid thee back with gallant interest one day, but all the money that comes into thy hands, must be mine—not for myself, but to use for thee. Remember, Nell, to use for thee!'

What could the child do with the knowledge she had, but give him every penny that came into her hands, lest he should be tempted on to rob their benefactress? If she told the truth (so thought the child) he would be treated as a madman; if she did not supply him with money he would supply himself; supplying him, she fed the fire that burnt him up and put him perhaps beyond recovery. Distracted by these thoughts, borne down by the weight of the sorrow which she dared not tell, tortured by a crowd of apprehensions whenever the old man was absent, and dreading alike his stay and his return, the colour forsook her cheek, her eye grew dim, and her heart was oppressed and heavy. All her old sorrows had come back upon her, augmented by new fears and doubts; by day they were ever present to her mind; by night they hovered round her pillow, and haunted her in dreams.

It was natural that, in the midst of her affliction, she should often revert to that sweet young lady of whom she had only caught a hasty glance, but whose sympathy, expressed in one slight brief action, dwelt in her memory like the kindnesses of years. She would often think, if she had such a friend as that to whom to tell her griefs, how much lighter her heart would be—that if she were but free to hear that voice, she would be happier. Then she would wish that she were something better, that she were not quite so poor and humble, that she dared address her without fearing a repulse; and then feel that there was an immeasurable distance between them, and have no hope that the young lady thought of her any more.

It was now holiday-time at the schools, and the young ladies had gone home, and Miss Monflathers was reported to be flourishing in London, and damaging the hearts of middle-aged gentlemen, but nobody said anything about Miss Edwards, whether she had gone home, or whether she had any home to go to, whether she was still at the school, or anything about her. But one evening, as Nell was returning from a lonely walk, she happened to pass the inn where the stage-coaches stopped, just as one drove up, and there was the beautiful girl she so well remembered, pressing forward to embrace a young child whom they were helping down from the roof.

Well, this was her sister, her little sister, much younger than Nell, whom she had not seen (so the story went afterwards) for five years, and to bring whom to that place on a short visit, she had been saving her poor means all that time. Nell felt as if her heart would break when she saw them meet. They went a little apart from the knot of people who had congregated about the coach, and fell upon each other's neck, and sobbed, and wept with joy. Their plain and simple dress, the distance which the child had come alone, their agitation and delight, and the tears they shed would have told their history by themselves.

They became a little more composed in a short

time, and went away, not so much hand in hand as clinging to each other. 'Are you sure you 're happy, sister?' said the child as they passed where Nell was standing. 'Quite happy now,' she answered. 'But always?' said the child. 'Ah, sister, why do you turn away your face?'

Nell could not help following at a little distance. They went to the house of an old nurse, where the elder sister had engaged a bedroom for the child. 'I shall come to you early every morning,' she said, 'and we can be together all the day.'—'Why not at night-time too? Dear sister, would they be angry with you for *that*?'

Why were the eyes of little Nell wet, that night, with tears like those of the two sisters? Why did she bear a grateful heart because they had met, and feel it pain to think that they would shortly part? Let us not believe that any selfish reference—unconscious though it might have been—to her own trials awoke this sympathy, but thank God that the innocent joys of others can strongly move us, and that we, even in our fallen nature, have one source of pure emotion which must be prized in Heaven!

By morning's cheerful glow, but oftener still by evening's gentle light, the child, with a respect for the short and happy intercourse of these two sisters which forbade her to approach and say a thankful word, although she yearned to do so, followed them at a distance in their walks and rambles, stopping when they stopped, sitting on the grass when they sat down, rising when they went on, and feeling it a companionship and delight to be so near them. Their evening walk was by a river's side. Here, every night, the child was too, unseen by them, unthought of, unregarded; but feeling as if they were her friends, as if they had confidences and trusts together, as if her load were lightened and less hard to bear; as if they mingled their sorrows, and found mutual consolation. It was a weak fancy perhaps, the childish fancy of a young and lonely creature; but night after night, and still the sisters loitered in the same place, and still the child followed with a mild and softened heart.

She was much startled, on returning home one night, to find that Mrs. Jarley had commanded an announcement to be prepared, to the effect that the stupendous collection would only remain in its present quarters one day longer; in fulfilment of which threat (for all announcements connected with public amusements are well known to be irrevocable and most exact), the stupendous collection shut up next day.

'Are we going from this place directly, ma'am?' said Nell.

'Look here, child,' returned Mrs. Jarley. 'That 'll inform you.' And so saying, Mrs. Jarley produced another announcement wherein it was stated, that, in consequence of numerous inquiries at the wax-work door, and in consequence of crowds having been disappointed in obtaining admission, the Exhibition would be continued for one week longer, and would re-open next day.

'For now that the schools are gone, and the regular sight-seers exhausted,' said Mrs. Jarley, 'we come to the General Public, and they want stimulating.'

Upon the following day at noon, Mrs. Jarley established herself behind the highly-ornamented table, attended by the distinguished effigies before mentioned, and ordered the doors to be thrown open for the readmission of a discerning and enlightened public. But the first day's operations were by no means of a successful character, inasmuch as the general public, though they manifested a lively interest in Mrs. Jarley personally, and such of her waxen satellites as were to be seen for nothing, were not affected by any impulses moving them to the payment of sixpence a head. Thus, notwithstanding that a great many people continued to stare at the entry and the figures therein displayed; and remained there with great perseverance, by the hour at a time, to hear the barrel-organ played and to read the bills; and notwithstanding that they were kind enough to recommend their friends to patronise the exhibition in the like manner, until the doorway was regularly blockaded by half the population of the town, who, when they went off duty, were relieved by the other half; it was not found that the treasury was any the richer or that the prospects of the establishment were at all encouraging.

In this depressed state of the classical market, Mrs. Jarley made extraordinary efforts to stimulate the popular taste and whet the popular curiosity. Certain machinery in the body of the nun on the leads above the door was cleaned up and put in motion, so that the figure shook its head paralytically all day long, to the great admiration of a drunken, but very Protestant, barber over the way, who looked upon the said paralytic motion as typical of the degrading effect wrought upon the human mind by the ceremonies of the Romish Church, and discoursed upon that theme with great eloquence and morality. The two carters constantly passed in and out of the exhibition-room, under various disguises, protesting aloud that the sight was better worth the money than anything they had beheld in all their lives, and urging the bystanders, with tears in their eyes, not to neglect such a brilliant gratification. Mrs. Jarley sat in the pay-place, chinking silver moneys from noon till night, and solemnly calling upon the crowd to take notice that the price of admission was only sixpence, and that the departure of the whole collection, on a short tour among the

Crowned Heads of Europe, was positively fixed for that day week.

'So be in time, be in time, be in time,' said Mrs. Jarley at the close of every such address. 'Remember that this is Jarley's stupendous collection of upwards of One Hundred Figures, and that it is the only collection in the world; all others being imposters and deceptions. Be in time, be in time, be in time!'

CHAPTER XXXIII

As the course of this tale requires that we should become acquainted, somewhere hereabouts, with a few particulars connected with the domestic economy of Mr. Sampson Brass, and as a more convenient place than the present is not likely to occur for that purpose, the historian takes the friendly reader by the hand, and springing with him into the air, and cleaving the same at a greater rate than ever Don Cleophas Leandro Perez Zambullo and his familiar travelled through that pleasant region in company, alights with him upon the pavement of Bevis Marks.

The intrepid aeronauts alight before a small dark house, once the residence of Mr. Sampson Brass.

In the parlour-window of this little habitation, which is so close upon the footway that the passenger who takes the wall brushes the dim glass with his coat-sleeve—much to its improvement, for it is very dirty—in this parlour-window in the days of its occupation by Sampson Brass, there hung, all awry and slack, and discoloured by the sun, a curtain of faded green, so threadbare from long service as by no means to intercept the view of the little dark room, but rather to afford a favourable medium through which to observe it accurately. There was not much to look at.

A rickety table, with spare bundles of papers, yellow and ragged from long carriage in the pocket, ostentatiously displayed upon its top; a couple of stools set face to face on opposite sides of this crazy piece of furniture; a treacherous old chair by the fire-place, whose withered arms had hugged full many a client and helped to squeeze him dry; a second-hand wig-box, used as a depository for blank writs and declarations and other small forms of law, once the sole contents of the head which belonged to the wig which belonged to the box, as they were now of the box itself; two or three common books of practice; a jar of ink, a pounce-box, a stunted hearth-broom, a carpet trodden to shreds, but still clinging with the tightness of desperation to its tacks—these, with the yellow wainscot of the walls, the smoke-discoloured ceiling, the dust and cobwebs, were among the most prominent decorations of the office of Mr. Sampson Brass.

But this was mere still-life, of no greater importance than the plate, 'Brass, Solicitor,' upon the door, and the bill, 'First-floor to let to a single gentleman,' which was tied to the knocker. The office commonly held two examples of animated nature, more to the purpose of this history, and in whom it has a stronger interest and more particular concern.

Of these, one was Mr. Brass himself, who has already appeared in these pages. The other was his clerk, assistant, housekeeper, secretary, confidential plotter, adviser, intriguer, and bill of cost increaser, Miss Brass—a kind of amazon at common law, of whom it may be desirable to offer a brief description.

Miss Sally Brass, then, was a lady of thirty-five or thereabouts, of a gaunt and bony figure, and a resolute bearing, which if it repressed the softer emotions of love, and kept admirers at a distance, certainly inspired a feeling akin to awe in the breasts of those male strangers who had the happiness to approach her. In face she bore a striking resemblance to her brother, Sampson—so exact, indeed, was the likeness between them, that had it consorted with Miss Brass's maiden modesty and gentle womanhood to have assumed her brother's clothes in a frolic and sat down beside him, it would have been difficult for the oldest friend of the family to determine which was Sampson and which Sally, especially as the lady carried upon her upper lip certain reddish demonstrations, which, if the imagination had been assisted by her attire, might have been mistaken for a beard. These were, however, in all probability, nothing more than eye-lashes in the wrong place, as the eyes of Miss Brass were quite free from any such natural impertinences. In complexion Miss Brass was sallow—rather a dirty sallow, so to speak—but this hue was agreeably relieved by the healthy glow which mantled in the extreme tip of her laughing nose. Her voice was exceedingly impressive—deep and rich in quality, and, once heard, not easily forgotten. Her usual dress was a green gown, in colour not unlike the curtain of the office-window, made tight to the figure, and terminating at the throat, where it was fastened behind by a peculiarly large and massive button. Feeling, no doubt, that simplicity and plainness are the soul of elegance, Miss Brass wore no collar or kerchief except upon her head, which was invariably ornamented with a brown gauze scarf, like the wing of the fabled vampire, and which, twisted into any form that happened to suggest itself, formed an easy and graceful head-dress.

Such was Miss Brass in person. In mind, she was of a strong and vigorous turn, having from her earliest youth devoted herself with uncommon ardour to the study of the law; not wasting her speculations upon its eagle flights, which are rare, but tracing it attentively through all the slippery and eel-like crawlings in which it commonly pursues its way. Nor had she, like many persons of great intellect, confined herself to theory, or stopped short where practical usefulness begins; inasmuch as she could engross, fair-copy, fill up printed form with perfect accuracy, and, in short, transact any ordinary duty of the office down to pouncing a skin of parchment or mending a pen. It is difficult to understand how, possessed of these combined attractions, she should remain Miss Brass; but whether she had steeled her heart against mankind, or whether those who might have wooed and won her, were deterred by fears that, being learned in the law, she might have too near her fingers' ends those particular statutes which regulate what are familiarly termed actions for breach, certain it is that she was still in a state of celibacy, and still in daily occupation of her old stool opposite to that of her brother Sampson. And equally certain it is, by the way, that between these two stools a great many people had come to the ground.

One morning Mr. Sampson Brass sat upon his stool copying some legal process, and viciously digging his pen deep into the paper, as if he were writing upon the very heart of the party against whom it was directed; and Miss Sally Brass sat upon her stool making a new pen preparatory to drawing out a little bill, which was her favourite occupation; and so they sat in silence for a long time, until Miss Brass broke silence.

'Have you nearly done, Sammy?' said Miss Brass; for in her mild and feminine lips, Sampson became Sammy, and all things were softened down.

'No,' returned her brother. 'It would have been all done though, if you had helped at the right time.'

'Oh yes, indeed,' cried Miss Sally; 'you want my help, don't you?—*you*, too, that are going to keep a clerk!'

'Am I going to keep a clerk for my own pleasure, or because of my own wish, you provoking rascal?' said Mr. Brass, putting his pen in his mouth, and grinning spitefully at his sister. 'What do you taunt me about going to keep a clerk for?'

It may be observed in this place, lest the fact of Mr. Brass calling a lady, a rascal, should occasion any wonderment or surprise, that he was so habituated to having her near him in a man's capacity, that he had gradually accustomed himself to talk to her as though she were really a man. And this feeling was so perfectly reciprocal, that not only did Mr. Brass often call Miss Brass a rascal, or even put an adjective before the rascal, but Miss Brass looked upon it as quite a matter of course, and was as little moved as any other lady would be by being called an angel.

'What do you taunt me, after three hours' talk last night, with going to keep a clerk for?' repeated Mr. Brass, grinning again with the pen in his mouth, like some nobleman's or gentleman's crest. 'Is it my fault?'

'All I know is,' said Miss Sally, smiling drily, for she delighted in nothing so much as irritating her brother, 'that if every one of your clients is to force us to keep a clerk, whether we want to or not, you had better leave off business, strike yourself off the roll, and get taken in execution as soon as you can.'

'Have we got any other client like him?' said Brass. 'Have we got another client like him now—will you answer me that?'

'Do you mean in the face?' said his sister.

'Do I mean in the face!' sneered Sampson Brass, reaching over to take up the bill-book, and fluttering its leaves rapidly. 'Look here—Daniel Quilp, Esquire—Daniel Quilp, Esquire—Daniel Quilp, Esquire—all through. Whether should I take a clerk that he recommends, and says, "this is the man for you," or lose all this, eh?'

Miss Sally deigned to make no reply, but smiled again, and went on with her work.

'But I know what it is,' resumed Brass after a short silence. 'You 're afraid you won't have as long a finger in the business as you 've been used to have. Do you think I don't see through that?'

'The business wouldn't go on very long, I expect, without me,' returned his sister composedly. 'Don't you be a fool and provoke me, Sammy, but mind what you 're doing, and do it.'

Sampson Brass, who was at heart in great fear of his sister, sulkily bent over his writing again, and listened as she said—

'If I determined that the clerk ought not to come, of course he wouldn't be allowed to come. You know that well enough, so don't talk nonsense.'

Mr. Brass received this observation with increased meekness, merely remarking, under his breath, that he didn't like that kind of joking, and that Miss Sally would be 'a much better fellow' if she forbore to aggravate him. To this compliment Miss Sally replied, that she had a relish for the amusement, and had no intention to forego its gratification. Mr. Brass not caring, as it seemed, to pursue the subject any further, they both plied their pens at a great pace, and there the discussion ended.

While they were thus employed, the window was suddenly darkened, as by some person standing close against it. As Mr. Brass and Miss Sally looked up to ascertain the cause, the top sash was nimbly lowered from without, and Quilp thrust in his head.

'Hallo!' he said, standing on tip-toe on the window-sill, and looking down into the room. 'Is there any-body at home? Is there any of the Devil's ware here? Is Brass at a premium, eh?'

'Ha, ha, ha!' laughed the lawyer in an affected ecstasy. 'Oh, very good, sir! Oh, very good indeed! Quite eccentric! Dear me, what humour he has!'

'Is that my Sally?' croaked the dwarf, ogling the fair Miss Brass. 'Is it Justice with the bandage off her eyes, and without the sword and scales? Is it the Strong Arm of the Law? Is it the Virgin of Bevis?'

'What an amazing flow of spirits!' cried Brass. 'Upon my word, it 's quite extraordinary!'

'Open the door,' said Quilp, 'I 've got him here. Such a clerk for you, Brass, such a prize, such an ace of trumps. Be quick and open the door, or if there 's another lawyer near and he should happen to look out of window, he 'll snap him up before your eyes, he will.'

It is probable that the loss of the phœnix of clerks, even to a rival practitioner, would not have broken Mr. Brass's heart; but, pretending great alacrity, he rose from his seat, and going to the door, returned, introducing his client, who led by the hand no less a person than Mr. Richard Swiveller.

'There she is,' said Quilp, stopping short at the door, and wrinkling up his eye-brows as he looked towards Miss Sally; 'there is the woman I ought to have married—there is the beautiful Sarah—there is the female who has all the charms of her sex and none of their weaknesses. Oh Sally, Sally!'

To this amorous address Miss Brass briefly responded 'Bother!'

'Hard-hearted as the metal from which she takes

her name,' said Quilp. 'Why don't she change it—melt down the brass, and take another name?'

'Hold your nonsense, Mr. Quilp, do,' returned Miss Sally, with a grim smile. 'I wonder you're not ashamed of yourself before a strange young man.'

'The strange young man,' said Quilp, handing Dick Swiveller forward, 'is too susceptible himself not to understand me well. This is Mr. Swiveller, my intimate friend—a gentleman of good family and great expectations, but who, having rather involved himself by youthful indiscretion, is content for a time to fill the humble station of a clerk—humble, but here most enviable. What a delicious atmosphere!'

If Mr. Quilp spoke figuratively, and meant to imply that the air breathed by Miss Sally Brass was sweetened and rarefied by that dainty creature, he had doubtless good reason for what he said. But if he spoke of the delights of the atmosphere of Mr. Brass's office in a literal sense, he had certainly a peculiar taste, as it was of a close and earthy kind, and, besides being frequently impregnated with strong whiffs of the second-hand wearing apparel exposed for sale in Duke's Place and Houndsditch, had a decided flavour of rats and mice, and a taint of mouldiness. Perhaps some doubts of its pure delight presented themselves to Mr. Swiveller, as he gave vent to one or two short abrupt sniffs, and looked incredulously at the grinning dwarf.

'Mr. Swiveller,' said Quilp, 'being pretty well accustomed to the agricultural pursuits of sowing wild oats, Miss Sally, prudently considers that half a loaf is better than no bread. To be out of harm's way he prudently thinks is something too, and therefore he accepts your brother's offer. Brass, Mr. Swiveller is yours.'

'I am very glad, sir,' said Mr. Brass, 'very glad

indeed. Mr. Swiveller, sir, is fortunate enough to have your friendship. You may be very proud, sir, to have the friendship of Mr. Quilp.'

Dick murmured something about never wanting a friend or a bottle to give him, and also gasped forth his favourite allusion to the wing of friendship and its never moulting a feather; but his faculties appeared to be absorbed in the contemplation of Miss Sally Brass, at whom he stared with blank and rueful looks, which delighted the watchful dwarf beyond measure. As to the divine Miss Sally herself, she rubbed her hands as men of business do, and took a few turns up and down the office with her pen behind her ear.

'I suppose,' said the dwarf, turning briskly to his legal friend, 'that Mr. Swiveller enters upon his duties at once? It 's Monday morning.'

'At once, if you please, sir, by all means,' returned Brass.

'Miss Sally will teach him law, the delightful study of the law,' said Quilp; 'she 'll be his guide, his friend, his companion, his Blackstone, his Coke upon Littleton, his Young Lawyer's Best Companion.'

'He is exceedingly eloquent,' said Brass, like a man abstracted, and looking at the roofs of the opposite houses, with his hands in his pockets; 'he has an extraordinary flow of language. Beautiful, really.'

'With Miss Sally,' Quilp went on, 'and the beautiful fictions of the law, his days will pass like minutes. Those charming creations of the poet, John Doe and Richard Roe, when they first dawn upon him, will open a new world for the enlargement of his mind and the improvement of his heart.'

'Oh, beautiful, beautiful! Beau-ti-ful indeed!' cried Brass. 'It 's a treat to hear him!'

'Where will Mr. Swiveller sit?' said Quilp, looking round.

'Why, we 'll buy another stool, sir,' returned Brass. 'We hadn't any thoughts of having a gentleman with us, sir, until you were kind enough to suggest it, and our accommodation 's not extensive. We 'll look about for a second-hand stool, sir. In the meantime, if Mr. Swiveller will take my seat, and try his hand at a fair copy of this ejectment, as I shall be out pretty well all the morning—'

'Walk with me,' said Quilp. 'I have a word or two to say to you on points of business. Can you spare the time?'

'Can I spare the time to walk with *you,* sir? You 're joking, sir, you 're joking with me,' replied the lawyer, putting on his hat. 'I 'm ready, sir, quite ready. My time must be fully occupied indeed, sir, not to leave me time to walk with you. It 's not everybody, sir, who has an opportunity of improving himself by the conversation of Mr. Quilp.'

The dwarf glanced sarcastically at his brazen friend, and, with a short dry cough, turned upon his heel to bid adieu to Miss Sally. After a very gallant parting on his side, and a very cool and gentlemanly sort of one on hers, he nodded to Dick Swiveller, and withdrew with the attorney.

Dick stood at the desk in a state of utter stupefaction, staring with all his might at the beauteous Sally, as if she had been some curious animal whose like had never lived. When the dwarf got into the street, he mounted again upon the window-sill, and looked into the office for a moment with a grinning face, as a man might peep into a cage. Dick glanced upward at him, but without any token of recognition; and long after he had disappeared still stood gazing upon

Miss Sally Brass, seeing or thinking of nothing else, and rooted to the spot.

Miss Brass being by this time deep in the bill of costs, took no notice whatever of Dick, but went scratching on, with a noisy pen, scoring down the figures with evident delight, and working like a steam-engine. There stood Dick, gazing now at the green gown, now at the brown head-dress, now at the face, and now at the rapid pen, in a state of stupid perplexity, wondering how he got into the company of that strange monster, and whether it was a dream and he would ever wake. At last he heaved a deep sigh, and began slowly pulling off his coat.

Mr. Swiveller pulled off his coat, and folded it up with great elaboration, staring at Miss Sally all the time; then put on a blue jacket with a double row of gilt buttons, which he had originally ordered for aquatic expeditions, but had brought with him that morning for office purposes; and, still keeping his eye upon her, suffered himself to drop down silently upon Mr. Brass's stool. Then he underwent a relapse, and becoming powerless again, rested his chin upon his hand, and opened his eyes so wide, that it appeared quite out of the question that he could ever close them any more.

When he had looked so long that he could see nothing, Dick took his eyes off the fair object of his amazement, turned over the leaves of the draft he was to copy, dipped his pen into the inkstand, and at last, and by slow approaches, began to write. But he had not written half a dozen words when, reaching over to the inkstand to take a fresh dip, he happened to raise his eyes. There was the intolerable brown head-dress—there was the green gown—there, in short, was Miss Sally Brass, arrayed in all her charms, and more tremendous than ever.

This happened so often, that Mr. Swiveller by degrees began to feel strange influences creeping over him—horrible desires to annihilate this Sally Brass—mysterious promptings to knock her head-dress off and try how she looked without it. There was a very large ruler on the table; a large, black, shining ruler. Mr. Swiveller took it up and began to rub his nose with it.

From rubbing his nose with the ruler, to poising it in his hand and giving it an occasional flourish after the tomahawk manner, the transition was easy and natural. In some of these flourishes it went close to Miss Sally's head; the ragged edges of the head-dress fluttered with the wind it raised; advance it but an inch, and that great brown knot was on the ground; yet still the unconscious maiden worked away, and never raised her eyes.

Well, this was a great relief. It was a good thing to write doggedly and obstinately until he was desperate, and then snatch up the ruler and whirl it about the brown head-dress with the consciousness that he could have it off if he liked. It was a good thing to draw it back, and rub his nose very hard with it, if he thought Miss Sally was going to look up, and to recompense himself with more hardy flourishes when he found she was still absorbed. By these means Mr. Swiveller calmed the agitation of his feelings, until his applications to the ruler became less fierce and frequent, and he could even write as many as half a dozen consecutive lines without having recourse to it,—which was a great victory.

CHAPTER XXXIV

In course of time, that is to say, after a couple of hours or so, of diligent application, Miss Brass arrived at the conclusion of her task, and recorded the fact by wiping her pen upon the green gown, and taking a pinch of snuff from a little round tin box which she carried in her pocket. Having disposed of this temperate refreshment, she arose from her stool, tied her papers into a formal packet with red tape, and taking them under her arm, marched out of the office.

Mr. Swiveller had scarcely sprung off his seat and commenced the performance of a maniac hornpipe, when he was interrupted, in the fulness of his joy at being again alone, by the opening of the door, and the reappearance of Miss Sally's head.

'I am going out,' said Miss Brass.

'Very good, ma'am,' returned Dick. 'And don't hurry yourself on my account to come back, ma'am,' he added inwardly.

'If anybody comes on office business, take their messages, and say that the gentleman who attends to that matter isn't in at present, will you?' said Miss Brass.

'I will, ma'am,' replied Dick.

'I shan't be very long,' said Miss Brass, retiring.

'I 'm sorry to hear it, ma'am,' rejoined Dick when she had shut the door. 'I hope you may be unexpectedly detained, ma'am. If you could manage to be run over, ma'am, but not seriously, so much the better.'

Uttering these expressions of good-will with extreme gravity, Mr. Swiveller sat down in the client's chair and pondered; then took a few turns up and down the room and fell into the chair again.

'So I 'm Brass's clerk, am I?' said Dick. 'Brass's clerk, eh? And the clerk of Brass's sister—clerk to a female Dragon. Very good, very good! What shall I be next? Shall I be a convict in a felt hat and a grey suit, trotting about a dockyard with my number neatly embroidered on my uniform, and the order of the garter on my leg, restrained from chafing my ankle by a twisted belcher handkerchief? Shall I be that? Will that do, or is it too genteel? Whatever you please, have it your own way, of course.'

As he was entirely alone, it may be presumed that, in these remarks, Mr. Swiveller addressed himself to his fate or destiny, whom, as we learn by the precedents, it is the custom of heroes to taunt in a very bitter and ironical manner when they find themselves in situations of an unpleasant nature. This is the more probable from the circumstance of Mr. Swiveller directing his observations to the ceiling, which these bodily personages are usually supposed to inhabit—except in theatrical cases, when they live in the heart of the great chandelier.

'Quilp offers me this place, which he says he can insure me,' resumed Dick after a thoughtful silence, and telling off the circumstances of his position, one by one, upon his fingers; 'Fred, who, I could have taken my affidavit, would not have heard of such a thing, backs Quilp to my astonishment, and urges me to take it also—staggerer, number one! My aunt in the country stops the supplies, and writes an affectionate note to say that she has made a new will, and left me out of it—staggerer, number two. No money; no credit; no support from Fred, who seems to turn steady all at once; notice to quit the old lodgings—staggerers, three, four, five, and six! Undcr an accumulation of staggerers, no man can be considered a free agent. No man knocks himself down; if his destiny knocks him down, his destiny must pick him up again. Then I 'm very glad that mine has brought all this upon itself, and I shall be as careless as I can, and make myself quite at home to spite it. So go on my buck,' said Mr. Swiveller, taking his leave of the ceiling with a significant nod, 'and let us see which of us will be tired first!'

Dismissing the subject of his downfall with these reflections, which were no doubt very profound, and are indeed not altogether unknown in certain systems of moral philosophy, Mr. Swiveller shook off his despondency and assumed the cheerful ease of an irresponsible clerk.

As a means towards his composure and self-possession, he entered into a more minute examination of the office than he had yet had time to make; looked into the wig-box, the books, and ink-bottle; untied and inspected all the papers; carved a few devices on the table with the sharp blade of Mr. Brass's penknife; and wrote his name on the inside of the wooden coal-scuttle. Having, as it were, taken formal possession of his clerkship in virtue of these proceedings, he opened the window and leaned negligently out of it until a beer-boy happened to pass, whom he commanded to set down his tray and to serve him with a pint of mild porter, which he drank upon the spot and promptly paid for, with the view of breaking ground for a system of future credit and opening a correspondence tending thereto, without loss of time. Then, three or four little boys dropped in, on legal errands from three or four attorneys of the Brass grade: whom Mr. Swiveller received and dismissed with about as professional a manner, and as correct and comprehensive an understanding of their business, as would have been shown by a clown in a pantomime under similar circumstances. These things done and over, he got upon his stool again and tried his hand at drawing caricatures of Miss Brass with a pen and ink, whistling very cheerfully all the time.

He was occupied in this diversion when a coach stopped near the door, and presently afterwards there was a loud double-knock. As this was no business of Mr. Swiveller's, the person not ringing the office bell, he pursued his diversion with perfect composure, notwithstanding that he rather thought there was nobody else in the house.

In this, however, he was mistaken; for, after the knock had been repeated with increased impatience, the door was opened, and somebody with a very heavy tread went up the stairs and into the room above. Mr. Swiveller was wondering whether this might be another Miss Brass, twin-sister to the Dragon, when there came a rapping of knuckles at the office-door.

'Come in!' said Dick. 'Don't stand upon ceremony. The business will get rather complicated if I 've many more customers. Come in!'

'Oh, please,' said a little voice very low down in the doorway, 'will you come and show the lodgings?'

Dick leant over the table, and descried a small slipshod girl in a dirty coarse apron and bib, which left nothing of her visible but her face and feet. She might as well have been dressed in a violin-case.

'Why, who are you?' said Dick.

To which the only reply was, 'Oh, please will you come and show the lodgings?'

There never was such an old-fashioned child in her looks and manner. She must have been at work from her cradle. She seemed as much afraid of Dick, as Dick was amazed at her.

'I haven't got anything to do with the lodgings,' said Dick. 'Tell 'em to call again.'

"WILL YOU COME AND SHOW THE LODGINGS?"

'Oh, but please will you come and show the lodgings,' returned the girl; 'it 's eighteen shillings a week and us finding plate and linen. Boots and clothes is extra, and fires in winter-time is eightpence a day.'

'Why don't you show 'em yourself? You seem to know all about 'em,' said Dick.

'Miss Sally said I wasn't to, because people wouldn't believe the attendance was good if they saw how small I was first.'

'Well, but they 'll see how small you are afterwards, won't they?' said Dick.

'Ah! But then they 'll have taken 'em for a fortnight certain,' replied the child with a shrewd look; 'and people don't like moving when they 're once settled.'

'This is a queer sort of thing,' muttered Dick, rising. 'What do you mean to say you are—the cook?'

'Yes, I do plain cooking'; replied the child. 'I 'm housemaid too; I do all the work of the house.'

'I suppose Brass and the Dragon and I, do the dirtiest part of it,' thought Dick. And he might have thought much more, being in a doubtful and hesitating mood, but that the girl again urged her request, and certain mysterious bumping sounds on the passage and staircase seemed to give note of the applicant's impatience. Richard Swiveller, therefore, sticking a pen behind each ear, and carrying another in his mouth as a token of his great importance and devotion to business, hurried out to meet and treat with the single gentleman.

He was a little surprised to perceive that the bumping sounds were occasioned by the progress upstairs of the single gentleman's trunk, which, being nearly twice as wide as the staircase, and exceedingly heavy withal, it was no easy matter for the united exertions of the single gentleman and the coachman to convey up the steep ascent. But there they were, crushing each other, and pushing and pulling with all their might, and getting the trunk tight and fast in all kinds of impossible angles, and to pass them was out of the question; for which sufficient reason, Mr. Swiveller followed slowly behind, entering a new protest on every stair against the house of Mr. Sampson Brass being thus taken by storm.

To these remonstrances, the single gentleman answered not a word, but when the trunk was at last got into the bedroom, sat down upon it and wiped his bald head and face with his handkerchief. He was very warm, and well he might be; for, not to mention the exertion of getting the trunk upstairs, he was closely muffled in winter garments, though the thermometer had stood all day at eighty-one in the shade.

'I believe, sir,' said Richard Swiveller, taking his pen out of his mouth, 'that you desire to look at these apartments. They are very charming apartments, sir. They command an uninterrupted view of—of over the way, and they are within one minute's walk of—of the corner of the street. There is exceedingly mild porter, sir, in the immediate vicinity, and the contingent advantages are extraordinary.'

'What 's the rent?' said the single gentleman.

'One pound per week,' replied Dick, improving on the terms.

'I 'll take 'em.'

'The boots and clothes are extras,' said Dick; 'and the fires in winter-time are—'

'Are all agreed to,' answered the single gentleman.

'Two weeks certain,' said Dick, 'are the—'

'Two weeks!' cried the single gentleman gruffly, eyeing him from top to toe. 'Two years. I shall live here for two years. Here. Ten pounds down. The bargain 's made.'

'Why you see,' said Dick, 'my name is not Brass, and—'

'Who said it was? *My* name 's not Brass. What then?'

'The name of the master of the house is,' said Dick.

'I 'm glad of it,' returned the single gentleman; 'it 's a good name for a lawyer. Coachman, you may go. So may you, sir.'

Mr. Swiveller was so much confounded by the single gentleman riding rough-shod over him at this rate, that he stood looking at him almost as hard as he had looked at Miss Sally. The single gentleman, however, was not in the slightest degree affected by this circumstance, but proceeded with perfect composure to unwind the shawl which was tied round his neck, and then to pull off his boots. Freed of these encumbrances, he went on to divest himself of his other clothing, which he folded up, piece by piece, and ranged in order on the trunk. Then, he pulled down the window-blinds, drew the curtains, wound up his watch, and, quite leisurely and methodically, got into bed.

'Take down the bill,' were his parting words, as he looked out from between the curtains; 'and let nobody call me till I ring the bell.'

With that the curtains closed, and he seemed to snore immediately.

'This is a most remarkable and supernatural sort of house!' said Mr. Swiveller, as he walked into the office with the bill in his hand. 'She-dragons in the business, conducting themselves like professional gentlemen; plain cooks of three feet high appearing mysteriously from underground; strangers walking in and going to bed without leave or licence in the middle of the day! If he should be one of the miraculous fellows that turn up now and then, and has gone to sleep for two years, I shall be in a pleasant situation. It 's my destiny, however, and I hope Brass may like it. I shall be sorry if he don't. But it 's no business of mine—I have nothing whatever to do with it!'

CHAPTER XXXV

Mr. Brass on returning home received the report of his clerk with much complacency and satisfaction, and was particular in inquiring after the ten-pound note, which, proving on examination to be a good and lawful note of the Governor and Company of the Bank of England, increased his good-humour considerably. Indeed he so overflowed with liberality and condescension, that, in the fulness of his heart, he invited Mr. Swiveller to partake of a bowl of punch with him at that remote and indefinite period which is currently denominated 'one of these days,' and paid him many handsome compliments on the uncommon aptitude for business which his conduct on the first day of his devotion to it had so plainly evinced.

It was a maxim with Mr. Brass that the habit of paying compliments kept a man's tongue oiled without any expense; and, as that useful member ought never to grow rusty or creak in turning on its hinges in the case of a practitioner of the law, in whom it should be always glib and easy, he lost few opportunities of improving himself by the utterance of handsome speeches and eulogistic expressions. And this had passed into such a habit with him, that, if he could not be correctly said to have his tongue at his fingers' tips, he might certainly be said to have it anywhere but in his face: which being, as we have already seen, of a harsh and repulsive character, was not oiled so easily, but frowned above all the smooth speeches—one of nature's beacons, warning off those who navigated the shoals and breakers of the World, or of that dangerous strait the Law, and admonishing them to seek less treacherous harbours and try their fortune elsewhere.

While Mr. Brass by turns overwhelmed his clerk with compliments and inspected the ten-pound note, Miss Sally showed little emotion and that of no pleasurable kind, for as the tendency of her legal practice had been to fix her thoughts on small gains and grippings, and to whet and sharpen her natural wisdom, she was not a little disappointed that the single gentleman had obtained the lodgings at such an easy rate, arguing that when he was seen to have set his mind upon them, he should have been at the least charged double or treble the usual terms, and that, in exact proportion as he pressed forward, Mr. Swiveller should have hung back. But neither the good opinion of Mr. Brass, nor the dissatisfaction of Miss Sally, wrought any impression upon that young gentleman, who, throwing the responsibility of this and all other acts and deeds thereafter to be done by him, upon his unlucky destiny, was quite resigned and comfortable: fully prepared for the worst, and philosophically indifferent to the best.

'Good-morning, Mr. Richard,' said Brass, on the second day of Mr. Swiveller's clerkship. 'Sally found you a second-hand stool, sir, yesterday evening, in Whitechapel. She 's a rare fellow at a bargain, I can tell you, Mr. Richard. You 'll find that a first-rate stool, sir, take my word for it.'

'It 's rather a crazy one to look at,' said Dick.

'You 'll find it a most amazing stool to sit down

upon, you may depend,' returned Mr. Brass. 'It was bought in the open street just opposite the hospital, and as it has been standing there a month or two, it has got rather dusty and a little brown from being in the sun, that 's all.'

'I hope it hasn't got any fevers or anything of that sort in it,' said Dick, sitting himself down discontentedly, between Mr. Sampson and the chaste Sally. 'One of the legs is longer than the others.'

'Then we get a bit of timber in, sir,' retorted Brass. 'Ha, ha, ha! We get a bit of timber in, sir, and that 's another advantage of my sister's going to market for us. Miss Brass, Mr. Richard is the—'

'Will you keep quiet?' interrupted the fair subject of these remarks, looking up from her papers. 'How am I to work if you keep on chattering?'

'What an uncertain chap you are!' returned the lawyer. 'Sometimes you 're all for a chat. At another time you 're all for work. A man never knows what humour he 'll find you in.'

'I 'm in a working humour now,' said Sally, 'so don't disturb me, if you please. And don't take him,' Miss Sally pointed with the feather of her pen to Richard, 'off his business. He won't do more than he can help, I dare say.'

Mr. Brass had evidently a strong inclination to make an angry reply, but was deterred by prudent or timid considerations, as he only muttered something about aggravation and a vagabond; not associating the terms with any individual, but mentioning them as connected with some abstract ideas which happened to occur to him. They went on writing for a long time in silence after this—in such a dull silence that Mr. Swiveller (who required excitement) had several times fallen asleep, and written divers strange words in an unknown character with his eyes shut, when Miss

Sally at length broke in upon the monotony of the office by pulling out the little tin box, taking a noisy pinch of snuff, and then expressing her opinion that Mr. Richard Swiveller had 'done it.'

'Done what, ma'am?' said Richard.

'Do you know,' returned Miss Brass, 'that the lodger isn't up yet—that nothing has been seen or heard of him since he went to bed yesterday afternoon?'

'Well, ma'am,' said Dick, 'I suppose he may sleep his ten pound out, in peace and quietness, if he likes.'

'Ah! I begin to think he 'll never wake,' observed Miss Sally.

'It 's a very remarkable circumstance,' said Brass, laying down his pen; 'really, very remarkable. Mr. Richard, you 'll remember, if this gentleman should be found to have hung himself to the bed-post, or any unpleasant accident of that kind should happen—you 'll remember, Mr. Richard, that this ten-pound note was given to you in part payment of two years' rent? You 'll bear that in mind, Mr. Richard; you had better make a note of it, sir, in case you should ever be called upon to give evidence.'

Mr. Swiveller took a large sheet of foolscap, and with a countenance of profound gravity, began to make a very small note in one corner.

'We can never be too cautious,' said Mr. Brass. 'There is a deal of wickedness going about the world, a deal of wickedness. Did the gentleman happen to say, sir—but never mind that at present, sir; finish that little memorandum first.'

Dick did so, and handed it to Mr. Brass, who had dismounted from his stool, and was walking up and down the office.

'Oh, this is the memorandum, is it?' said Brass, running his eye over the document. 'Very good.

Now, Mr. Richard, did the gentleman say anything else?'

'No.'

'Are you sure, Mr. Richard,' said Brass, solemnly, 'that the gentleman said nothing else?'

'Devil a word, sir,' replied Dick.

'Think again, sir,' said Brass; 'it 's my duty, sir, in the position in which I stand, and as an honourable member of the legal profession—the first profession in this country, sir, or in any other country, or in any of the planets that shine above us at night and are supposed to be inhabited—it 's my duty, sir, as an honourable member of that profession, not to put to you a leading question in a matter of this delicacy and importance. Did the gentleman, sir, who took the first-floor of you yesterday afternoon, and who brought with him a box of property—a box of property—say anything more than is set down in this memorandum?'

'Come, don't be a fool,' said Miss Sally.

Dick looked at her, and then at Brass, and then at Miss Sally again, and still said 'No.'

'Pooh, pooh! Deuce take it, Mr. Richard, how dull you are!' cried Brass, relaxing into a smile. 'Did he say anything about his property?—there!'

'That 's the way to put it,' said Miss Sally, nodding to her brother.

'Did he say, for instance,' added Brass, in a kind of comfortable, cozy tone—'I don't assert that he did say so, mind; I only ask you, to refresh your memory—did he say, for instance, that he was a stranger in London—that it was not his humour or within his ability to give any references—that he felt we had a right to require them—and that, in case anything should happen to him, at any time, he particularly desired that whatever property he had upon the premises should be considered mine, as some slight recompense for the trouble and annoyance I should sustain—and were you, in short,' added Brass, still more comfortably and cozily than before, 'were you induced to accept him on my behalf, as a tenant, upon those conditions?'

'Certainly not,' replied Dick.

'Why then, Mr. Richard,' said Brass, darting at him a supercilious and reproachful look, 'it 's my opinion that you 've mistaken your calling, and will never make a lawyer.'

'Not if you live a thousand years,' added Miss Sally. Whereupon the brother and sister took each a noisy pinch of snuff from the little tin box, and fell into a gloomy thoughtfulness.

Nothing further passed up to Mr. Swiveller's dinner-time, which was at three o'clock and seemed about three weeks in coming. At the first stroke of the hour, the new clerk disappeared. At the last stroke of five, he reappeared, and the office, as if by magic, became fragrant with the smell of gin-and-water and lemon peel.

'Mr. Richard,' said Brass, 'this man 's not up yet. Nothing will wake him, sir. What 's to be done?'

'I should let him have his sleep out,' returned Dick.

'Sleep out!' cried Brass; 'why he has been asleep now, six-and-twenty hours. We have been moving chests of drawers over his head, we have knocked double-knocks at the street-door, we have made the servant-girl fall downstairs several times, (she 's a light weight and it don't hurt her much,) but nothing wakes him.'

'Perhaps a ladder,' suggested Dick, 'and getting in at the first-floor window—'

'But then there 's a door between; besides, the neighbours would be up in arms,' said Brass.

'What do you say to getting on the roof of the house through the trap-door, and dropping down the chimney?' suggested Dick.

'That would be an excellent plan,' said Brass, 'if anybody would be—' and here he looked very hard at Mr. Swiveller—'would be kind, and friendly, and generous enough, to undertake it. I dare say it would not be anything like as disagreeable as one supposes.'

Dick had made the suggestion, thinking that the duty might possibly fall within Miss Sally's department. As he said nothing further, and declined taking the hint, Mr. Brass was fain to propose that they should go upstairs together, and make a last effort to awaken the sleeper by some less violent means, which, if they failed on this last trial, must positively be succeeded by stronger measures. Mr. Swiveller, assenting, armed himself with his stool and the large ruler, and repaired with his employer to the scene of action, where Miss Brass was already ringing a hand-bell with all her might, and yet without producing the smallest effect upon their mysterious lodger.

'There are his boots, Mr. Richard!' said Brass.

'Very obstinate-looking articles they are too,' quoth Richard Swiveller. And truly, they were as sturdy and bluff a pair of boots as one would wish to see; as firmly planted on the ground as if their owner's legs and feet had been in them; and seeming, with their broad soles and blunt toes, to hold possession of their place by main force.

'I can't see anything but the curtain of the bed,' said Brass, applying his eye to the keyhole of the door. 'Is he a strong man, Mr. Richard?'

'Very,' answered Dick.

'It would be an extremely unpleasant circumstance if he was to bounce out suddenly,' said Brass. 'Keep the stairs clear. I should be more than a match for him, of course, but I 'm the master of the house, and the laws of hospitality must be respected.—Hallo there! Hallo, hallo!'

While Mr. Brass, with his eye curiously twisted into the keyhole, uttered these sounds as a means of attracting the lodger's attention, and while Miss Brass plied the hand-bell, Mr. Swiveller put his stool close against the wall by the side of the door, and mounting on the top and standing bolt upright, so that if the lodger did make a rush, he would most probably pass him in his onward fury, began a violent battery with the ruler upon the upper panels of the door. Captivated with his own ingenuity, and confident in the strength of his position, which he had taken up after the method of those hardy individuals who open the pit and gallery doors of theatres on crowded nights, Mr. Swiveller rained down such a shower of blows, that the noise of the bell was drowned; and the small servant, who lingered on the stairs below, ready to fly at a moment's notice, was obliged to hold her ears lest she should be rendered deaf for life.

Suddenly the door was unlocked on the inside, and flung violently open. The small servant flew to the coal-cellar; Miss Sally dived into her own bedroom; Mr. Brass, who was not remarkable for personal courage, ran into the next street, and finding that nobody followed him, armed with poker or other offensive weapon, put his hands in his pockets, walked very slowly all at once, and whistled.

Meanwhile, Mr. Swiveller, on the top of the stool, drew himself into as flat a shape as possible against the wall, and looked, not unconcernedly, down upon the single gentleman, who appeared at the door growling and cursing in a very awful manner, and, with the boots in his hand, seemed to have an intention of hurling them downstairs on speculation. This idea, however, he abandoned. He was turning into his room again, still growling vengefully, when his eyes met those of the watchful Richard.

'Have *you* been making that horrible noise?' said the single gentleman.

'I have been helping, sir,' returned Dick, keeping his eye upon him, and waving the ruler gently in his right-hand as an indication of what the single gentleman had to expect if he attempted any violence.

'How dare you then?' said the lodger. 'Eh?'

To this, Dick made no other reply than by inquiring whether the lodger held it to be consistent with the conduct and character of a gentleman to go to sleep for six-and-twenty hours at a stretch, and whether the peace of an amiable and virtuous family was to weigh as nothing in the balance.

'Is my peace nothing?' said the single gentleman.

'Is their peace nothing, sir?' returned Dick. 'I don't wish to hold out any threats, sir—indeed the law does now allow of threats, for to threaten is an indictable offence—but if ever you do that again, take care you 're not sat upon by the coroner and buried in a cross-road before you wake. We have been distracted with fears that you were dead, sir,' said Dick, gently sliding to the ground, 'and the short and the long of it is, that we cannot allow single gentlemen to come into this establishment and sleep like double gentlemen without paying extra for it.'

'Indeed!' cried the lodger.

'Yes, sir, indeed,' returned Dick, yielding to his destiny and saying whatever came uppermost; 'an equal quantity of slumber was never got out of one bed and bedstead, and if you 're going to sleep in that way, you must pay for a double-bedded room.'

Instead of being thrown into a greater passion by

these remarks, the lodger lapsed into a broad grin and looked at Mr. Swiveller with twinkling eyes. He was a brown-faced sun-burnt man, and appeared browner and more sun-burnt from having a white nightcap on. As it was clear that he was a choleric fellow in some respects, Mr. Swiveller was relieved to find him in such good-humour, and, to encourage him in it, smiled himself.

The lodger, in the testiness of being so rudely roused, had pushed his nightcap very much on one side of his bald head. This gave him a rakish eccentric air which, now that he had leisure to observe it, charmed Mr. Swiveller exceedingly; therefore, by way of propitiation, he expressed his hope that the gentleman was going to get up, and further that he would never do so any more.

'Come here, you impudent rascal!' was the lodger's answer as he re-entered his room.

Mr. Swiveller followed him in, leaving the stool outside, but reserving the ruler in case of a surprise. He rather congratulated himself on his prudence when the single gentleman, without notice or explanation of any kind, double-locked the door.

'Can you drink anything?' was his next inquiry.

Mr. Swiveller replied that he had very recently been assuaging the pangs of thirst, but that he was still open to 'a modest quencher,' if the materials were at hand. Without another word spoken on either side, the lodger took from his great trunk a kind of temple, shining as of polished silver, and placed it carefully on the table.

Greatly interested in his proceedings, Mr. Swiveller observed him closely. Into one little chamber of this temple, he dropped an egg; into another some coffee; into a third a compact piece of raw steak from a neat tin case; into a fourth, he poured some water.

Then, with the aid of a phosphorus-box and some matches, he procured a light and applied it to a spirit-lamp which had a place of its own below the temple; then, he shut down the lids of all the little chambers; then he opened them; and then, by some wonderful and unseen agency, the steak was done, the egg was boiled, the coffee was accurately prepared, and his breakfast was ready.

'Hot water—' said the lodger, handing it to Mr. Swiveller with as much coolness as if he had a kitchen-fire before him—'extraordinary rum—sugar—and a travelling glass. Mix for yourself. And make haste.'

Dick complied, his eyes wandering all the time from the temple on the table, which seemed to do everything, to the great trunk which seemed to hold everything. The lodger took his breakfast like a man who was used to work these miracles, and thought nothing of them.

'The man of the house is a lawyer, is he not?' said the lodger.

Dick nodded. The rum was amazing.

'The woman of the house—what 's she?'

'A dragon,' said Dick.

The single gentleman, perhaps because he had met with such things in his travels, or perhaps because he *was* a single gentleman, evinced no surprise, but merely inquired 'Wife or Sister?' 'Sister,' said Dick. —'So much the better,' said the single gentleman, 'he can get rid of her when he likes.'

'I want to do as I like, young man,' he added after a short silence; 'to go to bed when I like, get up when I like, come in when I like, go out when I like,—to be asked no questions and be surrounded by no spies. In this last respect, servants are the devil. There 's only one here.'

'And a very little one,' said Dick.

'And a very little one,' repeated the lodger. 'Well, the place will suit me, will it?'

'Yes,' said Dick.

'Sharks, I suppose?' said the lodger.

Dick nodded assent, and drained his glass.

'Let them know my humour,' said the single gentleman, rising. 'If they disturb me, they lose a good tenant. If they know me to be that, they know enough. If they try to know more, it 's a notice to quit. It 's better to understand these things at once. Good-day.'

'I beg your pardon,' said Dick, halting in his passage to the door, which the lodger prepared to open. 'When he who adores thee has left but the name—'

'What do you mean?'

'—But the name,' said Dick—'has left but the name —in case of letters or parcels—'

'I never have any,' returned the lodger.

'Or in case anybody should call.'

'Nobody ever calls on me.'

'If any mistake should arise from not having the name, don't say it was my fault, sir,' added Dick, still lingering. 'Oh blame not the bard—'

'I 'll blame nobody,' said the lodger, with such irascibility that in a moment Dick found himself on the staircase, and the locked door between them.

Mr. Brass and Miss Sally were lurking hard by, having been, indeed, only routed from the key-hole by Mr. Swiveller's abrupt exit. As their utmost exertions had not enabled them to overhear a word of the interview, however, in consequence of a quarrel for precedence, which, though limited of necessity to pushes and pinches and such quiet pantomime, had lasted the whole time, they hurried him down to the office to hear his account of the conversation.

This Mr. Swiveller gave them—faithfully as regarded the wishes and character of the single gentleman, and poetically as concerned the great trunk, of which he gave a description more remarkable for brilliancy of imagination than a strict adherence to truth; declaring, with many strong asseverations, that it contained a specimen of every kind of rich food and wine, known in these times, and in particular that it was of a self-acting kind and served up whatever was required, as he supposed by clockwork. He also gave them to understand that the cooking apparatus roasted a fine piece of sirloin of beef, weighing about six pounds avoirdupois, in two minutes and a quarter, as he had himself witnessed, and proved by his sense of taste; and further, that, however the effect was produced, he had distinctly seen water boil and bubble up when the single gentleman winked; from which facts he (Mr. Swiveller) was led to infer that the lodger was some great conjuror or chemist, or both, whose residence under that roof could not fail at some future day to shed a great credit and distinction on the name of Brass, and add a new interest to the history of Bevis Marks.

There was one point which Mr. Swiveller deemed it unnecessary to enlarge upon, and that was the fact of the modest quencher, which, by reason of its intrinsic strength and its coming close upon the heels of the temperate beverage he had discussed at dinner, awakened a slight degree of fever, and rendered necessary two or three other modest quenchers at the public-house in the course of the evening.

CHAPTER XXXVI

As the single gentleman after some weeks' occupation of his lodgings, still declined to correspond, by word or gesture, either with Mr. Brass or his sister Sally, but invariably chose Richard Swiveller as his channel of communication; and as he proved himself in all respects a highly desirable inmate, paying for everything beforehand, giving very little trouble, making no noise, and keeping early hours; Mr. Richard imperceptibly rose to an important position in the family, as one who had influence over this mysterious lodger, and could negotiate with him, for good or evil, when nobody else durst approach his person.

If the truth must be told, even Mr. Swiveller's approaches to the single gentleman were of a very distant kind, and met with small encouragement; but, as he never returned from a monosyllabic conference with the unknown, without quoting such expressions as 'Swiveller, I know I can rely upon you,'—'I have no hesitation in saying, Swiveller, that I entertain a regard for you,'—'Swiveller, you are my friend, and will stand by me I am sure,' with many other short speeches of the same familiar and confiding kind, purporting to have been addressed by the single gentleman to himself, and to form the staple of their ordinary discourse, neither Mr. Brass nor Miss Sally for a moment questioned the extent of his influence, but accorded to him their fullest and most unqualified belief.

But quite apart from, and independent of, this source of popularity, Mr. Swiveller had another, which promised to be equally enduring, and to lighten his position considerably.

He found favour in the eyes of Miss Sally Brass. Let not the light scorners of female fascination erect their ears to listen to a new tale of love which shall serve them for a jest; for Miss Brass, however accurately formed to be beloved, was not of the loving kind. That amiable virgin, having clung to the skirts of the Law from her earliest youth; having sustained herself by their aid, as it were, in her first running alone, and maintained a firm grasp upon them ever since; had passed her life in a kind of legal childhood. She had been remarkable, when a tender prattler, for an uncommon talent in counterfeiting the walk and manner of a bailiff: in which character she had learned to tap her little playfellows on the shoulder, and to carry them off to imaginary sponging-houses, with a correctness of imitation which was the surprise and delight of all who witnessed her performances, and which was only to be exceeded by her exquisite manner of putting an execution into her doll's house, and taking an exact inventory of the chairs and tables. These artless sports had naturally soothed and cheered the decline of her widowed father: a most exemplary gentleman, (called 'old Foxey' by his friends from his extreme sagacity,) who encouraged them to the utmost, and whose chief regret, on finding that he drew near to Houndsditch churchyard, was, that his daughter could not take out an attorney's certificate and hold a place upon the roll. Filled with this affectionate and touching sorrow, he had solemnly confided her to his son Sampson as an invaluable auxiliary; and from the old gentleman's decease to the period of which we treat, Miss Sally Brass had been the prop and pillar of his business.

It is obvious that, having devoted herself from infancy to this one pursuit and study, Miss Brass could know but little of the world, otherwise than in connection with the law; and that from a lady gifted with such high tastes, proficiency in those gentler and softer arts in which women usually excel, was scarcely to be looked for. Miss Sally's accomplishments were all of a masculine and strictly legal kind. They began with the practice of an attorney and they ended with it. She was in a state of lawful innocence, so to speak. The law had been her nurse. And, as bandy-legs or such physical deformities in children are held to be the consequence of bad nursing, so, if in a mind so beautiful any moral twist or bandiness could be found, Miss Sally Brass's nurse was alone to blame.

It was on this lady, then, that Mr. Swiveller burst in full freshness as something new and hitherto undreamed of, lighting up the office with scraps of song and merriment, conjuring with inkstands and boxes of wafers, catching three oranges in one hand, balancing stools upon his chin and penknives on his nose, and constantly performing a hundred other feats with equal ingenuity; for with such unbendings did Richard, in Mr. Brass's absence, relieve the tedium of his confinement. These social qualities, which Miss Sally first discovered by accident, gradually made such an impression upon her, that she would entreat Mr. Swiveller to relax as though she were not by, which Mr. Swiveller, nothing loth, would readily consent to do. By these means a friendship sprung up between them. Mr. Swiveller gradually came to look upon her as her brother Sampson did, and as he would have looked upon any other clerk. He imparted to her the mystery of going the odd man or plain Newmarket for fruit, ginger-beer, baked potatoes, or even a modest quencher, of which Miss Brass did not scruple to partake. He would often persuade her to undertake his share of writing in addition to her own; nay, he would sometimes reward her with a hearty slap on the back, and protest that she was a devilish good fellow, a jolly dog, and so forth; all of which compliments Miss Sally would receive in entire good part and with perfect satisfaction.

One circumstance troubled Mr. Swiveller's mind very much, and that was that the small servant always remained somewhere in the bowels of the earth under Bevis Marks, and never came to the surface unless the single gentleman rang his bell, when she would answer it and immediately disappear again. She never went out, or came into the office, or had a clean face, or took off the coarse apron, or looked out of any one of the windows, or stood at the street-door for a breath of air, or had any rest or enjoyment whatever. Nobody ever came to see her, nobody spoke of her, nobody cared about her. Mr. Brass had said once, that he believed she was a 'love-child,' (which means anything but a child of love,) and that was all the information Richard Swiveller could obtain.

'It 's of no use asking the Dragon,' thought Dick one day, as he sat contemplating the features of Miss Sally Brass. 'I suspect if I asked any questions on that head, our alliance would be at an end. I wonder whether she *is* a dragon by the bye, or something in the mermaid way. She has rather a scaly appearance. But mermaids are fond of looking at themselves in the glass, which she can't be. And they have a habit of combing their hair, which she hasn't. No, she 's a dragon.'

'Where are you going, old fellow?' said Dick aloud, as Miss Sally wiped her pen as usual on the green dress, and uprose from her seat.

'To dinner,' answered the Dragon.

'To dinner!' thought Dick, 'that 's another circumstance. I don't believe that small servant ever has anything to eat.'

'Sammy won't be home,' said Miss Brass. 'Stop till I come back. I shan't be long.'

Dick nodded, and followed Miss Brass—with his eyes to the door, and with his ears to a little back-parlour, where she and her brother took their meals.

'Now,' said Dick, walking up and down with his hands in his pockets, 'I 'd give something—if I had it—to know how they use that child, and where they keep her. My mother must have been a very inquisitive woman; I have no doubt I 'm marked with a note of interrogation somewhere. My feelings I smother, but thou hast been the cause of this anguish my—upon my word,' said Mr. Swiveller, checking himself and falling thoughtfully into the client's chair, 'I should like to know how they use her!'

After running on, in this way, for some time, Mr. Swiveller softly opened the office-door, with the intention of darting across the street for a glass of the mild porter. At that moment he caught a parting glimpse of the brown head-dress of Miss Brass flitting down the kitchen-stairs. 'And by Jove!' thought Dick, 'she 's going to feed the small servant. Now or never!'

First peeping over the handrail and allowing the head-dress to disappear in the darkness below, he groped his way down, and arrived at the door of a back-kitchen immediately after Miss Brass had entered the same, bearing in her hand a cold leg of mutton. It was a very dark miserable place, very low and very damp: the walls disfigured by a thousand rents and blotches. The water was trickling out of a leaky butt, and a most wretched cat was lapping up the drops with the sickly eagerness of starvation. The grate, which was a wide one, was wound and screwed up tight, so as to hold no more than a little thin sandwich of fire. Everything was locked up; the coal-cellar, the candle-box, the salt-box, the meat-safe, were all padlocked. There was nothing that a beetle could have lunched upon. The pinched and meagre aspect of the place would have killed a chameleon: he would have known, at the first mouthful, that the air was not eatable, and must have given up the ghost in despair.

The small servant stood with humility in presence of Miss Sally, and hung her head.

'Are you there?' said Miss Sally.

'Yes, ma'am,' was the answer in a weak voice.

'Go further away from the leg of mutton, or you 'll be picking it, I know,' said Miss Sally.

The girl withdrew into a corner, while Miss Brass took a key from her pocket, and opening the safe, brought from it a dreary waste of cold potatoes, looking as eatable as Stonehenge. This she placed before the small servant, ordering her to sit down before it, and then, taking up a great carving-knife, made a mighty show of sharpening it upon the carving-fork.

'Do you see this?' said Miss Brass, slicing off about two square inches of cold mutton after all this preparation, and holding it out on the point of the fork.

The small servant looked hard enough at it with her hungry eyes to see every shred of it, small as it was, and answered, 'Yes.'

'Then don't you ever go and say,' retorted Miss Sally, 'that you hadn't meat here. There, eat it up.'

This was soon done. 'Now, do you want any more?' said Miss Sally.

The hungry creature answered with a faint 'No.' They were evidently going through an established form.

'You 've been helped once to meat,' said Miss Brass, summing up the facts; 'you have had as much as you can eat, you 're asked if you want any more, and you answer, "No!" Then don't you ever go and say you were allowanced, mind that.'

With those words, Miss Sally put the meat away and locked the safe, and then drawing near to the small servant, overlooked her while she finished the potatoes.

It was plain that some extraordinary grudge was working in Miss Brass's gentle breast, and that it was that which impelled her, without the smallest present cause, to rap the child with the blade of the knife, now on her hand, now on her head, and now on her back, as if she found it quite impossible to stand so close to her without administering a few slight knocks. But Mr. Swiveller was not a little surprised to see his fellow-clerk, after walking slowly backwards towards the door, as if she were trying to withdraw herself from the room but could not accomplish it, dart suddenly forward, and falling on the small servant give her some hard blows with her clenched hand. The victim cried, but in a subdued manner as if she feared to raise her voice, and Miss Sally, comforting herself with a pinch of snuff, ascended the stairs, just as Richard had safely reached the office.

CHAPTER XXXVII

THE single gentleman among his other peculiarities—and he had a very plentiful stock, of which he every day furnished some new specimen—took a most extraordinary and remarkable interest in the exhibition of Punch. If the sound of a Punch's voice, at ever so remote a distance, reached Bevis Marks, the single gentleman, though in bed and asleep, would start up, and, hurrying on his clothes, make for the spot with all speed, and presently return at the head of a long procession of idlers, having in the midst the theatre and its proprietors. Straightway, the stage would be set up in front of Mr. Brass's house; the single gentleman would establish himself at the first-floor window; and the entertainment would proceed, with all its exciting accompaniments of fife and drum and shout, to the excessive consternation of all sober votaries of business in that silent thoroughfare. It might have been expected that when the play was done, both players and audience would have dispersed; but the epilogue was as bad as the play, for no sooner was the Devil dead, than the manager of the puppets and his partner were summoned by the single gentleman to his chamber, where they were regaled with strong waters from his private store, and where they held with him long conversation, the purport of which no human being could fathom. But the secret of these discussions was of little importance. It was sufficient to know that while they were proceeding, the concourse without still lingered round the house; that boys beat upon the drum with their fists, and imitated Punch with their tender voices; that the office-window was rendered opaque by flattened noses, and the key-hole of the street-door luminous with eyes; that every time the single gentleman or either of his guests was seen at the upper window, or so much as the end of one of their noses was visible, there was a great shout of execration from the excluded mob, who remained howling and yelling, and refusing consolation, until the exhibitors were delivered up to them to be attended elsewhere. It was sufficient, in short, to know that Bevis Marks was revolutionised by these popular movements, and that peace and quietness fled from its precincts.

Nobody was rendered more indignant by these proceedings than Mr. Sampson Brass, who, as he could by no means afford to lose so profitable an inmate, deemed it prudent to pocket his lodger's affront along with his cash, and to annoy the audiences who clustered round his door by such imperfect means of retaliation as were open to him, and which were confined to the trickling down of foul water on their heads from unseen watering pots, pelting them with fragments of tile and mortar from the roof of the house, and bribing the drivers of hackney cabriolets to come suddenly round the corner and dash in among them precipitately. It may, at first sight, be matter of surprise to the thoughtless few that Mr. Brass, being a professional gentleman, should not have legally indicted some party or parties, active in the promotion of the nuisance, but they will be good enough to remember, that as Doctors seldom take their own prescriptions, and Divines do not always practise what they preach, so lawyers are shy of meddling with the Law on their own account: knowing it to be an edged tool of uncertain application, very expensive in the working, and rather remarkable for its properties of close shaving, than for its always shaving the right person.

'Come,' said Mr. Brass one afternoon, 'this is two days without a Punch. I 'm in hopes he has run through 'em all, at last.'

'Why are you in hopes?' returned Miss Sally. 'What harm do they do?'

'Here 's a pretty sort of a fellow!' cried Brass, laying down his pen in despair. 'Now here 's an aggravating animal!'

'Well, what harm do they do?' retorted Sally.

'What harm?' cried Brass. 'Is it no harm to have a constant hallooing and hooting under one's very nose, distracting one from business, and making one grind one's teeth with vexation? Is it no harm to be blinded and choked up, and have the king's highway stopped with a set of screamers and roarers whose throats must be made of—of—'

'Brass,' suggested Mr. Swiveller.

'Ah! of brass,' said the lawyer, glancing at his clerk, to assure himself that he had suggested the word in good faith and without any sinister intention. 'Is that no harm?'

The lawyer stopped short in his invective, and listening for a moment, and recognising the well-known voice, rested his head upon his hand, raised his eyes to the ceiling, and muttered faintly—

'There 's another!'

Up went the single gentleman's window directly.

'There 's another,' repeated Brass; 'and if I could get a break and four blood horses to cut into the Marks when the crowd is at its thickest, I 'd give eighteen-pence and never grudge it!'

The distant squeak was heard again. The single gentleman's door burst open. He ran violently down the stairs, out into the street, and so past the window, without any hat, towards the quarter whence the sound proceeded—bent, no doubt, upon securing the stranger's services directly.

'I wish I only knew who his friends were,' muttered Sampson, filling his pocket with papers; 'if they 'd just get up a pretty little Commission *de lunatico* at the Gray's Inn Coffee House, and give me the job, I 'd be content to have the lodgings empty for one while, at all events.'

With which words, and knocking his hat over his eyes as if for the purpose of shutting out even a glimpse of the dreadful visitation, Mr. Brass rushed from the house and hurried away.

As Mr. Swiveller was decidedly favourable to these performances, upon the ground that looking at a Punch, or indeed looking at anything out of window, was better than working; and as he had been, for this reason, at some pains to awaken in his fellow-clerk a sense of their beauties and manifold deserts; both he and Miss Sally rose as with one accord and took up their positions at the window: upon the sill whereof, as in a post of honour, sundry young ladies and gentlemen who were employed in the dry nurture of babies, and who made a point of being present, with their young charges, on such occasions, had already established themselves as comfortably as the circumstances would allow.

The glass being dim, Mr. Swiveller, agreeably to a friendly custom which he had established between them, hitched off the brown head-dress from Miss Sally's head, and dusted it carefully therewith. By the time he had handed it back, and its beautiful wearer had put it on again (which she did with perfect composure and indifference), the lodger returned with the show and showmen at his heels, and a strong addition to the body of spectators. The exhibitor disappeared with all speed behind the drapery; and his partner, stationing himself by the side of the theatre, surveyed the audience with a remarkable expression of melancholy, which became more remarkable still when he breathed a hornpipe tune into that sweet musical instrument which is popularly termed a mouth-organ, without at all changing the mournful expression of the upper part of his face, though his mouth and chin were, of necessity, in lively spasms.

The drama proceeded to its close, and held the spectators enchained in the customary manner. The sensation which kindles in large assemblies, when they are relieved from a state of breathless suspense and are again free to speak and move, was yet rife, when the lodger, as usual, summoned the men upstairs.

'Both of you,' he called from the window; for only the actual exhibitor—a little fat man—prepared to obey the summons. 'I want to talk to you. Come both of you!'

'Come, Tommy,' said the little man.

'I an't a talker,' replied the other. 'Tell him so. What should I go and talk for?'

'Don't you see the gentleman 's got a bottle and glass up there?' returned the little man.

'And couldn't you have said so, at first?' retorted the other with sudden alacrity. 'Now, what are you waiting for? Are you going to keep the gentleman expecting us all day? haven't you *no* manners?'

With this remonstrance, the melancholy man, who was no other than Mr. Thomas Codlin, pushed past his friend and brother in the craft, Mr. Harris, otherwise Short or Trotters, and hurried before him to the single gentleman's apartment.

'Now, my men,' said the single gentleman; 'you have done very well. What will you take? Tell that little man behind, to shut the door.'

'Shut the door, can't you?' said Mr. Codlin, turning gruffly to his friend. 'You might have knowed that the gentleman wanted the door shut, without being told, I think.'

Mr. Short obeyed, observing under his breath that his friend seemed unusually 'cranky,' and expressing a hope that there was no dairy in the neighbourhood, or his temper would certainly spoil its contents.

The gentleman pointed to a couple of chairs, and intimated by an emphatic nod of his head that he expected them to be seated. Messrs. Codlin and Short, after looking at each other with considerable doubt and indecision, at length sat down—each on the extreme edge of the chair pointed out to him—and held their hats very tight, while the single gentleman filled a couple of glasses from a bottle on the table beside him, and presented them in due form.

'You 're pretty well browned by the sun, both of you,' said their entertainer. 'Have you been travelling?'

Mr. Short replied in the affirmative with a nod and a smile. Mr. Codlin added a corroborative nod and a short groan, as if he still felt the weight of the Temple on his shoulders.

'To fairs, markets, races, and so forth, I suppose?' pursued the single gentleman.

'Yes, sir,' returned Short, 'pretty nigh all over the West of England.'

'I have talked to men of your craft from North, East, and South,' returned their host, in rather a hasty manner; 'but I never lighted on any from the West before.'

'It 's our reg'lar summer circuit is the West, master,' said Short; 'that 's where it is. We takes the East of London in the spring and winter, and the West of England in the summer-time. Many 's the hard day's walking in rain and mud, and with never a penny earned, we 've had down in the West.'

'Let me fill your glass again.'

'Much obleeged to you, sir, I think I will,' said Mr. Codlin, suddenly thrusting in his own and turning Short's aside. 'I 'm the sufferer, sir, in all the travelling, and in all the staying at home. In town or country, wet or dry, hot or cold, Tom Codlin suffers. But Tom Codlin isn't to complain for all that. Oh, no! Short may complain, but if Codlin grumbles by so much as a word—oh dear, down with him, down with *him* directly. It isn't *his* place to grumble. That 's quite out of the question.'

'Codlin an't without his usefulness,' observed Short with an arch look, 'but he don't always keep his eyes open. He falls asleep sometimes, you know. Remember them last races, Tommy.'

'Will you never leave off aggravating a man?' said Codlin. 'It 's very like I was asleep when five-and-tenpence was collected, in one round, isn't it? I was attending to my business, and couldn't have my eyes in twenty places at once, like a peacock, no more than you could. If I an't a match for an old man and a young child, you an't neither, so don't throw that out against me, for the cap fits your head quite as correct as it fits mine.'

'You may as well drop the subject, Tom,' said Short. 'It isn't particular agreeable to the gentleman, I dare say.'

'Then you shouldn't have brought it up,' returned Mr. Codlin; 'and I ask the gentleman's pardon on your account, as a giddy chap that likes to hear himself talk, and don't much care what he talks about, so that he does talk.'

Their entertainer had sat perfectly quiet in the beginning of this dispute, looking first at one man and then at the other, as if he were lying in wait for an opportunity of putting some further question, or reverting to that from which the discourse had strayed. But, from the point where Mr. Codlin was charged with sleepiness, he had shown an increasing interest in the discussion: which now attained a very high pitch.

'You are the two men I want,' he said, 'the two men I have been looking for, and searching after! Where are that old man and that child you speak of?'

'Sir?' said Short, hesitating and looking towards his friend.

'The old man and his grandchild who travelled

with you—where are they? It will be worth your while to speak out, I assure you; much better worth your while than you believe. They left you, you say, —at those races, as I understand. They have been traced to that place, and there lost sight of. Have you no clue, can you suggest no clue, to their recovery?'

'Did I always say, Thomas,' cried Short, turning with a look of amazement to his friend, 'that there was sure to be an inquiry after them two travellers?'

'*You* said!' returned Mr. Codlin. 'Did I always say that that 'ere blessed child was the most interesting I ever see? Did I always say I loved her, and doted on her? Pretty creetur, I think I hear her now. "Codlin 's my friend," she says, with a tear of gratitude a trickling down her little eye; "Codlin 's my friend," she says—"not Short. Short 's very well," she says; "I 've no quarrel with Short; he means kind, I dare say; but Codlin," she says, "has the feeling for *my* money, though he mayn't look it." '

Repeating these words with great emotion, Mr. Codlin rubbed the bridge of his nose with his coat-sleeve, and shaking his head mournfully from side to side, left the single gentleman to infer that, from the moment when he lost sight of his dear young charge, his peace of mind and happiness had fled.

'Good Heaven!' said the single gentleman, pacing up and down the room, 'have I found these men at last, only to discover that they can give me no information or assistance! It would have been better to have lived on, in hope, from day to day, and never to have lighted on them, than to have my expectations scattered thus.'

'Stay a minute,' said Short. 'A man of the name of Jerry—you know Jerry, Thomas?'

'Oh, don't talk to me of Jerry,' replied Mr. Codlin.

'How can I care a pinch of snuff for Jerrys, when I think of that 'ere darling child? "Codlin 's my friend," she says, "dear, good, kind Codlin, as is always a devising pleasures for me! I don't object to Short," she says, "but I cotton to Codlin." Once,' said that gentleman reflectively, 'she called me Father Codlin. I thought I should have bust?'

'A man of the name of Jerry, sir,' said Short, turning from his selfish colleague to their new acquaintance, 'wot keeps a company of dancing dogs, told me, in a accidental sort of a way, that he had seen the old gentleman in connection with a travelling wax-work, unbeknown to him. As they 'd given us the slip, and nothing had come of it, and this was down in the country that he 'd been seen, I took no measures about it, and asked no questions—But I can, if you like.'

'Is this man in town?' said the impatient single gentleman. 'Speak faster.'

'No he isn't, but he will be to-morrow, for he lodges in our house,' replied Mr. Short rapidly.

'Then bring him here,' said the single gentleman. 'Here 's a sovereign a-piece. If I can find these people through your means, it is but a prelude to twenty more. Return to me to-morrow, and keep your own counsel on this subject—though I need hardly tell you that; for you 'll do so for your own sakes. Now, give me your address, and leave me.'

The address was given, the two men departed, the crowd went with them, and the single gentleman for two mortals hours walked in uncommon agitation up and down his room, over the wondering heads of Mr Swiveller and Miss Sally Brass.